P9-DGY-840

OUR HOUSE

OUR HOUSE

LOUISE CANDLISH

BERKLEY
NEW YORK

Jefferson Madison
Regional Library
Charlottesville, Virginia
WITHDRAWN

30874 8399

R

BERKLEY
An imprint of Penguin Random House LLC
375 Hudson Street, New York, New York 10014

Copyright © 2018 by Louise Candlish
Penguin Random House supports copyright. Copyright fuels creativity, encourages diverse voices, promotes free speech, and creates a vibrant culture. Thank you for buying an authorized edition of this book and for complying with copyright laws by not reproducing, scanning, or distributing any part of it in any form without permission. You are supporting writers and allowing Penguin Random House to continue to publish books for every reader.

BERKLEY is a registered trademark and the B colophon is a trademark of
Penguin Random House LLC.

Library of Congress Cataloging-in-Publication Data

Names: Candlish, Louise, author.
Title: Our house / Louise Candlish.
Description: First edition. | New York: Berkley, 2018.
Identifiers: LCCN 2017029542 (print) | LCCN 2017047538 (ebook) |
ISBN 9780451489128 (ebook) | ISBN 9780451489111 (hardback)
Subjects: LCSH: Divorced parents—Fiction. | Parenting, Part-time—Fiction. |
Home—Fiction. | Children of divorced parents—Fiction. |
Secrets—Fiction. | Domestic fiction. | BISAC: FICTION/Suspense.
Classification: LCC PR6103.A63 (ebook) | LCC PR6103.A63 O97 2018 (print) |
DDC 823/.92—dc23
LC record available at https://lccn.loc.gov/2017029542

First Edition: August 2018

Printed in the United States of America
1 3 5 7 9 10 8 6 4 2

Jacket photos: magnolia tree © Le Do/Shutterstock; stormy sky © gyn9037/
Shutterstock; texture © releon8211/Shutterstock
Jacket design by Katie Anderson
Book design by Kristin del Rosario

This is a work of fiction. Names, characters, places, and incidents either are the product of the author's imagination or are used fictitiously, and any resemblance to actual persons, living or dead, business establishments, events, or locales is entirely coincidental.

For the inimitable and remarkable SJV

OUR HOUSE

1

She must be mistaken, but it looks exactly as if someone is moving into her house.

The van is parked halfway down Trinity Avenue, its square mouth agape, a large piece of furniture sliding down the ribbed metal tongue. Fi watches, squinting into the buttery sunlight—rare for the time of year, a gift—as the object is borne shoulder high by two men through the gate and down the path.

My gate. My path.

No, that's illogical; of course it can't be her house. It must be the Reeces', two down from hers; they put their place on the market in the autumn and no one is quite sure whether a sale has gone through. The houses on this side of Trinity Avenue are all built the same— redbrick double-fronted Edwardians in pairs, their owners united in a preference for front doors painted black—and everyone agrees it's easy to miscount.

Once, when Bram came stumbling home from one of his "quick"

drinks at the Two Brewers, he went to the wrong door and she heard through the open bedroom window the scrambling and huffing as her inebriated husband failed to fit his key into the lock of number 87, Merle and Adrian's place. His persistence was staggering, his dogged belief that if he only kept on trying, the key *would* work.

"But they all look the same," he'd protested in the morning.

"The houses, yes, but even a drunk couldn't miss the magnolia," Fi had told him, laughing. (This was back when she was still amused by his inebriety and not filled with sadness—or disdain, depending on her mood.)

Her step falters: the magnolia. It's a landmark, their tree, a celebrated sight when in blossom and beautiful even when bare, as it is now, the outer twigs etched into the sky with an artist's flair. And it is definitely in the front garden of the house with the van outside.

Think. It must be a delivery, something for Bram that he hasn't mentioned to her. Not every detail gets communicated; they both accept that their new system isn't flawless. Hurrying again, using her fingers as a sun visor, she's near enough to be able to read the lettering on the side of the vehicle: PRESTIGE HOME REMOVALS. It *is* a house move, then. Friends of Bram must be dropping something off en route to somewhere. If she were able to choose, it would be an old piano for the boys (please, Lord, not a drum kit).

But wait—the deliverymen have reappeared and now more items are being transported from van to house: a dining chair; a large, round metallic tray; a box labeled FRAGILE; a small, slim wardrobe the size of a coffin. *Whose things are these?* A rush of anger fires her blood as she reaches the only possible conclusion: Bram has invited someone to stay. Some dispossessed drinking pal, no doubt, with nowhere else to go. ("Stay as long as you like, mate—we've got tons of room.") When the hell was he going to tell her? Well, there's no way a stranger is sharing their home, however temporarily, however charitable Bram's intentions. The kids come first: Isn't that the point?

Lately, she worries they've forgotten the point.

She's almost there. As she passes number 87, she's aware of Merle at the first-floor window, face cast in a frown, arm raised for her attention. Fi makes only the briefest of acknowledgments as she strides through her own gate and onto the tiled path.

"Excuse me. What's going on here?" But in the clamor no one seems to hear. Louder now, sharper: "What are you doing with all this stuff? Where's Bram?"

A woman she doesn't know comes out of the house and stands on the doorstep, smiling. "Hello, can I help?"

She gasps as if at an apparition. *This* is Bram's friend in need? Familiar by type rather than feature, she is one of Fi's own—though younger, in her thirties—blond and brisk and cheerful, the sort to roll up her sleeves and take charge. The sort, as history testifies, to constrain a free spirit like Bram. "I hope so, yes. I'm Fi, Bram's wife. What's going on here? Are you . . . are you a friend of his?"

The woman steps closer, purposeful, polite. "Sorry. Whose wife?"

"Bram's. I mean ex-wife, really." The correction earns a curious look, followed by the suggestion that the two of them move off the path and out of the way of "the guys." As a huge Bubble Wrapped canvas glides by, Fi allows herself to be steered under the ribs of the magnolia. "What on earth has he agreed to here?" she demands. "Whatever it is, I know nothing about it."

"I'm not sure what you mean." There is a faint puckering of the woman's forehead as she studies Fi. Her eyes are golden brown and honest. "Are you a neighbor?"

"No, of course not." Fi is becoming impatient. "I live here."

The puckering deepens. "I don't think so. We're just moving in.

My husband will be here soon with the second van. We're the Vaughans?" She says it as though Fi might have heard of them, even offers her hand for a formal shake. "I'm Lucy."

Gaping, Fi struggles to trust her ears, the false messages they are transmitting to her brain. "Look, I'm the owner of this house, and I think I would know if I'd arranged to rent it out."

The rose-pink of confusion creeps over Lucy Vaughan's face. She lowers her hand. "We're not *renting* it. We've *bought* it."

"Don't be ridiculous!"

"I'm not!" The other woman glances at her watch. "Officially, we became the new owners at twelve o'clock, but the agent let us pick up the keys just before that."

"What are you talking about? What agent? No agent has keys to my house!" Fi's face spasms with conflicting emotions: fear; frustration; anger; even a dark, grudging amusement, because this *must* be a joke, albeit on an epic scale. What else *can* it be? "Is this some sort of prank?" She searches over the woman's shoulder for cameras, for a phone recording her bewilderment in the name of entertainment, but finds none—only a series of large boxes sailing past. "Because I'm not finding it very funny. You need to get these people to stop."

"I have no intention of getting them to stop," Lucy Vaughan says, crisp and decisive, just like Fi usually is when she hasn't been blind-sided by something like *this*. Lucy's mouth turns in vexation before opening in sudden wonder. "Wait a minute. Fi, did you say? Is that Fiona?"

"Yes. Fiona Lawson."

"Then you must be—" Lucy pauses, notices the querying glances from the movers, lowers her voice. "I think you'd better come inside."

And Fi finds herself being ushered through her own door, into her own house, like a guest. She steps into the broad, high-ceilinged hallway and stops short, dumbstruck. This isn't *her* hall. The dimensions are correct, yes; the silver-blue paint scheme remains the same and the staircase has not moved; but the space has been stripped, plundered of every last item that belongs in it: the console table and antique monks bench, the heap of shoes and bags, the pictures on the walls. And her beloved rosewood mirror, inherited from her grandmother, gone! She reaches to touch the wall where it should be, as if expecting to find it sunk into the plaster.

"What have you done with all our things?" she demands of Lucy. Panic makes her strident and a passing mover casts her a correcting sort of look, as if *she* is the threatening one.

"*I* haven't done anything," Lucy says. "*You* moved your stuff out. Yesterday, I'm assuming."

"I did nothing of the sort. I need to look upstairs," Fi says, shouldering past her.

"Well . . ." Lucy begins, but it isn't a request. Fi isn't seeking permission to inspect her own home.

Having climbed the stairs two at a time, she pauses on the upstairs landing, hand still gripping the mahogany curve of the banister rail as if she expects the building to pitch and roll beneath her. She needs to prove to herself that she is in the right house, that she hasn't lost her mind. Good, all doors appear to lead to where they should: two bathrooms at the middle front and rear, two bedrooms on the left and two on the right. Even as she lets go of the banister and enters each room in turn, she still expects to see her family's possessions where they should be, where they've always been.

But there is nothing. Everything they own has vanished, not a stick of furniture left, only indentations in the carpet where twenty-four hours ago the legs of beds and bookcases and wardrobes stood. A bright green stain on the carpet in one of the boys' rooms from a ball of slime that broke open during a fight one birthday. In the corner of the kids' shower stands a tube of gel, the one with tea-tree oil—she remembers buying it at Sainsbury's. Behind the bath taps her fingers find the recently cracked tile (cause of breakage never established) and she presses until it hurts, checking she is still flesh and bone, nerve endings intact.

Everywhere, there is the sharp lemon smell of cleaning fluids.

Returning downstairs, she doesn't know whether the ache has its source inside her or in the walls of her stripped house.

At her approach, Lucy disbands a conference with two of the movers and Fi senses she has rejected their offer of help—to deal with *her*, the intruder. "Mrs. Lawson? Fiona?"

"This is unbelievable," Fi says, repeating the word, the only one that will do. Disbelief is all that's stopping her from hyperventilating, tipping into hysteria. "I don't understand this. Please, can you explain what the hell is going on here?"

"That's what I've been trying to do. Maybe if you see the evidence," Lucy suggests. "Come into the kitchen—we're blocking the way here."

The kitchen too is bare but for a table and chairs Fi has never seen before, and an open box of tea things on the worktop. Lucy is thoughtful enough to push the door to so as not to offend her visitor's eyes with the sight of the continuing invasion beyond.

Visitor.

"Look at these e-mails," Lucy says, offering Fi her phone. "They're from our solicitor, Emma Gilchrist at Bennett, Stafford and Co."

Fi takes the phone and orders her eyes to focus. The first e-mail is from seven days ago and appears to confirm the exchange of contracts on 91 Trinity Avenue, Alder Rise, between David and Lucy Vaughan and Abraham and Fiona Lawson. The second is from this morning and announces the completion of the sale.

"You called him Bram, didn't you?" Lucy says. "That's why it took me a minute to realize. Bram's short for Abraham, of course." She has a real letter at hand too, an opening statement of account from British Gas, addressed to the Vaughans at Trinity Avenue. "We set up all the utility bills to be paperless, but for some reason they sent this by post."

Fi returns the phone to her. "All of this means nothing. They could be fakes. Phishing or something."

"Phishing?"

"Yes, we had a whole talk about neighborhood crime a few months ago at Merle's house and the officer told us all about it. Fake e-mails and invoices look very convincing now. Even the experts can be taken in."

Lucy gives an exasperated half smile.

"They're real, I promise you. It's all real. The funds will have been transferred to your account by now."

"What funds?"

"The money we paid for this house! I'm sorry, but I can't go on repeating this, Mrs. Lawson."

"I'm not asking you to," Fi snaps. "I'm *telling* you—you must have made a mistake. I'm *telling* you it's not possible for you to have bought a house that was never for sale."

"But it *was* for sale—of course it was. Otherwise, we could never have bought it."

Fi stares at Lucy, utterly disoriented. What she is saying, what she is *doing*, is complete lunacy and yet she doesn't *look* like a madwoman. No, Lucy looks like a woman convinced that the person *she* is talking to is the deranged one.

"Maybe you ought to phone your husband," Lucy says finally.

GENEVA, 1:30 P.M.

He lies on the bed in his hotel room, arms and legs twitching. The mattress is a good one, designed to absorb sleeplessness, passion, deepest nightmare, but it fails to ease agitation like his. Not even the two anti-depressants he's taken have subdued him.

Perhaps it's the planes making him crazy, the pitiless way they grind in and out, one after another, groaning under their own weight. More likely it's the terror of what he's done, the dawning understanding of all that he's sacrificed.

Because it's real now. The Swiss clock has struck. One thirty here, twelve thirty in London. He is now in body what he has been in his mind for weeks: a fugitive, a man cast adrift by his own hand. He realizes that he's been hoping there'll be, in some bleak way, relief, but now the time has come there is something bleaker: none. Only the same sickening brew of emotions he's felt since leaving the house early this morning, somehow both grimly fatalistic and wired for survival.

Oh, God. Oh, Fi. Does she know yet? Someone will have seen, surely? Someone will have phoned her with the news. She might even be on her way to the house already.

He shuffles upright, his back against the headboard, and tries to find a focus in the room. The armchair is red leatherette, the desk black veneer. A return to a 1980s aesthetic, more unsettling than it has any right to be. He swings his legs over the side of the bed. The flooring is warm on bare feet—vinyl or something else man-made. Fi would know what the material is; she has a passion for interiors.

The thought causes a spasm of pain, a new breathlessness. He rises, seeking air—the room, on the fifth floor, is ablaze with central heating—but behind the complicated curtain arrangement the windows are sealed. Cars, white and black and silver, streak along the carriageways between hotel and airport, and, beyond, the mountains divide and shelter, their white peaks tinged peppermint blue. Trapped, he turns once more to face the room, thinking, unexpectedly, of his father. His fingers reach for the red leatherette chair, grip the seat back. He does not remember the name of this hotel, which he chose for its nearness to the airport, but knows that it is as soulless a place as he deserves.

Because he's sold his soul; that's what he's done. He's sold his soul. But not so long ago that he's forgotten how it feels to have one.

2

March 2017

Welcome to the website of *The Victim*, the acclaimed crime podcast and winner of a National Documentary Podcast Listeners' Award. Each episode tells the true story of a crime directly in the words of the victim. *The Victim* is not an investigation, but a privileged insight into an innocent person's suffering. From stalking to identity theft, domestic abuse to property fraud, the experience of each victim is a terrifying journey that you are invited to share—and a cautionary tale for our times.

Brand-new episode "Fi's Story" is available now! Listen here on the website or on one of multiple podcast apps. And don't forget to tweet your theories as you listen using #VictimFi.

Caution: Contains strong language.

SEASON TWO, EPISODE THREE: "FI'S STORY" > 00:00:00

My name is Fiona Lawson and I'm forty-two years old. I can't tell you where I live, only where I *used* to, because six weeks ago my husband sold our home without my knowledge or consent. I know I should say "allege," that I should say it before everything, so how about this: I "allege" that what I say in this interview is the truth. I mean, legal contracts don't lie, do they? And his signature has been authenticated by the experts. Yes, the finer details of the crime are still to be revealed—including the identity of his accomplice—but as you can appreciate, I'm still coming to terms with the central fact that I no longer have a home.

I no longer have a home!

Of course, once you've heard my story you'll think I have no one to blame but myself—just like your audience will. I know how it works. They'll all be on Twitter saying how clueless I am. And I get it. I listened to the whole of season one and I did exactly that myself. There's a thin line between a victim and an idiot.

"This could have happened to anyone, Mrs. Lawson," the police officer told me the day I found out, but she was just being kind because I was crying and she could see a cup of tea wasn't going to cut it. (Morphine, maybe.)

No, this could only happen to someone like me, someone too idealistic, too forgiving. Someone who'd deluded herself into thinking she could reform nature itself. Make a weak man strong. Yes, that old chestnut.

Why am I taking part in this series? Anyone who knows me will tell you I'm a very private person, so why open myself to mockery or pity or worse? Well, partly because I want to warn people that this really can happen. Property fraud is on the rise; there are stories in the press every day. The police and legal profession are playing catch-up with technology. Homeowners need to be vigilant: there's no limit to what professional criminals will try—or, for that matter, amateur ones.

Also, this is an ongoing investigation and my story might nudge a memory, might encourage someone who has relevant information to get in touch with the police. Sometimes you don't know what's relevant until you hear the proper context. That's why the police don't mind my doing this. Well, they haven't asked me *not* to—let's put it that way. As you probably know, I can't be compelled to testify against Bram in a trial, thanks to spousal privilege (that's a laugh). We're still married, though I've considered us exes since the day I threw him out. Of course I could *choose* to testify, but we'll cross that bridge when we come to it, my solicitor says.

To be honest, I get the feeling she thinks there won't ever be any prosecution. I get the feeling she thinks he's got a new identity by now, a new home, a new life—all bought with his new fortune.

She says it's ever expanding, the lengths to which people will go to cheat one another.

Even husband and wife.

Speaking of which, you said this has a good chance of being heard by him, that it might be the factor that prompts him to get in touch? Well, let me tell you right now—let me tell *him*—and I don't care what the police think:

Don't even think about coming back, Bram. I swear, if you do, I'll kill you.

#VictimFi

@rachelb72 Where's the husband then? Has he done a runner?
@patharrisonuk @rachelb72 He must have disappeared with the cash. Wonder how much the house was worth.
@Tilly-McGovern @rachelb72 @patharrisonuk Her HUSBAND did this? Wow. The world is a dark place.

BRAM LAWSON,
excerpted from a Word document
e-mailed from Lyon, France, March 2017

Let me remove any doubt straightaway and tell you that this is a suicide note. By the time you read this, I'll have done it. Break the news gently, please. I may be a monster, but I'm still a father and there are two boys who'll be sorry to lose me, who'll have reason to remember me more kindly.

Maybe even their mother too, a one-in-a-million woman whose life must be a nightmare now, thanks to me.

And who, may I say for the record, I have never stopped loving.

3

Ruinous though the situation is, catastrophic even, it is also quite fitting that it's ended the way it has, because it has always been about the house. Our marriage, our family, our *life*: they seemed to make proper sense only at home. Take us out of it—even on one of the smart holidays we used to treat ourselves to when the kids were very young and we very sleep deprived—and the glue would ooze away. The house sheltered us and protected us, but it also defined us. It kept us current long after our expiry date.

Plus—let's be frank—this is London, and in recent years the house had earned more in capital growth than either Bram or I made from our salaries. It was the family's primary breadwinner, our benign master. Friends and neighbors felt the same, as if our human power had been taken from us and invested in bricks and mortar. Spare cash was sunk not in pension funds or private education or marriage-salvaging weekends in Paris, but in the house. You know you'll get it back, we told each other. It's a no-brainer.

That reminds me of something I'd forgotten till now. That day, that terrible day when I came home and discovered the Vaughans in my house, Merle asked them outright what I hadn't yet thought to ask: "How much did you pay for it?"

And even though my marriage, my family, my *life* had been annihilated, I still paused my sobbing to listen to the answer:

"Two million," Lucy Vaughan said in a broken whisper.

And I thought, *It was worth more.*

We were worth more.

We bought it for a quarter of that, though still a substantial-enough sum at the time to have caused us sleepless nights. But once I'd set eyes on 91 Trinity Avenue, I couldn't consider being an insomniac anywhere else. It was the bourgeois confidence of its redbrick exterior, with its pale stone details and chalky white paintwork, wisteria curling onto the wrought iron Juliet balcony above the door. Impressive but approachable, solid but romantic. Not to mention neighbors with the same sensibilities as ours. One after another, we'd rooted out this delightful spot, sacrificed a tube stop for that languidness you get in the suburbs, that sweetness, the air dusted with sugar like Turkish delight.

Inside was a different story. When I think now of all the improvements we made over the years, the energy the house absorbed (the cash!), I can't believe we took it on in the first place. There were, in no particular order: the remodeled kitchen, the refreshed bathrooms, the reimagined gardens (rear and front), the refurbished downstairs cloakroom, the repaired sash windows, the restored timber flooring. Then, when the "re-" verbs had run out, there was a slew of new: new French doors from kitchen to garden, new kitchen cupboards and worktop, new fitted wardrobes in the boys' bedrooms, new glazed partition in the dining area, new railings and gate for the front, new playhouse and slide out back . . . On it went, a constant program of renewal, Bram and I (well, mostly I) like the directors of a charitable body carving up its annual budget, all free time spent canvassing for price quotes, booking and supervising labor, searching on- and offline for fittings and fixtures and the implements needed to fit and fix them, curating colors and textures. And the tragic fact is, never, ever did I stand back and say "It's done!" The idea of the perfect house eluded me like a rake in an old romance novel.

Of course, if I had my time again I probably wouldn't touch a thing. I'd concentrate on the humans. I'd repurpose them before they destroyed themselves.

#VictimFi

@ash_buckley Wow, unbelievable how cheap property was back then.
@loumacintyre78 @ash_buckley Cheap? 500K? Not in Preston. There is life outside London, you know!
@richieschambers Reimagined gardens? Curating colors? Is this woman for real?

The previous owners were an older couple, just the kind I imagined we would become. Moderately successful in their teaching careers (they'd bought the place when you didn't need corporate careers like ours or, later, banking ones like the Vaughans', to afford a decent family home) and confident of the job they'd done raising their kids, they'd wanted to release equity, release themselves. They planned to travel and I imagined them as born-again nomads making a desert crossing under the stars.

"It must be very hard to say good-bye to a house like that," I said to Bram as we drove back to our flat after a visit to measure for curtains that had ended with a bottle or two of wine. He would have been breaking the speed limit, possibly the drink-driving one too, but it didn't bother me then, before the boys, when there were only our own lives at risk. "I thought there was something a bit melancholy about them," I added.

"Melancholy? They're crying all the way to the bank," Bram said.

BRAM, Word document

So, how did I get to this point? The point of terminal despair? Believe me, it would have been better for all concerned if I'd reached it a lot sooner. Even the short version is a long story (OK, so this is a bit more than a "note"—it's a full-scale confession).

Before I start, let me ask this: Was it in fact the house that was doomed? Did she simply take down all who sailed in her?

The old couple we bought it from were splitting up, you see. The estate agent let that slip when he and I nipped into the Two Brewers for a drink on the way back from a visit with our builder. ("Fancy trying out your new local?" he said, and I don't suppose I needed any second invitation.)

"Not the sort of information you share with prospective buyers," he admitted. "No one likes to think they're moving into a house that's witnessed marital breakdown."

"Hmm." I gripped the glass, raised it to my lips, as I would at that bar thousands of times to come. The pale ale was more than acceptable and the place had an old-school feel to it, hadn't yet gone the gastro route of most of the boozers in the area.

"You'd be surprised how common divorce is with these empty

nesters," he went on. "Pack the youngest off to university and then suddenly you and the wife have time to notice you hate each other and have done for years."

"Really?" I was surprised. "I thought it was only our parents' generation who stuck it out for the sake of the children."

"Not the case. Not in areas like this, people like this. It's more traditional than you'd think."

"Well, it's only divorce, I suppose. Could be worse. Could be body parts found in the drains."

"I definitely wouldn't have told you *that*," he said, laughing.

I didn't say anything about it to Fi. She had some romantic notion of this past-it pair collecting their final-salary pensions and riding camels across the desert like Lawrence of Arabia. Flying hot air balloons over Vesuvius, that kind of crap. Like they hadn't already had forty years of teachers' holidays to travel the world.

We'd seen at least a couple of dozen houses by then and the last thing I needed was her changing her mind about the first one to pass muster on the grounds that "melancholy" was some kind of airborne disease. Like smallpox or TB.

"FI'S STORY" > 00:07:40

Was I aware of the house's escalating value? Of course I was. We were all on Rightmove constantly. But I *never* would have sold it. The opposite: I had hopes of keeping it in the Lawson family, of finding some tax-efficient way for the boys to raise *their* kids there, my grandchildren's heads resting on the same pillows, under the same windows, as my sons' did then.

"How will that work?" my friend Merle asked. She lives a couple of doors down from my place (my *old* place; it's still hard to say it). "I mean, what're the chances their wives will want to share a house with each other?"

It went without saying that the women of the future would be making the decisions. Trinity Avenue, Alder Rise, was a matriarchy.

"I haven't thought about the official negotiations," I said. "Can't you just allow me my little castle in the air?"

"That's all it is, I'm afraid, Fi." Merle pulled that small secret smile of hers that made you feel so *chosen*, as if she bestowed it only on the very special. Of the women in my circle she was the least concerned with her appearance—petite and nimble-bodied, dark-eyed, occasionally disheveled—and that made her, inevitably, one of the most attractive. "You know as well as I do that we'll all have to sell up sooner or later to fund our nursing homes. Our dementia care."

Half the women on the street thought they had dementia, but they were really just overloaded or, at most, suffering generalized anxiety. That was what had caused Merle, Alison, Kirsty and me to gravitate toward one another: we didn't "do" neurosis. We kept calm and carried on (we hated that phrase).

When I hear myself now, it's laughable: didn't "do" neurosis? What about the kind caused by marital breakdown, betrayal, fraud? Who did I think I was?

You've probably already decided that. I know everyone will be judging me—believe me, I'm judging myself. But what's the point of me doing this if I'm not going to present myself honestly, warts and all?

#VictimFi

@PeteYIngram Hmm. IMO losing your posh house isn't on a par with being the victim of violent crime.
@IsabelRickey101 @PeteYIngram Wtf? She's homeless!

@PeteYIngram @IsabelRickey101 She's not on the street, though, is she? She's still got a job.

What do I do for a living? I work four days a week as an account manager for a large homewares retailer—recently I've been involved in our new line of ethically sourced rugs, as well as some beautiful pieces by Italian glassmakers inspired by spirals.

It's a great company, with a really holistic and forward-thinking ethos: can you believe *they* suggested my reduced hours to fit better with my parenting? And this is *retail*? They'd signed up for an EU initiative to support working mothers and I was in the right place at the right time. Well, you know what they say when *that* happens: never leave.

It's true, I could probably earn more working for one of the big cut-throat conglomerates, but I've always valued work-life balance over salary. Some of us don't want our throats cut, do we? It's a cliché, I know, but I love working with the kind of handmade products that really make a house a home.

Yes, even now that I no longer have one of my own.

BRAM, Word document

I worked for the best part of ten years for a Croydon-based orthopedic supplies manufacturer as one of their regional sales managers for the Southeast. I was on the road a lot, especially in the early years. I sold all kinds of braces—for knees, elbows, you name it—and neck pillows and abdominal binders, but really they could have been anything. Paper clips, dog food, solar panels, tires.

It was meaningless then and it's meaningless now.

4

Yes, Bram and I have been separated since last summer. Will I tell you why? I'll tell you precisely why, precisely *when*: 14 July 2016, at eight thirty p.m. That was when I discovered him fucking another woman in the kids' playhouse at the bottom of our garden.

I know, what a place to choose! A beautiful, secluded, sun-dappled oasis filled with hydrangeas and fuchsias and roses; home to a wonky rectangle of fraying lawn, with a blue and white football goal, scene of many a penalty shoot-out. A *children's den*.

Almost as unforgivable as the act itself.

I was supposed to be out for office drinks and Bram was on shift with the boys, but the drinks were canceled and rather than phoning ahead to let the family know, I thought I'd surprise them—you know, that cliché of swanning in for the bedtime story and seeing their little faces erupt with joy. *Mummy, you're here!* Get a bit of acclaim for what's usually taken for granted. I admit that I also thought I might check that Bram was sticking to the proper routine, but only because I hoped to see that he was.

Of course, *he* would argue that what I really wanted was to catch him messing up, and now I wonder if maybe there's a grain of truth in that. Maybe he sinned because he knew I expected him to; maybe this whole horror show has been a self-fulfilling prophecy.

(Victims tend to blame themselves. I'm guessing you know that.)

Anyway, the house was quiet when I let myself in—there'd been delays on the trains again and I'd missed catching the kids' bedtime after all. I assumed Bram was still upstairs, having nodded off reading *James and the Giant Peach* (there was not a man in Alder Rise who hadn't done that, soothed by his own voice, stupefied by the parallel narrative about work in his mind). But when I tiptoed upstairs to check, I found the boys in the right beds in the right rooms, blackout blinds pulled, night-lights aglow on their little blue-painted bedside tables. All was as it should be—except for there being no sign of their father.

"Bram?" I whispered. As I moved from room to room, I felt my annoyance rise in an unattractively righteous way. *He's left them,* I thought, marching back downstairs. *He's bloody left them home alone, a seven-year-old and an eight-year-old! Probably to go to the Parade for some revolting takeaway or even a quick pint at the Two Brewers.* But then I thought, *No, be fair; he's never done that. He's a good father, famously so. More likely, he's left his phone in the car and nipped out to fetch it.* We were rarely able to park outside the house, thanks both to our proximity to the Parade and to the fact that so many households on Trinity Avenue owned at least two cars, and it wasn't unheard-of for us to have to park all the way down past the intersection with Wyndham Gardens. I'd probably missed him in the street by seconds; he'd be coming through the door any moment. If we dug up the front garden for off-street parking we wouldn't have this palaver, he'd say, and he'd chuck the car keys into the designated dish on the hallway table.

But he didn't say that because he wasn't coming through the door, and the fact remained that had my drinks not been canceled, the kids would have been in the house without an adult to protect them.

Yes, of course I was concerned that something might have happened to him, but only very briefly, because as soon as I reached the kitchen I spied an open bottle of white wine on the counter. The frosting of condensation suggested it hadn't been out of the fridge long, so if he'd been abducted by aliens, then he'd gone with a glass of Sancerre in his hand.

The kitchen door was unlocked and I stepped out into the breeze-less evening, everything green and pink and gold. Though I wasn't aware of any human presence in the garden, some indefinable disturbance of the mood encouraged me to set off down the path toward the playhouse at the bottom. It was only a few months old then, a cute little thing with a ladder to the roof and a slide curving around the side, constructed and customized by Bram. The door, usually swinging open, was closed.

I could hear all the typical sounds of the street's gardens on a summer evening—husbands and wives summoning one another for dinner, last calls for children's bedtimes, dogs and foxes and birds and cats objecting to one another's proximity—but I did not add to them by calling Bram's name, because I was by now certain he was in the playhouse.

What was I expecting as I stepped over the lip of the slide and peered through the window? A crack pipe? An open laptop with the frozen image of something unspeakable? In all honesty, I expected to find him sneaking a cigarette and I was already calming down, planning a retreat. There were worse crimes, after all, and I wasn't his GP.

A second passed when the shapes were too abstract to identify, but only a short one because the rhythm was real enough, even banal: a man and a woman having sex. A married man and a woman who was not his wife having frantic sex, because time was of the essence here. Yes, *she* was out for the evening, but still, there were kids in the house—he couldn't have them waking up and finding the place abandoned. Telling Mum all about the scare in the morning in that breathless way of theirs, competing to make the most dramatic claim: "The *whole* house was *totally* empty!" "We thought Daddy had been *murdered*!"

There was a horrible chewing sensation in my gut as I stood there, overwhelmed by an unexpected sense of power. Should I fling open the door, as he deserved, or should I creep away and bide my time? (For what purpose? To see if he would do it again? This, surely, was proof enough that he would.) Then I caught a glimpse of his face, the sickening, feral grimace of excitement, and I knew I had no choice. I pushed open the door, watched them startle like animals. A half-full wineglass set to the left of the door wobbled but did not fall.

"Fi!" Bram mouthed, breathless, dazed.

You know, a year or so ago, I overheard my sister Polly talking to a friend of hers about me: "It's like she's a normal, intelligent person in every other way, but she has this blind spot when it comes to Bram. She'll forgive him anything." And I'd wanted to storm in and tell her, "Once, Polly! He did it once!"

Well, now it was twice. And I mean it when I say it was a relief to discover it, a relief so powerful it was almost pleasure.

"Bram," I replied.

BRAM, Word document

I'll kick off with the thing in the playhouse, which I have no doubt is where Fi would begin, even though it's a red herring—I can tell you that for nothing. But it was the official catalyst, our assassination of Archduke Franz Ferdinand, and so it has its place in this story—I accept that.

The name of my partner in crime is beside the point, and since I doubt her husband knows what she's been up to and won't relish her being associated with me and my crimes, I'll call her Constance in this document, after Lady Chatterley. (You'll allow that little joke, I hope. And no, I'm not a great reader of the classics. I saw the movie once—Fi's choice.)

"I thought I'd drop by," she said that evening at the door, with the unmistakable air of goods being offered. She seemed very drunk, but it could have been the exhilaration of being the initiator, an aphrodisiac in itself, as men have known for millennia. "You said you'd show me the inside of your playhouse, remember?"

"Did I? I'm not sure there's anything to see," I said, grinning.

She waggled her iPhone. "Can I take a photo to show my carpenter?"

"*My* carpenter?" I teased. "Well, you can, yes, but you do know you can just buy these things flat packed at B and Q? All I did was fix it together and then build the slide."

"But the slide is the best bit," she exclaimed. "Maybe I'll try it out—if my bum doesn't get stuck."

What was that if not an invitation to look?

She was wearing a white cotton dress, puffed at the shoulders and gathered under her breasts with a tie, the fabric so light it caught on her thighs every time she took a step.

"Any chance of a glass of wine?" she asked as we passed through the kitchen.

You know, it's not true that in moments of sexual temptation men degenerate into lower mammals, all rational thought obliterated. It's more a weakening by degrees. First, when I noticed the dress riding up, I thought, *Don't even think about it. No way.* Then, when I was opening the wine, I thought, *Well, you had to crack sometime.* Soon after, as I was leading her down the garden path (that sounds bad), I thought, *Come on, at least not here, not with your children sleeping inside.* Then: *All right, just this one time and then never again.*

By which time we were inside the playhouse, door closed, and she was pressing the full length of herself against me: her body was overheated, her hair humid, her face on fire. It was the heat that did it, not the softness or pertness or wetness, not the scent of sweat or Chanel or wine. There's such an urgency to hot skin, the nearness of the other person's blood, your own responds as if they're magnetized.

It tells you what's on offer is worth it.

It tells you it's worth everything you own. Everything you love.

OK, so maybe all rational thought *is* obliterated.

"FI'S STORY" > 00:17:36

No, I don't want to tell you her name. It's a question of sparing feelings, isn't it? These namings and shamings rarely damage the individual alone; people have families, loved ones who get caught in the crossfire. And, in the end, it really doesn't matter. She could have worn a mask and I would have felt the same: that's the truth. I didn't address her directly, not a word. I left them to scuffle to their feet and waited for him in the living room. I put the TV on so I couldn't follow the guilty whispers of her departure, but as soon as I heard the front door close I turned it off again.

His voice reached me even before the handle turned on the living room door: "Fi, I don't—"

I spun, ready, cutting him off: "Save your breath, Bram. I know what I saw and I'm not interested in discussing it. This is where it ends. I want you to leave."

"What?" He stood stranded in the doorway, trying to laugh off the strike, two parts bravado, one part fear. His hair was disheveled and damp at the temples and he still had the flushed skin, the odd vulnerability, of a man interrupted during sex.

"I want to separate. Our marriage is over."

I could see from his face, his struggle to find the right reaction, that my tone of dead conviction was more unsettling than the hysteria he'd expected.

"You thought I'd left the boys, didn't you?" he said.

I knew him inside out and I knew that in times of confrontation his technique was not to plead his case but to try to alter the emphasis of mine, in doing so undermining the central crime.

"You *really* thought I would just leave the house and not be here if they needed me?"

This was slick even by his standards: *I* was in the wrong for unjustly suspecting him of neglect. Not even voiced either—thoughtcrime. "You *did* leave the house," I pointed out.

"Not the premises, though."

"No, you're right. Let's put it in perspective: what you were doing was no different from taking out the bins, doing a bit of weeding."

He raised his eyebrows, as if sarcasm had no place in this discussion, as if *he* were in a position to take the moral high ground. But his fingers strayed to his lips as they did when he was uncertain.

"Go and stay at your mum's," I said coldly. "We'll talk tomorrow and work out when you can see the boys over the school holidays."

"The school holidays?" He was taken aback, as if he'd assumed any expulsion was no more than a time-out, a temporary cooling off in the sin bin.

"If you prefer, I'll take them and go to Mum and Dad's, but I think you'll agree it's less disruptive if you leave and we stay."

"Yes. Yes, of course." Committed now to a show of cooperation, he hastened upstairs to gather a few things. There was a brief lull in activity that I knew must be his lingering at the boys' doors, looking in on them before he left, and this caused a small tearing sensation inside me.

"Fi?" He was back in the doorway, a holdall at his feet, but I didn't make eye contact.

"I don't want to hear it, Bram."

"No, please," he begged, "I just need to say one thing."

I sighed, raised my gaze. What one thing could he possibly say? A hypnotist's spell to erase my short-term memory?

"Whatever I've done as a husband, I'm not that person as a father. I'll do whatever you want to make this OK for the boys. To stay in their lives."

I nodded, not unmoved.

He left then. He left with the air of a man who noticed that the ledge beneath his feet was crumbling only at the point of its giving way completely.

#VictimFi

@Emmashannock72 If my husband did that I'd f**king castrate him!

@crime_addict Should have taken him to the cleaners then and there, love.

5

You heard right: I said twice. He'd been unfaithful to me before.

Which doesn't mean we'd never been happy, because we were—I swear we were—for years. We were inseparable at the beginning; there was none of that keeping each other in compartments until we were sure. It was a physical attraction, yes, but a mental one too, a genuine fascination with a different kind of life-form. I was quiet on the outside but confident inside; he was noisy to the world but to himself, I don't know what. . . . Lost, I'd say, maybe even *empty*. I suppose I wanted to fill him. When we got married, I thought I'd done the impossible, settled down with a man who was never going to settle down—until he met me, of course.

OK, so I took my eye off the ball when the house needed attention, and then there were the kids, but so does everyone at that life stage. Dropped balls were rolling into the street the length of Trinity Avenue; you just got used to stepping over them.

Then, a few years ago, he slept with a colleague at a work team-building event. There was an overnight hotel stay, a free bar, a what-happens-in-Vegas mood: the usual clichés. I saw texts from her that made it impossible to deny, even for a man like Bram, who is pretty good at thinking on his feet.

I was at home with the boys while this "team building" was going on. They were young then, maybe four and five, as much of a handful as you'd imagine, even without my work and other pressures. It was a despicable betrayal, yes, but despicable in a familiar, classic way, and whatever people say, there is a certain solace in knowing others have felt the same pain.

"Don't tell anyone else what he did," I remember Alison saying, when I confided in her and Merle that I'd decided to forgive him (not quite the right word, but for the sake of simplicity, that's the one I'll use). "It will change how people react to you far more than how they react to him."

This was advice I'd have done well to follow, for even as I shared my distress with Polly, I knew it was an error. Naturally resistant to Bram's charms from the start, she now had evidence to prove her intuition, evidence she was not willing to excuse even when I did. And just as Alison had predicted, Polly instinctively found fault with *me*. "You can't be attracted to someone so obviously, well, *you know*, and not expect other people to be attracted to him as well," she said.

"So obviously what?"

"Sexy, Fi. And restless, you know, in that edgy way."

"Is that how everyone else sees him?"

"Of course they do. He's a type. A bad boy. However hard he tries, he can never be fully rehabilitated."

"That's stereotypical nonsense," I said.

As was the conversation I had with Bram himself.

"I don't know if I can ever trust you again," I told him.

"Try," he begged. "It will never happen again—you have to believe that."

Trying, trusting, believing: a thousand times more appealing than the alternative when you share two young children. And he *was* faithful after that. I'm certain he was—until that evening last July.

Was I faithful to him? Very funny. Of course I was. I refer you to the two small children. Even if I'd had the desire to stray—which I hadn't—well, I didn't have the time.

And no, Polly isn't married.

BRAM, Word document

If you haven't been told already, then you will soon: there had been a prior extramarital lapse. I won't dwell on that here, because as I say this isn't about the sex. Love and fidelity are not the same thing, whatever women say. (Again, there's no need for names. She was a girl at a work event, a one-night thing. She left the company soon after.)

Why did I cheat on the woman I love? The best way I can explain it is that it was not an addiction or even an itch, but more like the memory of hunger after years of good eating. The belief that I was better when I was desperate, my senses sharper, pleasure more intensely taken. A kind of egomaniac's nostalgia.

I won't go on. I have no doubt you're already rolling your eyes. You'll show your colleague that last bit and you'll say, "I've heard it all now."

"FI'S STORY" > 00:24:41

By the way, don't think I don't know that after that incident with the girl at work, Polly called him "Wham Bram Thank You Ma'am."

Pretty clever, I have to admit.

What she called him after the playhouse is too shocking for broadcast.

BRAM, Word document

When the boys were little and Fi was on the warpath, we used to call her "Fee Fi Fo Fum." Affectionately, of course, though it became less so on my part once I'd realized that nine times out of ten the English-man's blood she smelled was mine.

6

Friday, January 13, 2017

LONDON, 1 P.M.

The number you have dialed is no longer in service.

"Any luck?" Lucy Vaughan asks her.

"No." She needs to get rid of this woman with her fake e-mails and fantasies about owning someone else's home. Should she call the police straightaway? Or wait till she's located Bram, so they can tackle this outrageous invasion together? Now that so much of the Vaughans' furniture is installed, do they qualify for squatters' rights? Are they, technically, occupiers?

The questions have no answers. They feel as unreal as the images in front of her eyes. The whole experience is hallucinatory, not to be trusted.

She tries Bram a second time. A third.

The number you have dialed is no longer in service.

She can't even leave him a voice mail. "Where the hell *is* he?"

Lucy watches, her own phone in her hand. "You have children, don't you? Could he be with them?"

"No, they're in school." How does Lucy know things about her when she didn't know Lucy even existed until a few minutes ago?

Mum, she thinks. She'll ask her to pick up the boys from school and take them to her place. They can't come here; they'd be distraught to find their bedrooms gutted, their precious possessions spirited away.

Spirited away where? Owning the house might be this stranger's delusion (she continues to cling to the notion of a practical joke), but its rightful contents are starkly, incontrovertibly missing. Someone has physically removed them.

This is when it occurs—not a thought so much as an unleashing, a surge of foreboding that breaks into consciousness in the form of full-blown terror: if her property could vanish during her two-day absence, could her *children*? "Oh my God," she says. "Please, no. Please..." With trembling hands she scrolls through her phone contacts.

"What is it?" Lucy asks, agitated. "What's happened? Who are you calling?"

"My children's school. I have to— Oh, Mrs. Emery! This is Fi Lawson. My son Harry is in year three and Leo in year four."

"Of course. How are you, Mrs.—" begins the school secretary, but Fi interrupts.

"I need you to check on them for me—urgently."

"Check on them? I'm not sure I understand."

"Can you just make sure they're where they should be? In their classrooms or the playground, wherever. It's really important."

Mrs. Emery hesitates. "Well, year four will be in the lunch hall, I think—"

"Please!" Stronger than a wail: a shriek, offensive enough to cause Lucy to flinch. "I don't care where it is—just check they're there!"

There's a shocked pause, then, "Would you mind holding a moment...?"

Fi strains to follow a background exchange between Mrs. Emery and a colleague, ten or so agonizing seconds of low-voiced back-and-forth, and then Mrs. Emery comes back on the line. "I'm sorry, Mrs. Lawson, but I've just been told your boys aren't actually here."

"What?" Instantly, a terrible smacking starts up in her rib cage and her stomach threatens to empty itself.

"They're not in school today."

"Where are they, then?"

"Well, with their father, as far as we're aware. Look, I'm going to put you through to the head. . . ."

She is shaking now, the convulsions out of rhythm with the heart smacking. She is a machine that has lost control of its functions.

"Mrs. Lawson? Sarah Bottomley here. I can assure you there's absolutely nothing for you to worry about." The head teacher of Alder Rise Primary has a bracing manner, confident of order at all times, with just the subtlest sense of offense at Fi's current suggestion of *dis*order. "Your husband requested permission to take the boys out of school for the day and I agreed to give it. Their absence is fully authorized."

"Why?" Fi cries. "Why did he take them out of school? And why would you agree to that?"

"Pupils are taken out of school for all sorts of reasons. In this case, it was to do with pickup being difficult, what with neither of you being in London today."

"Neither of you?" Bram was supposed to be here, in this house, two streets from the school! "No, no, that's wrong. I've been away, but Bram has been working from home."

The home that continues to be stocked with a stranger's belongings.

"Is there a chance you might have got your dates muddled?" Mrs. Bottomley suggests. "When I spoke with your husband a few days ago, I got the impression you knew all about the request."

"I knew nothing. *Nothing.*" This is followed by a ghastly animal wail, and it is only when Lucy takes the phone from her that Fi understands she has become too unmanageable to be allowed to continue.

"Hello?" Lucy says. "I'm a friend of Mrs. Lawson's. Of course, yes, leave this with us. We'll try to track down the boys' father. I'm sure it's just a case of crossed wires and the children are quite safe. Mrs. Lawson has had a bit of a shock and isn't herself. Yes, we'll let you know as soon as we locate them."

As the call ends, Fi attempts to seize back her phone, but Lucy resists. "Would it be best if I tried your husband for you?" she asks, mildly.

"No, it wouldn't. This is nothing to do with you," Fi snaps. "You shouldn't be here! Give me my phone and get out of my house!"

"I really think you should sit down and take a deep breath." As Lucy pulls out a chair for her at the kitchen table, the dynamic is one of patient and nurse. "I'll make you a cup of tea."

"I don't want tea, for God's sake!" Her phone returned to her, Fi tries Bram again—*The number you have dialed is no longer in service*—before placing it facedown on the table. Something horrific is taking place, she thinks. *Knows.* Knows in her bones. This confusion with the house, this brazen Lucy woman, is only a part of it: Something has happened to Bram and the boys. Something very bad.

And in that instant, her waking nightmare becomes something so terrifying it has no name.

GENEVA, 2 P.M.

Already he hates the room. Hates the hotel. Hates what little he's seen and heard of this city. A plane screams in from the east, more earsplitting than the rest, and he braces himself for shattered glass. Maybe that's what it's going to take, he thinks, to allow *his* disaster to shrink. Something as earth-shattering—literally—as a plane crash.

It's not the first time today he's thought like this. When his own plane approached the city that morning, he had had the distinct idea that it wouldn't matter if the landing gear failed, if the belly of the thing split open on the tarmac and spilled him from its wounds. He would not have objected to dying that way. Despicably, given the two hundred fellow passengers he was prepared to take with him, he *prayed* for it.

Of course, the plane landed smoothly, his the only body clenched in agony. He alone pleading with the gods for a reversal of fortune that can never be granted.

Really, he should have known that escape was only prison by another name.

7

It was a strange separation initially, five weeks of limbo over late July and the entirety of August. Of course, given half the chance I would live it again and again, appreciate it for the mildly disruptive interlude it was, but at the time it felt like a bleak stretch to be endured.

No, I don't mean the practical impact of our being apart. Though I worked in Central London, a forty-five-minute commute that could take twice that on a bad day, and the school holidays added their usual complications, I had arrangements in place for that. My mother helped, and there were friends on the street with whom I traded childcare.

No, I mean emotionally. My aim was to break even, to stay sane.

Bram was staying at his mother's in Penge, awaiting my next move, his absence temporarily glossed over as far as the boys were concerned. "He's away for work," I'd say. "We'll see him on Saturday." When his Saturday visit arrived, it would extend past bedtime and the boys wouldn't know he'd left. In the morning I'd say he'd had to get up early to go to the office. It helped that they were too busy cracking each other over the head with cereal bowls to question the deception, but, still, it wasn't a sustainable tactic long term.

We canceled the family holiday to the Algarve and stayed in Alder Rise, upon which the whole city seemed to have descended. Thanks partly to a feature in the property section of the *Standard*, couples clustered around estate agents' windows to see what the damage was for a one-bed, a terrace, a status family four-bedder like the ones on Trinity Avenue. They rarely come up, the agents would say, though there was a rumor the Reeces at number 97 had just had a valuation.

It was virtually impossible to park on the upper section of Trinity Avenue, and I often forgot where I'd left the car.

"This is the price we pay for our houses being worth so much," Alison said. "To complain would be unseemly."

("Unseemly" was a very Alison word.)

She was the first to visit when I let it be known that Bram had moved out. She came over with those stiff lollipop hydrangeas that dry so nicely. They're hugely expensive; in Alder Rise you can get them only from the posh florists on the Parade.

"Oh, Fi," she said, hugging me. "Do you want to talk about it?"

"There's nothing to say," I said.

Her sea green eyes watered when she laughed—she was always wiping away smudges of eye makeup—but it was less usual to see them shine in sorrow as they did then. "Just tell me, do we have to choose between you?"

"Of course not."

"No elaborate plan for revenge, then? Or even a basic one?"

"Not every story has to be about revenge," I said.

"True. But most of them are."

OK, I admit there've been times when I've fantasized about Bram meeting his match, a woman who would run roughshod over him—albeit in a fashion that had no impact whatsoever on the well-being of the boys—but I've never come close to seeking direct retribution. I suppose I of all people knew he was his own worst enemy, a man with a self-destructive streak. If I waited long enough he would take revenge on himself.

"You know, I remember seeing an old interview with George Harrison," I told Alison. "It was after his wife had left him for Eric Clapton and you'd be expecting him to be spitting feathers, but he was so calm and philosophical. He said he'd rather she was with a friend of his than with any old Tom, Dick or Harry."

She considered this. "He was probably stoned, Fi."

Through my nose I made the little exhalation that passed for laughter during this unfunny time. "My point is I've released him. We've released each other. What I want now is to put the boys first and find a way to live in harmony. Like that old Paul McCartney song."

"You mean 'Ebony and Ivory'?" Her eyes widened. She feared I'd been body-snatched by a Stepford wife with a Beatles fixation. "Well, I'm not sure there are too many precedents for *that* in the history of marital breakdowns, but if anyone can do it, you can."

Like my parents, Alison had always adored Bram, seeming to understand instinctively that in spite of his drinking and his lies, the exhausting, cliff-hanger nature of being with him, there was a goodness at his heart.

"You're staying in the house?" she asked.

"Of course."

"Good. That's the most important thing."

There were three hydrangeas, one for each of us remaining Lawsons, though I don't think that had occurred to Alison when she bought them. She'd bought them because interior designers said you should always arrange things in threes. It was the rule of asymmetry, the same rule that made Merle dither constantly about having another child. Her existing duo neither matched nor contrasted. (There's always the risk of a third, her husband Adrian said once, and I remembered it for the tone, as if he were talking about a world war, his borders to be defended by Trident.)

"Just so you know," Alison said as she left, "I would have chosen you."

I'm sorry—do I sound a little too humorous? Was I not furious with the bastard? Of course I was. I despised him in a way you can only despise someone you deeply love. But I couldn't bear to let him make me weak. It took strength to keep a lid on my anger, to put it on ice the way I did, and I was proud of that strength.

Believe me, though, what I felt about the cheating was not comparable with what I feel about the house. This is far worse. This is grief.

BRAM, Word document

I don't remember much about that interim period. It seemed pretty painful at the time, but then I had no idea how dark and disabling pain could get.

It didn't help that I was staying with my mother. I remember her attempts to advise, her reliance on the kind of Christian learnings that had felt outdated (if not loony) in my childhood and now, in twenty-first-century South London, were irrelevant to the point of gibberish. Suffice it to say that the wisdom I had demonstrated fell short of my Old Testament namesake and I refused to discuss it with her—or anyone, frankly.

I remember thinking that the boys were surprisingly unaffected by my absence, almost unflatteringly so. They accepted my weekend gifts of crisps and jelly beans as if their parents' marriage had not imploded. As if the pleasure of posting Pringles through slotted mouths eclipsed any ill the universe could hurl at them.

As for Fi, seeing me seemed to fill her with none of the anguish I felt—nor the anger I deserved. We even went to the park together, the four of us, one sweltering Sunday in mid-August. "Pistachio or salted caramel?" she asked me at the ice cream counter in the café, as if she was acting the role of gracious host to a foreign exchange student.

"You choose," I said, and there was the faintest arching of her eyebrows. *You've chosen,* I read, *and your choice was the wrong one.*

It was an odd thing: the ingredients of her were just the same as before—blond hair cut smooth to the collarbone, puppy brown eyes with straight lashes, curves that drew the male gaze and yet were disavowed by their owner as excessive—but the flavor was different. It was as if she'd found a way to sugarcoat her sourness, to disguise her bitterness toward me.

We strolled across the threadbare grass to the playground. The place was heaving with day-trippers, half-naked twentysomethings in those trendy sunglasses with blue lenses that looked better on the women than on the men (or maybe I only noticed the women). There was even a queue for the swings.

"Where did all these people come from?" I said. I hadn't been out of Alder Rise for *that* long.

"Alison says this is the price we pay for our houses being worth so much," Fi said, and she somehow managed to make it sound like self-sacrifice, as if this were the most trying issue she faced. Being a property millionaire.

What about *me?* I wanted to whine. Living in Penge with a religious nut, sleeping on a blow-up bed with my head against a radiator! I'd been careful till then not to pressure Fi or make demands, but now the angst tumbled from me: "Speaking of which, we need to decide what to do about the house. I can't stay at my mum's forever. If we really are splitting, then we need to talk about how we divide the assets."

Now there was emotion in her eyes. Pure alarm.

I blundered on, both wanting to hurt her and willing her to take me back then and there and give me the chance never to hurt her again. "Have you been in touch with a solicitor? Or an estate agent? Are you waiting for *me* to?"

"No." As two swings came free, she took half-finished ice creams from the boys and urged them to take their turns.

"Fi," I began again, but she held up a dripping cone in protest.

"Please. Stop."

"But how much longer—?"

"Another week," she said. "Give me another week and I'll have some suggestions for next steps."

Next steps: project-management speak. The next steps would be to identify the deliverables, secure the assignees and nail down a time-frame.

"OK," I said.

"And, Bram?"

"Yes?"

"We *are* 'really' splitting. I just don't want to be knee-jerk about it. I want what's best for *them*." She turned to watch the boys swinging; she was hardly blinking, as if it were some new and hypnotic spectator sport—until I realized she simply couldn't bear to look at *me*.

I remember thinking, having returned to my mum's that evening, that this is what it must feel like to be a condemned man awaiting news of his appeal.

Condemned? I didn't know how blissfully free I was.

"FI'S STORY" > 00:28:49

Sorry about that little outburst—I'm fine now. My emotions are all over the place at the moment, as you can imagine.

So, what happened next? It was Bram talking about dividing the assets—that's what galvanized me into action. We'd put on a united front one afternoon for a family trip to the park, and I suppose it shouldn't have been as much of a shock as it was when he asked what we were going to do about the house.

That evening, I went to the window and stood for some time looking at the magnolia, always a source of consolation to me. It had blossomed early this year and we'd all gushed at its beauty; passersby took photos on their phones and the boys climbed the lower branches to stroke the blossoms, tenderly, as they might a newborn hamster, careful not to loosen any of the petals.

I would never get this beauty and tranquility somewhere else. Everyone knew that the property market exacerbated the hostilities of separation and divorce and that in London and its suburbs you could no longer expect to sell one large home and get two smaller ones in exchange. My work was reasonably paid, but I'd need to be headhunted by Saudi Oil & Gas to have any chance of buying Bram out of his half of Trinity Avenue.

I thought, or at least tried to think, how it might feel to have those precious pink petals open for someone else next spring. No, it was unthinkable. It would split my heart with a violence no adulterous spouse could achieve.

A For Sale sign at our gate? Over my dead body.

#VictimFi

@SharonHill50 She's a bit intense, isn't she? I don't get how people are so obsessed with their houses.
@Rogermason @ SharonHill50 Money. At least she's honest.

8

Yes, the custody arrangements were crucial to the crime, I would say, because they gave Bram access to both the house itself and the documents he needed to sell it—not just the shared homeowners' stuff, but my personal papers too. No, I didn't think to keep them separate from his after we parted, though obviously that's the first thing I would urge other women in that position to do. Keep your passport taped to your body, even when you sleep!

"Irony" doesn't begin to cover the fact that the solution I came up with was intended to let me *keep* the house. Bird's nest custody, it's called, and like all good ideas, it rang true from the very instant I heard it. I read about it first in the *Guardian* and then on parenting sites online; well past the experimental stage, it's a US-originated arrangement growing in popularity. The way it works is that the children remain at all times in the family home and the two parents take it in turns to be there with them. "Off" time is spent at their respective second homes or, in the case of tighter budgets like ours, a shared one.

Some couples even manage without a second residence, using their parents' spare room instead, or the sofa of a friend.

For Bram, the offer was less an olive branch than a whole sun-drenched Puglian grove.

"Why?" he asked me, not daring to believe my sincerity. "Why are you giving me this?"

"It's not for *you*," I told him. "It's for the boys. I don't want them to lose their home. I want as little to change for them as possible. You betrayed me," I added baldly, "but you didn't betray *them*."

Of course, the Internet had told me that not everyone bought into this interpretation, that many women insisted that by betraying the mother of his children a man betrayed them too, but I didn't agree with the Internet. Husband, father: the roles were linked, but they were still distinct. *"Whatever I've done as a husband, I'm not that person as a father."* And he wasn't. As I say, he was excellent, acknowledged by other parents as the one the kids gravitated toward, the one who built dens and tree houses (and playhouses) and who came up with Dodgeball Day and the Lawson Olympics and who assembled the street's kids one Sunday to help him pull down a dead tree with ropes, when the other dads were probably lying low with their phones, trying not to catch anyone's eye.

"If you're committed to making it work, there is no better setup for the child," our bird's nest counselor told us.

Except a happy marriage, I thought.

Her name was Rowan and she was precise and courteous, modeling the painstaking niceties we would need to practice if our reconfigured union was to succeed. "Bird's nest custody offers exactly what you would expect from a real bird's nest: strength, safety and continuity for the chicks. With the best will in the world, it can be unsettling for them to shuttle between two homes, especially if those homes aren't in the same area. This completely negates that disruption. In the best-case scenario, they'll hardly notice anything has changed."

She guided us through the nuts and bolts—or twigs and feathers, as she joked. We would have a trial period in which I handled the weekdays and Bram most of the weekends. Handovers would be seven p.m. on Friday and noon on Sunday, giving us each weekend time with the boys. He would also visit on Wednesday evenings to do the bedtime routine. "It works best if you can keep separate bedrooms in the main house," Rowan advised. "It helps with establishing boundaries."

I'd already given this thought, grateful that the house's size and layout suited our new purposes so readily. There would be no uprooting of the boys and no modification costs. "We can do that. We have four bedrooms, so we can use the spare for one of us, and there's a study downstairs that can become the new spare."

"You're very lucky," Rowan said. "Some couples have to take turns in the same bedroom. You'd be surprised how many negotiations I've had involving who changes the sheets."

"You keep our room," Bram told me, "since you're going to be there more nights than me."

Our room. Setting up new sleeping arrangements was one thing; adjusting the language of our home, our life, was another.

"The trick is to think of both places as your home," Rowan said. "Your house is your primary home, the other place your secondary. No one has the greater claim to either; you are co-owners and co-tenants. Above all, you're co-parents. Equals."

She showed us a diary app she recommended. "This is where it all goes: who's in the house, who's in the flat, who's away for work, who's picking up from school. The clubs, the playdates, the birthday parties: all color coded."

As for the financial arrangements, they required little adaptation in the short term. Bram and I earned similar salaries, contributed the same amount to the joint account, from which we paid mortgage, utilities and all the kids' expenses. This pooled figure would now increase to cover the rent on the second property in Alder Rise, most likely a studio or a room in a shared house, and left little to spare. For this reason, I suggested that the other expense, divorce lawyers, should be postponed for this trial period.

"That makes sense," Bram said, and there was enough raw optimism in his tone for me to glance across at him.

"You do understand, we are separated?" I said, struggling to keep the sharpness from my tone. "The divorce *will* happen, just not straight-away. There's no going back as far as I'm concerned."

"Of course," he said.

Rowan watched, composed, thoughtful. "In some cases, a clean break in living arrangements is preferred. The way you're choosing will inevitably bring a level of invasion of privacy, because it's not going to be practical to remove all traces of yourself every time you leave one property for the other. Are you certain that's what you both want? Fiona?"

I breathed so deeply I filled every recess of my lungs, and then I pictured the boys' faces, their Lawson curly heads, and I nodded.

Bram agreed with uncharacteristic earnestness. "Let's do it," he said, and his smile, unexpectedly self-conscious, made me remember why I'd loved him in the first place.

#VictimFi

@LydiaHilluk Sounds a bit hippy-dippy, this bird's nest idea.
@DYeagernews @LydiaHilluk I think the opposite—it's civilized, grown-up. Sounds like it could work.
@LydiaHilluk @DYeagernews Well, it obviously didn't, did it?

BRAM, Word document

You know that great Smiths line from "Heaven Knows I'm Miserable Now" about Caligula blushing? Well, the thing Fi was proposing, a *saint* would have blushed. Seriously, not a day went by without
there being some new article about divorced dads consigned to flat-
sharing bedlam, not a cat's chance in hell of getting a new mortgage
while they were still paying the old one. But Fi spared me this;
she spared me all the miseries she had every right to inflict on me.
Rather than exiling me, she was reintegrating me; rather than taking me to the cleaners, she was allowing current financial arrangements to stand.

She was doing what parents always say they'll do but never get
halfway to achieving: putting the kids first.

We drew up an agreement—nonbinding, but important to her—
and signed it. Of course, this is Fi we're talking about and so there had
to be some touchy-feely therapy attached. The counselor had a low, fil-
tered voice bordering on seductive. "Is there anything non-negotiable?"
she asked us. "Any no-no's?"

"No new partners in the house," Fi said immediately. "Only in the
flat. And no speeding, not with the kids in the car. He's already got
two sets of points on his license. And no drinking on duty."

"What a charming portrait you paint of me," I joked. She had a
point about my driving, but it seemed to me that the only difference
between my drinking and hers was that her drinks were a prettier
color. She liked mint green mojitos and ruby red kir royales; weird gins
made with rhubarb or blueberries or Christmas spices. They all went
crazy for gin, the women of Trinity Avenue.

Still do, I'm guessing.

"And you, Bram?" Rowan said. "Any conditions?"

"No conditions. Whatever Fi wants, I'm on board." And I meant it; I was being "authentic." I didn't even make any jokes about life jackets.

"She's a rare woman, is Fi," my mother said when I relayed the news. She's always had a little insecurity around Fi and her family, with their middle-class attachments to thank-you notes and regular theater, their trips to the Dordogne—or at least she might have if Fi hadn't always been so kind and attentive to her. But the fact remained that she thought I'd done well. I'd married up—and now I was separating up too.

"Don't go spoiling *this* as well, Bram," she warned me, and her gaze had traces of both disapproval and indulgence. "You might not get another chance."

There was a sense that the Lord had had mercy on me—for now.

"FI'S STORY" > 00:36:18

We agreed on Friday, 2 September, as the first day of the new plan. It was the weekend before the start of the school year, which gave us very little time to find our "second residence" (I thought of it like that, in quotation marks, as if it were artificial, somewhere I would never connect with in any real way).

But the project was charmed, it seemed, what with Bram never burning his bridges, at least not where his drinking buddies were concerned. He still had a pint now and then with the estate agent who'd sold us the house on Trinity Avenue, and this agent knew of a studio rental in an apartment block that had gone up a few years ago on the western side of Alder Rise, an easy ten-minute walk down the Parade and across the park from our house. Bought as a buy-to-let investment, the flat had since passed from tenant to tenant, evidently too small for people to want to stay longer than the minimum period.

The exterior was stylish enough. Designed in echo of the art deco building on the high street that had once housed the art school, it was sleek and white with steel window frames and curved terraces. "Baby Deco," the agents called the block (in Alder Rise, even architecture was expressed in family metaphor).

Bram handled everything: negotiated the rent, checked and signed the contract, even made a trip to IKEA for the kitchen supplies we needed.

At a viewing together, I took the opportunity to remind him of my condition about other women. "You can do what you like here, but the house is off limits."

"Got it," he said. "I'll run my crystal meth lab from here as well, shall I?"

"Very funny." I held his eye. "And I meant it about the speeding. I don't want any nasty surprises."

Was I imagining it or was there the briefest flicker of furtiveness in his face? Impossible to tell, even with my experienced eye, but something made me press the point. "I mean it, Bram. No secrets."

"No secrets," he said.

I should have got it in writing, had it put in the signed agreement. I should have set it as a notification daily—*hourly*—on our new shared diary app: *no secrets.*

And, yes, in spite of everything that's happened, I *still* think the setup was an excellent one—for people not married to a criminal, that is.

BRAM, Word document

I torture myself sometimes with the thought of how the bird's nest might have panned out if I'd just been able to keep past sins secret and avoid committing future ones. ("Just!") I think it would have succeeded—I genuinely do. In terms of the division of time and labor, it really played to our strengths: I'd take care of the weekend rough-and-tumble, the necessary letting off of steam (the Trinity Avenue mums always used to say that boys needed precisely the same amount of exercise as a Labrador retriever), while Fi handled the school needs, the laundry, the nutritious, balanced diet. OK, so most things.

That's not to say she didn't have fun with Leo and Harry. She was probably the only person who could defuse the fever pitch of competitive spirit between them, to remind them that they could choose to be a team of two. They'd clamor for quizzes, especially ones about capital cities, and just as they risked coming to blows over Bucharest, she'd derail arguments with a bad joke. Like: "Where do Tunisians buy their music? iTunis." And the boys would look at each other in affectionate resignation. "Oh, *Mum*. Be *serious*."

(She looked the jokes up in advance, I guess.)

It breaks my heart to know how deeply she'll be regretting those arrangements now. It will destroy her to realize that disaster could not have struck without the framework of logistics suggested by her, without the trust she continued to place in me as a family man, a fellow householder.

Even when she could no longer trust me as a husband.

9

It's hard to say what were the first clues to subterfuge, because obviously I didn't recognize them as clues at the time. The car was an issue even before we separated—I do know that.

It was April or May when I found the speeding tickets. Maybe I'm imagining it now, but I do recall having an uncertain feeling when we discussed them, the sense that more was being concealed than was being shared. Maybe that was why I brought up his speeding with the counselor later.

"Bram? What are these?" I held up a pair of letters from the Driver and Vehicle Licensing Agency that I'd discovered folded between the pages of the coffee machine manual when the thing had suddenly stopped working: two separate notes of confirmation that three points had been added to his license. His speeding had long been a source of contention between us, though in terms of detection he'd generally got away with it. The way he drove, it was not so much that he thought the rules didn't apply to him as that he'd identified one of life's chief pleasures in bending them. "Six points? I thought you took that speed awareness course a while back."

"I did," he said warily.

"So why have they given you points?"

"Because these are different tickets. The course was for the first one."

I frowned, tried to get the situation straight. "So there've been *three* in all? One course and then two sets of points?"

"Yep. You're not allowed to do the course more than once in three years."

More's the pity, I thought, since he'd clearly learned nothing the first time. "Where are the original tickets? Are they in the study?"

"Why?"

"I'm just interested to know the details, that's all."

He cut me off in my path to the filing cabinet. "I'll get them."

With supreme reluctance, he handed over the notices to prosecute, one from the Surrey Police and one from the Metropolitan Police. The Surrey incident had obviously been during a work journey: nine miles an hour over the seventy limit on an A road, not dissimilar to the first offense eighteen months ago, when he'd been "running late, not looking at the dial." The London one was more troubling: forty-three miles an hour in a twenty zone on a road between Crystal Palace and Alder Rise. With that speed limit, it was almost certainly a residential stretch like Trinity Avenue, and forty-three was easily fast enough to kill a pedestrian, a child like one of our own.

Then I noticed the dates: one from a year and a half ago and the other from nine months ago. "How am I only hearing about these now?"

Silly question: because I'd stumbled upon them by mistake. Clearly, he thought he'd removed all correspondence from sight. "You're only allowed twelve points before you lose your license, aren't you? So just two more mistakes and—"

He cut in, irritated. "I know my times table, Fi. Come on—there are millions of people with points on their licenses, including most of our neighbors on this street. Why d'you think they're suddenly catching record numbers of offenders? It's purely a money-spinner for the authorities."

"It's purely a deterrent," I said, "with the aim of saving lives. Have you told the insurance company?"

"Of course I have. Seriously, it's no big deal."

Not to him. "This local one—the kids weren't in the car with you, were they?"

"No, I was on my own." Insulted now, he roared from defense to offense in about five seconds. "Disappointing, isn't it? I'm not quite as feckless as you hoped I was?"

"Don't turn this into a criticism of *me*!"

Even at the time I recognized the exchange as a perfect illustration of what was failing in our marriage. Not his crimes per se—I hardly need say that this one paled into insignificance compared with those to follow—but the role in which he so readily cast me in the aftermath. Cop, teacher, killjoy, snitch. Grudge holder.

Victim.

"You'd better let me drive from now on," I said. "Minimize your chances of reoffending." Oh God, now I sounded like his parole officer.

"Be my guest," he said sullenly.

Later, when I went to the filing cabinet, I found that the drawer marked CAR was empty.

BRAM, Word document

Like I say, the adultery was a bit of a false trail. Far more destructive in the long run were the speeding tickets, which I would have preferred not to share with her—to be honest, it was easier to avoid the grief. This is the flip side of good citizens like Fi: they find it hard to make concessions for their husbands.

I thought I'd squirreled away all evidence (I'd never known her to look in the file marked CAR) and so I was unprepared when she came brandishing the DVLA letters, demanding to know if I'd had the boys in the car with me (for the record, I did not, not for any of the offenses).

"I would never risk harming our kids," I told her. "Surely you know that."

"Then why risk harming someone else's?" she said, and she looked at me with a distaste that should have warned me that a separation was imminent, with or without the shenanigans in the playhouse still to come.

"Well, at least I know the truth now," she added.

But she didn't. She didn't know the half of it. The truth was that by the time she found out about those two speeding tickets there'd already been two further ones, two further sets of three points, and, with the final infraction, a court appearance.

The truth was, I'd been fined one thousand pounds and banned from driving for a year, lasting till February 2017.

Of course, now she *had* found part of the evidence, there was nothing to stop her double-checking my story by ringing the insurance company to see if our premium had gone up, though I'd been careful to ensure that the policy was set up in my name and password protected. Even so, I feared she would look at bank statements, notice that the premium had in fact gone down, not up, since she was now the sole driver of our Audi.

The sole *named* driver.

"FI'S STORY" > 00:42:52

I know some listeners might think I was too hard on him about the speeding tickets, and it's true that one of the other dads at school also had six points on his license and many others three. Even Merle had been stopped by the police for running a red light in Herne Hill and let off with a warning. There was a culture in our circle of such misdeeds being a badge of honor, as if these were victimless crimes.

Right.

I'm not saying I'm a paragon of virtue myself, but I honestly don't think I've ever broken the speed limit, at least not by more than a mile or two per hour. I mean, we have pedestrians and cyclists to navigate around; we have kids in our care; there are traffic lights and crossings every two minutes and most of us have cruise control on our cars: When is the situation ever so frantic that you can disregard all that? And does five miles an hour, ten miles, even twenty, *really* make such a difference to your arrival time? Is it *really* worth risking a catastrophic outcome?

But I guess most speeders aren't thinking about outcomes.

They leave outcomes to other people.

BRAM, Word document

No, the catastrophically wrong decision was not to conceal the ban. The catastrophically wrong decision was to ignore it. That's right—I'm admitting it formally: I defied a court-ordered driving disqualification and continued to drive.

If I hadn't done that, I wouldn't be in this position now.

Of course, at first I'd told myself it would be just one journey. It was a Saturday afternoon, a couple of weeks after I'd appeared in court, and I was in trouble with Fi for having an especially bad hangover when I was supposed to be fresh for the weekend's janitorial duties. She was demanding that I take the garden waste to the recycling center and, Sod's law, it was the only time in months there'd been a parking space right outside our door, so I couldn't just lug the stuff out of sight and ditch it in someone's skip.

Fi even came out to the car with me, issuing additional instructions. "Just swing by Sainsbury's on the way back and pick up dishwasher tablets and some more milk. Oh, I forgot! Leo needs a mouth guard for PE on Monday. They're starting hockey. Can you go to that sports shop on the South Circular?"

Under her scrutiny, I got into the vehicle I'd been forbidden by law to operate, turned the ignition and drove down Trinity Avenue to the junction at the Parade. Through muscle memory rather than conscious thought, I drove to the recycling center and then I drove to Sainsbury's and then I drove to the sports shop. I held my breath a few times but at no point did the sky fall in.

So I just kept driving. Essential trips only, I hasten to add, unavoidable family chores or work client calls that were impossible to manage by public transport. I hadn't driven this timidly since I was a seventeen-year-old learner in my neighbor's Fiesta. Speed limits: check. Red lights: check. Not a bumper over the parking line, not a hazard light flashed, not a cyclist cursed.

Once, when I looked in the rearview, I saw there was a patrol car behind me and I almost went blind with fear. I considered pulling over, just parking in someone's drive and waiting till the coast was clear, but at the next set of lights, the police car indicated left while I kept going and I was glad I'd held my nerve.

When the bird's nest scheme was proposed, I knew there was no way I could stop. "How is this going to work if we can't both drive?" Fi would demand. "You know what weekends are like, with swimming and playdates and visits to the grandparents. Maybe we should forget this whole idea."

No, I had no choice but to brazen it out until the end of the ban.

This is how criminals think, I see now. We tell ourselves other people have backed us into a corner and we're simply reacting, cooperating, surviving.

And we're so convincing we believe it.

10

"Murder. Assault. Rape. The kidnapping of our infants." They're *real* crimes.

Who was it who said that? Alison or Kirsty, perhaps. Whoever it was, Fi remembers there was laughter.

Lucy is touching her arm, cautiously, as if she expects Fi to rear up and hurl her chair through the window. "You need to stop crying. I know this is overwhelming, but we have to stay calm and start contacting people who might be able to help. Is there anyone else your husband might have made plans with? Or asked to look after the boys? A relative or a babysitter?"

Her mother. Of course, she had been going to try her before she phoned the school! She snatches up the phone again, selects the number, speaks the moment the ringing ends and before her mother can say hello. "Mum, thank God! It's me."

"Fi? Are you crying? What's—"

"Bram's taken the boys out of school and his phone is dead. Are they with you?"

"Bram's what? No, they're not with me—of course they're not." Another smooth, reasonable voice, just like Lucy's, just like Sarah Bottomley's. "Aren't you supposed to be away with your new man?"

"I came back early. Bram's disappeared and taken the kids."

"Don't be silly, why would he do that? Have you tried Tina? She might know where they are."

Bram's mother. Still working full-time but always happy to swap shifts and help out if given enough notice. He spoke to the school "a few days ago"; whatever he's doing with the boys has been planned and he's more likely to have involved his mother than hers.

She cuts off the call and rings Tina's mobile, again crying into the phone the moment she connects. "Tina? Do you have any idea where Bram is?"

"Is that you, Fi? Yes, he's at the house today. I thought you agreed that. Is anything wrong?"

Is anything wrong? The dismay that her obvious ignorance causes is brutal. "Useless," Fi wants to scream, "you're all useless!" It takes a Herculean effort to keep her voice steady. She doesn't want Lucy intervening again and speaking for her. "He's not at the house, Tina. *I'm* at the house."

"You're back from your trip already? Why?"

"It doesn't matter why, but I need to find Bram urgently, so if you have any idea where he might have gone, you *have* to tell me." Losing the battle, she begins to sob again, sees Lucy's grimace of concern. "He's taken the boys out of school and I don't know where they've gone and there's a—"

"Fi, shush a moment," Tina interrupts. "They're here. The boys are here."

"Say that again?" Did she hear correctly over the roar of her own fear, over the thumps of the removals team on the other side of the door?

"They're with me, right here, watching TV. I wasn't supposed to phone you until later to ask about getting them back to you in the morning."

"Oh, thank God. They're staying with you tonight? Is that what Bram's arranged?"

"Yes, if that's all right with you?"

"Of course, yes, thank you."

She's aware of Lucy's shoulders going slack with relief. This isn't going to be *that* story then, the worst, and can go back to being *this* one, the one about the house. She stands and reaches for the kettle. Tea making can finally get under way.

Fi wipes her eyes with a square of Lucy's kitchen roll. In spite of her relief, she remains rigid with anxiety. "Why aren't they in school, Tina? Are they OK?"

"They're fine. Bram just thought it would be easier for them not to go in. And I doubt he's far away, so if I were you I'd get out of the house before he sees you."

What on earth is she talking about? "Tina, please listen to me. There's a crisis here. The house has been completely emptied and Bram's phone is out of service and there's a woman who says . . ." Fi stops, can't repeat it, it sounds so absurd: *who says she's bought my house.*

"I know all about that." Tina's patience is exaggerated, a sign of impatience in her. "It's supposed to be a surprise, Fi."

"What surprise? Will you please tell me what's going on?"

"The redecoration. Isn't it obvious? Poor Bram, he'll be upset you've arrived before it's finished. Maybe you should go to the flat, ask the decorators not to let on you've been there? Or you're welcome to come over here. Shall I tell the boys you're home early?"

"No, no, don't do that." She has to stem this flow of questions, more questions she can't answer, and try to think. "You just carry on with whatever you've planned. Thank you. I'll phone you later. Give my love to the boys."

She hangs up. "She says you're here to decorate," she tells Lucy. "There's no other explanation for all our stuff having been cleared out. Where have you put everything? *Where are our things?*"

Abandoning her kettle, Lucy comes to sit next to her. Her movements, her breathing, are soft, as if she's making herself as unobjectionable as possible. "I'm not decorating, Fi—I think you can see that. I'm moving in. As I understand it, you and your family moved out yesterday. It sounds as if you were out of town—were you?"

"Yes, I'm not supposed to be back yet, but I needed my laptop." The sound she utters is supposed to be laughter but it comes out wrong, broken. "Pointless to ask where *that* is."

Lucy just smiles, gentle, encouraging. "Look, your kids are safe. That's the main thing, isn't it? Let's just catch our breath and think where else your husband might be. What about trying his office?"

"Yes." Fi looks at Lucy, this stranger in her kitchen now guiding her thoughts and actions, and she thinks, *What's the connection, Bram? Why have you lied to Tina? To me? Where have you gone?*

Her hands tremble as she takes up the phone once more.

What have you done?

GENEVA, 2:30 P.M.

He cannot stay in the room a moment longer; if he does, he will hurl himself at the sealed window—over and over until he slumps to the floor. He'll go out, find a bar, have a beer. Tomorrow, he'll move on. He won't risk staying more than a single night here. He'll go to the train station and he'll look at the departures board and take his pick. Cross into France, like he thought he might, to Grenoble or Lyon.

Good, he thinks, a plan. Or at least something better than *this*, this suffocating limbo.

Pocketing his wallet, he senses the lightness, the absence of counterbalance, the missing items he has carried habitually for as long as he can remember:

House keys.

11

I haven't said much about the boys, I know. I suppose I've been hoping I could keep them out of this. The thing is, I haven't even broken the news to them yet about the house. My latest lie is that it's been flooded after all the rain we've had, but I can't expect to fob them off for much longer, especially once *this* is released and people start talking. Primary schools have grapevines too, pruned with dedication by the parents at the gate, which I've avoided since Bram disappeared. (Mum has been doing the school run.) I've avoided Alder Rise altogether.

Their names are Leo and Harry and they are eighteen months apart. Leo has just turned nine and Harry will be eight in July. They both have Bram's dark, unruly hair and pale, gentle mouth and we all think they'll have his height too. Being so close in age, Harry follows in Leo's footsteps even while the prints are fresh. Harry's year three teacher was Leo's the year before; at swimming lessons, Leo moved from Dolphins to Stingrays the term Harry entered Dolphins. On paper, they look to be taking identical paths.

But they are utterly different in character.

Harry is bold. He makes eye contact with adults and his voice is a foghorn with a single setting. It's a point of principle to him that he doesn't seek consolation or comfort. He'll injure himself, slip down wet steps or crash-land from the magnolia, and he'll look for the exit through his tears, grimly resisting the outstretched arms, the offers of comfort.

Leo is the crier, the cuddler, the obliger. Inevitable, then, that I sometimes think my bond with him is stronger. He had quite bad allergies as an infant as well, which led to a couple of A&E visits before the right medication was prescribed. We still keep it to hand, in case of a flare-up.

I discussed the new living arrangements with him as we unloaded the dishwasher together. Harry claimed table laying as his chore, but the dishwasher was Leo's department.

"What do you think of our new plan?" I asked him.

"It's OK."

"You understand how it's going to work?"

"Mmm, I think."

"Things aren't going to be *that* different. We'll all still live here. It's just that Dad and I will take it in turns."

How important was it to see your parents together? If we hadn't announced it semiformally as we had, how long before the boys noticed of their own accord that we were never in the same place at the same time? It was possible it might have been some time.

"Do you have any questions for me?" I said. I saw him think, looking down at the last of the clean utensils in his hands. He was not the questioner. Harry was the questioner; Leo was the accepter. "Anything?" I prompted. "Anything that doesn't make sense?"

I could see him trying to summon something as he gazed down at his fistful of cutlery. Perhaps he just wanted to please me. I had no idea if he thought of me as being a victim to be supported or as an instigator to be resented. Neither, perhaps.

At last his face cleared. "Why do we have so many spoons?" he said.

He was so happy when I burst out laughing.

Oh, Leo. My Leo. I pray he hasn't been permanently scarred by all of this, though it's hard to imagine how he hasn't.

BRAM, Word document

Bless his heart, Harry cried his eyes out when I talked to him about the new setup, and he *never* cries. He's the family stoic.

"Are you and Mummy still married?"

"Yes, absolutely. For now."

"Then why won't you be in the house together?"

"It's a peace process, mate. We *will* be in the house together, just not long enough to argue. Because arguing's not very nice for anyone, especially you and Leo."

"Will we still go on holiday together?"

"Probably not for a while. We won't have as much spare cash."

"Mum said we can still go to Theo's house in Kent at half term. We always do that."

"Well, there you go."

Theo was Rog and Alison's kid. It was inevitable, I supposed, that Team Fi was assembling—the women, the mothers—closing ranks around her.

"Will you get a new wife?" Harry asked. "Will she move into the house as well?"

"Certainly not," I said. "Mummy's my wife. We're not getting divorced."

I should have said "yet" out loud rather than just mouthing it when he'd already looked away. It was wrong to give him hope, but I couldn't help it, because I was already suspecting that it was my hope too.

Which, if it's true, may prompt you to ask why I destroyed my marriage in the first place. I suppose because I didn't know how much I wanted it until after I'd destroyed it. I suppose I must have had a death wish.

Hence the suicide note.

12

So, back to the bird's nest.

The first Friday handover was casual to the point of anticlimax, especially as the main event appeared to all intents and purposes to be Bram moving back in. As if we were reuniting, not separating. The sight of his clothes draped on the gingham-covered armchair in the spare bedroom was not so different from the times when he'd slept there after a night out, not wanting to disturb me with his snoring.

"Can we camp out in the playhouse tonight?" Harry suggested, the new favorite way to mark a special occasion (they sometimes lit a campfire), and I saw the quick look Bram sent my way.

"It's a bit wet out there," I said. There'd been rain for days and by now the drains had overflowed, the lawn become spongy. Streams ran down the slide and puddled at its foot, and when the boys took off their shoes after playing outside, their socks squelched on the kitchen floor.

"Maybe we can put up a tent *inside*," Bram said, and my departure was lost in the outbreak of excitement that this provoked. Still, that was the point of this setup, wasn't it? For the boys scarcely to notice who was there and who was not. Continuity.

I walked slowly through the park to Baby Deco. At dusk, with its windows alight, it was seductive, a white and gold confection against the pink-blushed sky. But when I let myself into the lobby, I found it all much smaller and blander than I had remembered from the viewing. The lift was claustrophobic, the corridor narrow, and I had the peculiar feeling of being an intruder, here without permission or purpose. There was the chemical smell of just-dried emulsion, far removed from the Trinity Avenue aroma of muddy trainers and leftover Bolognese.

As for the unit itself, the space was so small, more like a hotel room than a flat. You could see everything it contained without turning your head: bed (three-quarters, not a full double), coffee table, shelving unit, two snug little armchairs. No dining space, only a short breakfast bar with the pair of cheap stools Bram had picked up at IKEA.

The shower ran cold and the fridge's purr grew into a jet engine as the hours passed, but I did not phone Bram for instruction. Except in the event of an emergency, we'd agreed on a single text each night after the boys were tucked up in bed. Nothing more.

At least I had no trouble working the TV, for it was an old one of ours, the small screen suiting the compact space. With an old episode of *Modern Family* to divert me (the aptness did not pass me by) and a bowl of ravioli on my lap, I downgraded my earlier disquiet to the temporary flatness you feel in one of those corporate-serviced apartments.

"It will take a bit of getting used to," Rowan had warned. "You'll wonder what on earth you're doing on your own, how you can possibly spend a day there without the kids to run around after. Just go with your feelings. Don't be hard on yourself for finding it strange. What you're feeling is natural."

Was this how Bram had felt these previous few nights, not to mention during his month of banishment to his mother's? Isolated from the pack, a solo pilot forced into a holding pattern.

I added my toiletries to the few he had assembled in the shower room, keeping them separate. As agreed, he had put his bedding in the washing machine and, as agreed, I hung it on the small clotheshorse in the kitchen.

Yes, I *did* wonder if it was going to be difficult to coexist in this way, to scrupulously separate all those mundane elements we'd shared for so long (we each had our designated kitchen cupboard space for groceries, like students!). There would be times when it felt petty, beneath us somehow, and others when it struck me as deeply, profoundly sad. But I didn't allow myself to think about that on the first night. I certainly didn't allow myself to cry. I just cleaned my teeth, washed my face, changed into pajamas. When I got into bed, I fell asleep straightaway, though I'd expected to lie awake all night.

The next day, I FaceTimed the boys in the lull between their swimming lesson and the birthday party they were attending at a city farm. They were bickering about who had been the first to pick llamas as his favorite animal, because it was against the law that they should choose the same. That second night, I went to visit my parents in Kingston and told myself that it was too late to head back to Alder Rise on the train, that I should save the taxi fare and stay over.

If you had told me then that in a few months' time I'd be moving back in with Mum and Dad semipermanently, I would have thought you had lost your mind.

BRAM, Word document

I surprised myself by liking the flat from the off, and not only because it was an escape from my mother's place. Perhaps it was the knowledge that I would soon be back home for my rotation, but I didn't feel lonely. I enjoyed its silent welcome, the fact that it demanded nothing of me. To my knowledge, the address had been distributed to no one but the utilities companies, and it was a good feeling in 2016 to be uncontactable, off grid.

It didn't hurt that the car was back on Trinity Avenue and I could push that particular item of fucked-upness from my mind.

I was on my best behavior now, ready to toe the line—however, wherever Fi chose to draw it. OK, maybe later, when things got truly hellish, I indulged in the fantasy that we might get back together, that she'd save me from myself, once and for all, but for now I gained pleasure simply from knowing that the flat was something only the two of us shared. Even though it was the very space that facilitated our separation, I liked that we were the only people to breathe its air. In the beginning, at least, it felt like somewhere only we knew.

"FI'S STORY" > 00:51:18

The house had century-old sash windows, with beautiful, watery imperfections in the original glass. The flat had state-of-the-art double glazing that I seem to remember was self-cleaning—not that I ever thought to notice.

The house had cornicing and ceiling roses and geometric floor tiles in rust and beige and a beautiful cobalt blue. The flat had cheap skirting and that laminate flooring that glows orange in artificial light.

The house had tall French doors leading to a stone terrace with weathered teak steamer chairs and potted Japanese maples. The flat had a balcony overlooking a busy approach road to the park that was disliked by locals for its constant congestion.

But none of it mattered. This was not a situation for direct comparison; it was a question of horses for courses.

Houses for spouses, as Alison put it.

The second Friday, I invited Polly to come and keep me company. I'd been up to Milton Keynes for a meeting and had spent the homeward journey of signal failures and delays dreaming of my first glass of prosecco (prosecco was the elixir of the female community of Trinity Avenue; some among us wept when the newspapers warned of a shortage).

"I don't understand," she said when we met at the main doors. "How on earth can you afford a flat here on top of the expenses of the house?"

"Well, you know how being incredibly old means we don't have a huge mortgage? At least not huge by current, crazy standards." Old grievances on my sister's part that I had bought a house back when prices were real-world had been laid to rest when our parents helped her with the deposit for her flat in Guildford, but there was still the occasional gripe.

As the lift delivered us to the second floor, it occurred to me there was no security camera. What happened if you got stuck? Who answered when the emergency button was used? There was no caretaker or concierge and I'd yet to make eye contact with any of the neighbors. Those I'd seen were young professionals, uninterested in interacting with a middle-aged crone like me.

I opened our door with the same sense of trepidation I'd felt the previous weekend and let Polly sweep in ahead of me.

"It's really cute, Fi. Wait, you've got a balcony as well?"

"Yes, but it doesn't get the sun, and the road's so noisy. Bram thinks there was some sort of affordable-housing remit and this is one of those units."

She laughed in scornful amusement. "So they've rented it to a couple who can already afford a massive house on Trinity Avenue? Hmm. Social housing policy at its most penetrating."

"Maybe Bram didn't tell them that," I admitted. This was an element of doing things differently that I hadn't anticipated: you weren't quite sure if you were selling it to other people or apologizing for it.

She'd explored the flat's remaining features in the time it took me to pour drinks, and we settled into the two stiff little armchairs as if about to have an interview filmed. The upholstery, an insipid puddle gray, was rough to the touch.

"So, how's he handling it all?" Polly asked.

"Pretty well. In fact, I'd say he's been almost, I don't know . . ."

"What?"

"Well, almost submissive."

"*Submissive?* Bram?" She gave a shout of laughter. "No, that can't be right. That must be the good twin he never told you about. They've swapped identities. The real Bram will be at a beach party in Goa. Or at least down the pub."

"I know it sounds crazy, but it's true. When he came to the house on Wednesday he looked, I don't know, *grateful*. I think he might really be appreciating how special the setup is."

"I should hope so!" Polly exclaimed. "Even he must realize how close he came to losing everything. And *would* have with any other wife."

Even now I'd split from him, even now scar tissue hardened my heart, I was deemed too soft on him. (How easy it was to imagine Polly telling her friends: "Get this: she's finally sent him packing—to the room across the landing!")

"The thing is, Fi, this bird's nest scheme all sounds great on paper—it's very fashionably liberal and all that—but do you trust him to do his share? Every Friday and Saturday, sole charge? You'd have no problem getting full custody, would you? You could be in the house seven days a week and he could be here. Why throw him a bone like this?"

"Because he's the center of the boys' world—in many ways, he's a better parent than I am. He makes them laugh and shout and dash around like mad things."

"*That's* a good parent? I think I prefer the boring kind that keeps them quiet—oh, and protects them from the effects of adultery."

I smiled. "Well, they've got one of each. And the boring one wants them to be able to stay in their home and sleep in their own beds every night, not on cots somewhere like this. She wants them to have what they've always had: football in the garden with their dad, building dens for the dog we'll probably never get . . ."

"Hmm." Her nephews' welfare held Polly's interest only so far. A year into her current relationship and not yet a parent, she was doubtless thinking she would never be foolish enough to find herself in my predicament. "How does it work if you or Bram start dating someone new?"

"There's no rule against it, obviously, but we've agreed, no third parties at Trinity Avenue."

"Third parties?" She raised an eyebrow. "That's not what they call them on Tinder."

"Well, whatever they call them, I'm too old to find out, so it's not going to be an issue."

"You're only in your early forties, Fi."

"I feel in my early hundreds."

"That's what marriage to Bram does to you. *He* won't have any qualms about bringing people back here."

"And I won't have any qualms about him not having any," I insisted.

My sister considered her verdict, which, when delivered, was in my favor only by chance. "I have to say, Fi, it really is the most perfect setup. You get the best nights here: Friday and Saturday. The grown-up nights. You can have a private life and keep it completely separate from him and the kids. From *everyone*."

I laughed. "Did you not just hear me say there isn't going to *be* a private life?"

"Maybe not at first. I give you a month."

That's Polly's way: she's so certain she knows what's going to happen before it does. She thinks she's seen it all before.

But even she admits now that she could never have predicted *this*.

#VictimFi

@LorraineGB71 Something really horrible is going to happen in that flat.

@KatyEVBrown @LorraineGB71 There's a reason why no one stays longer than six months . . . *turns on menacing soundtrack*

BRAM, Word document

Right, enough scene setting. Lies, infidelity, best bird's-nest intentions, you get the picture: I was already a fucking moron before we even get to the main event. To the tragedy that should never have happened. The grave I dug for myself.

(Second thoughts, maybe that's not the best metaphor.)

It was the third Friday of the new custody arrangement and I had a company away day at a country-house hotel near Gatwick. I was second on the bill to present, along with another sales manager, Tim, who, conveniently for me, had written the thing. It was a complicated journey involving a change of trains at Clapham Junction and a taxi at the other end, and when I missed the first train from Alder Rise, even before the DELAYED sign flashed up for the next, I calculated that I wasn't going to get to the venue in time. Standing there on the mobbed platform, I found it impossible not to think of the Audi parked a minute away on Trinity Avenue, especially when the calendar app showed no activities that might require its use after school. Best of all, Fi was not at home, as she usually was on a Friday, but had left early with Alison to go to some antiques fair in Richmond, driving in Alison's Volvo, which meant I could nip to the house and get the car keys without running into her.

So I slipped from the station and took the back route past the school and along Wyndam Gardens to the house. I considered texting Fi that I was entering the property without prior agreement, but I couldn't spare the half a minute that would take.

Thank God I didn't. A message stating my intention to drive that day could have buried me.

Speeding only when I knew for certain there were no cameras, and with the last of the rush-hour traffic against me, I reached the hotel with minutes to spare, copresented the mumbo jumbo Tim had strung together and then suffered the demoralizing tedium that is a full day's program of strategic team building.

(Basketmaking. I've just remembered. After lunch—at which I restrained myself and had only two glasses of wine—we did a basketmaking workshop. For fuck's sake.)

Now fast-forward to the drive back home. Not only was I exhausted, but I was antsy as well, thanks partly to the need to get the car back and partly to the darkening of my door by a new HR executive called Saskia. She'd been e-mailing me for the last few weeks about the firm's reissued contracts following our merger with a competitor earlier in the year, contracts that required disclosure, among other things, of any motoring convictions. (Did I mention I hadn't yet declared my driving ban to work? Even at this stage, the blunders were stockpiling.) I'd stalled her for as long as I could, avoided eye contact during the day's activities, but just before I left the venue, she materialized by my side.

"Everyone else in Sales has got their contract back to me," she said. "I just need yours. Can you make sure you bring it in on Monday?"

She was young and attractive and aware of it and somehow this only added to my agitation.

"If not, I'd be happy to issue a new one and find you a quiet spot to read it through during office hours," she offered.

"Sure," I said. "No problem." And I hung back so she wouldn't see me walking to my car, which I'd parked in a different car park from the assigned one just in case the ban came to light and someone like Saskia remembered seeing me driving off.

I can't go on like this, I thought. The constant just-in-case precautions. *I have to tell people. I have to tell Fi.* Without a doubt, she would consider the lying as egregious as the ban itself, so perhaps I could present it as a brand-new development? A six-month ban that began in August, when we were out of touch? What was the worst she could do?

Well, she could pull the plug on the bird's nest, keep herself at Trinity Avenue with the kids and consign me to the flat full-time. Maybe not even that. Once the need to economize lost its appeal, I'd be out of there too, just another sad fuck living with his mates or parents. Penge. Childhood meals. Godliness.

Now, of course, I see how lucky I would have been to settle for those consequences. I could have negotiated with Fi. Even when at the end of her tether, she was no monster. Besides, the law protected fathers' visitation rights, and far worse scumbags than me had regular access to their kids.

So, I was driving home, avoiding the main arteries in favor of unsurveilled parallel roads as I'd learned to do while driving "rogue," taking long residential stretches such as Silver Road in Thornton Heath, which was where I was when I got clogged behind a white Toyota.

I began flashing him to get a move on. *"Can you make sure you bring it in on Monday?"* I was thinking, screwing my face up at the memory of Saskia's voice, low-pitched and syrupy, as if HR was psychotherapy, not bureaucracy, when I lost my patience and pulled out to overtake the guy. I shouldn't have bothered—*obviously* I shouldn't have bothered—but if I was the kind of person who regularly exercised restraint, then I wouldn't have been in that mood in the first place; I wouldn't have been churning myself up about what I was going to say to Saskia or Fi; I wouldn't have lost my license; I wouldn't have been at the wheel illegally. I wouldn't have been estranged from my wife. But instead, I was *this* kind of person: sick with self-pity, prickly with the urgent, petty, short-term desire to get the upper hand over a stranger.

So, evidently, was he, because just as I was beginning to cut in front of him he accelerated, forcing me to straighten and abort my overtaking. For a second or two we drove side by side without acknowledging each other, our cars inches from touching. I could tell he was scowling and swearing at me, and I set my own face in a sneer before glancing left. He was just the kind of bloke I'd known he'd be: hard jaw, hard eyes, built in that solid way, like a weapon. And not just scowling but raging. The adrenaline rush I had on facing his fury was so powerful that all reason was lashed into its flow; as I put my foot down in a second attempt to overtake him, I felt an intense release of all the fear and impotence of the last few months.

Then I saw the car coming toward me and I changed my mind and braked, ready to concede defeat now, expecting to slot back in behind the Toyota and suffer the sight of a finger raised in victory as we reached the junction. But that wasn't the way it played out. To my confusion, he braked as well, blocking my attempts to slip back in behind, and we were continuing side by side, as parallel as if the cars were joined. Every mile an hour my speed dropped, his matched it. We were going thirty, twenty-five, twenty, and the oncoming car didn't seem to be slowing, a little Fiat 500, snub-nosed and innocent, with a driver who'd either decided to trust us to sort this out in time or wasn't concentrating fully, until suddenly there wasn't any time left. One of us had to get out of the lane or we would smash head-on. The Fiat swung sharply with a split second to spare, seeming to accelerate instead of brake, screeching off the road at speed and into an off-street bay with a parked car.

The force blasted the parked car against the front of the house. The noise was horrendous, not a crash so much as a crumpling, deafening even through sealed windows; God knows how it must have sounded outside. *Now* I moved into the correct lane, not daring to look over my shoulder at the wreckage before pulling over. A little way ahead of me, the Toyota waited, idling, and I could see the guy holding up his phone, calling for help, I assumed. Then, not quite believing it, I watched his brake lights go out and the car roar off.

I sat there, nauseated and immobilized, the pleading in my ears some shrill, desperate version of my own voice:

Pull yourself together. Turn around.

Go back. Get out of the fucking car and help.

At least phone *for help!*

Do it!

My hands floundered, hunting for my phone in my pockets, on the dashboard, in the door pocket, which was full of coffee cups and bits of plastic toy. It was on the backseat, possibly. My right foot was on the brake pedal and the leg had begun to spasm. I put the hand brake on, turned to reach over my left shoulder, but the seat belt locked.

Then I remembered who I was. I was a man banned from driving, on the road without insurance, against the law, probably over the alcohol limit. A man with prior criminal convictions (we'll come to that). What had just happened was dangerous driving by anyone's standards, even before the question of human injury or damage to property. There was no way around this—I was looking at a prison sentence. Shame. Confinement. Violence. Leo and Harry taken from me. The end of everything.

Breathe. Think. The road ahead was empty, the pavements clear. The Toyota was long gone. Light-headed now, scarcely capable of conscious thought, I took the hand brake off, hit the accelerator and pulled away.

Miraculously, I was able to drive fifty meters to the next junction without anyone passing in the opposite lane. The only moving car I saw was in my rearview, its driver having clearly come to the crash scene and stopped to help, just as any normal citizen would have.

Looking in the mirror before making a left turn, I expected to see smoke or some other evidence of carnage, but there was nothing. Only the same rooftops, the same sky.

"FI'S STORY" > 00:57:22

On the third Friday, I arranged to stay overnight with friends in Brighton. While not following any formal strategy, I was once again avoiding time alone in the flat—this in spite of being exhausted after a day out with Alison, not to mention concerned about the expense of all this gadding about.

When Bram arrived at the house for the seven p.m. handover, he was subdued and I wondered if he too was still adjusting to the new regime, trying as I was to align the serrated edges where practice joined theory.

"It takes a bit of getting used to, doesn't it?" I said. While not looking to be buddies, I was aware that he was the only other person in the world who knew exactly how I felt.

"Huh?"

"This. The new us."

Before he could reply, the boys descended from their rooms, Harry first, then Leo, who shouldered ahead of the noisy upstart and misjudged the maneuver, so they arrived in a sharp-elbowed tangle.

"Daddy, we're staying up late, aren't we? Aren't we?"

"Shut up, Harry," Leo snapped.

"*You* shut up."

"I said it first. But we are staying up, aren't we?"

It had plainly been established that Bram's nights were for fun, following the austerity of school nights, *my* nights. This was an unavoidable consequence of carving up the week the way we had, Rowan had warned, and I needed to remember it was not a popularity contest. Bram and I were comrades, not rivals. No longer a couple but still partners.

"Not *too* late," I told the boys. "But Daddy will decide—he's in charge. You OK, Bram?" I noticed now the telltale pallor of the mortally hungover.

"Sure. You know these team-building days—by the end of it you've lost the will to live."

I nodded, my sympathy waning. I hadn't been aware that he'd had a work event, but if he was stupid enough to indulge in a drinking session the night before, then what did he expect? Besides, one of the benefits of our being separated was that I was no longer duty bound to listen to his complaints about work (nor he mine—let's face it). So long as we each made our financial contribution and respected the terms and conditions, we had a free pass on that. "Anything I need to know about the flat?"

"No." He gathered his concentration. "The hot-water issue finally seems to have resolved itself. There's milk in the fridge, should be OK for the morning."

"Thanks, though I won't be there till later tomorrow. I'm going down to Brighton tonight."

Bram looked faintly alarmed. "You're taking the car?"

"No, I assumed you'd need it for swimming tomorrow, and Leo's got a party in Dulwich, remember? I'll take the train. I'm visiting Jane and Simon," I added, though he hadn't asked. I supposed it was on the phone calendar in case he was interested. "Kiss Mummy good-bye," I said, trying to encourage Harry and Leo toward me, but they evaded my affections.

"Only boys allowed," Harry said with cheerful callousness.

#VictimFi

@IngridF2015 He's obviously got a drink problem, poor #VictimFi having to deal with that.
@NJBurton @IngridF2015 Or he's just a normal guy and she's a sanctimonious b*tch?
@IngridF2015 @NJBurton WTF?!!! She's the victim here. #VictimFi, get it?

BRAM, Word document

Sitting watching anime with the boys that evening, I stopped myself from using my phone or laptop to search for news reports of the crash, which meant an agonizing wait for the local bulletin after *News at Ten*.

Nothing. Did I dare gather then that any injuries caused by the accident had not been serious, much less fatal? Did I dare picture a figure staggering from the driver's seat, shaken but unscathed? A figure whose focus during the incident had been on the irresponsible roadhogging of the Toyota and not on the recklessly overtaking Audi? After all, the whole thing had taken place in a matter of seconds, too fast and terrifying for any of us to absorb the detail.

Then again, *I'd* absorbed the detail.

I'd absorbed the crashed car's brand, model, even the year of registration: 2013.

I'd absorbed the fact that there'd been in the front seat not one figure but two.

An adult and a child.

14

BRAM, Word document

That weekend was hands down the most harrowing of my adult life: I was incarcerated in my own mind, incapable of thinking of anything but the crash. On Saturday morning, I took Leo and Harry to their swimming lesson by bus, resisting their clamor to be chauffeured by claiming I couldn't find the car keys. I'd get away with it this time but I wasn't going to be able to stop driving them indefinitely without their commenting on it to Fi. I wondered, semideliriously, if I might be able to fake an illness that precluded being at the wheel: epilepsy, perhaps, or a vision condition of some sort.

As luck would have it (luck—there's a relative concept), the library across the road from the pool was open and after the lesson I was able to dump the boys in a drop-in storytelling session while I used one of the public PCs. It didn't take long to find what I was looking for:

MOTHER AND DAUGHTER CRASH VICTIMS
IN CRITICAL CONDITION

Two victims of a collision yesterday on Silver Road in Thornton Heath are fighting for their lives in the intensive care unit of Croydon Hospital. Police from the Serious Collisions Investigation Unit are appealing to anyone in the area between 5:45 p.m. and 6:30 p.m. to come forward with information.

The owner of the parked Peugeot into which the victims' Fiat plunged came out of her house in time to see a dark-colored car—possibly a VW or Audi—turning in the distance, but was too far away to identify the model or registration. Her own car was written off in the incident. "That's nothing compared to what this poor family is going through," said Lisa Singh, a GP, who has in the past petitioned, without success, for the introduction of speed cameras on Silver Road. "It's a rat run during morning rush hour," she added.

A spokesman for the Met Police said, "The dark-colored car did not stop at the scene and we are currently working to trace its identity and whereabouts."

My first thought: a dark-colored VW or Audi—I'd been seen and was going to jail. My life was over. It took a superhuman effort to conceal my urge to roar with terror at this, to reason with myself that there'd been no definitive recognition, only an approximation. How many hundreds of thousands of dark VWs and Audis were there on the British roads? Black was, I knew, one of the most popular colors.

Then (and, I'm ashamed to say, only then): "fighting for their lives"—what did that mean? I prayed it was the standard exaggeration of local news reporting, the reality being closer to some serious bruising and a broken rib or two.

Back to: galling that the Toyota had not been mentioned—but wait, wasn't that also *good* news? Were this other guy to be apprehended, he would be able to identify not only the model of my car but also my face. Far better that he stayed out of the frame.

Then: what about cameras? Great, so there were none on Silver Road, but we were led by the media to believe they were on virtually every corner, that we were under constant surveillance by the authorities, not to mention on a more accidental basis by one another. After fleeing the scene, I'd zigzagged through more residential streets before eventually heading back to Alder Rise, and I was fairly sure I hadn't passed any shops or public buildings that might have had security cameras. Did bus shelters have them? And what about private residences? Could the police access satellites?

No, that was foolish. I was being paranoid.

Then I thought about forensics. Might there be something on my car, tiny bits of paint or dust from the wrecked Fiat, that could incriminate me? If I took the car to a car wash, would that signal guilt? Did car washes have CCTV? Likely, yes. If I hosed it myself, neighbors would remember, even note it as unusual ("Well, some of the guys would be out washing their cars at the weekend, but never *him* before."). Detectives looked for anomalies, didn't they? Breaks in routine.

All this in a matter of minutes. I could see it was going to be very easy to lose my mind.

"FI'S STORY" > 01:00:14

I remember the Sunday of that weekend well, but not for anything related to Bram. Having returned from Brighton on Saturday evening and gone straight to bed with a book, I made the morning Pilates class at the gym behind the Parade for the first time in years. Walking in with my kit bag and water bottle, I felt like an actress playing the role of a child-free mistress of her own destiny. I imagined myself recalling the class to younger female colleagues on Monday, ones like Clara, whose smile had occasionally drooped when I recounted my weekend schedule with the boys.

On my way out, I saw a familiar figure through the glass wall that divided the reception area from one of the fitness studios: Merle. A yoga class was beginning and she'd arrived a little late, scanning the room for a space to unroll her mat. I thought of her as the most self-confident woman I knew and yet she looked in that moment so . . . so *defenseless.*

Not so long ago, we'd enjoyed mocking the yoga bunnies and fitness freaks of Alder Rise. Didn't they have anything better to do? we'd said; did Emmeline Pankhurst give two hoots about *muscle tone*?

Now look at us. Not so immune to the virus of middle-aged insecurity as we'd thought.

Yes, that was probably my big epiphany of that whole period: *we're getting old—whether we like it or not!*

Seriously, talk about navel-gazing.

BRAM, Word document

When Fi arrived home on Sunday at noon to relieve me of the boys, I barely said two words before heading straight to the station to catch a train to Croydon. I found a scruffy, half-forgotten Internet café on a shopping parade and quickly learned the additional details released that morning regarding the condition of the two people in the Fiat.

It was far worse than I'd hoped: both had sustained head, chest and pelvic injuries and it was believed that one of them had also suffered cardiac arrest. Neither was reported to have yet regained consciousness.

Their names had not been published, for which I was grateful. Nameless, faceless, they were somehow less human to me, not so much flesh-and-blood victims as symbols of a more generalized injustice. As for the perpetrator, nothing new had come to light, and he—he was referenced without exception in the male singular—had "not yet been apprehended."

I looked up the address of the hospital—not far from West Croydon Station—and headed there without clearly knowing why (to send healing vibes through the walls? to whisper anonymous apologies?). But approaching the main entrance, I spotted the CCTV cameras by the doors and turned on my heel.

Instead, I took the northbound hopper bus that served Silver Road; I was grimly pleased to get a window seat on the right side for viewing the accident site. Both the Fiat and the Peugeot had been removed, but the drive was still cordoned off by the police. The gatepost had been obliterated, shrubbery flattened and two of the windows in the front bay boarded up, presumably shattered in the impact. A police board stood nearby—WITNESS APPEAL. A SERIOUS COLLISION OCCURRED HERE FRI 16/09 6 P.M.–6:15 P.M.—with a phone number to call with information.

It was six oh five, I thought. I'd noticed the time on my dashboard computer as I fled the scene.

Near the shrubbery lay a collection of bouquets, most still in their supermarket wrappings, as if to protect them from the same offender who'd harmed the humans.

You could see that each separate bunch had been placed in its spot with care.

15

Two days off, Bram's boss, Neil, is saying. It wasn't ideal, so soon into the new year, but to be honest he hasn't been himself since . . . well, since his marital troubles began. But anyway, they haven't seen him since mid-afternoon on Wednesday and don't expect him back until Monday.

"I thought he was helping his mum put some stuff in storage?" he says from his mobile, voice loud and bright. She can hear the Friday lunchtime laughter of a restaurant or bar in the background.

"No, he's definitely not with her," Fi says. She doesn't tell him about the decorating ruse Bram used on Tina. The idea of storage can't be a coincidence, though: if not Tina's, then surely theirs?

"Hang about," Neil says, and exhales in a low whistle. "He hasn't gone and checked himself into rehab, has he?"

"Of course not!" Even through the fog of shock, she's taken aback by this suggestion.

"Good, because that would be a hell of a lot longer than a couple of days. He'll turn up, Fi. You of all people know what he's like."

But what if she doesn't, she thinks, hanging up. What if she *doesn't* know what he's like? Not anymore.

"They haven't seen him either," she tells Lucy Vaughan, who is back at her kettle in a renewed attempt to civilize Fi with tea. Fi can tell from the subtle alteration to her manner since the business with the school that she thinks she might be dealing with someone of unsound mind. Not amnesiac, but *psychotic*. She is humoring Fi, managing her as best she can until backup arrives in the form of her husband, en route with the second van. She's no doubt regretting telling the removals guys they can grab a coffee on the Parade while they wait.

In fact, Fi is managing herself better now. She must be, because she's started noticing details, like the fact that Lucy has a chrome kettle where hers is black, white mugs where hers are sage green, an oak-topped table instead of the industrial-style steel one Alison helped Fi choose. All items that have, like the rest of her Trinity Avenue reality, evaporated.

"When was the last time you actually saw Bram?" Lucy asks, pouring steaming water into the mugs and dropping the squeezed tea bags into a Sainsbury's carrier, her makeshift moving-day bin.

"Sunday," Fi says. "But I spoke to him yesterday and Wednesday."

The gulf between the innocent arrangements of the last few days and the nameless mysteries of today already feels unbreachable. Bram was leaving work after lunch on Wednesday to pick up the boys from school and allow Fi her early start to her two-night break, which was also supposed to involve a leisurely return this evening and an over-nighter in the flat. She wasn't due to relieve Bram of the boys until Saturday morning, a departure from their usual bird's nest routine, but normal service was to be resumed the following week. Had she not needed to dash back for her laptop, or had she left it in the flat and not here, she wouldn't have known the boys were at their grandmother's;

she wouldn't have known the Vaughans were in her house. Not yet. She'd be in a state of grace.

Lucy unpacks a carton of milk and adds a dash to each mug. "Here, finally." She hands Fi hers with an air of it being a leap of faith to expect that Fi will not throw it back at her. "Don't worry. I'm sure he'll be back in touch soon and we'll sort this misunderstanding out."

She keeps using that word—"misunderstanding"—as if it's some farcical mix-up like when Merle's Biscuiteers delivery went to Alison's house and the Osborne kids ate them without checking the card. Easily solved, quickly forgiven.

Fi stares past Lucy, out to the garden. This, at least, is exactly as she left it, every plant rooted loyally to its spot. The goal net. The swing. The slide snaking from the roof of the playhouse to the patch of lawn worn to dirt.

"I was planning on taking a sledgehammer to that playhouse," she says, "when the kids grow out of it."

Lucy tries to conceal a look of shock, licks dry lips. As if preempting further violent impulses, she tries another helpful suggestion: "Should we phone the school and let them know the boys have been located? You probably gave them quite a scare."

"Oh yes, I should do that. . . ." Startled from her reverie and unable to locate her phone immediately, Fi starts to shower the table with items from her handbag before remembering the phone is in her pocket. Having redialed the school, she goes through to voice mail and leaves Mrs. Emery a garbled apology.

Hanging up, she sees that Lucy's attention is fixed on the items spilled from Fi's bag, specifically on a slim box of pills lodged in its mouth. Her face is that of someone whose worst suspicions have just been confirmed.

"They're not mine," Fi tells her, and she stuffs the items back into her bag, keeping the phone in front of her.

"Right." Pity crosses Lucy's eyes, followed by redoubled wariness. Perhaps she suspects that Fi has a personality disorder and has somehow appropriated the name of the former owner, presenting herself here in some dissociative state. "I don't mean to pry, but is the medication new? Did the doctor warn you about side effects? Maybe short-term memory loss or something . . ."

"I just told you, it's not mine!" Fi can feel her expression distorting, struggles to straighten it. She can't predict her emotions any more than she can control the way they express themselves.

Lucy nods. "My mistake. Oh!" At the sound of the doorbell, relief floods her face and she springs to her feet in near joy. "They're here!"

She hurries to the door and soon Fi hears two new voices—one male, belonging to one of the removals team or perhaps Lucy's husband, the other immediately identifiable as Merle's.

Merle! She was at the window, watching. She must have waited until the second van arrived and then decided she could delay intervening no longer. She'll be on Fi's side, won't she? See this as Fi does, know that Lucy is the deluded one, not her.

Lucy returns first, newly emboldened: "Right, now David's here, I suggest we both try to get hold of our solicitors."

Before Fi can protest that she doesn't have one, because she *hasn't sold her house*, Merle bursts in, all but forcing Lucy against the kitchen counter to take command of the space.

"Have you invited these people to move in, Fi?" Ardent with indignation, her scarlet top billowing, she is like a guru, her energy magical, transformative.

"No," Fi says with a surge of spirit, "definitely not. I don't know who they are or why their things are here. This is all completely against my will."

As Lucy begins to object, Merle silences her with a raised palm inches from her nose. "In that case, this is illegal occupation and harassment," Merle declares. (She worked years ago as a housing officer, which is always worth remembering.) "And I'm reporting them to the police!"

GENEVA, 2:45 P.M.

He's hungry, though it takes him a minute or two to recognize the sensation, because it's without urgency or anticipation. It's simply a variation on the new constant: Rawest anguish. Grief. Loss.

But you have to eat, even if it *is* going to remind you of all the times you doled out sausages to ravenous boys, coaxed broccoli into their mouths while privately agreeing it was food fit for the devil. Or maybe it will remind you of a face across the table at La Mouette, the best restaurant in Alder Rise, back when the face still smiled at you, back when the woman the smile belonged to still believed in you. Wanted to know your story, defend your frailties. When you all lived together in the house the woman loved and to which both the boys came home from the maternity ward.

Stop, he thinks. *You have no right to be sentimental. Or self-pitying.*

He leaves the bar, the first he'd come to on exiting the hotel, and follows signs to the nearest restaurant. He finds himself climbing through a building in a lift, which makes him think of Saskia and Neil and of the resignation e-mail that will be sent to them automatically on Monday at nine a.m. The request that Fi be sent his remaining salary payments—for what it's worth.

The top-floor restaurant has windows facing the airport and from his table he has a clear view of the planes coming in, touching down as if toys controlled by some capricious child. Everyone around him has the disengaged air of those in transit: too early to check in or too tired on arrival to make anything of the day. Might as well have some lunch.

He orders something with potatoes and cheese. Swiss mountain food. The glass of red wine doesn't help the anxiety any more than the beer did, but at least the action of drinking it is familiar. He supposes he should be grateful for every last minute of this borrowed time, grateful it didn't end at airport immigration when he negotiated passport control. Somehow, his impersonation of old Bram, family holidaymaker and occasional business traveler, had satisfied both the human officer and the thermal camera that scanned arriving passengers for fever and virus (though not, as he'd feared, guilt), and he'd been waved through.

Crazy, but even after he'd cleared baggage reclaim and customs and was out among the general public, he still expected to be approached and asked to step aside.

To be asked if the name on his passport was really his own.

16

Have I considered alternative theories about Bram's disappearance? Believe me, I've considered everything. Even the police acknowledge that his continued absence might be owing to circumstances unrelated to the house fraud, that he might never have got as far as being a fugitive from the law. He might have been killed in a brawl and his body hidden, or he might have gone on a drinking binge and fallen into the river—you wouldn't last five minutes in the Thames in January temperatures. We're talking about someone with a volatile temperament here; we're talking about a heavy drinker.

I know it sounds awful, but when the police ask me what Bram was like, *really* like, what made him tick, the first thing I think of is the boozing. I don't remember a day when he didn't drink. Mind you, that didn't make him unique on Trinity Avenue. There were men—and women—who would come home from work and within an hour have inhaled a bottle of wine. I used to think it was pure luck that their fix of choice happened to be a socially acceptable one, but then I realized it was their fix of choice *because* it was socially acceptable.

(I say "their" but I mean "our": it's not like I'm teetotal myself.)

One of Bram's little quirks was that he disliked lime; he joked that it was an allergy and that this was where Leo got *his* allergies from, but in fact it was to do with some epic tequila session when he was a student. He mocked mocktails; he mocked low-alcohol lager; he mocked Dry January; he mocked anything that didn't have alcohol in it.

I realize I'm using the past tense, which I shouldn't do. But you see why I'm so certain that if he *is* dead, then he won't have died sober?

I know now of course that September was a significant time for Bram and his misdemeanors, but my own crime-related concerns during this period were about the wave of incidents that had suddenly swept Trinity Avenue.

First, one of the tenants in the flats on the corner of Wyndham Gardens returned from holiday to discover his place ransacked by people renting it in his absence through some Airbnb-type website. Though avid in our interest, we all agreed he probably shouldn't have been subletting in the first place.

Deeper sympathies were extended to Matt and Kirsty Roper soon after when they were burgled in broad daylight. Kirsty was one of us, hers a misfortune we could get on board with: a side gate left on the latch while the family nipped out to the garden center; the alarm not activated (they were going to be gone only twenty minutes); a Stonehenge of laptops and other devices left enticingly on the kitchen table; a barking spaniel that the neighbors had been trained to ignore—it was a perfect storm that might have broken over any of us.

"The police think he must have been watching the house," Kirsty told us. "In a way, that's the most upsetting bit."

Gripped by the drama, her son Ben, Merle's Robbie and my Leo formed a detective society, meeting in our playhouse to hypothesize. I delivered biscuits and juice to them, at no time pointing out that their meeting place had itself once been the scene of a crime of sorts.

There was no news of the culprits being caught, and soon Kirsty reported that the police had decided not to investigate. "They haven't got the manpower. They have to prioritize real crimes."

"Burglary isn't considered a real crime?" I said.

"You know what she means," Alison said. "Murder. Assault. Rape. The kidnapping of our infants. The kind of thing that gets on *Crime-watch* or *The Victim*."

Though I *did* know what she meant, I personally thought breaking and entering a most unsettling violation. The idea of criminals soft-footing around my house, touching the boys' possessions, seeing how we shared our lives (or didn't, in the case of Bram's and my separate bedrooms): it was not so much an invasion of privacy as of the soul.

BRAM, Word document

If I can just keep my job, I thought, riding the lift up to the HR department on Monday morning and thinking it couldn't climb high enough as far as I was concerned, *I'll happily stay in this little mirrored box for hours, days, perpetually between places, between problems. If I can somehow keep all of this a secret from Fi,* I thought, *if those poor people in the car pull through and the police close their investigation owing to lack of evidence, then I'll never sin again. I'll become a missionary. I'll be celibate. I'll—*

"Bram?" Saskia said.

I started. I hadn't noticed that I'd exited the lift, navigated the corridor, reached her desk.

"Did you want me?" she prompted, with an impressive game face. She wondered perhaps if I was a simpleton, employed here on some minorities quota.

"Yes, sorry. I've got your contract," I said.

"It's *your* contract, but thank you." She gave me a small smile as she took it from me, prim but pleased.

I cleared my throat, reached for the prepared lines. "As you'll see, there's some personal information I've disclosed and I wanted to chat to you about it face-to-face. Can we . . . ?"

"Of course." Professionalism not quite veiling human curiosity, she led me from the open-plan area into a nearby meeting room and discreetly pushed shut the door. We sat opposite each other, the contract and Saskia's notebook on the table between us. "Go ahead."

"Well, it's the bit about motoring convictions. . . . The thing is, Saskia, I've received a driving ban."

"Received": it didn't seem like the right word—you received an award or praise, something desirable, whereas this was something so undesirable that the person I was saying it to was compelled to take written notes.

"I see. Well, given your sales role, that could be problematic. When did this happen?" she asked.

"In February." The truth.

"February? That's seven months ago!"

"I know, and I'm really sorry I didn't declare it straightaway. To be completely honest, I haven't even told my wife yet. I've been covering up the fact that I've not been able to drive." Perhaps it was the relief of the thing, or simply the intimate dimensions of the room, the comfort of her body heat, but I began to get more confessional than I'd planned. "There was this one time—it was awful. She was at the window of our house, expecting me to go off somewhere in the car, and I unlocked the door, got in the driver's seat, just sat there pretending to fiddle with the heating, until she moved away. Then I got out and caught the bus."

Actually, this was not such a bad thing to confess; it was the sort of story you might remember if called to testify in a court of law. ("Was it your understanding that Mr. Lawson had continued to drive?" "No. But I do know he was pretending to, to his wife.")

I swallowed. "I was like one of those blokes who's been made redundant but keeps putting on his shirt and tie and leaving the house every morning to go to work."

This addition was more regrettable: it might give her ideas.

"Oh." Saskia blinked and I saw that her lashes were weighted with mascara. It took a moment because my sensibilities were rerouted, but the signs were there for me to read: that lavish eye makeup, the snugly fitting shirt with the pendant signaling the route to the hidden cleavage; poking from under the table, heels an inch higher than was comfortable. Not inappropriate, but with a defiant message for those who cared to receive it: I'm a professional, but no less female for it. No less single.

"I should say my soon-to-be ex-wife," I said, sensing a lifeline. "Not that there's any reason you should know, but we've split up. It's all been a bit of a nightmare, and I suppose . . . I suppose I just didn't need there to be yet another thing I've done wrong."

It was quite a betrayal to imply that Fi had been unjustly on my case, when she'd in fact been more generous than any cheated wife I'd ever heard of, but needs must and to my relief Saskia was regarding me with the beginnings of compassion.

"Sounds like you've got yourself into a bit of a tangle. I'll have to check the files, but you don't have a company car, do you?"

"No, I use my own."

This was the one pinprick of sunlight in my stormy sky: when I'd joined the firm I'd opted out of the standard sales perk in favor of the cash alternative. The Audi was privately owned and registered to Fi and me at Trinity Avenue; if the police came calling, they would have no need to involve my employers.

"Used," I corrected myself. "Obviously, I've made no claims for fuel since February." I'd taken the hit myself, paid for petrol in cash so Fi wouldn't question any debits from our joint account.

"How have you been getting to your appointments? You can claim for train travel and taxis, you know, assuming Neil signs them off. Or has he arranged for a driver for you?"

I said nothing and she smothered a grimace.

"You have told him, haven't you, Bram?"

"No. You're the first person I've told." I could feel myself doing it, giving her the look that said, "You're the first because you're special." I let the moment extend, glanced very briefly at the pendant on her breastbone. Borderline sexual harassment of an HR executive of all people was insanity by most people's standards, but mine no longer bore any relation to most people's.

"You'll need to tell him," she said finally. "Would you like me to be present?"

"No, I'll be OK. He's not in today, so I'll do it tomorrow."

Having finished her notes, Saskia carefully placed pen on notepad. "It's at his discretion whether this will have an impact on your future here. Sales roles do require you to have a current driver's license."

"I know." I sighed. Another look, this more lingering than the first. "But I'm glad I've come clean."

I kept using that term, both in speech and in my mind. It was starting to feel disingenuous.

"FI'S STORY" > 01:05:34

It was only days after the Ropers' burglary that another Trinity Avenue resident, an older woman who'd been recently widowed, was the victim of a scam worrying enough for Merle to get straight on the phone and arrange for a community police officer to come and talk to us—and for me to phone Bram at work. "Did you hear what happened to Carys?"

"Who?" he said.

"You know, the lady at number 65? Teaches piano? She was ordering a new bank card and her call to the bank was intercepted by scammers. They phoned her back and got her to divulge her PIN and then they sent a courier to her house to pick up her old card. By the time she realized, they'd almost emptied her account. *Thousands*, apparently."

There was a delay before he spoke. "Banks never send couriers to pick up old cards."

"*We* know that, yes. It just shows how convincing they must have been. Alison says even the couriers don't know they're in on a scam— they've just been booked for a regular job. Poor Carys was distraught. I've already phoned Mum and Dad about it, and you should tell your mum as well."

Another pause, then, "Why?"

He was beginning to frustrate me. "Because these fraudsters obviously prey on older people! You know, they're more trusting than we are, not so confident to challenge a change in procedure."

"Right."

I frowned to myself. "You don't seem very interested in this, Bram. I think we all need to be really vigilant if criminals are operating in Alder Rise."

He gave a weary sigh. "Come on, Fi. Carys was just a bit gullible. Everyone knows you never give PIN numbers or passwords over the phone. Let's not get carried away."

I felt a surge of indignation. Though he'd never been community spirited (except in the alcoholic sense), I'd always felt certain of his respect for my efforts, but the way he was dismissing poor Carys's ordeal was flippant, almost arrogant. "This kind of crime is on the rise, apparently. We got a booklet from the police."

"The police have been round?" He sounded startled.

"No, it came through the door. It tells you about all the current scams, how they work, how you can protect yourself."

"Sounds more like a catalog to me. If we didn't know how to rip off our neighbors before, we will now."

"Bram!" It was a while since he'd been obstructive like this. Since our new arrangements had begun, he'd been, as I'd told Polly, meekly obliging. "How can you make a joke of this? The victims are our neighbors—ordinary hardworking people like us."

"Sorry, Fi. I'm a bit distracted, just waiting to go into a meeting with Neil. Of course we must all be vigilant. We could be in the grip of some Ukrainian crime ring. Or Nigerian. I don't know who our underworld enemies are these days."

I'd had enough of this. I had work to do myself. "Anyway, the reason I'm calling is, there's a meeting with a community officer tomorrow evening at eight, so I wondered if you could stay a bit late with the boys while I go along."

"Sure."

I ended the call. He was preoccupied—that was obvious—and I presumed there was something going on in his private life. Maybe I thought I'd even have a casual look around the flat on Friday evening for signs of female habitation. I certainly wasn't going to ask him outright, because that way lay the fraught waters of emotional complication, maybe even the temptation to swim back downstream.

Yes, of course I wish I'd asked. I wish I'd *demanded* to know.

#VictimFi

@val_shilling Aargh, I'm not going to get anything done today, am I?

BRAM, Word document

"Jesus Christ, Bram," Neil barked, "how the fuck did that happen?"

I readjusted, pulled the hangdog face he was expecting, not the haunted contortion I'd seen reflected in the glass wall of his office moments earlier.

"Was it in one of those new twenty-mile-an-hour zones? I thought they weren't enforceable yet."

"No, it was out of town, mostly."

"'Mostly'? There speaks a serial offender."

His response bordered on admiration, which reminded me of something the instructor had said in my speed awareness course. "Would you be so quick to tell your mates if you'd been caught driving drunk instead of speeding? No? And yet they're equally life-threatening." And she'd caught my eye, mine especially.

"So, what's it been like, not driving?" he said.

"You get used to it—it's already been a while. I'm really sorry for not saying anything sooner, mate. What I need to know is, is it going to be a problem? Workwise?"

"Technically, yes, a big problem. But since it's you . . ." As improper as Saskia had been proper, Neil now laughed. "You muppet. We'll just get one of the interns to drive you around. Till when?"

"The middle of February. That would be great, Neil. Thank you. Just on the days when the routes between calls are a bit awkward. I'm happy getting the train to and from home."

"Happy? You're kidding, right? I wouldn't get on one of those commuter trains if you paid me. I'd rather *roller-skate* in."

"They're a nightmare," I agreed. "Constantly delayed. I was almost late for the conference last week."

Another seed scattered, but I needn't have bothered, because he was too busy singing the lyrics to "Breaking the Law" to notice. I had never been more grateful to have such a clown as my direct superior. There weren't enough David Brents left in the working world.

"Five points if you can name the band," he challenged me.

"AC/DC?"

"Judas Priest." He was pleased with the victory. "What did Fee Fi Fo Fum say, then? About the ban?"

He'd met her several times—family parties, dinners with his wife, Rebecca, birthday drinks in the Two Brewers. Once, when Fi was a bit stressed, she'd found us smoking and hissed at me like I was some juvenile offender. I'd seen the look of shame on Neil's face before it rearranged itself into laughter.

"I haven't told her yet," I said.

He whistled. "Well, good luck with that. I'm guessing it's going to affect your new henhouse arrangements, is it?"

"Not 'henhouse.' Bird's nest."

"Sorry, bird's nest. Clipped your wings a bit, I would have thought." He cackled, never more amused than by himself. "They'll grow back. You know she's been in touch with Rebecca? Rallying the sisterhood. She sent her the link to that podcast and now they tweet together when they listen. What's it called, again?"

"*The Victim*?"

"That's the one."

The Victim was a cheap, sensationalist bit of entertainment with which Fi and her crowd had developed an obsession. Every episode, a new victim—invariably female—gave her unvarnished account of some terrible injustice, safe in the knowledge that there was to be no opposing argument, no investigative reporting, nothing that might contradict her version of events. Instead, listeners were invited to draw their own conclusions. "There but for the grace of God go I," Fi had said by way of explanation (she liked to listen to it while ironing the boys' school uniforms).

"Goes on for *hours*," Neil said. "Just one woman slagging off some man. It's never woman-on-woman, is it? And what if it's not true, just someone venting? Doesn't that make it slander?"

"Hmm, yeah," I said, no longer really listening. Why was there no further news about *my* victims? How long could people remain unconscious before their chances of recovery faded? Was it less disastrous for me for the mother and child to die, removing any risk of their identifying me, or to recover and reduce the severity of the criminal charges brought against me if I *was* identified? (Assuming the driver of the Toyota hadn't made a report—and if he hadn't already, then surely he must have decided not to at all.)

Scrub that—I know how it sounds. I wanted them to live—*of course* I wanted them to live. If I thought my life was somehow worth more than theirs, I wouldn't be writing this now; I'd be somewhere far-flung, beyond extradition.

Lost in some savage place where only the damned take their pleasures.

"FI'S STORY" > 01:09:04

To my surprise, when I returned from the community meeting at Merle's on the Wednesday evening, Bram was standing in the front garden under the dripping magnolia. There was a large rain puddle on the paving stones and he seemed oblivious to the fact that one of his feet had sunk into it.

"Why are you out here in the dark? Keeping a lookout for burglars? I don't think we're in any danger, with a police officer still on the premises two doors down." I noticed he was smoking, which answered my question for me.

"Meeting go OK?" he said.

"Yes, really good. They gave us these special pens with forensic fluid to mark all our valuables, so if they're stolen and get recovered, they can be returned to us. I'll get the boys to do it—they'll enjoy that. And we're going to get new signs that say 'criminals beware: this is a policed neighborhood,' or something like that."

"Sounds useful." His tone was mechanical.

"I didn't know you were smoking again."

He didn't answer, which was fair enough; I had no jurisdiction over him now, and in any case he'd stepped outside. The boys were upstairs in bed, their lungs safe.

"Thanks for staying late. Are you coming in?"

"No, I'll just finish this and then go." He startled at the sound of Merle and some of the other neighbors coming from the house to say their farewells to the police officer at the gate.

"You look a bit uneasy," I said. "Guilty conscience?" As our eyes locked, I kept my expression free of challenge. "Your teenage brush with the law, I mean. What else?"

His face flickered with some emotion I couldn't track. "Oh. Right."

It was sly to bring this up, a schoolboy conviction for cannabis possession almost thirty years ago. He'd been unlucky to have just had his eighteenth birthday and qualified for adult prosecution.

He looked away, ground out the cigarette and kicked it into the deepest part of the puddle as if expunging all evidence of it. Of course

I interpreted that as symbolic of a desire to expunge far greater transgressions than a sneaky smoke.

"I'll head off, then," he said. He really did look wretched.

Don't waver, I told myself. *Remember the playhouse. He didn't stop to think how wretched that would be for* you, *did he?*

I noticed he took a left at our gate, not the right that would have taken him in the footsteps of the police officer and the most direct route to the Parade and the park, but I didn't dwell on it.

17

Were the women of Trinity Avenue control freaks? Is that a serious question? Because we pulled together as a community to prevent crime?

No, no, I know you didn't mean to offend. Let me answer your question this way: if a control freak gets up every morning to dress and feed her children (herself too, if she's really on form), take them to school and head straight to the station to cram onto a commuter train to Victoria and then a tube to the West End; if, after working a full-on day, she then comes home and gets on with the kids' reading, bath-and-bedtime routine (sometimes still with her coat on for the first part), segueing seamlessly into making dinner while unloading and reloading the dishwasher, her e-mail open on the iPad on the counter or, every now and then, a friend propped nearby with a glass of wine because it's so hard to catch up any other time, even though she gamely signs up for book groups and residents' association and, yes, meetings with community police officers; if she finishes the evening by making the kids' packed lunches for the next day and sorting out the recycling and putting the laundry on and ordering groceries online or birthday presents or whatever else needs finding or replacing that day; if she climbs into bed thinking her greatest achievement of the day has been to not scream at her children, not argue with her colleagues, not divorce her husband . . .

If that's what a control freak does, then yes, I was one.

BRAM, Word document

Rog Osborne and I used to joke that it was like the Pink Ladies and the T-Birds on Trinity Avenue, everything done along gender lines. (The kids went with the women, of course, unless it suited the Pink Ladies otherwise.)

Fi was Sandy through and through, blond and wholesome and hardworking. Moral in a sweet, old-fashioned way. Totally on top of her assignments. I'd failed as her Danny long before we separated, long before I had my own greased-lightning moment behind the wheel and consigned us all to purgatory.

"FI'S STORY" > 01:13:01

It's not that I lied to Polly—I really hadn't intended getting involved with someone new. Burned fingers, better things to think about, and all the rest of it. But intentions are a little more fluid than you think, I've found, and though it was true that I had no heart for the Gomorrah that was online dating, I did still have a heart—and other body parts.

I met Toby the old-fashioned way, in a bar, the bar of our local restaurant La Mouette, where Alison and I were marking my new Friday night availability at the expense of hers. Both of us were surprised by the place having grown so much livelier since our last visit that it now had need of a bouncer.

Neither I nor the guy waiting next to me at the bar was having any success catching the bartender's eye.

"I've done a bit of bar work in my time," he told me, "and I'm wondering if I should offer to help out."

"If you were female and over forty you'd be used to waiting," I said. As lines go, it was not one designed to seduce, but he grinned as if in agreement.

"This place is crazy." He was gray eyed, dark browed, uncomplicated in style, younger than me by about the same number of years that Bram was older (impossible not to make comparisons, much as I set out to avoid them), and my impression was of someone unafraid to be direct when he needed to.

"It's not as bad as the Two Brewers," I said, and then, at his lack of recognition: "The pub at the other end of the Parade? You don't live around here, then?"

"No, Alder Rise is a bit swanky for me."

"Swanky? You make it sound like Beverly Hills or something." So conditioned was my small talk that I almost ran on as if I hadn't heard him say he didn't belong: *The way house prices are going it might as well be Beverly Hills. Isn't it* awful *how we're all suddenly millionaires? People don't get how* trapped *we feel! Plus, there are suddenly all these* crimes. *Will that affect house prices, do you think?*

But I caught myself, and in any case he was skipping the property talk altogether to ask: "Here with your husband, are you?"

"No. We're divorcing." I was better-get-used-to-it breezy. "You?"

"Been there. Few years ago now."

So far, so abbreviated. But the way he looked at me was full and uncompromising. (Was this how Bram was now looking at other women? Maybe even did before—? *Stop.*)

"Where's he now, then?" he asked. "Your ex?"

"Still in the area. We share a house, actually. We have two sons."

"So you've split but you're living together? How does that work?"

I shrugged. "It's an unusual setup. I won't go into details."

"No, I'm interested."

"You don't have to say that. Other people's children—is there anything *less* interesting? Oh, two mojitos, please!" By the time I turned back from the bartender, my new friend had his phone out.

"Why don't I call you sometime." Not a question. And, in a way, that's what caused the abrupt lurching sensation of desire, the self-confidence of him.

I gave him my number. "Fi," I added.

"Toby."

It wasn't awkward; it was natural and that was why I didn't fight it.

When I returned to our table with the drinks, Alison was laughing.

"Well, you certainly have a type," she said.

"We were just talking, Al."

"But he took your number!"

"I neither confirm nor deny it," I said. "And you couldn't be more wrong about my type. That guy's easy and uncomplicated."

"So is everyone when you've only spoken to them for two minutes," she said. "So was Bram once, probably."

"Bram was *never* uncomplicated," I said. "In fact, he was acting a bit weird the other night. Have you seen much of him on his days at the house?"

"No." She pulled a face. "You know what weekends are like."

Comments like this brought me up short: I was no longer at home on the weekends, at least not till Sunday afternoon, because we had chosen to do things differently from other people. Yes, our friends were supportive, but there was an element of spectacle to the dynamic, as if they were watching us from the stalls, any show of faith provisional.

"Teething problems with the bird's nest?" she suggested on cue.

"I don't think it was that. I don't know what it was."

We looked at each other and I sensed what was coming.

"So, listen, we haven't really talked about how this is going to work."

As I watched her stir her cocktail with the straw, I hoped Bram wasn't drinking on duty at the house.

Stop thinking about him!

"For instance, can I invite you both to the same thing? I mean, I wouldn't be so insensitive," she added, hastily, "but what about things that I've already invited you both to?"

"Alison," I said, "I told you before, you don't have to pick sides. You can invite whoever you like to whatever you like and I'll be nothing but courteous to all concerned."

"I'm sorry, but *no one* can be this forgiving," she said.

"I'm not forgiving. I'm just doing my best to control the impact events have on me. If I have to make adjustments to my life, then I'll be damned if anyone else decides what they'll be."

I let my eyes drift to Toby, still standing alone at the bar and now in possession of a drink. Perhaps he was early meeting someone for dinner—her choice, then, since he was a newcomer to Alder Rise. An online date, no doubt. As if sensing my attention, he rotated slowly, missing me in his surveillance before returning to his drink.

BRAM, Word document

I was with the kids at the farmers' market on Sunday morning when I first saw Wendy. It was nine days after the Silver Road incident and frequent checks online at the Internet café, as well as of the various local papers left on the train, had yielded no further news on the victims. I continued to function in a state of high agitation; as I surveyed the stalls of cheeses and honeys and wild boar burgers, it was as if I had never seen such a spectacle before, had been stripped of my middle-class credentials. My citizenship.

I didn't fancy her that day. I was in a different mode (the mode of father trying to act normal, feel normal, while looking over his shoulder for the squad car at the curb), but I noticed her noticing me. Fi used to say that a huge part of attraction was simply being made aware that the other person is interested in you, that deep down we didn't develop much from our teenage selves, flattered by the first head to turn our way. In other words, we'll take anyone who'll take us. True, of course. This woman was interested, and had she caught my eye two weeks ago I might have been interested in return.

Ten minutes of queueing for artisan fudge made with Pop Rocks and when I next looked, she'd gone. After that it was all about whose mouth explosion was the more violent and whether a piece should be saved for Rocky, the Osbornes' dog, or would that be cruelty to animals and if it was cruelty to animals, then didn't that mean it was cruelty to humans too, since Mrs. Carver in year three said humans were animals too, and maybe they should call the police and get Dad arrested.

"Nine-nine-nine, you have to phone," Harry said.

"No, one-oh-one if it's not an emergency," Leo corrected him, with a tone of moral superiority he often used with his brother.

"But it *is* an emergency. Someone could *choke to death*!" Now Harry began chanting—"Dad's going to pri-son, Dad's going to pri-son!"— loudly enough for people to look.

"Don't joke," I said, and I made a passable job of finding the whole thing funny as opposed to wanting to lean into the nearest bin and vomit up breakfast.

"FI'S STORY" > *01:18:44*

In a way, I didn't care if Toby phoned me or not. The feeling that I might like to sleep with him was enough, a feeling matched only by the exhilaration of knowing I was free to choose either way. I was no longer loving and cherishing and being faithful to Bram as long as we both shall live.

According to Polly, I had been institutionalized by my marriage. I'd labored under a form of Stockholm syndrome.

Still, I was a free woman now—at least I *thought* I was.

#VictimFi

@Tracey_Harrisuk LOL Stockholm syndrome
@crime_addict @Tracey_Harrisuk She's not free if she's still legally married #justsaying

BRAM, Word document

Tuesday brought my semiregular slot with Rog Osborne at the Two Brewers and I headed there straight from the station, even though we weren't meeting for another hour. It was becoming obvious that I could deal better with the crushing weight of guilt and uncertainty if I avoided time alone and spent my idle hours with a drink in my hand.

Rog managed roughly half the number of pints I did before calling time on the grounds of being middle-aged and/or under his wife's thumb, and he was just draining his last when, glancing past him, I saw her again: the woman from the farmers' market. As I say, I'd had a bit to drink, and I started making some connections: the flat was mine and, God, it was eleven days since the horror and it had been such a strain to be my usual self at work and with the kids and even here with Rog, and I suppose I thought I deserved something to take my mind off it. (Even *I* wouldn't use the word "reward.")

She was wearing skinny jeans and a very tight pink top. You could see the outline of her bra, the way the elastic cut into her skin, and dark spots under her arms—it was humid for late September, more like late summer. Her eyeliner had run and maybe her lipstick too. Even in repose her lips didn't quite meet.

"What?" I said, seeing Rog watching me.

"I'm not saying anything, mate." He winked. "By which I mean I'm not saying anything to Alison."

"You can say what you like. I'm a free agent."

"Are you?"

"Yep. We're both allowed to see other people—it's agreed. Just not at the house."

"Which gives you, what, five nights a week on the pull?"

"You think it's that easy?"

Gunshots of laughter from a group of women at a table by the window saved me from answering. The woman I had my eye on was not with this group—she was younger, in her early to mid-thirties.

"Oh," Rog remembered, "Alison said the mums' book group are meeting here. Not theirs, a rival one. You'd think they could confine that sort of thing to the kitchen."

"I know. Is nothing sacred anymore?"

This was the shtick among us emasculated husbands (and soon-to-be ex-husbands): faux old-school chauvinism. In the same spirit, when Rog headed for the door and I said I'd hang about for one for the road, he just grinned at me like it was the 1950s and boys will be boys.

I crossed the bar and, without asking, bought her another glass of the white wine she was drinking. Caught her eye and held it, bold but respectful. Twelve years of marital devotion (those two lapses notwithstanding), and it was as if I was a bachelor in my early thirties again. Maybe it *was* this easy—so long as I didn't think about the horror, of course.

She told me her name was Wendy and she lived in Beckenham, had come to Alder Rise that evening to help a friend paint the kitchen of her new flat on Engleby Close.

"She's not out tonight?"

"Was. She went home. It's been a tiring day."

"You're not too tired, then?"

"Not yet." She made no attempt to mask her desire, leaning close as she spoke. "Were they your boys at the market the other day?"

"Yep. Leo and Harry, a real pair of rascals."

"I thought they were cute."

She had a South London accent, with a slight "f" to her pronunciation of "th" and an attractively grainy quality to it.

"You got kids?" I asked.

She rocked back slightly. "No."

I made no reaction to this. In any case, she was as keen to get on with it as I was, and after half an hour of small talk, we left. In the street, she slipped her arm through mine, the first physical touch between us, and it was a relief that even in the grip of my situation I responded like a normal man.

There was no moon that night, I remember.

As we reached Trinity Avenue, she gave a tug of my arm as if to turn.

"Why're you going down there?" I said.

"I thought you said this is your street?"

"No, I'm in the block of flats on the other side of the park. The white building."

"Oh, OK." She moved closer, mouth in my ear. "Lead the way, sir."

"We'll walk through the park—if you're not afraid I'll molest you."

Fi would have said I should be very careful making jokes like that these days, but Wendy did not. I had the distinct thought that I was free to choose different women now, that they didn't have to be the Alder Rise kind, with their educated, entitled, postfeminist sensibilities. Obviously, prefeminist was too much to hope for. (Joke.) The thought sent a back draft of optimism, for a moment generalized but then narrowing into the instinct that I might have got away with that thing that day. In the space of a few hours I'd downgraded "horror" to "situation" to "that thing that day," and I had that last pint or two to thank for it. I had Wendy.

"Cool building," she said when we arrived at Baby Deco.

"Lower your expectations," I told her. "It's just a rented studio. Kind of the caretaker's quarters."

"Wow, you make it sound like quite the lair."

We'd hardly closed the door behind us and we were falling on each other, kissing with unexpected force, and she was pulling at my clothes and groaning about what she wanted me to do to her and I had the brief, ungallant thought that the less attractive a woman was the better she tended to be at this bad-girl sort of thing, which worked—it really worked—and I thought just in time to push out of my sight line the novel Fi had left on the table by the bed and that only the previous night I had flicked through, imagining the same sentences flowing through her mind and making her frown. The idea that I should have done that was excruciating now.

Yes, this was long overdue.

"Something on your mind?" Wendy murmured.

"Why?"

"You seem a bit distracted."

"Sorry. Allow me to show you how hard I'm concentrating."

She laughed. I could see she was pleased with the repartee (if you could call it that), that she wanted to make something memorable of this encounter, and I played along because I couldn't exactly announce that what *I* wanted was something utterly forgettable.

18

"FI'S STORY" > 01:19:13

Alison texted me on the Wednesday morning with a message that could not have been sent lightly:

> Do I tell you if I hear something about Bram?
> *What kind of thing?*
> Extracurricular.

I didn't pause.

> *You tell me.*
> Sure?
> *Yes.*
> OK. He took someone home last night, or so Rog thinks.
> A woman in the pub, no one we know.

I waited for the knife wound through the ribs but it didn't come, or at least it hit the bone and bounced off again.

Interesting.
Don't say anything or he'll know where it came from.

I thought of the man at La Mouette.

You wouldn't tell R who I'm taking home, would you?
No way. I'm not a double agent.
Better not be, Mata Hari.
She was a triple agent, actually, or so the French claimed.

Seeing Alison as I usually did, wiping snot from a child's nose or squirting antibiotic drops into a dog's ears, I could forget how clever she was. Her history master's from Durham, her three days a week as a lecturer.

Say if you'd rather not know this stuff.
No, I want to know. Thank you.

She was a good friend, Alison. The best. When I think about my situation now, I see that I couldn't have survived without her. Merle and her.

BRAM, Word document

In the morning, after we'd had sex again, Wendy dressed quickly and accepted a coffee. This she drank standing, her phone in her other hand—I assumed she was checking the trains. This encouraged me to hope she'd leave before me, thus eliminating the awkwardness of walking through Alder Rise together or even bumping into Fi at the station. She and I took trains from opposite platforms and I could just picture her face across the tracks as she saw this woman canoodling with me, murmuring and giggling, making our intimacy clear.

I reminded myself that I was a free man, like I'd told Rog.

Free so long as I didn't think about the thing (still the "thing"; it hadn't reverted to the "horror"). As I perched there at the kitchen counter next to Wendy, it struck me as so simple I didn't know how it hadn't occurred before: *just don't think about it*. Not so much denial as rejection. Selective amnesia.

"You look very happy about something all of a sudden," Wendy said, amused. Placing the used mug in the sink, she added, very casually: "You have no idea, do you?"

"No idea about what?" I said.

"That I saw you."

"What, at the farmers' market? Of course I know. We discussed it last night—don't you remember? How our eyes met over the artisanal Scotch eggs." I marveled at my own jocularity.

"Not there," she said, watching me. "Silver Road."

I went completely cold, as if I'd been shoved overboard into the Atlantic in December. "What did you just say?"

"I said Silver Road." Her gaze over the top of her coffee mug was sly, nerveless. "I saw the crash, Bram."

"What crash?" It was miraculous that I was still intelligible, when my internal organs were in seizure.

"Come on—don't give me that. They're still in intensive care. I'm sure you've followed the news and heard about the police investigation." Then, in the same light tone, so light as to be sinister: "Actually, there was a detective there when I dropped by the hospital, but I don't think they were in any state to be interviewed. Both on ventilators," she added, and the insincerity in her frown was unmissable. It bordered on glee.

Slow to recover, I sounded foolish when I asked, "I thought you said you lived in Beckenham."

"I do. I was at my cousin's place. She lives about halfway down Silver Road. Her living room window is right on the street, so I had a front-row seat."

There was the sensation of piranhas fighting in my Atlantic depths; it was all I could do not to double over. "And you thought you saw some sort of an incident, did you?"

She chuckled. "Nice phrasing. All right, I 'thought' I heard crazy-loud accelerating and I looked out of the window and 'thought' I saw two cars racing and then a Fiat plow into a parked car and smash into a house. Then I 'thought' I saw you driving away in an Audi. A black A3. I didn't catch the full registration but I got the first few letters." She moved to observe me from a side angle. "You're a great-looking guy, Bram. I'm pretty sure I'd be able to recognize your profile in a lineup."

There was silence between us as I struggled to hear my own thoughts over the banging of my heart. "There's no way you'd be able to recognize someone from the distance you're describing," I said finally, but I'd been well and truly trapped. Had she followed me home that evening? Studied my face as I exited the car and scurried to my front door? Taken photos of me like some sort of stalker? Clearly, our encounter in the pub had been no coincidence. The friend on Engleby Close she'd been with—did she even exist? "This cousin of yours on Silver Road—did she see this as well?"

"No. She was in another room. Don't worry—I didn't tell her I'd seen you."

"*Don't worry?*" "Why were you at the hospital?"

"Just interested. You know how it is—you're drawn there."

As I had been. "Did you . . . did you speak to the detective you saw there?"

If she had, then there'd been a delay, possibly, in my having been apprehended because the car was registered to Trinity Avenue. The police had called there, perhaps, when no one was home. I had a very clear picture of myself fleeing, of leaving the flat right now and making my way to Heathrow.

When she shrugged no, I relaxed a fraction, summoned the old Bram bravado. "Well, Wendy, then it sounds like we're guilty of the same thing. Neither of us reported something we know we probably ought to have."

There was a sudden sharpening of her features. "Oh, I don't think we're guilty of the same thing at all, Bram. It wasn't *my* dangerous driving that put two people on life support."

Her statements rained on me as brutally as a rockfall and yet she was very cool, unnaturally so. If she really thought I was capable of a violent rampage like that, why wasn't she frightened I'd attack her here? She must have texted someone the address, I thought.

I became aware of a wild, accelerating rage displacing the fear, a dangerous leap in body temperature. "Since you seem so clear about what happened, why don't you go after the other driver, the bastard who *really* caused the crash?"

"Oh, come off it," she said. "*You* were the one in the wrong lane."

"Only because he wouldn't let me back in the right one! If the Fiat hadn't swerved, we'd have smashed headlong and we'd all be dead."

"You shouldn't have been overtaking. You were speeding when you tried to get around him—you can't deny *that*."

I said nothing.

"So you *did* cause the crash? Come on, Bram. I was there."

"Of course I fucking did. I told you, I had no choice! Because of *him*."

It was an admission of guilt and I hastened to smother it with a show of aggression: "I'd like to know why you don't find him and spring this shit on him ten minutes after getting out of his bed?"

"Maybe I will," she said agreeably, and put down her coffee mug.

"*Will*," I noted, not "*already have*." It was all very well arguing that

Toyota Man and I were equally at fault, but I was the one whose car had been semi-identified in the news reports.

It was clear she was preparing me for some sort of blackmail demand.

She stepped around me and reached for her jacket, a cheap denim thing she'd flung onto an armchair last night. I remembered the painful suction of her mouth on mine. "So, I thought we might do business," she said.

As I'd thought. "Well, I'm sorry to disappoint you, Wendy, but I don't have any money to do business *with*. Seriously, I'm broke. I can show you my latest bank statement if you like."

She shook her head, a grim smile on her lips. "Come on—you've got that big house on Trinity Avenue."

I recalled the way she'd pulled me in its direction the previous night. She *must* have followed me on the evening of the crash. I hadn't questioned it; I'd been thinking about getting her into bed. Thinking she was exactly the simple, no-strings partner I needed for the night.

She continued undaunted: "You can afford this place as well. That's two properties in this posh area. You've obviously got cash."

"I don't, I'm telling you. I'm going through a divorce." Not technically true—yet—but what did that matter?

"Even so." In a sudden move, she placed warm fingers on my wrist and I recoiled.

"Don't touch me!"

"Hey, don't be like that." She withdrew the hand, used it to smooth her hair, touch her mouth, as if she had all the time in the world to indulge me my foibles. "Since we're going to be involved for a while, we might as well get some pleasure out of it. I really enjoyed last night. I thought you did as well."

I was at a loss as to how to respond. If her aim from the start had been to extort money, I could not see why she had needed to sleep with me. There had been no need for a honey trap; she could have delivered her cowardly message in the pub. "I want you to leave, Wendy. Is that even your real name?"

"Wow, you *are* paranoid."

"What's the name of the company you work for? You said it was commercial cleaning services? Which department are you?"

"Why?" She laughed. "You going to complain to my manager?"

She knew full well I couldn't complain to anyone. I couldn't breathe a word to a soul about this squalid little episode.

"You going to tell him I didn't report a crime?" she taunted. "Maybe I didn't realize it was serious until I read about it in the paper. Maybe it was only when I saw you in the pub last night that it triggered my memory of a hit-and-run."

"It wasn't a hit-and-run," I snapped.

"As good as. As *bad* as."

"No, it was an accident. That's all."

"That's all." The words startled us both and there was a pause, a moment of shared honesty, maybe even disgrace.

"Whoever you are," I said, "and whatever you mistakenly think you've seen, you've got the wrong man. Please don't contact me ever again."

Any confidence gained or expressed by this punchy little display was short-lived, for the look she gave me as she left was full of exaggerated regret. "Sorry, Bram. You don't get out of it that easily."

19

Did hearing about his liaison with someone new make me nostalgic for how it was between *us* in the beginning?

You'll have to forgive me, but I prefer not to think about that now, the "before." Before the boys, before the house, before our life in Alder Rise. The bit they call falling in love—though no one ever really *falls*, do they? In reality, half of us seek, reach, *climb*; the other half simply stand still in surrender.

I say that, realist that I am, but then an image will surface before I can stop it, an image that defies cynicism and persuades me we were the exceptions: the two of us in a crowded West End bar—our first date—eyes too fascinated by each other to stray to the hundreds of other faces; or an aerial view of a car speeding through the emerald English countryside—our first holiday together—too fast and yet never fast enough. You don't need to point out the irony of that. The fact that it was the speed, the sense of the headlong, that got me addicted. That his impact on me was like a collision.

There's another image from the beginning, a more painful one: a female figure cartwheeling on a California beach, her long hair touching the sand. A new wife, married after less than a year of knowing him, coming upright to find her husband unbuttoning his shirt, staring out to sea, as if he intends to swim and swim, leaving his vows on the shore with his clothes.

Crazy, really, to have ever imagined that a wife and children could be anything but shackles to a man like Bram.

BRAM, Word document

This afternoon I got close. I almost did it, even though I've hardly started my story and I've committed myself to telling it in full before I act. But you forget how you get ambushed by music here, because the radio stations love their nostalgia and there's always the potential for an old song that stirs memories you don't want stirred. "Our" songs when there isn't any "our" anymore. And they were playing that song "Big Sur," a hit when Fi and I started going out. Maybe it was played at our wedding; I don't remember, but we had our honeymoon in California and drove to Big Sur to see the famous coastline for ourselves. Listening to the song, I could picture myself so clearly on the cliff's edge, the Pacific monstrous and baying below, ready to smother a million times over the pain of my past. And I thought, since it was all utterly meaningless, why bother leaving my statement behind? Why not go back to my miserable little room and end my life right now, let my version of events die with me? Sitting there, I could feel my toes twitching in my shoes; I could feel the balls of my feet rocking forward.

Jump, Bram.

20

Lucy Vaughan's husband, David, is a solid, fair-skinned man of about forty, his powers of leadership evident the moment he enters the house, his air of *ownership*. No sooner has he dissuaded Merle from phoning the police than he is making the calls he clearly thinks Lucy should have made the moment it became clear that allegations of a legal—and possibly financial—catastrophe had been made. If it angers him that neither his solicitor nor estate agent is immediately available, he does not show it. Colleagues of both proffer the "strange misunderstanding" theory, he reports, and promise urgent returns of call.

"Well, these are odd circumstances in which to meet," he says to Fi. Though his speech is self-assured, he regards her with perplexity, even caution.

"They are," she says, unsmiling. It is remarkable how Merle's presence has fortified her.

"Mrs. Lawson is a bit calmer now," Lucy tells him, as if to excuse

Fi's poor manners. "There was a scare about the whereabouts of her sons, but we've just found out they're fine."

That's the working hypothesis, then: it is Fi's interpretation of events that is at fault and not the events themselves. She isn't on top of arrangements; she gets confused. As it has been proved with the boys, so it will with the house—and Bram is not here to support her.

Merle, however, is. "Bram should have told Fi he was letting the boys miss school," she says. "*Any* mother would've had a nervous breakdown to discover that." She eyes Lucy sternly, as if she should be thoroughly ashamed of herself. "I'm guessing you don't have children."

"Not yet," Lucy says.

"Then you'll have to take my word for it that there is no more terrifying thought than their going missing. Now, I'm sure Fi is very grateful for the help you've given her in tracking them down, but we seem to have another mystery on our hands, don't we?" She blazes with intensity, never more charismatic than now, and Lucy gazes at her spellbound. "You obviously understand that Fi disputes this claim about the house and would like you to leave. My suggestion is you do that while we locate Bram and all the paperwork that proves he and Fi are the owners, and then we can arrange a meeting to discuss this formally—perhaps on Monday at your solicitor's office? In terms of your—"

"Wait a minute," David interrupts sharply, breaking Merle's hold. "We're not going anywhere. This house was sold to us fair and square."

"I think you'll find it wasn't," Merle says.

"And yet we've had all the verifications that completion took place this morning." He brandishes his phone and begins scrolling for the relevant e-mails, just as Lucy did earlier.

"They must be fake," Merle says, just as Fi did. "Don't click on any links, will you? They could trigger Trojan malware."

"Trojan malware—what on earth are you talking about? Look..."

As David hands her his phone, Merle scrutinizes the screen with skepticism before passing it to Fi. Though two of the messages are those from Bennett, Stafford & Co that Lucy has already shared, a third is from another conveyancing solicitor, Graham Jenson at Dixon Boyle & Co in Crystal Palace, who confirms receipt of the funds from Emma Gilchrist's client account. It is dated 13 January and was sent just before eleven a.m.

"Dixon Boyle are the Lawsons' solicitors," David tells Merle, and a burning sensation starts to spread across Fi's chest.

Merle, however, remains cool. "'The Lawsons' in quotation marks," she corrects him. "And I don't see any proof of the transfer of deeds." Her manner is professional, as if the meeting is being monitored for official purposes and any time she fails to dispute an assertion of David's, it will be entered into the record as fact.

"That's all done electronically," David says. "Perhaps it might be helpful if you check your bank account," he suggests to Fi.

"If she doesn't know anything about the sale, she's hardly likely to have received the money," Merle points out, just short of scorn.

"Sure, but just in case. We'd know the transaction definitely took place, even if she's . . ." He falters.

Forgotten, he means. That chronic attack of amnesia she's suffering from. But when she sees an unusually colossal deposit among the debits for train tickets and groceries and school shoes, she'll think, *"Oh yes, I did sell my children's home."*

An iPad is produced, her bank's website found, and it is all she can do to remember her customer ID and PIN. At last, with David bearing down on her, she clears security.

"Is it there?"

"No." Both her own account and her joint account with Bram are untouched.

"He has an individual account as well, does he?" David persists.

"Yes, but I don't know the password for that. And his phone is out of service."

Merle makes a fresh bid for command. "As I've been saying since I got here, we need to get the police over here. If Bram's phone's out of action, there must be something wrong."

"A phone could be off for all sorts of reasons," David says.

"Yes." Merle's attention moves between the Vaughans and Fi. "But since *Mrs.* Lawson knows nothing about this, don't you think it's possible that *Mr.* Lawson doesn't either? Maybe his identity has been stolen by mobsters, Fi. Maybe he was on to them in some way and they, I don't know, retaliated."

"Mobsters?" Fi echoes, a deeper, new shock seizing her. "Retaliated?"

"Yes, he could have been abducted or something. Perhaps he knew he was in danger and that's why he arranged to keep the boys at his mother's while you were away. Maybe he's already involved the police and you're under their protection without realizing it."

"That all sounds a bit melodramatic," David says. "You can't just go around passing yourself off as other people in order to sell their property. You need passports, birth certificates, proper proof of ownership. Funds of this size are checked for money laundering—there are all sorts of hoops to jump through. I know because we've just done it."

"Even so, I can't think of any better explanation," Merle says. "Can you?"

There is silence in the room, a collective sense of held breath. Fi feels her face clenching as she struggles to keep from crying.

"If you're right, then this is horrific," says Lucy, finally.

"It *is* horrific," Merle agrees. She turns to Fi with the air that the Vaughans may have an interesting contribution to make but it's only Fi's that matters. "If you want my opinion, Fi, we need to report an identity theft."

Fi nods.

"We need to report Bram missing. Missing and in danger."

GENEVA, 3 P.M.

As he leaves the restaurant, the wine having done nothing to ease the ferment of nerves in his gut, he is unsettled by the presence of a man standing close to the lift controls, his head angled in query as he watches Bram's approach. He is in his early thirties, lofty, rough skinned, dressed in a dark gray suit and well-polished shoes. Business traveler—or plainclothes policeman? A concerned member of the public who has seen an Interpol appeal containing his photograph?

Bram considers bolting through the doors to the stairwell, but resists. *No. Calm down. Act casual.* Interpol appeal? There is self-preservation and then there are delusions of grandeur. Not unlike the sales career he has left behind, his survival is a matter of confidence trickery and the person he most needs to trick is himself.

Even so, when the lift operates normally, not a word spoken between its occupants, and Bram soon deposited safely to the ground floor, the relief he feels is savage.

Even so, when he slips into a pharmacy on his way back to the hotel, searching the aisles for a good pair of scissors, he glances over his shoulder more than once before he makes his selection and pays.

21

BRAM, Word document

For the next twenty-four hours, I heard nothing from Wendy and I wondered if I'd imagined what she'd said. What *I'd* said. Maybe she'd left before I woke up and I'd had that exchange in the kitchenette with an apparition—Lord knows that between Macbeth and me, countless men have been so demented by guilt they've given their conscience voice and mistaken it for retribution.

Better still, perhaps I'd never met her; she didn't exist! But, no, that really was wishful thinking. There'd been a text from Rog in the morning, asking, *Good night?* complete with the "lucky bugger" subtext of a winking-face emoji. No doubt he'd told Alison I'd been on the pull. Definitely she'd told Fi. But Fi was the least of my worries, for once.

Nothing happened, I texted back. No emojis.

I didn't go near the car—by now, I couldn't even look at it—and as I took the train to and from work, I abused myself ceaselessly for not having stayed on the platform that morning of the conference and bitten the bullet of a commuter delay. What would a late start have been, or even a no-show, a job loss, compared to this inferno of misery?

Then, on the Friday evening, a text came from her. I hadn't been aware of having given her my phone number, but evidently she had it. Easy enough to discover by calling my office, I supposed, or even snooping while I slept. The message consisted of a link to a story on a Croydon news website:

REWARD OFFERED IN HUNT
FOR SILVER ROAD CRASH DRIVER

A £10,000 reward for information has been offered by the husband of the Silver Road collision victim, a forty-two-year-old woman recovering from critical injuries sustained in the collision on Friday, 16 September. The couple's ten-year-old daughter was also severely injured in the incident.

The police have yet to identify the other party in the collision and are keen to hear from motorists and pedestrians in the area at approximately 6 p.m., the time of the incident.

A spokesperson for the victims' family said: "Two innocent people have sustained terrible injuries as the result of a cold-blooded and cowardly act and we will do everything in our power to help the police find this criminal."

A ten-thousand-pound reward. Jesus. It was a bounty on my head.

Or—have a beer, a cigarette, *think*—was it possible that the announcement of a reward was a *useful* development? Might it not bring unreliable witnesses and charlatans into the mix, both of which would waste police time?

As I read the item a second time, searching each word for new meaning, my stomach heaved. It wasn't the money—a sum that Wendy clearly expected me to improve on in my compensation of *her*—but a single word buried in the paragraph:

"Recovering."

It sounded as if the driver of the Fiat was now conscious and improving. It sounded as if she was now in a fit state to be interviewed by the police.

I made no reply to Wendy. I wouldn't have replied to her even if I hadn't lost the use of my hands to uncontrollable shaking.

"FI'S STORY" > 01:21:40

So, I'd say it was probably only a few days before the guy from La Mouette got in touch, inviting me to have a drink with him the next Friday. I suggested a bar in Balham, striking distance for both of us but a safe enough distance from home turf to avoid any neighborhood gossip. Not that Bram had worried on that score, brazenly picking someone up in the most popular drinking hole in Alder Rise, but I had different standards.

Yes, it was surprisingly easy to get back in the game. Toby was such effortlessly good company. I told him about my job in homewares and he spoke about his work as a data analyst for a think tank commissioned by the Department of Transport.

"It's not a study of inveterate speeders, is it?" I laughed. "If so, you might want to interview my ex. He's had three tickets in the last eighteen months."

Toby grinned at me. "We're interested in the exact opposite: why the average speed for a journey through Central London has slowed so dramatically. You know that it's getting down toward eight miles an hour? Everyone agrees the congestion charge isn't effective anymore, so we're working with a big engineering consultancy to put together a new strategy."

"It's all the white vans, I suppose?" I knew from my work that people expected same- or next-day delivery on even the cheapest, smallest items.

"Partly." He described his team's surveillance of freight vehicles and minicabs, cycle lanes and construction projects, before apologizing for boring me. "I sometimes think talking about work should be against the law."

I lifted my wineglass. "I'll drink to that." It was true that I wasn't looking to share career angst. I wasn't looking to share *lives*. This was a physical attraction, the interesting conversation a delightful bonus. "Just tell me one thing: *I'm* not under surveillance, am I?"

"No," he said. "Not the kind you mean, anyway."

We slept together that night. My flat was closer than his and so that was the natural venue. Also, I'm not totally irresponsible; I wouldn't go back to a complete stranger's place.

"I really like you, Fi," he said before he left. "We should do this again."

"OK," I said. Obviously, I'm simplifying it now, but honestly, it was that uncomplicated. "I'll phone you," I told him, because I was damned if I was going to revive the passive role of my twenties. I would drive this, if any driving were to be done, and I would decide whether there was. Which dated me right there, as Polly pointed out when we next talked on the phone.

"'Hard to get' doesn't exist as a concept anymore. Everyone is *easy* to get."

"What's the protocol, then?" I asked.

"The protocol is, there *is* no protocol. You have to get your head around the fact that it's not like when you and Bram were going out. Those were innocent times. People interacted differently."

"Right," I said, "because telecommunications didn't exist then, only semaphore and messengers on horseback."

"They *didn't* exist—at least not the kind that tells you anything useful. I wouldn't tell Bram about your congestion expert, by the way. If he thinks you're interested in someone new, he'll start chasing you again."

"It's too late for that." I cut the conversation short then. There was nothing to be gained from another character assassination of Bram. He was the father of my children and, as the cliché went, I would always respect him for that.

I would also need to monitor his fitness for the task. On my way home from the station an evening or two earlier, I'd seen him standing alone by the closed park gates, a wisp of blue smoke rising from a cigarette held by his side, and I'd felt genuinely quite disturbed. It wasn't the smoking; it was the solitude, the way he was standing: helpless, shrinking, as if stranded by the encroaching tide.

Hearts have muscle memory like any other and, I admit, mine squeezed at the sight of him.

I'd phoned Alison. "Will you do me a favor? Call round ours this weekend, if you have time. Get Bram and the boys to go out with you or just get invited in for a cup of tea. See if everything's OK with him—I don't mean this woman you told me about, just generally. He seems a bit down. I need to know he's in good spirits for the boys' sakes, but I'm not sure I can judge anymore."

"Leave it with me," Alison said.

#VictimFi

@natashaBwrite She's too passive-aggressive with the ex—getting the friend to ask for her!

@jesswhitehall68 @natashaBwrite Not sure I trust this Alison character either.

@ richieschambers @jesswhitehall68 @natashaBwrite Can lover boy please do something about the new traffic system at Elephant & Castle? #deathtrap

22

BRAM, Word document

That Saturday afternoon, the doorbell rang and from the hallway I saw two tall, darkly-dressed figures through the stained glass. *This is it,* I thought, and fear tore through me so violently I lost my balance as I put out my hand to open the door, landing heavily against the frame. I wasn't ready to explain, to understand, to atone. I was a mess.

"Bram, look at your face! Who were you expecting? A Mafia hit man?" Alison and Roger cackled at my expression. "We wondered if you and the boys wanted to come to the dog show in the park."

Incapacitated with relief, I was slow to respond. "Oh, right. Is that today?"

"It is. Rocky's in the Handsomest Hound category. Come on—it's not to be missed."

Previously, the prospect of watching the Osbornes' arthritic Lab stagger around the ring and retreat, without a rosette, into the arms of a flock of howling kids would not have floated my boat, but on this occasion I accepted gratefully and told Leo and Harry to put their jackets and trainers on. Did the police even make calls on the weekend? Well, if they did, I'd be out, buying myself one more night, one more day, with my boys.

In the street, I had to turn my face away and consciously recalibrate before engaging with my companions. Next to their carefree state of being, their simple joy in *dogs*, I was a Martian.

"Everything all right on your end?" Alison said as we walked, the kids scampering ahead. "You look a bit stressed."

"I'm fine. Just a bit worried about work," I said.

"Well, don't think about it. This is *le weekend*—and the prettiest bitches in Alder Rise await us."

A throng worthy of Woodstock awaited too. A well-known actor had moved to the area, Alison said, and was one of the judges. Rog had got talking to him at the vet's and now she had hopes of socializing together. I couldn't spot him through the crush, though everyone else I'd ever met was in view: the whole of Trinity Avenue, familiar faces from the boys' school, the pub, even the station platform. It was unseasonally warm again, the air a sickening soup of dog breath and the deep-fat frying of a pop-up churros stall. In the ring, puppies were being paraded and as the audience surged forward I hung back slightly, Harry's hand in mine, as if I'd developed a phobia of crowds. I felt the pain of a need for a drink like appendicitis.

"Hello, Bram," said a voice behind me.

I didn't recognize it. Expecting another neighborhood face, I prepared myself for the teasing and backslapping required of a local dad, and yet even as I turned my body responded differently. Skin, muscles, internal organs: they all shrank as if to protect themselves from violent attack.

It was him. The guy in the Toyota. At the time, I'd seen him only in profile glimpses, but there was no doubt about it—I recognized the angular bones of his skull, the jutting nose and flat-set ears, the hair shorn close to the scalp. His eyes were some indeterminate color and yet the energy in his gaze was keen, almost rapacious.

"How do you know my name?" I said.

He pushed out his lower lip, a facial shrug. "I hear you've had a visit from a mutual friend."

"What?"

"You heard."

"Daddy? I can't see!" Over the bellow of the MC, Harry was clamoring for me to press closer to the ring. I'd lost sight of Leo.

"Wait . . . will you?" I held up an index finger to Skullface—one minute—and steered Harry closer to the Osbornes. Checking that Leo was within range, I asked Alison to keep an eye on them for five minutes.

"This way." I led Skullface around the tattered edge of the crowd toward the café building, coming to a halt by the rear doors for the toilets.

He rolled his eyes at the GENTS sign. "Interesting place to choose, Bram. Wouldn't have thought you were the type."

He was every bit as loathsome as I'd imagined, as I'd prayed I'd never have to discover.

"What are you doing here?" I said. "How did you find me?"

He shrugged, impatient with my questions. "I was talking about your visitor. Tuesday night, wasn't it?"

"If you mean Wendy, then yes, our paths crossed."

You have no idea, do you?

Don't be like that. . . .

"She told you she saw what went down?" There was a note of relish in his voice. He was enjoying this, the sadistic bastard, the power of intercepting me on my home turf, where I'd thought I was safe. How had he known I lived in Alder Rise? Presumably from Wendy. Had he kept watch on my street or just turned up at the station and followed the crowd?

I glared at him. "Clearly, and since she can't have tailed both of us that night, she must have made a note of our registrations. Don't ask me how she managed to get our personal details from them, because I have no idea."

"Easy enough if you're willing to spend the money," he said dismissively. "You can pay for that sort of information online."

"Really?"

"Yeah. Never heard of the dark web, Bram? I would have thought it could be quite useful to you at this difficult time."

A baby's cry started up, echoing from the back walls of the houses on Alder Rise Road, rising in that commanding way that was so out of scale with its tiny form. Harry's had been like that, swelling with fury if Fi or I failed to materialize fast enough.

"She obviously wants money," I said, keeping my voice low as a café customer passed by, eyeing us. "More than ten thousand pounds, I think." It was an absurd sum, now that I said it out loud. This whole situation couldn't be real. "I told her where to go and I suggest you do the same." I was aware that I was talking more and more roughly, blurring my consonants as if in response to his brutish manner.

Whether unimpressed by the content or the delivery, he listened with open mockery. "Oh, I don't think so. In fact, I've taken a more collaborative position."

"What the hell are you talking about?"

"She's not going away, Bram, and the sooner you face up to that, the better. We're better off sticking together."

A warning pulse started up in my neck. "I'm not sticking with anyone," I said. "You can do whatever you like to stop her from going to the police, but I'm not getting involved."

"I'm not sure it's that straightforward." There was a pause, a grinding of teeth, a bitter stare. Applause from the distant show ring rose and fell; then he said, in the lull, "We know about the ban."

"What?"

"Your driving ban. You were only seven months into a twelve-month ban that day, weren't you? A bit too eager to get back on the road, eh?"

"But how . . . ?" I sucked air, unable to complete the question. How could he possibly know the status of my driver's license? Did he work for the DVLA? Or the police? Or was it as he had said—you could find out anything online if you were prepared to pay? "Forget it. I'm not interested in discussing it," I said. "I need to get back."

He actually rolled his eyes then. "You know what? I haven't got time for this denial act. You need to get a bit more real about the trouble you're in." As the announcement of a winner and an outbreak of cheering split the air, he dug into his pocket and withdrew a phone. "When you're on your own, take a look at this and get in touch. Don't use your regular mobile, all right?"

"Wrong. I'm not taking a look at anything." But trying to reject his offering, a smeared old Samsung, proved difficult without getting into a scuffle and drawing attention to us, and in the end I pocketed it, glaring at him as I did.

"Don't bin it," he said, reading my thoughts. "What's on there, I guarantee you'll want to see."

"I have to go," I said, trying to edge past him.

He stepped aside. "Of course. Better get back to your kids. You never know what kind of scumbags might be lurking about the place."

"FI'S STORY" > 01:25:19

When Alison phoned, she had little to report in her assessment of Bram's mental health.

"He was a bit quiet, but nothing weird. Oh, he did disappear for a while early on, but it was total chaos, dogs and kids all over the place, so he might have just lost us."

I frowned. "Disappeared?" Impossible not to flash back to the empty house, the open wine bottle, the steamed-up windows of the playhouse.

"It wasn't a big deal. Leo and Harry were with me the whole time."

I raised my eyebrows and pictured Alison doing the same: there was not a father in Alder Rise who would refuse a woman's offer to keep an eye on his charges while he checked his e-mail or gamed or simply stared into space. Merle once said, "Why do men find it so easy to accept help and women find it so hard? We need to reverse that."

We certainly did. "How long was he gone?" I asked.

"I don't know. Twenty minutes, maybe? The puppies had finished and the Best Tricks were on. All collies, obviously. I started to think he must have gone home, but then he reappeared and bought all the kids churros, which was sweet of him."

"Probably nipped to the pub for a pint." I tutted. "Did he smell of booze? Oh, don't answer that—it's none of my business. I'm sorry, Al—I don't mean to use you like a private detective."

"Use away. I enjoy it."

"How did Rocky get on? Was he in the Waggiest Tail again?"

"Handsomest Hound. And I can't believe I haven't told you the news: he came in third! It was the last category of the day and our new local celeb presented the rosette!"

"Well done, Rocky. Congratulations!"

"Seriously, it's the most exciting thing to happen in this house all year," Alison said. "We're having champagne tonight, maybe even marital relations."

Forgetting Bram, I laughed out loud.

Oh, my old friend laughter, I miss you.

BRAM, Word document

I waited until the boys were in bed before turning on the phone. Not a model I was used to, it was clearly several years old and, though fully charged, took an age to get through its welcome sequence and display the main screen.

There was a single text message waiting for me from a number I neither knew nor was in a position to give a name to, and it contained a link to a newspaper article:

DISQUALIFIED DRIVERS FACE STIFFER JAIL TERMS

Banned motorists who continue to drive and then injure or kill in a collision will now face far steeper punishment than in the past following years of campaigning by victims' groups to close a legal loophole.

If a disqualified driver causes serious injury, he or she will now face four years in jail, whereas formerly they might only have been fined, while the sentence for causing a death has leaped from two years to ten.

"Disqualified drivers should not be on our roads for good reason," the justice secretary said yesterday. "Those who choose to defy a ban imposed by a court and go on to destroy innocent lives must face serious consequences for the terrible impact of their actions."

The thump of my heart filled my rib cage, my lungs tender as they struggled to inflate. Just as I finished reading, the picture arrived. It was a shot of my black Audi, my blurred head behind the windscreen. The number plate was not quite legible at maximum zoom but obviously decipherable enough on whatever device Wendy had used. With the benefit of enhancing software, police forensics would have no trouble identifying it, or the place it had been captured. What was not in dispute was *when*: the date and time were stamped on the image.

It was hardly surprising, now I was presented with it. Like the rest of the world, Wendy had had her phone in her hand, ready to capture something interesting.

Though common sense told me not to engage, just as I had not when she had texted, some survival mechanism—or was it suicidal urge?—prompted my fingers to work a response:

Have you shown this to anyone else?
Why would I do that? We're mates, Bram.
We're not mates. I don't even know your name.
Thought you'd never ask. Mike.
Mike what?

No reply.

Well, Mike, you should assume she's also got a picture of your Toyota. 2009 registration, was it?

That'll rattle him, I thought, until his next text came:

Since you mention it, the Toyota is no longer in my possession. Nicked by some joyrider.

Nausea began to surge through my gullet.

When did that happen?

Work it out, Bram.

Four years, I thought. And that was just the beginning—this bas-tard didn't know the half of it.

But the police would certainly know.

Would Fi bring the boys to visit? Would she ever let them see me again?

Four years! I couldn't survive four *days.*

23

Before I tell you about the car, you have to understand something. You have to understand that none of these things looked related. Unlucky things happen all the time; it doesn't mean you should suspect some larger evil—that would make you one of those conspiracy-theorist nutjobs or just plain egocentric. So when Bram told me the car had been stolen, I just thought the car had been stolen.

I was the one who noticed it was gone. It was the Tuesday after the weekend of the dog show and I'd just got home from work. I needed to pick Harry up from a playdate on the other side of Alder Rise, but I couldn't find the Audi anywhere on Trinity Avenue. I phoned Bram, who was on his way back from work, his train about to pull into Alder Rise Station.

"Have you used the car since the weekend? Where did you park it?"

"I haven't driven for ages. When did you last use it?"

I cast my mind back. "I went to fill up with petrol at Sainsbury's on Sunday afternoon. Then I parked up by the Parade."

"Then that's where it must still be."

"It's not. I've walked up and down twice and I can't see it."

"I'll come and help you look," Bram offered.

"No, don't worry." I avoided proposals to meet outside the agreed times. "I'll borrow Mum's car—she's here with Leo. I'll have a proper look later when I've got more time."

But he beat me to it, phoning an hour later to say, "You're right, the car's nowhere on Trinity Avenue or any of the usual streets."

"Well, I definitely parked up by the corner, just around from the florist's."

"Then I think it must have been stolen," he said.

"Seriously? How can you do that without the key?"

At the meeting at Merle's house, the community officer had warned of the ease with which thieves could steal keyless cars, but ours was old enough to use traditional keys to start the ignition.

"I don't know," Bram said. "I'll ask the police. Have you got both sets of keys there?"

I went to check. "There's only one in the dish."

"What about the other set? Would you mind looking in your bag?"

I rummaged through my handbag, laptop bag and any likely coat pockets, but there were no car keys.

"OK," Bram said, "I'll say they've been mislaid."

"Of all the cars on the street, it had to be ours! Why didn't they take the Youngs' new Range Rover? Do you need me to help with the police?"

"No, I'll take care of it," he said. "I'll handle the insurance claim as well, and let you know when a courtesy car is coming."

"Thank you." I certainly wasn't going to insist on taking over this most tedious of projects. In spite of the cooperative nature of the bird's nest, I still kept mental tabs on who did what, and since the car was one of Bram's few areas of sole responsibility, I wasn't about to relieve him of it.

More fool me.

The courtesy car provided by the insurance company arrived on Thursday morning. I huffed a bit when it transpired that the paperwork had to be signed by Bram because the policy was in his name, but in the end we managed to catch him on his way to the station and it wasn't such a big deal.

BRAM, Word document

Days went by without any further contact from my tormentor, or tormentors—having thrown her hat into the ring with Mike, Wendy had presumably granted him leadership of their blackmail campaign. But already I knew better than to hold my breath.

As for the phone he'd given me, I treated it like a grenade. When at Trinity Avenue I kept it in a locked file and when at the flat I wedged it behind a stack of tins in a kitchen cupboard, as if at any time expectant of an armed raid. As if a simple locking mechanism or a barrier of tinned lentils would save me.

When the next message came, early on Thursday morning, I fully expected it to announce a new figure: either lower because they understood I really didn't have any money or higher because that was what happened in movies when an opening bid was treated with disrespect.

Instead, it contained another link, this time to the site of a national tabloid:

Take a look at this. . . .

The article was nothing to do with motoring offenses or the Silver Road incident, but about a couple in West London whose house had been sold without their knowledge by fraudsters—Russian Mafia or some such—an elaborate scam involving identity theft and a criminally negligent conveyancing solicitor. A man and woman in their sixties were pictured outside a Victorian town house, with the caption: "The Morrises clung on to their beloved property only because the Land Registry smelled a rat."

Mike must have set up the phone to receive notifications when I opened his messages, because his next came a thoughtful fifteen minutes after I'd read the first:

Interesting, don't you think?
Not particularly. What's it got to do with anything?
Meet me at the Swan at 6:30 p.m. and I'll enlighten you.

"Enlighten you"—pompous knob. The Swan was the pub nearest my office. I shouldn't have been as surprised as I was that he knew where I worked, since he seemed to know everything else about me.

All day I reiterated the vow that I would not go. I even asked Nick in Digital if he was getting the six thirty-five p.m. train that we'd caught together a couple of times lately. He was. (I'd started doing this, establishing a network of informants as to my public transport usage. Too little, too late, I know.) Then, at six twenty p.m., with the inevitability of a sunset, I messaged him an excuse and headed to the pub.

I asked the barman for a Coke. I would have preferred a pint but was damned if I was going to make any concession to male bonding. The day I shared a drink with Mike was the day I was discharged from hospital following a lobotomy. It was disconcerting how deep my hatred for him was, how rich and complicated, as if there'd been a whole lifetime of hostilities between us, not a few weeks.

The Coke, served at room temperature, was sweet enough to make me wince.

"You read the article?" Mike was at my side. No greeting this time, like I wasn't worth the extra seconds it would cost him. He had the bruised eyes of the hungover (it took one to know one) and a nasty shaving rash. It was impossible to judge from his clothing—jeans, nondescript gray shirt—whether he'd been in an office all day or at home passed out on the floor.

"I skimmed it," I muttered.

"Bram, my friend, I'm very sorry to hear you didn't take it more seriously than that."

I was getting used to his persona by now, which evidently included expressing dismay at my inadequacies, as if I were an apprentice taken on against his better judgment and, lo and behold, proving to be not quite up to scratch.

"No one could take it seriously," I said, terror and loathing preventing me from making the connections I guessed I was expected to make. "It's just sensationalist pap. Pandering to homeowners' fears. Do you own your own place, Mike? Where do you live? I don't think you've told me."

He ignored the questions, of course, taking a moment to order himself a pint. He was polite to the point of obsequiousness to the barman. "It happens more often than you think," he said, turning back my way. "What with all these cheap online legal services, there's hardly any face-to-face in the house-buying process. Things slip through the net."

"Oh, come on," I said. "It happens once in a blue moon; otherwise it wouldn't be news. These people are professional criminals."

Again, he ignored the comment entirely. "How much is *your* house worth, Bram?"

"What? No idea." I kept both my gaze and tone dead flat, giving him nothing.

"Two mill, would you say? Two and a half?"

"I told you, I don't know. It's not even mine."

"Fuck off. I know it is. You own it fifty-fifty with your wife, Fiona Claire Lawson. Date of birth eighteenth of January 1974."

This, presumably, had been ascertained the same way all his other information had.

"My soon-to-be ex-wife," I corrected him. "We're divorcing and she's getting the house in the settlement. It's already been agreed."

There was a long pause. Did he believe me?

"We'd better get on with it, then," he said cheerfully.

Even though I'd anticipated them, his words stole my breath from me, and the contempt in my reaction was pure bluster: "Get on with *what*, you dickhead?"

The insult didn't register. "Selling the house, of course. What's the timeframe on the divorce?"

"That's none of your business. None of this is. And if you think I'm selling my house, you're insane." I'd raised my voice, attracted glances, and he allowed the energy to dissipate before speaking again.

"How much have you got left to pay on your mortgage, Bram?"

I glowered at him. "What, you haven't found that out yourself?"

"I could, but it would be so much more efficient if you just told me. Let's say half a million. More? No. Less? Closer to four hundred K? Good. So, if the place is worth two million, that's well over one and a half million profit after fees. There's a house on your street on the market at the moment—did you know?"

I didn't. Fi would, of course.

"Two point four, it's on at. Just a couple along from you, actually.

They haven't got your pretty little tree out front, but it's still a very desirable family home. Big conservatory. Chrome fittings in the master bathroom. Nice little cellar that could be converted into a den. They use it for the laundry at the moment."

I gaped. "You mean you've been there?"

"Anyone can arrange to view a house that's for sale, Bram. Estate agents are the last of the egalitarians, eh?"

I couldn't bear his pomposity, his look of pride when he used a word of more than three syllables. As for the idea of him strolling past our gate—our pretty little tree—and walking through one of our neighbors' into a house like ours, probably with children like ours, it caused a molten fury at the deepest core of me. Had he arranged the viewing for last Saturday, then stalked me up Trinity Avenue to the park? I leaned forward, my breath hot. "Keep away from my family— do you understand?"

"Calm down," Mike said, palm raised between us. "No one said anything about your family."

"Yet" was the implication.

"Look," I growled, "you don't seem to realize, these house prices, they're meaningless. It's Monopoly money. They're people's homes, that's all."

"Valuable homes. Easy enough to sell up and move somewhere cheaper. You could start from scratch at your age, two decent salaries like yours."

"We're not together—aren't you hearing a single word I'm saying?" I released the Coke glass before it shattered in my grip. "What pathetic delusion do you have here? That you'll do what those criminals did and steal my house right under my nose?"

"*Now* he comprehends."

It was laughable; he couldn't expect me to take him seriously. He was a fantasist, mentally ill. "You said yourself it's jointly owned. How are you going to get around that, huh? Unless you've also got incriminating pictures of my wife. Well, I'd be interested to see those, because she's completely, one-hundred-percent clean."

"Great, so she won't suspect anything's going on, then."

"Except when you ask her to sign a pile of legal contracts," I scoffed.

He inhaled, taking a moment to choose his words, and it was then that I saw it. Had the context been different, I would have been pleased with the speed of my deduction, but instead I was only sickened.

"Wendy," I said.

He smirked. "From what I've seen of your wife on social media, their looks aren't a million miles apart. Got a bit of a type, have you, mate? Bit of a cliché, the shapely blonde, if you ask me."

The muscles in my throat and stomach convulsed with the sensations of seasickness. "It's not a matter of looking the part. You're talking about serious fraud. Theft. You're talking about being locked up for life. Seriously, you're both fucking idiots if you think that could work." Fucking idiots who'd struck up a miraculously fast and trusting friendship . . .

Something in his expression—a secrecy, a smugness—caused another sudden deduction: Wendy had spoken of identifying my face in profile and yet the image I'd been texted had not been taken from the side. It had been taken from the front and from quite a distance away. *He* had taken it, not she.

My pulse began to throb wildly. "She didn't see anything that day, did she? *You* took that photo. I saw you at the time holding up your phone—I remember now. I thought you were calling for help. Why did you take it? I don't understand. You didn't know me from Adam."

He shrugged. "Just covering my back in case you decided to stick some story on me."

But I hadn't. Instead I'd fled, never expecting to encounter him again, never expecting him to investigate me and decide he'd hit pay dirt.

"Wendy wasn't even there, was she? She made up that business of standing at the window. You told her exactly what to say to me."

"Get you, Sherlock."

My face was flushed with rage. I could feel the heat beating under the skin. "You're in this together, the two of you. You have been from the start."

"No, no, the *three* of us, Bram," he said, as if generously including me in a treat.

"Who is she? Your wife? Girlfriend? She slept with me—did you know that?"

His expression turned unpleasantly lascivious. "What two consenting adults do in the privacy of their own home is nothing to do with me. She probably just felt like a shag, fancied her chances in the fleshpots of Alder Rise."

She must have followed me from the station to the pub. What the hell was going on here?

"Why did she bother?" I demanded. "Why didn't you just approach me yourself straightaway? Why send her as your special reconnaissance agent?"

He chuckled. "Reconnaissance agent—I like that. To answer your question, we thought she might be better than me at buttering you up. Like I say, we see this as a three-way project—excuse the innuendo."

Again, a private slyness in his countenance was as clear a hint as the words he spoke: *"buttering you up . . ."*

Wendy must have recorded our conversation about the crash. I remembered my admissions—*"If the Fiat hadn't swerved, we'd have smashed headlong and we'd all be dead!" "So you did cause the crash?" "Of course I fucking did!"*—and felt the last of any self-control slide from my grip. Was he recording *this*?

"You're both deranged," I said, lip snarling. "Don't come near me again—do you understand? Find someone else's house to steal. I'll enjoy following your trial in the *Daily Mail*."

With this, I dropped the phone he'd given me to the floor and stamped on it. As other drinkers frowned, intolerant of argy-bargy so early in the evening, Mike had the gall to look entertained.

"Careful there, Bram. You don't want to be seen engaging in senseless acts of violence, do you? If the police start nosing around, these sorts of things get remembered, you know what I mean?" He turned to the bartender and said, "Bram here's had some bad news. I'll clear the mess up, mate. Don't worry."

I scooped up the fragments myself; it had not passed me by that he'd used my name, very loudly. "Fuck off, *Mike*," I hissed.

"I'm not going anywhere," he said, raising his drink to me as I exited.

And I knew he meant it. Even as I cast the plastic shards into a bin in the street, even as I slotted the SIM card through the grating of a nearby drain, still growling with anger as I did so, I knew it would make no difference.

I knew he'd be back.

24

Even when a detective came to the house to ask about the car, I remained unsuspecting. You know how it is; you focus on the short-term inconvenience of these things. You assume everyone gets the same prompt service: it was the Friday of the same week it had been stolen.

"You need my husband," I said at the door. "He made the original report."

"Even so, I'd just like to clarify a couple of things with you, if I may."

"Of course. This is impressively quick. Do you work with Yvonne Edwards, by any chance? She's the community support officer who came to talk to us about neighborhood crime. She was very helpful."

"No, I'm with the Serious Collisions Investigation Unit based in Catford."

I stared at him in confusion. He was not in uniform and it wasn't a police team I'd ever heard of, and as I led him inside, I chided myself for not taking a closer look at his ID. I'd read in the paper about innocent residents of a village in Leicestershire being hoodwinked and robbed by an imposter in a police costume. As we settled in the kitchen, I eyed my escape route.

"So, the vehicle was reported missing on Tuesday, but your husband was unable to say when you last saw it. Might it have been several days before? Even weeks?"

"Weeks?" I echoed, surprised. "No, I used it on Sunday. I parked it up near the junction with the Parade at about four o'clock and neither of us have seen it since."

"So that's last Sunday, the second of October?"

"Yes."

There was a pause, a faint hardening of attention. "And do you remember who was driving it on Friday, the sixteenth of September?"

I looked blankly at him. "No, not off the top of my head."

"Do you keep a diary or a calendar that might help you remember?"

He'd come to the right place there: I cross-referenced my work schedule with the kitchen calendar and the bird's nest app. "Friday the sixteenth, here we are. Neither of us used it. It would have been parked in the street all day. Bram had a sales conference out of town and I was at an antiques fair in Richmond for most of the day with a friend."

"Neither of you drove to these appointments?"

"No. Well, I drove with a friend in her car. Bram took the train to his conference."

"You saw him go to the station?"

"No, not personally. We're not together anymore. We're separated. He was at the flat." I gave him details of the address and its proximity to the house and train station. "But I know he leaves well before eight, and when I came back from the school run the car was definitely there. I remember because my friend and I had second thoughts about whose car to take. I showed her the Audi's boot space and we decided to take her Volvo, as planned."

"What time did you leave for this trip?"

"About eight fifteen. We put our kids in the school breakfast club to get an early start." Not sure who I was so eager to help, him or Bram, I added: "If you need to double-check that Bram took the train, you could always look at the station security film. They definitely have cameras there."

The corners of his mouth pulled, causing a stitch in the flesh on the left side. A detective with a dimple, I thought. "I see you know your police procedures, Mrs. Lawson," he said.

I smiled. "Sorry. I do like a crime drama."

"So, you left at eight fifteen and then you returned when?"

"In time for school pickup. Three thirty."

I talked him through my likely movements between pickup and handover to Bram at seven p.m., though the finer points of domesticity eluded me. "Pasta or sausages—I'm afraid I can't tell you," I said wryly.

"Did anyone stop by the house?"

To vouch for my having been there, he meant. I strained to recall. "I think my friend Kirsty came by. That's right—our kids had taken each other's PE kit home, so we swapped them back. I remember I had to leave the grill to answer the door. It *was* sausages."

A second appearance of the dimple. "And what about later, after your husband arrived? Might you have used your own car then?"

"No, I went to Brighton for the night, and I took the train. I know I used the car that Sunday, though, because I took the kids for lunch at my parents' in Kingston."

"Busy weekend."

"Yes, it was." I looked up, tried to read his expression. "Why are you asking all this? What happened that Friday?"

"There was a collision in Thornton Heath that we're investigating. You may have read about it in the local papers."

"I don't think so," I admitted. "But I've used the car a few times since then, so it can't have been involved in any crash. Oh, hang on, is this because of the missing key?"

"Missing key?" There was a flicker of fresh energy. "House key?"

"No, car key. We could only find one set—I thought Bram mentioned that in his report. It can be a bit chaotic around here. We take turns to be here with the kids, you see. We're never here at the same time." I answered his look of surprise with a brief piece of evangelism about bird's nest custody.

"Right, so in terms of the car keys, might this second set have been missing for some time?"

"Maybe. I guess." A thought struck. "You don't think someone might have broken in and stolen it? We've had a burglary on the street recently." The community officer had mentioned this trend at the meeting, I remembered. Alison had raised the notion that you should always leave car keys out in the open, counterintuitive as it was, so as to avoid burglars ransacking the place in search of hidden keys, but the officer had cautioned against leaving them visible through a window.

"Have you noticed any signs of forced entry?" the detective asked.

"No," I conceded. "But I know thieves can use wires and hooks through the letter box, can't they?"

"That's right." He paused. "Alternatively, you might simply have mislaid the key."

I agreed that this was more likely and he asked if I'd noticed any scratches or other damage to the car over the last few weeks.

"No, it looked the same as ever. There were some marks on the tires from parking—you know, curb damage—but they've been there for ages."

As soon as he'd left, I Googled "Thornton Heath car accident," adding the News filter. Here it was: an accident on Silver Road on Friday the sixteenth at about six p.m. A dark-colored VW or Audi had been seen close to the scene.

Remembering the officer's name, I found he was indeed a detective sergeant in the Serious Collisions Investigations Unit, which handled cases throughout southeast London and its suburbs. They must be visiting the owners of every dark-colored VW or Audi reported stolen in South London, even those taken after the incident, like ours. That struck me as an inefficient way to investigate, but what did I know?

Don't answer that.

#VictimFi

@crime_addict Where's the car then? Husband involved in this crash maybe?
@rachelb72 @crime_addict Must've been, that's why he's done a Lord Lucan
@crime_addict @rachelb72 Why no damage then? He got it fixed?
@rachelb72 @crime_addict Or maybe when they finally find it, they'll discover his rotting body in the boot . . .

BRAM, Word document

At that Friday's handover, Fi said, "Did you know the police thought one of us might have been involved in some car crash down in Thornton Heath a few weeks ago?"

I concealed a split second's paralysis. "They did? When did they say that?"

"A detective came round this morning. Obviously, I checked the diary and told him neither of us used the car that day, but I guess there's a process of elimination they have to follow, isn't there?"

"Yes." I swallowed.

"I wondered if it was possible someone stole the keys before they took the car," she went on, musing. "But the police said that was unlikely since there've been no signs of a burglary. Still, we should have been more careful, Bram."

Though taken aback by this, I saw how fortunate it was that it had been she, genuinely in the dark, who had been the one to field the police's inquiries. Would my own responses have sounded so natural, so guileless? How appalled she would be if I told her the truth about the Audi. That I'd thought seriously about finding a dark stretch of canal, or even the Thames, and taking the hand brake off to let it roll into the water, but then I'd decided it was better to hide it in plain sight.

Contrary to my reports to both insurer and police, I'd last seen our car late on Sunday night, last driven it then too. Left it in a street in Streatham with no parking restrictions, key dropped down the nearest drain. With any luck, the battery would go flat and it would sit there for years.

"I doubt we'll ever know what happened." I sighed. "But I really don't think we should beat ourselves up about it. We're still getting used to a whole new way of living. How are we supposed to know where the car keys are at any given moment?"

"You're right." The way she was looking at me, thankful for the solidarity, the shared attention to this latest aggravation—it not only flattered me, but it calmed me too.

"We're pretty security conscious generally," I said. "Especially after what happened to the Ropers. And poor old Carys."

She looked pleased that I'd remembered Carys.

I considered the issue of my ban: if the officer she had spoken to had known about it, then he obviously hadn't seen fit to divulge it. She must have explained early on that we'd split up and he'd erred on the side of diplomacy. "Tell the police to phone me if they have any more questions," I said.

I was already formulating my responses for just such a follow-up. "The sixteenth? Oh, that was the day of the conference. It was at a hotel down near Gatwick—I'd have to look up the name." "Did you drive there?" "No, I took the train. There was a delay, now I think about it. I only just made it to the first session." Surely they wouldn't go so far as to check the station's CCTV footage? If they did, crowds had accumulated quickly that morning and it was possible I wouldn't be easily identifiable on the platform, which was unfortunate. On the other hand, when I'd left I'd been part of a swarm too—hidden by it, with any luck.

But what if they checked at the other end? There'd be no pictures of me hurrying through any station on the Gatwick line. "Where did you get off the train, Mr. Lawson?" they'd ask. I needed to Google the station, I thought, check the exits. Or was it more natural to be vague—who remembered this stuff? What about CCTV at the hotel? Had cameras clocked the Audi near the collision site? And the police had number plate recognition technology, didn't they?—oh God, could it be applied retrospectively?

I became aware that I was blinking, over and over, a tic that was hard to control.

"Are your eyes all right, Bram?" Fi asked.

"Fine, just a bit of grit." I recovered my cool. "You know . . . No, now might not be the right time. . . ."

"For what? Tell me."

"Just a suggestion, but I was reading a thing in the *Guardian* about families going car free and I wondered if that might be something we could do. Get the boys involved, appeal to their inner eco-warrior."

She looked as surprised as any sentient human would to hear Bram Lawson, no stranger to *Top Gear* and hardly a soul-searcher regarding his carbon footprint, speaking in this way. "Are you serious?" she said. "You've always driven. I can't imagine you without a car."

"We all have to try new things now and again," I said.

25

Toby texted on the Saturday morning:

> *Let me guess—you've Googled me and discovered I don't exist? You think I must be a serial killer with an assumed identity?*

I smiled.

> Not quite.
> *I'm just a social media refusenik. You're lucky to get this text.*
> You're lucky I'm replying.

There was a companionable silence, during which I grew steadily more aware of the beat of my own pulse. It was no coincidence that he'd waited till the weekend to make contact. I'd explained my un-usual living arrangements, that this was my time at the flat.

Free later? I asked, before he could.

At your command, he answered.

BRAM, Word document

Hell-bent though I was on eliminating Mike from my consciousness, I found myself outmaneuvered yet again when, the Monday after our meeting in the Swan, a replacement phone, this one a Sony, was delivered by hand to my office. There was a charger attached, but no packaging, no envelope, no note.

"The guy said he saw you leave it charging in the pub just now," Nerina on reception told me. "He must have followed you back. Wasn't that nice of him? I do like a good deed, don't you?"

"I do," I agreed. What I don't like is a psychotic stalker, I thought. (A lesser gripe: it was good of him to give the impression I'd been in the pub at midday on a Monday rather than at the meeting with a local minor injuries clinic marked in my diary and duly attended.) I took the phone reluctantly and, as if in response to my touch, a message notification lit up the screen:

Uh-oh, looks like someone's getting her memory back. . . .

I read it right there, in reception, my bag of samples at my feet.

ROAD RAGE CAUSED SILVER ROAD CRASH, SAYS VICTIM

A victim of the Silver Road collision on 16th September has told police that the incident was caused by a reckless overtaking maneuver that may have been the result of road rage.

"From what the victim remembers, a black hatchback was accelerating past a third car, which was traveling well within the speed limit, and mistimed the maneuver, forcing her Fiat off the road and causing serious injury to her and her daughter," said Detective Sergeant Joanne McGowan.

Until now, the victim has been too unwell to give police her account of events. Her daughter is still being treated in intensive care at Croydon Hospital for life-threatening injuries and is believed to have undergone multiple surgeries.

"We are very keen to speak to the driver of this third car, thought to be a white sedan, and work together to establish the identity of the speeding driver," DS McGowan continued.

The victim's account confirms that of the owner of the house where the collision occurred, who saw a black VW or Audi turning off Silver Road soon after.

The victim's husband has offered a £10,000 reward for information leading to a breakthrough in the investigation.

I swore under my breath, ignoring Nerina's curious gaze. It defied belief: the police might have been mouthing Mike's own lines, so well did they serve his cause. The bastard hadn't *let* me overtake; that was what caused the collision, but no, in the official account I was reckless and he blameless. And what were the chances that his car's brand had eluded recognition, while mine had not? A white sedan: was that *all* she'd noticed?

Once again, I consoled myself that it was in my interest for him to escape the attention of the police; thanks to the evidence he'd collected against me, he'd be even more dangerous in their interview room than he was in his harassment of me now. Far worse was the fact that the car was no longer dark colored, but definitively black—and a hatchback.

Any thoughts? a text prompted.

I did not reply immediately. There was enough time before I left for an early-afternoon client visit in Surrey to find an anonymous local shop and buy an unregistered pay-as-you-go phone. I knew better now than to trust that any phone supplied by Mike came free of invisible weaponry to be used against me. I'd ditch it in the flat later.

I texted him in the car on the way to the client. In a week heavy with external meetings, a new intern had been charged with chauffeuring me, less convenient than it might have been had he not also shadowed me to the meetings themselves, forcing me to reach for a level of professionalism I was fairly sure I would never produce again in my lifetime. (What did it matter if a hospital or clinic repeated its order of cervical collars? Doubled it or canceled it? I was going down here.)

I might be able to get you some cash.
This you, Bram?
Yes.
I'd prefer you to use the phone I left you.
Well, I'd prefer to use this one.

I took petty pleasure in challenging him, enjoyed the pause that followed.

"Do you not have an iPhone?" said Rich, the intern, from the driver's seat, noticing my cheap pay-as-you-go of dubious brand. He was young, didn't spot my nervous breakdown, only my uncool phone.

"I do, yes, for work. This one's for my work for MI5," I said. It beggared belief that I was now in possession of three mobile phones, like a drug trafficker or a polygamist.

"Yeah, right." Rich laughed, and I resisted the urge to lecture him about valuing his life and all those in it, to warn him against making the same mistakes I had, because if he did not, then nothing less than a living hell awaited.

Mike was back:

What cash? Not interested in shrapnel.
Not shrapnel. 15K, better than the reward money.

Fifty percent better. Surely that would satisfy him.

Let's talk. I'll come to Trinity Avenue tonight.
No! I keep telling you, I'm in rented digs.

I added the address for the flat, an unnecessary courtesy since he appeared to know already every last detail of my circumstances.

I'll be there at 8 p.m. You'd better not be scamming me.

That was his sign-off. Not a trace of irony.

The client meeting was pure torture. Throughout my presentation of new products, my mind churned the same phrases: *"life-threatening injuries . . . multiple surgeries . . . identity of the speeding driver . . ."* The client, marginally more emotionally intelligent than the intern, remarked on my being off-color.

"All right, Bram? You're away with the fairies today."

Realizing I was chewing my fingers in an agitated, simian way, I dropped my hand to my side. "Sorry, no, I'm fine. Just got a few things on my mind."

"Ah, yes, I heard about your domestic troubles," he said. "Happens to the best of us, mate."

He'd told me previously that his wife had left him to shack up with a colleague of hers, consigning him to a bachelor existence of Netflix, ready meals and porn.

"Who's she dumped you for?" he asked, kindly.

"No one," I said. "There wasn't anyone else involved."

Mercifully, he gave me the benefit of the doubt on that. He saw us as kindred spirits, godforsaken—*wife*-forsaken.

He didn't have a clue.

26

BRAM, Word document

I have no problem saying I fantasized about cracking him over the head as he came through the door. Or sliding a knife between his ribs and watching him crumple to the floor, a jointless puppet. But then what? When you think it through, when you try malice aforethought for yourself, you quickly realize there really isn't any foolproof method for murder, what with security cameras everywhere and phones betraying our every step, not to mention DNA and forensics.

No, of course I wouldn't kill the bastard. I could only hope to pay him—and that grasping slut Wendy, wherever she'd got to—to go away.

I watched for him from the balcony. One after another, the vehicles of Alder Rise crawled up to the traffic lights on the eastern side of the park—silver-blond mothers chauffeuring their charges from late sports clubs and music lessons; the evening Ocado deliveries of avocados and sauvignon blanc—and I experienced the physical cramp of grief. I missed Fi and the boys the way you miss a sense, like sight or touch. I missed *driving*. Being behind the wheel had been, I saw now, a genuine passion. I'd offered lifts; I'd volunteered for chores; I'd whizzed here and there with the kids. Fitting the child seats that foxed Fi, securing the belts, ruffling the boys' hair before clunking shut their doors and sliding into the driver's seat. I'd felt so relaxed, so in command—apart from when I got riled up by other motorists or by cyclists or pedestrians, but that was par for the course in London, wasn't it? All drivers had their lapses.

Except *mine* had had terrible consequences.

Consequences that were about to get worse.

A filthy white Toyota pulled up and reversed into the only available space in range. The driver's and passenger's doors opened simultaneously and I watched as Mike and Wendy stepped out. He stood staring up at Baby Deco, at me—I resisted the instinct to duck out of view, but made no acknowledgment—while she consulted her phone, and then together they approached the main doors.

I waited in the hallway for them, already blazing with fury.

"What the fuck are you playing at?" I hissed, as soon as they emerged from the lift, and the brute hostility attracted a startled look from my neighbor leaving her flat (Sod's law, the only time I saw another soul on my floor, and it was when I was with these two).

Mike had the gall to look offended. "What? You knew I was coming—what's the problem? You don't mind that I've brought Wendy along? Thought you might like to get reacquainted."

I hustled them in, closed the door behind them. "I mean the car! The Toyota. I thought you said you got rid of it."

Mike frowned. "Why would I do that."

"You said joyriders took it!" Thirty seconds in and already I was on the back foot, speaking in just the wild exclamations I'd been determined to avoid.

Wendy, who had not uttered a word until then, said conversationally, "If *I* were the police and someone said they'd seen a Toyota at the scene of a crime, the first one I'd check out would be the one that's just been reported stolen. I'd think, a bit of a coincidence, that."

"You haven't gone and got rid of the Audi, have you, mate?" Mike said with unconvincing concern. "That would be a mistake."

Now he said it, it was obvious. I'd been played. I'd reacted to his text about joyriders exactly as he'd hoped, heedlessly incriminating my own vehicle and giving him even more leverage than he already had. The A3 would have been a needle in a VW/Audi haystack had I not left it for the police to find, had I not reported it missing. How many others had been stolen in the last month? Even in the whole of the Southeast there couldn't be more than, what, ten, twenty? Few enough for each owner to be given reasonable consideration, even before you added the new detail of it being a hatchback. Even before you cross-referenced said owners against the database of motoring convictions . . .

I was a fuckwit. At this rate, I was going to jail and I was throwing away my own key.

"Mind you," Mike said pleasantly, "even the other driver hasn't mentioned a Toyota, so it's a moot point." He paused to savor the phrase, before glancing about the flat with an amiable air. "Not a bad little place, this, is it, mate? Compact. Not a patch on the main house, obviously, but needs must. This is what happens when your wife finds out you've been a naughty boy, eh?"

What? How the hell did he know that? Guesswork, I supposed, based on my present circumstances, based on my willingness to fall into bed with Wendy.

"You don't know anything about my wife," I said bitterly. "You've never been in my house and you never will."

He smirked. "Someone got out of bed on the wrong side this morning, didn't he? I won't ask whose."

"Sadly, not mine," Wendy said, with a ghastly simper.

Without being invited, they seated themselves in the two arm-chairs, their heads turned to me at symmetrical angles, as if operated by a single brain. The blinds were drawn, the lamplight creating a terrible intimacy between the three of us.

"You not going to offer us a beverage, then?" Mike said.

"Got nothing in," I said, perching on a barstool, too agitated to settle.

"Not very domesticated, is he?" Mike said to Wendy.

"He had plenty of refreshments last time," she said, as if puzzled by the discrepancy.

"I bet he did."

I loathed them. I wanted to lock them in their Toyota and put a bomb under it. "So, what's the deal with you two?" I demanded. "It's obvious you knew each other before all this."

"Irrelevant background," Mike said, his agreeable tone at odds with my belligerence. "So, tell us about the money. Found an account you'd forgotten you had, have you?"

"It's the car insurance money," I said. "But it may be another week or two before they pay out—they have to be satisfied it was definitely stolen."

It struck me that the claims investigator might have been referred to the Collisions Unit, which may in turn have served to remind detectives of a vehicle they'd all but discounted following that preliminary chat with Fi. It was only a matter of time, surely, before they returned, this time to question *me*. I was the originator of the report, after all, even if Fi had stated she was the last to drive the thing. Tomorrow, perhaps? They must know about the second residence by now; they might come before I leave for work, escort me to a squad car as the school-run mums drive by. . . . Who would I call? Fi? My mother? Why hadn't I thought to line up a solicitor?

"I got the impression you had the cash ready to go," Mike said, frowning. "Fifteen won't be enough, by the way. Twenty would be better, and you'd better chase it up sharpish because we need it for the new documentation."

I snapped to attention. "What documentation?"

He adopted the air of exaggerated helpfulness I now knew to be his trademark, as if he were obliging an elderly tourist's request for directions. "Well, for starters, we're going to need new passports, and we're looking at five grand a pop minimum for the kind that gets you across borders. Plus, we'll need help with the bank account, probably in the Middle East, somewhere like Dubai, beyond the tentacles of the British taxman."

I bounced in my seat. "What the fuck . . . ? Who needs a new passport? Who needs to cross borders?"

"Well, *you* will, for one. When the sale goes through, your ex isn't just going to walk away, is she? She'll go mental. She'll want to get the police involved, find out what's happened to her share, and chances are they'll alert the Border folks, maybe even Interpol. You won't be able to travel on your own passport, and new ones can't be magicked up overnight. They're works of art, Bram."

I gaped. *"When the sale goes through"? "Interpol"?* The understanding that the money I'd offered had not slaked his lunatic appetite entered me through my open mouth, a monster cockroach blocking my airway. Finally, I managed to rasp: "Come on, Mike. Forget this fantasy about the house. I'll try to get twenty for you. Take it and move on. It's a decent payoff."

His expression remained phlegmatic. "It's not a fantasy. It's a plan, and it's time to get it under way. The first thing we need from you is a look at Mrs. Lawson's passport photo, so Wendy here can do a bit of restyling."

At this, Wendy pulled a theatrically modest face, as if receiving news of a promotion.

"Just take a picture of the relevant page, will you, next time you're home, and ping it over on the new phone. And a shot of her signature as well, please."

"Hang on a minute. What the hell are you talking about, 'restyling'?" I said.

"She'll be Fiona Lawson, of course. I *told* you this last time," Mike said. "Keep up."

I laughed, the demented tone of it belying my certainty that this had to be halted *now*. "Look, this has gone *way* too far." I sprang to my feet. "You've left me with no choice but to go to the police. I should have gone straightaway."

"Why didn't you?" Mike rose too, took a step toward me. In the lamplight the bones of his face were cadaverous. "Go on, tell us. We're fascinated. It wasn't just because of the ban, was it? A looker like you, you'd probably be able to persuade a judge to stick to the minimum sentence."

"I have no idea what you're on about," I said, apprehensive in a whole new way.

He pulled an expression of faux surprise. "Your assault conviction, of course. You can't have forgotten *that*."

I felt a smash of cold, like a ridge of ice collapsing on my upper body.

"A suspended sentence, wasn't it? What, four years ago now? In return for a guilty plea, I'm guessing. Quite a record you've got there, Brammy boy. If you ask me, going to the police is the last thing you should do. Does your boss know, by the way? What about your wife?"

I said nothing.

He whistled. "A hell of a lot of secrets you've been keeping, Bram. But you can't keep them from the police, can you? It all counts as evidence of bad character, when the time comes."

"When the time comes"?

The blood roared in my skull. "Get out," I said. "The deal's off. No money, nothing."

Mike did not reply, simply looked at Wendy, who produced her phone and began dialing. I hovered, impotent, as she selected speakerphone mode and placed the phone on the coffee table between them.

A voice emerged: "Croydon Hospital."

"Critical care ward, please," Wendy said, her tone grave.

"What are you doing?" I hissed, lunging forward. "Why are you ringing the hospital?"

With her eyes fixed blankly on mine, she continued to speak loudly into the phone. "Oh, hello. I'm inquiring about little Ellie Rutherford, the victim of the Silver Road accident. How is she?"

"Stop!" I gasped. My pulse hammered viciously.

"But you just said you wanted to cut your losses," Mike murmured, voice close to my ear, as if genuinely puzzled by my protest.

"What?" Wendy was speaking over him. "No, no, I'm not a family member, just a concerned member of the public. I think I witnessed the crash, you see, and I'm not sure who I need to speak to."

"Can I take your name?" the hospital worker said. "And a contact number, please."

"Sorry, could you repeat that?" Wendy picked up the phone, covered the mouthpiece, and appealed to me with a phony tone of dilemma: "She wants me to leave a name and number to pass on to the police. Shall I? It's your call."

"No!" I sank to my knees. "Hang up, please!"

Two sets of eyes did not move from me until, at last, Wendy looked at Mike for a signal.

She uncovered the mouthpiece. "No name. Please pass on my best wishes for her recovery."

She ended the call.

"That was despicable," I said, my breathing tight. "Saying you have information and then . . ." My voice cracked.

"Bless him," Wendy said to Mike. "I'm sure Karen Rutherford would be touched."

"How do you know their names? They haven't been released to the public." Quite apart from the stress of this latest stunt, the exposure of the victims' names was unwelcome to me: Karen and Ellie—they could be a mother and daughter at the boys' school gate. I wished I could unlearn them.

"Unofficial channels, mate," Mike said.

The same channels he'd used to discover my financial assets, my assault conviction and God only knew what else.

"Bram, I think you need to understand how serious this is," he went on, his manner suddenly gentle, paternal. "Like I say, we're ready to get the process under way and there's plenty to get on with while we wait for the funds."

"Yes, you said. The insane and not at all traceable act of stealing a house by impersonating me and my wife."

"Oh, there's no need for anyone to impersonate *you*," Mike said, chuckling. "Even if I had the acting skills, I couldn't hope to match your matinee idol looks. *Fading* matinee idol. No, you can play yourself, mate."

"Get your plot straight," I snapped. "You just said I'm going to need a new passport. Which is it?"

"Well, you'll be yourself for the transaction, but when it's done, like I said, you'll have a bit of explaining to do and you'll probably want to move on with a nice new identity."

"Over my dead body."

"Interesting choice of words. Just so long as it's yours and not little Ellie's. I hear she's hanging on by a thread, poor thing, getting new infections all the time."

I gaped at him. "You're evil."

His shrug was so casual it involved only one shoulder. "Not evil, just practical. You need to understand that you're not going to get your hands on the picture or the recording until we complete on the house. Meanwhile, there's always a chance the victim's memory will improve, especially if Wendy here gives her a call."

As I buckled at this confirmation that Wendy had indeed recorded our morning-after exchange, he steamed on: "So you see, time really is of the essence here. The faster we work, the faster you can escape. As I understand it, if we get the place on the market now, we should be able to do it in under three months."

"Three months?" I laughed, grimly. "I'll be arrested long before then, with or without your sidekick's tip-off."

"I was getting to that," Mike said. "If the police *do* come calling, then so long as you cooperate nicely, I'll help you out with an alibi for the night of the crash. We got talking in the Half Moon in Clapham Junction—how about that? I assume it would need to be a train station, eh? Since you're not meant to be on the road."

I could feel my right fist itching to smack him, fought to keep it by my side. "Fuck your alibi and get out. I won't ask you again."

For the first time his manner edged toward annoyance. "You know what? I'm beginning to find these knee-jerk outbursts of yours a bit tedious. Don't go wrecking another phone, will you? If you do, we'll have to contact you on your work phone. Better still, leave a message with your boss. Neil Weeks, isn't it? I imagine he'd be *very* interested to hear what you've got yourself involved in. I wouldn't be surprised if he was already a bit dismayed by your performance lately. Sales figures down this quarter, are they?" His hand fell on my shoulder, bony fingers grasping powerfully. "So what I suggest is that you have a proper think. I know you'll reach the right decision."

Wendy was slower to stand, taking a moment to scope the room.

Her gaze came to rest on the bed and, noticing this, Mike said, "Shall I go on ahead, give you two some time on your own?"

A flash of memory of bare skin and groaning, the names she'd urged me to mutter in her ear. The thighs splaying and then gripping.

"No, thanks," I said.

"Shame." She was right next to me, letting her fingertips touch my arm, before following Mike from the flat.

"Don't forget about the twenty K, Bram," Mike called.

I watched them leave in the same way I'd watched them arrive. Judging by the easiness between them, I felt sure they'd known each other for years. Was I one in a line of victims, or were they first-time grifters? Certainly, this could only be a crime of opportunity: first, at the scene, Mike had taken the photo to protect himself, and then, once establishing both my assets and liabilities, had dispatched Wendy to the Two Brewers to collect any admissions of guilt I was foolish enough to make. If she fancied sleeping with me in the process, then that was her call. To them, sex was cheap, easy to give and easy to take. What *was* worth something was property. A house on Trinity Avenue. A once-in-a-lifetime scam.

But it was a reckless plan by any standards. What did they know about counterfeit passports and bank accounts in Dubai? How had they intended meeting their expenses before I'd blundered in yet again with an offer of cash? They were amateurs. Clowns.

The fact that they seemed able to run rings around me only meant I was even less intelligent than they were.

Seriously, I should have just hurled myself off the balcony then and there.

27

"The police are on their way," Merle announces, and Fi falls silent, concentrating her energy on not trembling. The kitchen where she has cooked and eaten thousands of meals with her family and friends is no longer hers to command, but she prefers Merle over either of the Vaughans as its new ruler.

The prospect of the arrival of the authorities has not stopped David Vaughan from continuing with his private investigations, and he now ends a call to the Lawsons' solicitors (Lawsons in quotation marks), shaking his head in disbelief. "The guy we need to speak to has got his phone turned off while he's at a hospital appointment. He'll be back this afternoon."

Merle raises an eyebrow. "Let's hope he's getting his vision fixed. No, his whole *brain*."

The absent lawyers are becoming not only the missing links, but also the group's scapegoats.

"Well, it certainly looks like we've got a fraud on our hands," Merle goes on. "This will kill Bram. He's not as strong as you, Fi."

"Hang on a minute," David says. He is not having this, this tendency of Merle's to speak as if Fi's position is the rightful default. He addresses Fi directly: "If you're so sure your husband knows nothing about this, then who was the guy we met? The one who was here with the agent? I'm sure he was introduced to us as the owner. If he was some sort of imposter, then where was the real Mr. Lawson? Tied up in the playhouse?"

"What?" Fi says, startled.

"What does he look like? I'm serious. Have you got a photo on your phone?"

"Wait a minute!" Merle preempts any heedless cooperation on Fi's part: "*You* tell *us* what the man you met looked like," she tells David. There is little trust in this room; all they have in common is the object of their claim.

"He was good-looking, mid- to late forties, about six foot two, dark curly hair starting to go gray," Lucy says. "He was quite restless, I thought—you know, pacing about a bit. He went to have a cigarette, didn't he, David? He had quite an intense way of looking at you."

Fi stares at her, utterly chilled. Her impression is astute (women tend to notice the details of Bram), but how on earth has she come to form it?

"That does sound like him," Merle concedes.

Prickling with fresh dread, Fi fiddles with her phone to find a picture; she still has a couple of Bram with the boys.

"Definitely him," the Vaughans agree.

"I don't understand," Lucy says to David, semiprivately. "You think her husband cheated her?"

"Bram wouldn't do anything as evil as that," Merle says with profound certainty. "Would he, Fi?"

But shock has swept her in a fresh tide, making it impossible for her to follow the exchange with a rational mind.

"When exactly did you meet him?" Merle asks the Vaughans.

"At one of the viewings. He was only here that once, though," David says. "The next two times it was the agent on his own. So yes, just at the open house."

"Open house?" These two words cause the hairs on Fi's arms to stand on end. A memory; a connection on *her* part, in *her* experience, between blameless past and treacherous present.

Lucy turns to her, her memory jogged. "That's right! You were out of town, he said. I remember now. The way he said it, I assumed you were still married."

We are, Fi thinks. However deep Bram's ship has sunk, legally, financially, she goes down with it.

Merle, however, is still clinging to the prow. "I'm sorry, but there's no way there could have been an open house here without my noticing. I live two doors down."

"Well, there was," David says, exasperated. "It was a Saturday in October."

"Saturday the twenty-ninth," Lucy adds. It has sentimental value to her, Fi can tell. The day she first saw her dream house, her forever home.

As Fi's eyes meet Merle's, she sees the beginnings of doubt in her friend's response. "Kent," she says. "Half term."

Fi turns to David, his features blurring through the gathering of fresh tears. "So you're saying Bram was a part of this? He actively tried to sell my home?"

"I'm saying he *did* sell it," David says. "In which case, he's not likely to have been abducted, is he? He's probably gone of his own accord."

As Fi covers her sobbing face with her hands and Merle strokes her slumped shoulders, the doorbell rings.

"Let's see what the police think," Merle says.

GENEVA, 3:30 P.M.

In the hotel bathroom, he plays Nick Cave on his phone and sets about cutting his hair. The curls fall in chunks, only the dark visible on the white porcelain, the gray imperceptible. The lighting, the music, his anxiety: together they create an artificial mood, almost ceremonial, as if he's an actor playing an outlaw and this is the scene in which he must alter his appearance, become someone else. He's a great train robber, perhaps, or Jesse James.

No, Samson, he thinks. *He's* a more edifying point of reference. A man blessed with superhuman strength. The boys loved the children's Bible stories gifted by Grandma Tina. Harry, in particular, relished the violence of Samson's story: the tearing apart of a lion, the ripping of gates from their hinges with his bare hands, the slaying of a whole army (Bram remembers explaining what "slay" means following initial confusion with Santa's sleigh).

Having given it brief, desperate thought, he gave no clue to his mother that he was leaving. He may have no faith of his own, but he does have faith that hers will sustain her. And Fi won't cut off contact; she is scrupulous about grandparental rights. If anything, they will close ranks, once the police reveal the extent of his crimes; they'll prepare their assault on a shared enemy.

All he can pray for is that they'll temper their denunciations around Leo and Harry, that they'll let them remember him at his best—whatever that was.

He rakes up the shorn hair with his fingers and transfers it to the toilet for flushing. When he stands back and looks in the mirror, he is alarmed. Though he is altered, it is in an undesirable way: he looks younger, more striking, the fear in his eyes more candid and memorable. He remembers again the man by the lifts at the restaurant and he knows now that he must trust his instinct, that it is the only thing left *to* trust. Someone—if not that man, then another—is in Geneva, watching him, biding his time before . . . what? Forcing him back to Mike? Arresting him? *Killing* him?

At once, the compulsion to be on the move overcomes him and he repacks the few items removed from his rucksack and leaves the room.

The receptionist, at the start of her shift, has no way of knowing that his appearance has changed and makes no comment about his premature departure, his room having been paid for in cash on check-in.

As he exits, he tries not to think of Samson's end, how he brought down the temple, killing not only himself but everyone in it.

28

BRAM, Word document

Are you beginning to see how appalling it looked on paper? How trapped I felt, how terrorized? The confessed—and recorded—guilt for the Silver Road crash, the driving ban, the suspended sentence for assault, not to mention a conviction for possession . . . The last was ancient history, of course, but what did that matter? As Mike said, it all counts when the time comes.

Counts against me.

I can only defend myself by saying these have been my only crimes in forty-eight years and I believe that there are very few people who haven't committed some variation of at least one of them and simply never had the law involved. Seriously, have you never gone over the speed limit? Have you never tried drugs or got a bit lairy outside a pub? I didn't say did you get caught doing one of these—I just asked, did you do it?

Well, I got caught for all of them. Which meant that when the big one came along there could be no barrister in the land convincing enough to argue that Silver Road was a onetime mistake. Not when the record showed that I was someone who was always in the wrong place at the wrong time.

Doing the wrong thing.

OK, so the fight at the pub—it was pretty damn serious. I didn't *start* it, but I certainly finished it: the guy was hospitalized, off work for weeks. I was lucky the sentence was suspended and that, miraculously, I managed to hide the prosecution process from Fi. I won't go into the labyrinthine logistics of *that* (it helped that there were renovations going on at the house and, the boys not having started school yet, she had based herself with them at her parents' place, leaving me to my own devices). Nor will I explain what I imagined would happen if my remorse had not convinced the court and I'd been sent down ("Fi? I'm calling from a prison pay phone. I need to tell you something. . . .")

"In return for a guilty plea, was it?" Mike said that night at the flat, his gaze voyeuristic, as if he was able to see into my soul and measure my pain. And his instinct was sharp—I'll give him that. I would have pleaded guilty to far worse if it meant avoiding jail time. I won't say prison was a phobia, because that would make it irrational, all in the mind.

Whereas it was real. So real that I would have done anything, sacrificed anyone, to avoid it.

"FI'S STORY" > 01:37:11

I really hope I'm not giving the impression that I allowed a new relationship to distract me from what was, in retrospect, taking place right under my nose, but I'm sure you'll understand that it *was* an exciting time. We all know the beginning is the best bit— who would begrudge a woman that? Especially one whose marital breakdown had left her with no heart for anything more than beginnings.

Even beginnings came with a level of weirdness. It was maybe our third weekend of seeing each other, the first time Toby had stayed the night at the flat, when I had a completely unexpected fight-or-flight reaction. Waking to find him in bed next to me, I got trapped in the delay of recognizing him, of recognizing the bed itself, the four walls around us. *Why am I not in my home with my family?* I thought. *What is this sordid setup?* Even when my brain caught up, I was convinced I couldn't sleep with him again. Not here, with Bram's clothes in the wardrobe, his shaving gel in the bathroom, the air still fresh with the breath from *his* lungs. It was almost as if he were in the room with us, watching us.

Of course, by the time we were up and I was walking Toby through the park to the station, I was myself again and he was oblivious to the episode.

"So, do kids not play with conkers anymore?" he said. "Or are they all too busy indoors bullying one another on social media and self-harming?"

"Not *all* of them," I said, laughing. "Some still venture into the real world now and then." But as the spiky fruits rolled in our path, no children scampered forward to claim them, as they would have done in my day, the biggest seeds polished and threaded onto string for competition. (Polly and I had become quite vicious as we took turns to strike each other's, as I recalled.) It was possibly the most beautiful day of the month too, when the fire of autumn had not yet faded to ash. *Leo and Harry should be here,* I thought. "Maybe there's some mass maths tutoring event I don't know about. I'm going to get my two out here tomorrow afternoon. Enforced outdoor fun."

"Quite right." Toby had two almost grown-up children, Charlie and Jess, whom he saw every few weeks; relations with the ex were fraught and she'd moved to the Midlands to be close to her parents.

"You mustn't have been much older than a teenager yourself when you had your kids," I said to him. He was in his late thirties, almost a decade younger than Bram. "I can't imagine not talking about Leo and Harry the way you don't talk about your two." Hearing myself, I laughed my apologies. "That sounds bad. What I mean is, I'm impressed how you've let go."

Toby examined the path ahead. "Just because I don't talk about them doesn't mean I don't think about them," he said mildly.

"I know, of course. I didn't mean you aren't a fantastic dad."

"I'm not sure about that," he said, smiling. "You just do the best you can, don't you?"

"You do."

I remember thinking, *Bram would fight harder than this to be in his kids' lives.* Then, *Stop comparing!*

(Comparison is the thief of joy: that's one of Merle's favorite sayings. So true.)

Anyway, that was when I saw them, Bram and the boys. Under a big old horse chestnut by the gates to Alder Rise Road. The boys' hair was damp from swimming—Bram tended to forget hats. The wind was up and there was a sudden shower of prickly missiles as the fruit dropped from the tree, causing Harry to shout with excitement and throw up his hands to try to catch one. Leo, ever cautious, stepped away, but Bram pulled him back and though he yelled in protest, his face shone with excitement.

They didn't see me and I didn't point them out to Toby—who was in any case easing slightly ahead of me, checking his phone—but kept the sighting to myself.

I still think about it now sometimes, the three of them together and the way it made me feel to be watching them from across the park. It left me with an odd melancholy I didn't know how to explain at the time, though I now think it was directly connected to that feeling I'd had in bed. It was the day I let go of some last secret subconscious instinct that Bram and I might be reconcilable.

#VictimFi

@SarahTMellor This woman is still in love with her ex #BlindinglyObvious
@ash_buckley @SarahTMellor Don't forget she said at the start she wanted to kill him.

BRAM, Word document

There was a Saturday morning in October when I took the boys to the park that I think about a lot now. It was probably the last time, premedication, that I had the facility to clear my mind temporarily and be in the moment. I used to hate that phrase, "in the moment"—a bit too *mindful* for me—but it does describe it pretty well. As if I had no past and no future but had been transplanted to that corner of Alder Rise with two hilarious little boys to catch the conkers as they came flying down. I told them about the sign someone put on a tree a couple of years ago reading FALLING CONKERS and Leo said, "Wouldn't it be funny if the person putting up the sign had been hit on the head by one?" and Harry added, "Yes, and he *died*."

Oh, it was all fun and games until we got home and they strung their favorites to have a game and within seconds Harry had hit Leo in the eye and Leo had to sit with a bag of frozen peas on his face and I swore the two of them to secrecy because Fi was exactly the kind of person who'd have thought that a warning sign about conkers was a good idea.

I kept apologizing to them—I remember that—and they kept saying, "It's not *your* fault, Dad," partly because they *always* blamed each other (it was their default setting), and partly because they didn't know what it was I was really apologizing for.

Perhaps I didn't either, not truly. Not until the next morning.

I can record exactly the moment my final fingerhold slipped from the rock face, causing a loss of altitude so extreme, I came close to fainting: ten thirty a.m. on Sunday, the sixteenth of October, as I sat at the kitchen table playing Pokémon Monopoly with the boys while browsing the local news on the pay-as-you-go.

POLICE HUNT KILLER IN MOTHER-AND-DAUGHTER HORROR CRASH

The young victim of a suspected road rage incident in Thornton Heath last month has died in hospital from her injuries. Ten-year-old Ellie Rutherford, in the passenger seat of her mother's Fiat 500 at the time of the crash on the evening of September 16, lost her fight yesterday following multiple surgeries.

Karen Rutherford remains in Croydon Hospital recovering from her own injuries. Neither she nor her husband was available for comment.

A police spokesperson said: "This is incredibly sad news and we would like to assure Ellie's family that we are committed to bringing the offender to justice. We are particularly interested in hearing from a woman who phoned Croydon Hospital to say that she had witnessed the incident. We would like to emphasize that any information she shares will be treated with the utmost confidentiality."

Flowers have been left in tribute at both the family's
home and the collision site on Silver Road.

The words will be scored on my soul for as long as I continue to draw breath. A child was no longer critically injured, but dead. *A child was dead. . . .*

"Put the phone down, Dad," Leo said in Fi's voice. "You have to concentrate on the game."

A child was dead!

"Daddy? Are we going to buy Nidoqueen?" Harry asked.

"You decide," I told him, sounding ghostly even to myself. "Do we have enough cash?"

"It's *really* expensive, three hundred fifty Pokédollars," Leo said, needling him. "Can you even count that high?"

"Of course I can!" As Harry began to count the money in his slap-dash way, I sensed my impatience grow and feared the rage I might unleash: I pictured myself overturning the table, roaring like a monster, throwing myself through plate glass. It frightened me that the violence I felt toward Mike, Wendy, *myself*, might expose itself to the two people I most passionately wished to protect.

A child was dead. The charge would be upgraded from causing serious injury to manslaughter or death by dangerous driving—I didn't know what the hell it would be called.

Not four years in jail but ten. Maybe more.

"Give me a minute, boys, will you, while I just go to the loo? Help Harry count his cash, will you, Leo?"

"But he's not on my team!" Leo whined.

"Just do it!" I yelled.

Defiantly opposed though the two of them were, the shock on their faces was identical as I ran from the room and vomited in the downstairs toilet.

"FI'S STORY" > 01:41:20

On my return to Trinity Avenue that Sunday, Harry was the first one I saw as I let myself in. Though by now accustomed to the comings and goings of his separated parents, he always came into the hallway to announce the news headlines.

"Leo hurt his eye!"

"Did he? How?"

"Totally by accident—it wasn't *my* fault. And we've finished marking everything with the special police pen!"

"Well done! Did you do all the phones and iPads and things?"

"Yes, every single one. Oh, and Daddy's being sick again," he remembered, as Bram appeared from the bathroom.

"Really?" I said. *Again?* "Are you all right, Bram?"

"I'm fine," he said. "Just a bit of food poisoning. How was your weekend, Fi?"

"It was good. I . . . I spent it with a friend." We held each other's gaze and I surprised myself by blushing. Bram's response was peculiar, to say the least: one side of his face began to convulse, as if sustaining blows from an invisible opponent. He looked, in fact, just as a more vengeful ex-wife might fantasize about him looking: at her mercy, crushed.

Hypothetically—because I wasn't that woman—it didn't feel nearly as satisfying as I might have expected.

"Let me go and have a look at Leo's eye," I said.

29

BRAM, Word document

I was ready with my next move even before the inevitable provocation came on Monday morning:

> *I take it you've seen the latest news? Whole new ball game now.*

If I were really paranoid, I'd think he'd arranged for the poor child to die for his own benefit. I couldn't countenance seeing him again and so I phoned.

"Nice to hear from you, Bram," Mike said. "You've finally seen the error of your ways, have you?"

"I got your text," I said coldly. "Your compassion is over-whelming."

He sniggered. "I'm not in the business of compassion. You must know that by now."

"Then you're a sociopath."

He sighed. "Must we go through the same routine every time? Is this *really* all you called to say?"

I collected myself. "I called because I have a proposal for you."

"Oh yeah? Then we should—"

"No, I have no interest in meeting again. I'll tell you now, over the phone. Take it or leave it."

His scornful puff of laughter made me want to hunt him down and smash my phone into his face.

"Go on, then. Let's hear it."

I sucked in a lungful of air, enough to expel my words without pause: "You do what you need to do. If you're crazy enough to steal passports from me or whatever else you need, then I won't stop you. But I'm having nothing to do with it. You commit the crime and if by some miracle you succeed, you do whatever you like with the cash, go wherever you like. Either way, I'll play dumb. I'll have never met you, never heard your name."

"Steal passports from me . . . I won't stop you": that was the offer, buried in the speech, and I knew he would unearth it straightaway. *"Take what you need from me."* Just don't ask me to be an active conspirator.

In the twenty-four hours since I'd read of little Ellie Rutherford's death, this scenario—absurd, foolish, wicked though it was—had established itself as a comparatively desirable option. I would be the victim, just like Fi. We'd lose the house but we'd lose it together; we'd have each other. It might be the making of us—the *re*making of us. I imagined myself comforting her, telling her we would get through it together, that material possessions were nothing next to health, family, love. It would take years, but I would start to forget that poor girl and the family she left behind. I might even find a way to atone.

"Is that it?" Mike said.

Another long breath and I sped on: "In return, I'll need the photo from the incident and whatever this recording is that Wendy made. I'll need your word that there's nothing left that could connect us or incriminate me." Even as I spoke, I understood how flimsy any such promise would be: he and Wendy were *blackmailers*; of course they would keep copies, with or without each other's knowledge. Fresh anxiety followed: there was also a text message I'd overlooked. The one I'd received from Wendy after our night together—with the link to the news piece about the cash reward, before Mike had entered the frame—had been sent to my "official" registered phone, the one provided by my employer. I'd deleted it, of course, but couldn't messages and files be recovered by police even after being deleted? Even if those fools were satisfied they'd fulfilled their side of the bargain, even if Mike alibied me convincingly in the event of capture, would technology betray me?

Having felt close to euphoria when devising this solution, I was now free-falling through its holes, my soul screaming.

"Hmm." Mike's voice slid into my ear, sticky, poisonous. "I really don't think you're in a position to make demands, Bram, even if you've deluded yourself into thinking what you're actually making is an offer."

"But I don't see why you need me," I said in a whine, already reduced to a pleading child. "You can do it without me."

"Oh, but we can't," Mike said. "I thought we established that last time: you're inimitable." A pause as he relished having pulled off the word. "So why don't I make *you* an offer: stop the crap and we'll keep this between the adults."

I swallowed. My throat was raw from the retching I'd been doing several times daily—anytime I tried to eat, basically. "What does *that* mean?"

"It means we won't need to involve the kids. How about that?"

"What?" My stomach contracted.

"Leo and Harry, isn't it? Dog lovers, I'm guessing."

Of course, he'd seen them at the dog show, if only fleetingly. The thought of his having been close enough to touch them brought bile to my mouth.

"I'm sure you'd like to keep them safe, wouldn't you, Bram? So would I, and like I say, that's my offer."

"It's not an offer. It's a threat, and you know it."

"Interpret it how you like. I'm trying to be nice here. Now, let me remind you what you're going to do first."

"No, I need to know—"

"Shut the fuck up now, Bram, all right? I want those shots of your wife's passport photo and signature by the end of the day. Do you understand? If they don't arrive, the evidence from Silver Road goes to the police at nine a.m. tomorrow. I reckon you'll be arrested before midday—what d'you think? And with you in a police cell, those two boys'll have only their mum to look out for them. Let's hope she's up to the job, eh?"

He hung up, leaving me to swear into a dead line that if he mentioned Fi and the kids one more time I would kill him.

"FI'S STORY" > 01:42:33

When Bram asked to drop in on the Monday evening for some documents he needed for the car insurance claim, I reminded him that the file was empty. "You took all the paperwork months ago."

"I did, but I can't find the original no-claims certificate from when I switched the policy last year. I must have put it with the house insurance stuff. It won't take me a minute to find it."

"When do you think they'll pay up?" I asked him, when he reappeared from the study. It was now two weeks since the Audi had been reported stolen and it had still not been recovered. I'd heard nothing more from the police officer who'd come to the house. "Is it like missing persons—a certain period has to pass before you can be declared dead?"

He looked so suddenly, so inexplicably sad, that I reached to put a hand on his arm. Normally, I was careful to avoid physical contact with him, but this was instinctive, almost maternal. "I know you loved that car. Leo's upset too. But we'll get a new one or, as you suggested, try managing without one for a bit. We could spend the insurance money on something else. You know I want to have the house repainted. It's been years since we did upstairs. Whatever happens, I'll definitely need to keep the hire car for the half-term trip to Kent," I added. This was a long weekend at Alison's holiday home on the coast, an end-of-October tradition for mothers and kids now in its fifth year.

"I didn't think you'd go to that this year," Bram said.

"Why wouldn't I?"

He grappled visibly with a response before saying, finally, "I don't know, Fi. It's entirely up to you."

Well, not *entirely*, I thought. Bird's nest custody was about give-and-take, and I needed his cooperation just as much as he needed mine. "When we're away, you should just decide yourself where to hang out," I told him. "I don't know if you prefer to be based in the house or the flat. We didn't discuss this with Rowan, did we?"

It was clear he couldn't remember who Rowan was. "Our bird's nest counselor? Are you going to the rugby with Rog and everyone on the Saturday?"

Traditionally, the husbands marked the same weekend by going to Twickenham or, if the dates didn't fit, to Crystal Palace for the football. In previous years, Bram had been in the thick of it, leading the pub crawl, censoring the war stories (I usually got the more colorful details care of Merle or Alison).

"I'll probably stay in the house," he said, continuing his new habit of conversing at a half-minute delay. "I might have some friends from work over. A few of the guys and their wives."

"Good idea. You've looked a bit stressed-out lately." I thought about the previous time I'd seen him, when his face had begun twitching uncontrollably. "And I realize you'll be missing two nights with the boys, so we can swap with some weekday nights, if you'd like. When would be good for you?"

The way he looked at me then was so grim, he might have been a man who'd just been diagnosed with an incurable illness.

"Sooner rather than later," he said.

BRAM, Word document

Her passport was exactly where it was supposed to be, with the rest of the family's in the drawer of the filing cabinet at Trinity Avenue, where they'd remained, I suspected, since our return from our last family holiday. A week at Easter on the hot volcanic beaches of Lanzarote: it might have been a submarine trip to the bottom of the Mariana Trench for how fantastical it seemed now.

The drawer was marked CONFIDENTIAL DOCUMENTS and had I still had a sense of humor, I would have pointed out to Fi the helpfulness of this to the tsunami of criminals who'd swept Alder Rise. But I did not, possessing only the sick, humorless knowledge that I was the most wicked criminal of them all.

The enemy within.

I sent the photos to Mike by the deadline and received an immediate acknowledgment:

That's better, Bram. Your next job is to ring this estate
agent and make an appointment to get the house valued.

He added the details of the private sales arm of a branch of Challoner's Property in Battersea.

Are they in on your plan?
NO. You, me, Wendy, NO ONE ELSE. Understand?
Yes.

The thought of a normal person, a third party, becoming involved
in this insanity made me nauseated. What if this agent grew suspicious
of me and came back to the house when Fi was in to double-check?

Just as I was about to shut down the phone, a final text popped up:

Don't fuck this up or you know who will pay.

30

BRAM, Word document

Act natural. Normal. Just be yourself.

I opened the door, smiling as I would with a new client. "Hello, I'm Bram. You must be Rav?"

"Challoner's Property. This is a beautiful house, Bram."

"Yes. Yes, it is. Come in and see it properly."

Mike had done his research and found Wheeler's in Battersea was one of the foremost staging posts for buyers priced out of more central areas and open to migrating to the next zones out, to neighborhoods that included Alder Rise.

I'd arranged the valuation for Wednesday morning, when the shared diary showed that Fi was leaving early for a trade show in Birmingham and I could claim easily enough to be working from home. I wasn't worried about neighbors mentioning my presence to Fi—most who knew us well enough to have been briefed on the custody arrangements were at work, and even if the odd one was at home, she (it would only be a "she") was hardly likely to know I didn't have Fi's consent to be there or that my guest was an estate agent.

Still, letting myself into the house had felt exactly like the violation it was, even before I'd made a cursory sweep of the place, picking up clothes from the floors and removing—at Mike's instruction—all photographs of Fi. At least he had not insisted that images of Wendy be inserted in their place or, worse, that she should be by my side for this meeting. "You'll be fine on your own," he said magnanimously, the subtext being, "I'll be the first to know if you're not."

If Rav picked up on my subdued mood during the tour, it was to interpret it as reluctance of a more conventional kind. "How certain are you and your wife that you want to sell?"

"Oh, one hundred percent certain. As quickly as possible. That's why we want to price realistically. And we want to be discreet to the point of secrecy; that's why we're doing it through your private sales department. We don't want neighbors to know we're selling, so there mustn't be details in the shopwindow or online. We can't have people here on weekday evenings either. The boys have an early bedtime on school nights."

"Understood." Clearly Rav, noting this last request in his obliging, attentive manner, had met more troublesome sellers than I. "I would propose an open house. Get everyone in and out in one fell swoop. Anyone who needs a follow-up viewing can come at a time convenient for you, or perhaps when you're at work?"

I told him the day that suited us best was a week from Saturday, the twenty-ninth of October.

"That's the last weekend of half term," he said. "Not ideal—some of my candidates will be traveling back from holiday and won't be able to come."

It had been a jolt when Fi had started talking about arrangements for half term, as if the world held a future to be anticipated with plea-sure, while I was living—breathing—by the day, my only emotion to-ward tomorrow abject dread. But from a fraudster's point of view the timing was helpful: half the street would be away on holiday or visiting relatives, including those who would be with Fi at Alison's place in Kent.

Admittedly, the husbands would be left behind, but in my experi-ence men noticed very little.

"There's no other day that works for us," I told Rav.

"Then that's the one we'll go for. There'll still be plenty of interest. A lot of people have younger children, not in school yet, so half term won't be an issue for them. They're after the school district for Alder Rise Primary, of course."

"Of course," I agreed.

I didn't think about my own boys and whether they would con-tinue at the excellent state primary with the pet guinea pigs and the teaching assistant whose eyes teared up when her class sang to their parents at the end-of-year concert. I didn't think about them as I dis-cussed commission percentages and, when an agreement was pro-duced on the spot, signed my name. I told myself that the legal system, law and order, morality, *something* would intervene to bring an end to the lunacy into which I'd plunged. To stop Mike holding my head underwater until my lungs burst.

"As soon as I get back to the office, I'll start calling my candi-dates," Rav said.

Candidates, he kept saying. Candidates for *our* lives.

After he'd gone, I returned the clothes to the bedroom floors and the photographs to their rightful spots.

Mike was loitering outside my office building when I arrived just be-fore lunchtime.

"How much?" he demanded.

"We agreed two point two."

"Undercutting the neighbor. Good work. Accept any offer over two mill."

"Yes, sir."

He didn't move. One of my colleagues passed, a lunch bag from the sandwich bar next door in her hand. "Hi, Bram!" she called.

Great. She knew my name even if I'd forgotten hers. And she'd seen me with Mike. Though he wore a black woolen hat low to the eyes, his bony facial features and brick-wall build were distinctive. ("Yes, that was *definitely* the man I saw Bram with. They looked a bit shifty together, to be honest.")

"Look, Mike, you need to go. We can't be seen together like this. Can you contact me in the usual way next time?"

He gave me a long look that said, "*You* don't give orders—*I* do."

"Just make sure you keep on top of this agent, OK?" he said finally. "And we need the money from the car by the end of next week—I'm meeting a guy."

"What guy?"

"Trust me, better if you don't know."

Trust him? Right.

"If the check hasn't come through by then, you'll have to find another way to get the cash," he added. He stood, hands in pockets, body language maddeningly relaxed. "Still heard nothing from the police?"

"No. Not since they spoke to my wife."

"You can use her name, Bram. Fiona. Fi, did you call her?"

"*I* can use her name, but I'd prefer *you* not to."

"Oh, well, in *that* case," he sneered.

I ignored this. "Listen, the alibi you mentioned?"

"Yep. Half Moon, Clapham Junction."

"I need your full name and a number, just in case."

"Just say Mike. I'm there all the time. The bar staff'll point them my way. We're not mates, didn't exchange numbers or anything gay—we just got talking, had a bit of a session."

Though his instincts were right, it was infuriating to continue to be denied his full name. My investigations online into his and Wendy's identities had yielded laughable results: you try Googling "Mike South London." And of the commercial cleaning companies I'd found in and around Beckenham, none had a permanent member of staff named Wendy. "Not a session. I had to be back in Alder Rise by seven for the boys."

"Fine. We had two pints between five thirty and six thirty. How's that? We talked about the football. Nothing too deep. Can't be expected to remember the details. I know one of the barmen there—he'll vouch for us for a few quid."

"On the subject of money," I said, "if we do this, when it's over, what's my cut?"

He laughed, releasing streams of smoky breath into the cold air. "I wondered when you'd ask that."

"Well, tell me the answer, then."

He drew his face closer to mine, eyes baleful. "Your cut is your liberty, mate. Ten years, I reckon you'd get, *minimum*. And we all know killing a kid is the lowest of the low inside. Imagine ten years of being beaten up and buggered and God knows what else, a middle-aged child murderer in a cell with a twenty-year-old psycho. Or is it three to a cell these days? Sooner you than me."

I sucked in my breath, my heart hammering.

"Hit a nerve, have I?" he taunted. "Just think of all the nerves they'll be hitting inside, eh? They'll be queuing outside your cell."

I began to back away, as if from the Prince of Darkness himself.

"Don't worry about the money," he called. "We'll send a little something your way on completion. Call it a finder's fee."

"FI'S STORY" > 01:46:26

No, I hadn't introduced Toby to Bram. I hadn't introduced him to anyone. I didn't wish to parade him on the Trinity Avenue dinner party circuit, and he, for his part, had no interest in the social structures of Alder Rise.

"Why doesn't he ever invite you to his place?" Polly asked.

"Reading between the lines: it's not somewhere he thinks I'll be impressed by," I said. "He downsized after his divorce, so I'm guessing it's pretty modest."

"He's not married, is he?"

"Well, if he is, I can hardly object, since I am as well."

"You're *separated*," she corrected me. "Has Alison met him?"

"No one has. It's just a casual thing, Polly."

"Even so, not knowing where he lives? Maybe you should ask his wife," she drawled.

It would not be the last time she would propose the married-man theory—and to be fair, Bram's two infidelities gave her good cause to question my judgment—but I chose to close my ears to the clanging of warning bells. I didn't want to spend my time finding fault or preparing for the worst. Maybe such an attitude doesn't fit well in our cynical world, but I'm not going to apologize for trying.

Besides, I was busy at work and by then it was full steam ahead for half term and our weekend in Kent, which took a certain amount of planning. Having missed a summer holiday, Harry was so excited to be going away that he couldn't sleep for most of the week before. It didn't help that one night there was a police helicopter hovering over Alder Rise for hours. This is South London; it happens sometimes.

"It's nothing to worry about," I said when he climbed into bed with me. "It's just the police out catching criminals."

"How can they catch them in the dark?" he asked.

I told him about an article I'd read about police helicopters' thermal imaging cameras. You thought you were safe in your hiding place under the bushes, but you glowed bright white on the screens above.

"It's just like your forensic pen. They use special light to see what we can't see."

"They're cleverer than the baddies," Harry said.

"Much cleverer," I agreed.

Ironic though it may sound, as I lay in bed listening to the relentless staccato of those spinning blades, I genuinely thought how awful it must be to be a fugitive from the law with all this new twenty-first-century technology to contend with. There was nowhere the police couldn't find you once they were on your tail. I even thought, briefly, *Poor guy.*

Well, I assumed it was a man.

BRAM, Word document

There was one news report—and only one—that I haven't needed to remember word for word, because I kept a printout. You'll find it among my paltry last effects in the hotel room.

PARENTS MOURN THEIR "SPECIAL SUNBEAM"

The funeral of the tragic victim of the Silver Road collision, Ellie Rutherford, took place today at St. Luke's Church, Norwood, with the ten-year-old girl's mother released from hospital to say farewell to her beloved daughter.

Many mourners wore yellow, Ellie's favorite color, and a yellow and white floral arrangement was placed on her coffin. Tim Rutherford, who spoke at the service, described his daughter as "our special sunbeam," a child who loved writing stories and singing and who was proud to have been voted class captain for her final year at primary school. "Ten years old is old enough for you to be able to see the wonderful adult she would have become," he said.

Ellie died a week ago following an incident in September when her mother's car was run off the road by a speeding vehicle. As relatives and road-victim groups called for increased manpower in the police investigation, the girl's uncle, Justin Rutherford, said, "You would think they'd have a suspect in custody by now. The whole family is desperate from knowing that this criminal is still on our roads, putting other children's lives at risk."

Detective Inspector Gavin Reynolds said, "Police work is often a painstaking process of elimination, but we are confident we will find the offending driver and discover exactly what caused this fatal collision. Our thoughts are with Ellie's family today," he added.

Writing this, I can only assume the Rutherfords know my name by now. Certainly by the time you read this, they will. I can only assume they must be hoping I'll rot in hell.

31

There were four of us for the half-term weekend—Alison, Merle, Kirsty and me—each with two children, so we made an easy dozen. When I arrived on the Thursday, the light on the Channel already in silvery decline, Leo and Harry didn't even bother taking off their coats, but merged yelling into the spill of children and dogs in the wide garden that edged the sands. They would spend most of their time outdoors, though we drew the line at camping: the coastal winds could be biting at night.

I found the women in the sitting room, wine open in front of the fire. Though this was our fifth year, it was the first since the breakdown of my marriage, and I could hear the echo in the room of a sworn vow to avoid the subject. Fine with me, I thought. Any horror stories this weekend would be purely Hallowe'en based.

"Hello, all!" I displayed my offering: artisan gin from the farmers' market.

Alison jumped up to hug me hello. "Oh my God, that stuff is moonshine—it'll turn us blind. Glasses, girls!"

"I'll do it," Merle offered, taking the bottle from me and heading for the kitchen.

"You're shaking. Come onto the sofa nearest the fire," Alison said. "We've put Daisy in charge of the kids. Eleven is old enough to report a murder, isn't it?"

I laughed. It was all too easy to settle into the lamplit room, its old stone walls shutting out the elements and the gin and tonics Merle distributed smothering any real-world tensions.

"Please can we not talk about school applications this weekend," Kirsty said, a statement, not a request. "If we do, I'll spontaneously combust."

"Fine with me," Alison said. "If I had my way, children would stay in primary school forever, and it would never occur to them that we're not always right about absolutely everything."

"That's the joy of having boys," I said. "As I understand it, they *do* believe it forever."

"Oh, and house prices as well," Merle said. "I've reached saturation point."

Alison's eyes went very wide. "*That* will be hard, but we can certainly try. First, though, can I just ask if anyone else has heard about the house on Alder Rise Road that's just broken the three-mill ceiling?"

"Three million? Seriously?"

A familiar frisson of satisfaction sizzled between us: the only thing better than being a millionaire was being a millionaire without having lifted a finger.

(If that sounds smug and entitled, then just remember why I'm here talking to you now. There are no millions in *my* bank account, I can assure you.)

"Was that an estate agent I saw at your place the other day?" Kirsty asked me.

"No, you must mean the Reeces'," I said. "I think they've changed agents."

"It's been on the market for a while, hasn't it?" Alison said. "I wonder what the problem is."

"Sophie Reece told me they've turned down three low offers," Merle said. "They're holding out for two point three."

"Where are they going, Sophie and Martin?"

"Just to the other side of the park," I said. "A garden flat. They want to downsize."

"Downsize" had to be one of the most feared words in the Alder Rise lexicon, associated as it was with divorce, empty-nesting, financial hardship—perhaps all three at once.

"It will happen to us all sooner or later," Merle said, "and from what I've seen, when it's time, you don't fight it."

She might have been talking about death.

"Well, I can't accept that," Alison said.

"Funny, but I can. That must make me more middle-aged than you."

Of course, Merle looked good enough to be able to make these remarks without a smidgen of self-doubt. Once upon a time, I might have had doubts enough for the two of us, but these days, what with my Pilates and the general overhaul involved when sleeping with someone new, it was different.

"I agree with Merle. I dream of downsizing," Kirsty said. "Or at least *my* house with less stuff in it."

"Maybe that's why you were the one who got burgled." Alison laughed. "They sensed your inner minimalist."

"Well, they won't dare do it again, not with the nice yellow neighborhood police signs up everywhere," I said.

"They are a bit of an eyesore," Merle said. "But they're definitely working, because there hasn't been anything since."

"Fi's car," Alison reminded her. "How long ago was that now?"

"Almost a month," I complained. "We're still waiting for the claim to be processed."

"The words 'blood' and 'stone' spring to mind," Kirsty said. "I told you we got nothing, didn't I?"

"And Carys said her son is still in dispute with the bank about her fraud," Alison said. "The police have said the money's untraceable, so it's down to whether or not the bank agrees to reimburse her."

"Bet they don't!"

"It's almost reached the point where they're more likely to pay out to the criminals than to the victims," Alison said. "They probably have the unassailable human right not to be made to feel guilty."

On it went. To the casual ear it was the same old, same old, the easy banter of friends growing steadily tipsy, but I couldn't help being sensitive to a new hairline fracture between the others and me. I was different now, single—or half-single—a woman who had been humiliated and deceived. When they quizzed me about Toby, which they would soon enough, it would be with that vicarious relish that disguised real fear—fear of their own kingdoms crumbling. There but for the grace of God.

Don't get me wrong. I don't mean that critically. All three have been great friends to me. It's just that I'm the odd one out and I see now that it was a process that began not when my house was stolen but when my trust in my husband was.

"So, to get this straight," Alison said, "we're not talking about schools, we're not talking about property, we're not talking about aging. . . ."

"What is there left?" Kirsty giggled. "Men?"

Here we go, I thought.

"More gin?" Alison's eye swept the room's surfaces, a searchlight exposing empty glasses. "So, Fi, give us an update on the traffic expert. . . ."

Into the glasses sloshed the rest of the gin. It wouldn't be long before the bottles began to amass and we joked about how it might look to a child-protection officer stumbling across us. Maybe when the kids were back inside waiting for their supper, occupying themselves as they had one year by lining up the empties and blowing across their tops. Making music out of their mothers' ruin.

#VictimFi

@alanaP Sounds like she's as big a boozer as the ex.
@NJBurton @alanaP Wonder what he's doing back home?
@alanaP @NJBurton Party time in the bird's nest! Did you notice they joked about kids being murdered?
@NJBurton @alanaP Don't! The house thing is enough to cope with without someone dying.

BRAM, Word document

Survival, however temporary, owed a lot to compartmentalization, and I was becoming adept at sealing every last edge and corner of those compartments. The alternative was to lose my mind, take myself to the psychiatric ward, or to Waterloo Bridge, whichever happened to be closer. Even as Rav arrived with a colleague from Challoner's to set up for the open house, I was picturing my own body falling, watching its unstoppable trajectory into the river, the greedy swallow of the water. And the spectators to this suicide: Did people call for help anymore or did they just film death on their phones and tweet it?

"I've had a lot of interest," Rav said, and I feigned enthusiasm as he reported several booked appointments and more still to be confirmed.

"They all know not to talk to other agents, right?" My latest fear: a viewer who had seen the Reeces' house would discuss this lower asking price, use it to negotiate with them. Sophie Reece would come around to discuss the situation with Fi. "I think you must have the wrong end of the stick," Fi would say, her brow creasing in that bemused way I used to find so cute. She hated discord between neighbors, went out of her way to protect the status quo. "Trust me, I think I'd know," she'd say, and Sophie would agree, there must have been a misunderstanding.

More usefully, the Reeces had a second home in France and went there every school holiday without fail. Unless I was very unlucky, they'd be away from the street exactly when I needed them to be.

"Your wife's not going to be here today?"

"No, she's away with the kids for a long weekend. Women and children only." The idea of that group of women spending three days drinking and putting the world to rights was an unsettling one—then again, it was hardly the most unsettling thing on my mind. If they had any notion of what I was doing now, a marital atrocity so heinous it made adultery seem like charity . . .

"You drew the short straw, then, eh?" Rav's assistant said. She was busy with a spectacular arrangement of lilies for the hall table, their green stems forked like antlers, pink mouths ready to seduce all who entered.

As Rav had promised, there were several interested parties, too many to recall individually but not enough to cause congestion. I skulked in the shadows, concentrating on not smoking, throwing ghostly smiles to anyone who approached.

"You have a *gorgeous* house," they said, one after another. "Are you definitely in the area for Alder Rise Primary?"

"Yes, *and* the Two Brewers," I said, but the joke fell flat, possibly because I looked so convincingly like a man in need of rehab.

Finally, as the last candidates of the day toured, I allowed myself a cigarette at the bottom of the garden, sitting on the edge of the playhouse deck. The ground was hardening with the first cold, curling golden leaves waiting to be kicked and crunched by the kids. It had been soft underfoot that night in July when my luck had finally expired. Nature had issued no helpful warning when Fi crept down the garden path toward us.

Oh, Fi. No woman deserved less what she had coming.

"That went very well," Rav said, when the doors were closed. "I'm confident we'll have requests for second viewings after the weekend, if not our first offers."

I fetched us beers from the fridge; playing the game was easier with alcohol—even this game. "How can they even afford this sort of price?" I asked. "They can't *all* have big banking jobs."

"They're selling a flat or a cottage in Battersea or Clapham or Brixton. Maybe two. But you're looking for a chain-free purchaser who isn't selling as well—I know."

"Yes, we'd prefer not to be caught in a chain. We need this done quickly."

"That will be our priority. There's often an inheritance floating around, so let's see if we can't find one of those."

Which made me think of Fi—again—and her determination that the house should be inherited by Leo and Harry, and for a moment the fact of my standing here with the aim of selling the house from under them struck me as scientifically impossible, utterly severed from reality. Some karmic interconnectedness would stop this from proceeding: no one would make an offer, however low the price, and then I'd have done Mike's bidding without inflicting any real damage. He and Wendy would slink from my life and into some other sucker's.

Yeah, right.

In the end, it was the eerie familiarity of the viewers that I most disliked: the wife radiating social ambition, the husband more cautious or at least better skilled at hiding his aspirations. He prided himself on his negotiator's poker face, perhaps, just as I had all those moons ago. "I'll beat them down," I'd told Fi of those divorcing teachers, and soon we were celebrating with champagne, thinking ourselves quite the conquering heroes.

No, I would have preferred it to be a millionaire's daughter from Beijing or a lottery winner from Burnley. Not Fi and me in a previous life.

32

Saturday night's Hallowe'en party was traditionally the crowning glory of the trip. Custom decreed there be a large bowl of tinned lychees and another of spaghetti in tomato sauce, the blindfolded children taking it in turns to plunge their hands into the "eyeballs" and "brains" respectively. Then, vision restored and faces painted, they danced and screamed under spiderwebs of fairy lights, ate cake with lurid green icing (slime) and drank cherry juice (vampires' blood) through curly straws.

It was the kids who were in costume, but when I looked in the mirror at the end of the evening I saw a transformation in myself too. In contravention of the laws of Hallowe'en, I looked *less* ghoulish, more human. *I've survived this,* I thought. *I feel good.*

Then: Is it because adultery is not the worst crime in the world, not by a long shot? People are murdering one another out there, abusing the vulnerable and stealing from the elderly; there are bombed cities and drowned refugees. Why not forgive Bram, then—forgive him a second time?

Because there'd be a third and a fourth and a fifth, that was why not. I extinguished the bathroom light and, with it, the thought.

"Oh, Ali, it's so beautiful here," Merle was saying, when I returned downstairs. Kirsty was supervising bedtime, the kids in rows of blow-up beds under the eaves. Bingo, Kirsty's spaniel, and Alison's Lab, Rocky, had passed out on the rug in the sitting room, no one fully sure what they might have ingested during the festivities.

"We all helped make it nice," Alison said, surveying the debris over the top of her prosecco glass.

"Not the party stuff, the whole house. I wish I had your eye."

Merle had never been a house-proud type, not like Alison with her on-trend paint finishes and dawn raids on New Covent Garden Market for her flowers. I remember seeing Merle once trimming her fingernails with kitchen scissors, brushing the cuttings onto the floor. She'd exit the kitchen with handfuls of G&Ts and turn off the light switch with her nose. She was spontaneous, playful, with a joie de vivre I'd always envied.

Still do.

As she took a deep gulp of wine, as if quenching thirst with a soft drink, I noticed the liquid in her flute was more effervescent than ours, bubbles leaping from the surface. "You're not drinking, Merle?"

She pulled a face: the game was up. I sensed that she might have denied it had it been one of the others who'd asked. "Sparkling elderflower," she confessed.

"Just this glass or the whole time?"

She shrugged.

"You snake." Alison gasped. "I can't believe you've infiltrated our nest. What's going on?"

"Nothing exciting," Merle said. "I've just been going sober in October."

"Why? The charity thing?"

"Not exactly. Maybe I just liked the rhyme?"

Alison snorted. This was too silly for Merle, and she knew we knew that.

"I'm *never* going sober," I said. I had an ancient instinct to protect her from further interrogation. "And I don't care if *Shakespeare* said it in iambic pentameter. . . ."

"Oh, but you're in a new relationship," Alison said. "That's always a time of intoxication—in all senses of the word."

I chuckled. "In my experience, it's the old relationships that drive us to drink."

Alison's eye returned to Merle, who gazed past her to the clotted black world beyond the window.

"Well, at least this is the last day of the month," Alison said, sighing.

BRAM, Word document

After Rav and his sidekick had gone, I poured myself a vodka large enough to stun a farm animal and took a shower to scrub away the day's toxins. The ingratiations and the avarice. The cold sweats. The *strain*. I'd arranged what I knew would be at best a distraction, at worst the introduction into my freak-show existence of another variable, another complication, another opportunity for regret.

The doorbell rang. In the hall mirror I looked passably human, if you didn't peer too closely.

"What a beautiful house, Bram!" my guest exclaimed. She wore black—for sex, not for mourning, but it might have been the latter as far as I was concerned.

"Funnily enough, you're not the first to say that today," I said. I could tell there was something weird going on with my face, not as bad as once before, in front of Fi, when I'd thought I was having a stroke, but bad enough for my guest to notice.

"What's the matter? You look upset. Has something happened?"

"No, nothing." A smile, the broadest I could muster, pushed the cracks to the edges. "Just a tiring day. Come in and let's have a very large drink."

"I like a man with a plan," Saskia said.

"The clocks go back tonight," she said later, in bed, and it was inevitable that I would wish they could go back far longer than an hour. That they could take us back to September, undo everything that had been done. Maybe earlier than that. How much earlier? When I'd slept with that girl from work years ago, perhaps. Was that when the bindweed had started to grip?

Jodie, she was called. She was young, only twenty-three or something crazy like that. I remember the feeling I had as I drove home from the hotel the next day. Not guilt—at least not *real* guilt, as I now know it—but more a need to acknowledge my own disgrace. To mark the passing of one era to the next.

"If you could choose, how far would you turn back the clock?" I asked Saskia. "I don't mean hours—I mean months or even years. Where would you stop?"

"I wouldn't," she said. "I don't do regret. Seriously, it's one of my life philosophies. Don't look at me like that."

"Like what?"

"Like you've suddenly realized I'm an alien."

"You're not the alien," I said. "I am."

I kissed her again, not only because that was why she was here but also to end the conversation, which was getting maudlin and in danger of giving me away. She must have sensed some new element of yearning, though, because she broke off and said, "What is this, Bram?"

"What's what?"

"This. Tonight."

Oh God. Already. "What do you want it to be?" I said.

She sighed, clearly understanding that I'd used this line many times before, that it was the only answer I was likely to give. At least she'd known what she was dealing with coming here tonight: a soon-to-be-divorced philanderer with a criminal record. The published version of myself I felt almost nostalgic for now.

Really, it was amazing I'd lasted as long as I had.

33

Police constables Elaine Bird and Adam Miah have arrived and all available seating at the Vaughans' kitchen table is taken, every one of their moving-day tea mugs now in use. Lucy has asked Fi's advice about the central heating system, because it's starting to get drafty (apparently there's even the possibility of snow tonight), and it seemed churlish not to show her how it worked.

The movers have long gone, their vans leaving in convoy. David wasn't so flustered as to forget their tip, and Fi imagines them in the pub spending it, saying to one another, "That was a weird one, wasn't it? Who was that other woman? The one they couldn't get rid of?"

The formal state of affairs is this: Bram is not missing, or, rather, an adult has a legal right to disappear himself and there is not yet any good reason to believe this particular one is not safe and well and exactly where he wants to be. After all, no one has yet checked his second residence (he's not going to be there kicking back with an episode of

Game of Thrones—Fi can tell them that for nothing), or he might be with another family member.

"There's only his mother," Fi says. "I've tried, and he's not with her."

"A friend, then, or a work colleague? And you might ring around the local hospitals."

David Vaughan says he personally volunteers to put Bram in hospital, if he is not in there already, but he's misjudged his audience and the joke is ignored.

"If you still haven't located him by Monday," PC Bird tells Fi, "and you have good reason to think he might have come to harm, get back in touch."

The same circumspection is applied to the group's house-sale crisis. Like Bram, the proceeds of the sale are not technically missing, or even in dispute, not until deposits into *his* account are inspected. No fraud has taken place, at least not until it has been logged with Action Fraud and referred for investigation to Falcon, the Met's fraud and cybercrime unit. Meanwhile, if there is any suspicion that either of the solicitors has been negligent, the aggrieved party might consider contacting the Solicitors Regulation Authority. (That's what Fi is now, the aggrieved party.)

"Conveyancing fraud *is* on the rise," PC Miah says. "You've probably seen it in the news lately, have you? We've just issued a statement urging estate agents and solicitors to be more vigilant, especially when sending bank details via e-mail, which is when fraudsters tend to intercept. Typically, it happens when a tenant is in the property and they've never met the owner, so they're less likely to question visits by agents and surveyors."

"This is different, though," David points out. "This has been done with the cooperation of one of the owners."

"We don't know that for sure," Fi objects. "Like Merle said, Bram might have been acting under duress."

"That's why we called you," Merle tells the officers. "This house fraud and Bram's disappearance are clearly linked. We're worried he might be the victim of professional criminals."

"We've been through this," David says. "We met the guy at the open house. No one had a gun to his head. All the documents and questionnaires were signed by him. It will be simple enough to get the signatures verified, won't it?" he asks PC Miah.

"If and when we decide to investigate, yes."

"He must have let our surveyor in as well," Lucy says. "He came in December—I can check the date."

"I'm sure when you hear from your solicitors, they'll be able to shed light on the situation," PC Bird tells them, and it seems to Fi it's as if she and her colleague are mediating a dispute about parking or loud music rather than responding to a report of serious crime.

"But if they don't," David insists, "you can't expect us to wait months for it to be investigated, can you? We need to know who has the right to live in this house now. Today and tomorrow and the fore-seeable future."

"Fi, obviously," Merle says.

"Then give us back the two million," David snaps. Lucy gives him a look as if to say, "Don't get nasty. When all of this is resolved she'll be our new neighbor. We'll want to invite her to our barbecues and Christmas drinks. Her kids might babysit ours."

Fi looks around the table and has the perverse urge to laugh. Not just chuckle but scream. It's surreal, absurd. The fact is, they have no facts. Bram is missing; the solicitors are unavailable. No wonder the officers are so keen to depart, kindly advising a follow-up call on Monday "when we know more."

Lucy and Merle see them out together, uneasy cohosts, and no sooner has the front door closed than David's phone rings. "Finally, Rav!" he exclaims and leaves the room.

"Rav is the estate agent," Lucy explains to Fi and Merle.

"I still don't understand how an agent managed the sale," Merle says. "I've never seen this house listed on any of the property sites. I look regularly."

"It was done through the private sales department," Lucy says. "We were registered with another agent there and Rav just phoned us out of the blue, said a new property on Trinity Avenue had come up."

I had a chance to stop this, Fi thinks. She uses the downstairs bathroom, her fingers touching the smooth lip of the basin, the shiny curves of the taps. The toilet roll is patterned with a puppy motif, Harry's choice, but the soap and hand towel are the Vaughans'. Afterward, she lingers in the hall, which is stacked with boxes and fold-up chairs, and runs her hands over the chalky walls, the polished banister rail. The lights are out in all rooms except the kitchen; if you walked by the house now, you wouldn't know it has changed hands. You wouldn't know one family has been replaced by another. She has a strange thought then: Does the house still mean to her what it used to? Hasn't she already started to think of it as disputed territory? Hasn't she known, subconsciously, that in the end the bird's nest would topple and someone, if not all of them, risked being wounded? Maybe the fall has simply come sooner than she imagined.

In the kitchen, their war room, there is a temporary armistice between Merle and Lucy, a regathering of energies as they await the news from David's phone call. Lucy has produced biscuits and is eating one with nervous speed. Fi sees her eye Merle's clothing, consider making a comment, decide against it. She takes a biscuit too, chews, tastes nothing.

In the lull, Merle's phone pings constantly with updates. (Alison has collected Robbie and Daisy from school for her and taken them home for tea. Adrian is away on a skiing holiday with old university friends.) In contrast, Fi's has not rung once since she arrived. The only incoming communications have been texts from her mother asking after the boys and one from Clara at work, who reassures her the presentation document has been found after all and there is no need to go out of her way to send it. ("Sorry to interrupt your romantic break!") Whatever the presentation was, Fi's brain has erased it, Clara's words as unintelligible as if they were from some lost tongue.

When David returns, he looks for the first time quite shaken. "This is getting out of control."

"What, it wasn't before?" Merle says, straight back to her feet, punches ready.

"What do you mean?" Lucy asks. "What's happened?"

"Rav says Mrs. Lawson has been on the phone in a panic. She says the funds haven't arrived in her account, even though we all had confirmation from both solicitors that completion took place, which was why he released the keys to us this morning."

Fi stops breathing.

"She's spoken to Graham Jenson, so at least we know he's back in contact, but he's insisting everything's gone through OK and she just needs to keep checking her account. Apparently, she hasn't been able to track down her husband—"

"Bram's not her husband," Merle corrects him. "Can we all please agree on that? Whoever this woman is, she has absolutely no claim to this house."

"I don't understand," Lucy says. "What does that mean in terms of the money?"

David turns his palms upward. "Well, it means that either there's been some technical glitch with the transfer and, like Jenson says, it will resolve itself any minute . . ."

"Or?" Merle prompts.

"Or—and this seems more likely since we had confirmation of

completion hours ago—the money's been transferred to the wrong account. And that means yet more complications."

Fi makes a choking noise.

"Fi?" Merle says. "Are you OK?"

Still she can't seem to breathe. *Mrs. Lawson*, David said. *She* called the agent. *She* can't get hold of her husband. *She* needs to check her account.

Whatever Bram's done, he's done it with another person. A woman.

At last, she exhales.

Of course a woman.

GENEVA, 4 P.M.

Though the train station for services to France is seven kilometers from the hotel, he has decided to walk. This way he can weave and dive and double back, shake off any interested party. Exhaust himself too, with any luck.

Instinct causes him to reach for his phone for navigation before he remembers he has no connectivity, having disabled every digital means of drawing the authorities to him. What he does have, however, is an old-style foldout map; he did not arrive here a free and easy tourist, content to go with the flow. He knows from his research—indeed, it is one of the reasons he chose Geneva as his starting point—that passports are not checked at railway stations here because all countries that border Switzerland are in the Schengen Agreement.

Countries like France. Cities like Lyon, where he's never been before but which he has earmarked as being sizable enough to absorb him, easy enough to shop for food and drink in bars without standing out from the crowd. It's not what you'd call leading the police a merry dance, but it's a decent attempt at misdirection: if some observant soul at Gatwick recognized his mug shot, if he were to be traced to Geneva, the trail would be suspended here while he slipped away *there*. It might buy him a few weeks.

"Hideout," "mug shot," "police trail": these are the sorts of words he used to use with his sons in their elaborate setups in the garden—cops and robbers, spies and double agents—but there's no fun to be had now.

He's fairly certain he's thrown off his pursuer—if there ever was one.

Soon, the chill from Lake Geneva meets his newly cropped head, and the fact that he is even registering the pain of a late afternoon in subzero winter feels perversely like progress.

34

Did no one else suspect Bram of anything criminal back then, even if I did not? That's right, my mother helped us with childcare and was probably in and out of Trinity Avenue more than anyone else.

But certainly not her, no. I would go so far as to say that not only was she oblivious to any illegalities but she also privately wished for a reunion between us. Not that she had any desire to see her daughter humiliated, of course. It was just that she wasn't in possession of all the facts and she regarded his second infidelity as I had regarded the first: not excusable, but maybe, just possibly, pardonable.

"It seems to me he's going out of his way to make things nice for you," she said. "The lilies he left for you were beautiful."

This was undeniable. After the Kent weekend, he'd left a huge and stunning bouquet for me, even using my favorite vase. The last time he'd bought me flowers . . . Well, I couldn't remember—before the be-trayal, certainly. He'd been too exposed afterward to being accused of empty symbolism.

(You're probably thinking, "God, the poor man can't win," but I think we already know that he found a way.)

"You're obviously on his mind," Mum added. "He still loves you" was the subtext.

I don't say any of this in order to criticize her. No one could be more grateful to a parent than I am to her. It's more to try to show you that we were all susceptible to Bram's charms one way or another. (Alison always said this included Polly, whom she suspected disliked him because she feared an attraction.)

Don't get me wrong. I'm not saying he was psychopathically charismatic or anything like that. He didn't set out to use his powers for evil.

More likely, his powers were no match for the evil he chanced upon.

I'm bracing myself now, because I know that more than any other scene I've described, this next one will make you question my intelligence. I mean, *come on*, you'll think, how could you *possibly* not have suspected?

It was a few days after we'd come back from Kent, the first week of November, when in the evening, just before Harry's bath time, the doorbell rang.

A fortysomething couple stood on the doorstep, well-mannered and hopeful. "Sorry to interrupt your evening—this is a bit cheeky, but . . ." the woman began, and I thought at once it might be a scam, some apparently respectable pair with a broken-down car needing twenty pounds for a taxi. "We missed the open house and happened to be passing and wondered if we could have a quick look around now? We've been looking in this area for *months*."

"Open house?" I said.

"Yes." They exchanged looks. "This is the one for sale, isn't it? On the market with Challoner's?"

Ah, not a scam, an honest mistake. People like us, after all. "No, you must mean number 97," I told them. "I don't know which estate agent they're using."

As the couple retreated, apologetic, I felt sheepish for having jumped to conclusions. Until the recent spate of crimes on the street, I'd prided myself on giving strangers the benefit of the doubt.

Minutes later, Harry was in the bath and Leo was doing his reading homework while balancing on the banister and there was the usual chaos and clamor, so when the bell went again I didn't bother going back down.

Later, when I remembered the episode to Merle, she told me, "Don't be silly. There are a thousand possible outcomes to every one of our actions. Say you left Harry in the bath and got involved in a conversation on the doorstep. What if he'd hit his head and slipped under the water? Leo might not have noticed; he might have followed you downstairs or wandered back into his bedroom. That would have been far, far worse."

"You're right," I said.

And, to be fair, I did look at Challoner's website a day or two later and there was no listing for Trinity Avenue. On Rightmove, the Reeces' place was still there, now with an UNDER OFFER banner across the photo.

The only other listing for Trinity Avenue was one of the flats in the block on the corner with Wyndham Gardens. I remember wondering if it was the same one that had been ransacked a few weeks earlier and what would become of the tenants if they were to be given notice. A burglary and then an eviction in the space of a few months.

I reminded myself that I was one of the lucky ones.

#VictimFi

@LuluReading I'm sorry, but this #VictimFi *is* a bit of a
f*ckwit. The friend also mentioned estate agent on wknd away.
@val_shilling @LuluReading That's so unfair, the neighbor was
selling! #easymistaketomake
@IsabelRickey101 @val_shilling @LuluReading I agree. She's
really brave to admit all this now.

BRAM, Word document

I could delay no longer in breaking the news to Fi about the car.

"Our insurance claim has been turned down," I told her, at our
next Friday handover.

"What?" She flushed with shock. "Why?"

"They weren't a hundred percent clear about it—you know what
they're like—but it seems to be to do with the keys. Because we
couldn't say exactly where they were, there's a case that we were negligent."

"That's unbelievable! We thought we were going to get, what?
Twenty thousand? Even ten would have been *something*. What now?
We're just supposed to magic up the funds ourselves after years of pay-
ing premiums?"

"Or do without." I couldn't have felt more wretched. She'd been
right when she'd suggested there was a required period before the ad-
juster released payment—twenty-eight days in our case. The policy
was in my name and the check issued to me.

"Those bloody keys. If we'd known, we could have got our stories
straight about them," she railed. "I bet they talked to that detective
who questioned me. I made it sound like we had no clue who had
them and when, like we just handed them over to the first passing

criminal." In her eyes, distress hardened into determination. "Let's take it to the ombudsman, shall we?"

"To be honest, Fi, I don't think there's much they could do."

"You don't want to at least give it a try?"

"I don't, no. It's all in the small print—we haven't got a leg to stand on. And don't forget there's always a chance the car will still turn up, in which case we can get it fixed at our own expense. Better than nothing."

Fi nodded, still very agitated. "When do we have to return the courtesy car?"

"Tomorrow. I'm sorry. I'll come over and take care of it."

"So soon? This is crap timing with Christmas coming up—money's getting so tight. And it's all going to be so much more of a pain in the dark and cold, schlepping around on packed buses with the boys."

"They won't mind," I said. "Kids just accept whatever their parents say is normal. The main thing is they have two parents who love them and are there for them. It's not about money or presents or new cars." While this didn't sound at all like me, it benefited from being exactly the sort of thing Fi might say herself.

"That's true," she said, reaching for a sense of humility. "We have our home. We have our health."

I tried to agree, but struggled to yield any intelligible sound.

She gave me a concerned look. "How long have you been sitting on this, Bram? Have you been worrying about telling me?"

"A bit."

"Is that why you bought the flowers? There's absolutely no need to shield me from this sort of thing. Where the kids and the house are concerned, we're still a team, remember?"

The fierce loyalty in her expression was almost too much to contend with; I had a ghastly kaleidoscopic flash of Mike, of Wendy, of Rav, of the couples who had viewed her beloved house.

"I'm sorry," I said again. "I'm really sorry."

No offers yet, I take it?

No. Three second viewings booked for Saturday.

Why not sooner?

Not my days at the house, so too risky. I have no control over Fi's schedule.

Just make sure the place is looking its best, eh?

No, I thought I'd get all the neighborhood dogs in to piss on the walls.

You're a funny man, Bram. Bet you make Leo and Harry laugh, do you?

I turned off the phone. It was my policy now, whenever he mentioned the boys.

35

BRAM, Word document

I was starting to loathe my time at the flat, to associate it with booze-drenched, dread-filled solitude and with ugly, inescapable meetings—not all of them with Mike and Wendy. There was also one, a few days after the open house, that I would have preferred to shirk.

When the buzzer went at about eight p.m., my natural thought was that it was the police.

This is it, Bram. You knew it was coming.

There was a shocking moment of regression to childhood, a flood of that half-resentful, half-grateful feeling you get when a parent collars you for some dishonesty. *At least I don't have to lie anymore,* you think. *At least I don't have to hide.*

Before I went to answer, I turned down the volume of the music, too sorry to interrupt my task to turn it off completely. I know it will sound crazy, but I'd been compiling the playlists I would take when I had to disappear. Yes, I know I should have been devoting my time to strategizing some twist-in-the-tale defeat of Mike and Wendy, but I'd found that small, mechanical jobs, especially those that allowed me to sink into memory, were the only way my sanity could be salvaged from one day to the next.

"Hello," I said into the intercom. "Can I help you?"

"Bram?" The voice was female, low and indignant.

An arresting officer wouldn't call me Bram, I reasoned. It must be Wendy, she and Mike come to harass me about the second viewings of the house on Saturday. Slightly, *marginally*, better than the police.

"Bram? What's the matter? Buzz me in!"

Not Wendy, I realized. Saskia? The absence of any follow-up text or visit to my desk since our weekend liaison had encouraged me to assume she'd done the sensible thing and quit while she was ahead.

Then I registered who this actually was. "Ah. Come up."

I waited at the door, exhausted and confused. "Constance" from the playhouse. Her arrival reminded me that I'd not responded to a voice mail from her some time earlier—when? Last week, perhaps. I admit I considered her a small fry in the context of the circling sharklife—our original encounter, so catastrophic at the time, now almost quaintly sinful in the light of intervening events.

"Sorry about the delay," I said from the doorway, when she appeared from the lift. "I thought you were someone else."

"How many of us are there? Don't answer that—I'm not interested." There was no kiss or touch, of course; I wouldn't have expected that, but nor did I expect the current of hostility flowing from her. My brain was too bruised to register a reaction either way. If my night with Saskia had proved anything, it was that consolation and indifference were the same to me now.

"We need to talk." Reading reluctance in my frown, she snapped, "If you can spare me the time?"

"Of course I can." I paused the music, then immediately wished I hadn't. Silence, unbearable to me at the best of times these days, felt dangerously exposing. It was going to be a strain to focus on this.

"What was that song you were just playing?" she asked.

"Portishead. You remember, 'Sour Times'?"

"How appropriate." Her hair was pulled tightly back, her skin glowing in a faintly sickly way, as if she was being overtaken by fever right in front of me. "Is it all right if I sit down?"

"Sorry. Over here." I cleared one of the chairs of its jumble of dry cleaning. "Can I get you a drink?"

"Water, please."

I got myself a beer, delivered her glass of water, and waited. I noticed she was wearing the same dress she'd worn that evening in the playhouse, this time with opaque black tights and high-heeled ankle boots. I didn't know her well enough to know if that was a deliberate allusion; all I knew was that if I never had any dealings with women again it would be a good thing. For me *and* them.

"All right," she said, "I'll get straight to the point. I'm pregnant, Bram."

I stared, appalled.

"It's not yours." She raised her chin, gave a mirthless chuckle. "That's not what this is about—don't worry."

"Oh. OK." My skull ached terribly; I tried to think if there was any ibuprofen in the flat. "What *is* this about, then?"

She took a sip of her water, her hand trembling. "It's about the fact that I'll start to show soon and I don't need you putting two and two together and making five. *Or* anyone else."

Her husband, she meant.

"He still doesn't know about us?" I said.

"No. It was a mistake, a one-off act of insanity. There's nothing to be gained from telling him now." She eyed the four walls, her expression dismal. "I don't need to tell *you* that."

There was a damning edge to this last comment, reminiscent of nobody so much as Fi, and I felt annoyance rise. I wanted to hiss at her, "Is this *really* your biggest problem? Try being blackmailed. Try facing a death-by-dangerous-driving charge. Try losing your partner and children and everything you love. . . ."

But maybe she thought she would—if I were to get it into my head to challenge the new baby's paternity. To her, I was a threat. I was her Mike.

"So I can count on you to keep quiet?" she demanded.

"I've kept quiet this long. There's no reason for that to change."

"And to deal with any questions?"

I caught something then and looked more searchingly at her. If not from her husband, she could only mean from Fi. Was she saying . . . ? There was a silence, a suspended moment that emitted its own energy, caused her eyes to meet mine with new pleading.

"When is it due?" I asked, quietly.

"May. Don't insult me by counting the months."

Of course I *did* count, in silent torment. It was only one month out. But I couldn't allow myself to think about another man raising my child, unaware of the true paternity or of the existence of two half brothers. I couldn't allow it to be true. And, terrible as it sounds, it paled into insignificance now. A child had died at my hand and there wasn't space in my head to think about an unborn one.

"Well, congratulations, then," I said at last, and watched as tension left her chest. I resisted the urge to touch her hot face, to take her restless hands in mine. "That's great news."

"Thank you." She stood, cast another glance around the bland, claustrophobic space. "You need to sort yourself out, Bram. You're obviously in a bad way."

"Am I? Wow, I had no idea."

Like Fi, she reacted spikily to sarcasm, lecturing me even as she made for the door. "Seriously, you don't want to be one of those sad aging leopards who can never change their spots, do you? People run out of forgiveness, you know, and then you're just another unforgivable man."

These last words sounded scripted, but that wasn't to say they didn't ring true. That wasn't to say they didn't burn. I closed my eyes, no longer able to cope with her, and when I opened them she was gone, the door closing behind her.

"Thanks for the advice," I said.

"FI'S STORY" > 02:05:03

What with everything going on at Trinity Avenue—not just the Ropers' burglary and our car theft, the yellow police signs everywhere, but also the interactions with Bram that were about to come to a head—the flat was becoming a bit of a sanctuary.

There was time to breathe there, to relax. I'd got into the habit of lighting a scented candle the moment I walked through the door, putting on Classic FM or the sort of arts documentary I couldn't hope to follow with the kids running in and out yelling about Pokémon and Chelsea FC and whatever the latest grievance was between the two of them. Unless I had a guest, I aimed for no alcohol, brewing an herbal tea and treating myself to a bar of chocolate with some witty artisanal twist, like cardamom or sea salt or lavender. Maybe "sanctuary" isn't the right word. Maybe it was more of a retreat.

Once or twice, I even caught myself thinking I should bring the boys here for a sleepover, but of course I was only *here* so that they could be *there*.

36

BRAM, Word document

And then, at last, the police came. Not to the flat, but to my office in Croydon. A detective arrived the next Tuesday morning—thank God he was plainclothes and not in uniform. I handled it OK. I must have done, because it was a while before it was followed up.

I commandeered a small, windowless meeting room just off reception for our chat. On the table was an array of our new semirigid neck collars with adjustable Velcro strapping and I pushed them to the side without commenting. *No wisecracks. Don't antagonize him.*

"So, Mr. Lawson, you are the joint owner with Mrs. Fiona Lawson of a black Audi A3?" he asked, quoting the registration. He was in his forties, pale haired and thick necked, his experience of human fallibility unsettlingly underplayed as he searched my face for liars' tics.

Don't think like that—just answer his questions!

"Yes—at least I was. It was stolen back in early October. Is this about the insurance claim?"

Make him think that's your only concern.

"No, nothing to do with that," he said.

"Oh, hang on. Are you the officer who spoke to Fi a few weeks ago?"

"That's right."

"She said something about the keys having been stolen? I have to say, I think they're far more likely to be down the side of the sofa."

"If you do find them there, let me know." His manner was affable, as if he were here to pass the time in small talk.

"Of course. The thing is, the insurance claim is all settled now," I said. "I wasn't sure if they'd been in touch with you." *Not a question; it doesn't bother you either way, since they've already paid out the check.*

Though he did not reply to this, I felt fairly secure that this interview was not going to end in arrest.

"Do you remember where you were on Friday, the sixteenth of September, Mr. Lawson?"

My pulse quickened. "Yes, that was the day of my work sales conference." Silly to pretend I didn't remember when I'd already suggested I'd discussed details of Fi's interview with her.

"It took place here?"

"No, it's always off-site. This year it was at a hotel down near Gatwick."

"What time did it finish?"

"It would have been about five, maybe a bit earlier."

"That was when you left?"

Don't second-guess him—just answer each question as it comes.

"Yes. Some people stayed on for drinks, but I had to get home."

"You drove yourself in the Audi, did you?"

"Actually, no." I looked sheepish, hesitated as if embarrassed to admit the truth. "I didn't drive at all around that time."

"Why was that?"

I sighed. "If you're investigating our car, then you probably already know, don't you?"

"Know what, Mr. Lawson?"

"I've got a driving ban. It happened back in February. I was caught speeding a few times. So my wife has been the only driver since then."

He did not react, which encouraged me to continue.

"She didn't mention it when you spoke to her, did she? That's because she didn't know. She still doesn't, I hope." I paused, as if taking a moment to grapple with my own shame. "We've split up, you see, and I've found it's not always helpful to tell her everything I've done wrong. And if you're speaking to her again, I'd be grateful if you didn't let on."

It was too much to expect a law enforcement officer to collude with me in marital subterfuge, but I thought I detected the faintest flicker of sympathy.

"I don't expect to have to speak to her again," he said, and I felt like punching the air. This could only be routine, then, part of the police's painstaking process of elimination. *Get through this and you'll be off the list!*

"So, how *did* you travel home that Friday, Mr. Lawson?"

"I got the train. The station was right near the venue." *True.*

"Which station?"

"I can't remember the name—one or two before the airport. But the hotel was called Blackthorn something. I can look it up if you like."

He didn't ask me to do so, which I took to mean he did not intend to waste manpower on this particular line of inquiry.

"So, you left before five and were home by, what, six o'clock?"

"No, I had to change trains at Clapham Junction, so I stopped for a couple of pints. I was desperate for a drink, to be honest—it had been an exhausting day. I was due at the house at seven, so I got the connecting train at about six forty. It's only a couple of stops from Alder Rise."

"Which pub did you drink in?"

This seemed less good. If he accepted that I'd taken the train, then why probe the drinking? Perhaps because it was extraneous detail *I* had introduced. Why would I feel the need to say I'd been desperate for a drink? *Stop asking why—just answer the bloody questions!* "The one right next to the station. Is it the Half Moon, maybe?"

"See anyone you knew there? Talk to anyone?"

I narrowed my eyes as if straining to remember. "I was on my own, like I say, and it's not really a regular haunt. I flicked through the *Standard*, probably. Oh, that's right, I chatted to a guy at the bar for a bit. He seemed to be well-known there." *Don't give any more detail—too obvious!* "Then I had to get home. I take over with the kids at seven o'clock."

You've already said that. Calm down.

"When you got home, do you remember seeing your car parked in the street?"

"I don't. I mean, that doesn't mean I *didn't* see it. It's just, I've walked home from the station a thousand times—I can't remember every distinct occasion. I do remember I'd cut it a bit fine, so I probably wasn't noticing much, just rushing to get there. Sorry, I know that's not very useful."

He nodded. "OK, well, perhaps we'll have something more useful for *you* when your car is found."

Useful for me? Or for *him*? I could hear my pay-as-you-go start up in my pocket, felt the Pavlovian opening of my pores as I began to sweat. My thoughts turned wild: *I can't let them find the car! Maybe I should go back to it, move it out of London. Where's the second key? Has Fi still got it?*

Then: *No, no, if you do that, you might get stopped. Remember the police use automatic number plate recognition—you see those ANPR signs all over the place. Maybe—*

"Your phone's ringing," the detective said, rising. "I'll let you take it."

I recovered myself. "No, it's fine. I'll see you out."

And that was it. Bar my needless reference to the pub and that last-minute attack of nerves, it had gone as well as I could have hoped.

I waited a safe half hour before checking the phone and finding news from Rav: there were two offers on the house.

"FI'S STORY" > 02:07:21

You asked when it was that I got properly worried about Bram. Well, it was in early November at about the time of an upsetting incident with Toby, which I'll tell you about now. I remember thinking I had absolutely no idea what Bram was going to do next, that I'd lost the natural instinct I'd always had for his actions, his *reactions*. For *him*.

Toby had been consumed by work and had seen his kids the previous weekend, so when he told me he was free only in the early part of the week I made the decision to relax—OK, break—the bird's nest rule about third parties at Trinity Avenue and invited him there for dinner on the Tuesday. I asked him to arrive at eight thirty p.m. so the boys would already be asleep. I wasn't ready yet for introductions.

"Nice place," he said, following me into the kitchen, and, as I took his coat and handed him a glass of wine, I was more than usually charged by his presence, as if I were the forbidden guest and not him.

"Thank you. It's a shame you can't see the garden properly."

He moved to the kitchen window, wineglass in hand, and peered out. At the bottom of the garden, fairy lights traced the roofline and doorframe of the playhouse like lines iced on a gingerbread house.

"Is that the famous playhouse?" he said. "Looks innocent enough."

"It does." It surprised me sometimes how much I'd told him about my breakup with Bram. The traumas of marriage, like those of childhood, are permanent points of reference, I suppose. They hoard themselves within you, fuse into your body tissue.

"Want to get even?" he said.

"What do you mean?"

"You, me, the bottom of the garden . . . ?"

"Seriously?" I was genuinely nauseated by this idea, not because of the discomforts involved in alfresco intimacies in November, but because of the thought of Leo and Harry upstairs, trusting in the protection of their mother while she sneaked out to their den like some primitive woman in heat. . . . What Bram had done that night in July was and remained unconscionable, whatever impulse I'd had to the contrary that night in Kent, whatever my mother hoped I might come to excuse.

"It's a bit damp out there. I think I'd rather stay in the warmth and have another one of these," I said, raising my glass, and Toby accepted my demurral with an easy laugh. Interesting, though, to know that he had this daring in his personality, when I'd taken him to be a conventional, risk-averse sort of person like me.

Anyway, it wasn't long after, just as I was serving dinner, that the doorbell rang.

BRAM, Word document

Though I'd invited Saskia to the house, I'd reasoned that it had been in the boys' absence and so not strictly breaking the bird's nest rules. What *was* breaking them, however, was my decision to visit Trinity Avenue on one of *her* nights.

The impulse had been gathering since the police interview that morning and my state of distraction had become noticeable enough for Neil to send me home from work early. "Sort it out," he said, not without feeling.

And then there was that message from Rav. In spite of Mike's frequent texts pressing me for updates, I'd decided not to tell him about the offers on the house, not yet. Instead, agitation grew into a mania to jump off the ride—or at least to dangle myself over the edge—my thinking being that if I could keep his repulsive face from my mind, his serpent murmurs from my ear, and focus instead on Fi, I might be able to do it. I might be able to confess, do the right thing before the wrong one possessed me entirely.

"FI'S STORY" > 02:09:56

The bell was already ringing a second time as I reached the door. I expected to be greeted with an after-hours sales pitch or a local councillor on the campaign trail. "It's a bit late," I'd say, mildly reproachful but also sympathetic because everyone had to make a living (my main objection was the doorbell waking the children).

What I found, however, was the one man who had a key of his own. "Bram!"

"Sorry, I know I'm not supposed to come on a Tuesday. I—"

"That's right," I cut in, "you're not. It's too late to see the boys, anyway. They're already asleep. It's almost nine thirty."

"I know, but I needed to see you."

He was charged with an energy I couldn't diagnose, though my guess was that he'd been drinking. "Is something wrong?" I said, not masking my impatience.

"I just need to talk to you, Fi. Can I come in?"

I felt exasperation run through me in a way I recognized from when we were together. (Perhaps there was also an undercurrent of relief that he had not let himself in and caught me in the playhouse in a grisly reenactment of his own sin.) "It's not the best time, actually. We're just eating—I've got a friend here."

"Oh. Any way you can get rid of her? This is important."

Before I could register relief at his gender assumption—I didn't want to have to admit to breaking a condition of our bird's nest agreement—the matter was taken out of my hands, for Toby had followed me to the door, clearly ready to offer his protection.

"Everything all right here, Fi?"

Midbreath, before making the introductions I would have preferred to defer, if not avoid entirely, I could only watch, stunned, as Bram barreled past me, knocking me off balance, and launched himself full throttle at Toby. The two of them crashed violently into the stair paneling, the back of Toby's head smacking against the spindles.

"Get the fuck out of my house!" Bram yelled, making an unsuccessful attempt to grapple Toby toward the front door. Tall though he was, he was a terrier to Toby's mastiff.

"Come on, mate," Toby groaned. "Get off me and let's talk about this."

"Bram!" I rushed forward and clawed angrily at his jacket. "What are you *doing*?"

His eyes frightened me: protruding, unblinking, fixed with savage intensity on poor Toby. "Keep away from her or I'll fucking kill you!"

I couldn't believe what I was hearing. "Stop this, Bram! *Stop it now!*"

Inevitably, the boys, woken by the commotion, were soon at the top of the stairs. "Daddy!" Harry shouted.

"Daddy's just leaving," I called up. "*Aren't* you, Bram?" Again, I tried to haul him off Toby, succeeding only in getting a fingernail bent back, which caused me to cry out in pain.

"Mummy? Are you all right?" Leo was on his way down the stairs and I abandoned the men to cut him off halfway.

"You go back to bed, sweetheart. I'll come up in a second."

"Is there a burglar?" Harry asked his brother, and as Leo spoke to him I could hear the alarm in his voice.

"Nothing like that," I called, but my voice was shrill, frantic, exposing my own panic.

At last Bram released Toby, who retreated to the kitchen, rubbing his head and swearing.

"Wait out front," I instructed Bram and hurried upstairs to settle the boys.

Lights blazed in Leo's room, where they'd taken refuge, their faces pale with fright. "Who was Daddy fighting? Are the police coming?" they asked.

I hugged them close. "No, it was just a disagreement with a friend. Try to forget about it and get some sleep."

"Remember to lock the door, Mum," Leo said as I left, and I could have sobbed at his innocent trust in a locked door, in *me*.

Sorry, I'm getting upset. I can't stress enough how this was everything I'd been striving to avoid: a scene between estranged man and wife, the children disrupted and scared, uncertain who was in the house and where the crucial loyalties lay.

Deep breath. Anyway, when I joined Bram in the front garden, I was hot with anger. He was pacing the paving stones, cigarette smoke rising through the stripped branches of the magnolia. Nine thirty on a Tuesday in November was practically the dead of night on Trinity Avenue and in every visible window the curtains were drawn; it felt as if the whole neighborhood's allotment of drama and rancor had gathered in *my* house. "What the hell do you think you're doing?" I spoke through clenched teeth. "Are you drunk?"

He glared at me, clearly as enraged as I was. "Of course I'm not. We agreed no dates, not here."

"How do you know that's what he is? That he's not just a friend?"

"Is he?"

I paused. "I am seeing him, yes, but that doesn't mean that what you just did wasn't completely out of order."

He sucked the cigarette, its tip firing. "The boys are here."

"They were *asleep*. At least they were until you barged in. You assaulted him, Bram. You're lucky he didn't fight back properly!" I smoothed my hair from my face and throat. The chill air was astringent on my skin. I sighed heavily. "But you're right. We agreed on conditions and I've broken one of them. I'm sorry. This was just meant to be a one-off visit because we couldn't make it work any other time. It's dinner—that's all. He's not staying the night."

"He will *never* stay the night in this house," Bram said with a ferocity I hadn't seen in all our years together. "I will burn it to the ground before that happens."

"Bram, stop this. You're scaring me." We stood face-to-face, both breathing hard. His eyes were a wild animal's. I tried again. "If we're going to continue with our arrangement, then I need to know you can be a reasonable, civilized participant in this family." But I should have known this remark would rouse the precise opposite.

"I'm not a 'participant.' I'm their fucking father!"

"Don't shout," I hissed. "The neighbors will hear you."

He tossed the cigarette end into the border. "I don't give a shit who hears me. I don't want that man anywhere near my kids."

"*Our* kids. And I haven't even introduced them yet! If you hadn't caused this scene they wouldn't have known he was here. This is not Toby's fault." I regretted giving his name, because Bram seized on it at once.

"Toby, is that what he's called? What's his surname?"

I didn't answer. Agitated though I was, I had the presence of mind to consider that Bram might take it upon himself to pursue Toby at a

future time and threaten him. I imagined Toby phoning me and saying, "I'm sorry, it's not working out. I like you, but I'm just not up for
this sort of harassment."

It was just as Polly had warned: Bram hadn't wanted me himself
enough to be faithful to me and yet he couldn't bear the thought of
someone else taking his place. Such dog-in-the-manger instincts were,
I knew, typical of marriage breakdown. My mistake had been in believing we weren't typical.

"You're seeing other people as well, I assume?" I hugged myself as
I began to shiver. The cold was numbing the pain in my finger, at
least.

"No one special," he muttered, and I saw, to my horror, that he was
close to tears.

Was I flattered to see him reduced to this because of his feelings
for me? Maybe. But the incident is more important, I think, because
it shows how volatile he was becoming, how unpredictable. And, I'm
sorry to say, how quick to turn aggressive.

"Look, you have my word that I'll only see him at the flat from
now on."

"The flat," he echoed.

"Yes, which is where you're going now, right?" To my relief he began backing away toward the gate, nodding to himself. "Don't do anything stupid," I cautioned, which made him stop midstep and stare
at me.

"I already have," he said, and of course I assumed he meant the
attack on Toby. He looked so utterly heartbroken that I moved toward
him, my fury easing a little.

"Then don't do anything *else* stupid. I'll talk to the boys in the
morning and we'll see you after work as usual, OK?"

No, I didn't find out what he'd come to talk about. If anything had been made clear by this dysfunctional scene, it was that I was no longer the right person to hear it.

In the kitchen, Toby was standing drinking, our tuna steaks cold on their plates. I could see on his left cheekbone a red mark that would deepen to bruising.

"Are you all right?" He was composed, civilized, a different species from the wild man I'd just seen off.

"Are *you*? You hit your head quite badly. And look at your face. Do you need ice? I'm so, so sorry, Toby. I can't believe that just happened."

He pulled me toward him. "You don't have to apologize, Fi."

His body was flaming, not yet readjusted after the raised temperature of the fight.

"I do, though. I feel so ashamed."

He took a step back and regarded me with unusual scrutiny. "Are you sure . . . Are you sure you're over this guy? He obviously doesn't *want* you to be, does he? It's a complicated setup, I know. You're still living together but you're not living together; you're married but you're not married. . . ."

For the first time, I felt unequal to this, overwhelmed by the experiences I'd accrued these past six months, as if they were stacked, interlocking, on top of me, their weight deadly. Was Bram going to make life impossible for me, after all? Had I made a terrible mistake "still living together but not living together"?

I felt a deep, guttural lurch remembering the sensation I'd had when waking with a man who wasn't my husband in a bed that should have felt new, separate from my marriage, but that in reality I shared with Bram.

"I'm sure," I said. "He's sure too—he just doesn't realize it. But when he meets someone himself, he won't care who I'm with."

"I thought you said he'd already started shagging around."

I flinched at the term. "I mean someone he's *really* interested in, someone he considers special."

"I would question whether he's capable of recognizing that," Toby said with a certain significance to his tone, and I wondered what was coming next. I broke the silence myself.

"Well, he should be capable of recognizing how special his children are. I'll talk to him tomorrow and make it clear this can never happen again."

"If you want my advice, I wouldn't make a big deal of it," Toby said. "It was mainly bluster—I'm not injured. He'll come to his own conclusion that he was out of order."

"That's very understanding of you." I doubted he would feel so charitable when he'd had the time and solitude to reflect.

"Everyone comes with baggage," he said, shrugging.

"I was just thinking the same thing," I said. "The problem is that some of us have exceeded the weight limit."

He smiled, rubbing absently at his sore cheek. "All the more interesting to unpack."

"What, even when you realize there are false bottoms and hidden compartments?"

He laughed. "Especially then."

"Good, because we can't stretch this metaphor any further."

It was very sweet of him to act as if the evening had not been catastrophically wrecked. Two boys in the rooms above our heads believing him to be an intruder, a jealous ex baying at the door: there were plenty of men out there who would have just walked away.

#VictimFi

@Tilly-McGovern Stick with Toby, girl!
@IsabelRickey101 Bram is like one of those abusers who kills his whole family and then gets called a tortured hero.
@mackenziejane @IsabelRickey101 I know. "I'll burn the house to the ground." He gives me the creeps.

BRAM, Word document

In the morning, my head a Catherine wheel of pain, I stumbled into the bathroom and splashed cold water over my face. After leaving Trinity Avenue, I'd gone straight to the Two Brewers, where I drank until every image of the evening had been obliterated. I'd missed Roger and the other guys, but that suited me. I was in no mood for banter with men whose lives were everything mine used to be, everything I'd thrown away.

Catching sight of myself in the mirror, I recoiled from the creature gaping back at me. I'd aged badly since the last time I'd looked: my skin was puffy and threaded with the crimson veins of a drunk; my eyelids were hooded and blinking madly; general neglect was resulting in the beginnings of a beard and too-long hair. I looked like the old man who lived rough in the park before the so-called Friends of Alder Rise had had him removed.

(He was probably dead now.)

For the record, I'm not proud of attacking him. Quite apart from anything else, it was yet another witnessed incident of violence that could come back to haunt me. But what can I say? Either you've experienced the onrush of pure anger or you haven't, the brief feeling of concussion chased by a superhuman energy that can't be summoned by any other emotion, not even lust. They call it red mist but it's not red—it's white. It obscures your reason; it blinds you to consequences; it holds you in its atmosphere—and then it flings you back to the ground.

Which is when you discover that everyone who might have supported you has scattered in terror.

I checked myself for wounds beyond the minor bruises of our scuffle in the hallway and, finding none, deduced that there'd been no drunken blackout of my having gone back to the house and killed him.

Because I wanted to kill him: I state that explicitly. I despised him from the pit of my black heart.

Turning from my own ghastly reflection, I vowed to make an appointment with the GP, get some medication. Antianxiety, antipsychotic, antibreakdown.

On the kitchen counter, next to a coffee mug I'd used as an ashtray last night, my pay-as-you-go pinged. He knew to use this number now, the one element I'd been able to dictate, for what it was worth. I opened the message with a new sense of surrender:

Just passing, were you? One word to her about us and she will suffer. Do you understand me?

I understood. I had no idea if I'd have had the guts to go through with my confession to Fi last night, but he was very, very lucky he'd been there when I rolled up. The bastard had wormed his way into her affections, and withholding the fact that he'd met me before was a deliberate act of torture. He had my balls in his grip. He planned not only to steal my property, but to help himself to my wife.

He had hijacked my life.

Mike. *Toby.* Cunt.

37

"This is totally screwed up," David Vaughan says in exasperation. He is starting to fray now: any human would, exposed to this sort of strain for long enough. It is Russian roulette in the suburbs, with solicitors holding the gun. "This other woman says she's Fiona Lawson and hasn't received proceeds of the sale that are rightfully hers. *You* say you're Fiona Lawson and never sold the house in the first place."

"I don't 'say' I'm Fiona Lawson; I *am* Fiona Lawson. Look—here's my driving license. Is that enough to convince you?" This man might be claiming her house, but he will not take her identity. Both the Vaughans examine the license, but there is little discernible alteration to their manner toward her.

"Any chance of getting a phone number for this fake Mrs. Lawson from the estate agent?" Merle says.

"I asked, but Rav says he's only ever had *Mr.* Lawson's, which I'm assuming is the same number you have for him."

"Bram's phone has been out of service all afternoon," Fi says.

But when they check the number, they find it is *not* Bram's official one, the one paid for by his employer and used by Fi to contact him from day to day. Blood pulses through her head at the discovery, but when she tries phoning the unfamiliar number, the line rings on and on.

"You didn't think he'd actually answer?" David says. "She must have been trying it all day."

She. Who is this rival, this usurper with whom Bram would share the Lawson fortune? Is it a case of bigamy? He's married a second wife and together they've conspired to steal the house belonging to the first? (He has children with her too, perhaps, half-siblings for Leo and Harry.) Or is it the other extreme and she is merely an actress he hired for the transaction? The "Mrs. Lawson" who phoned the solicitor could be anyone; the Vaughans didn't meet her, the legal process not requiring buyer and seller to be in the same room at the same time. Perhaps he simply photocopied Fi's passport and submitted it online. The police officers openly acknowledged how faceless the conveyancing process has become, how fraudsters are slithering through loopholes unchallenged.

And if not to fund a new relationship—new *love*—then why? Why does Bram need such a sum of money? What could be worth sacrificing both his children's security and his own relationship with them? A huge debt from a gambling addiction? Drugs?

She massages her temples, failing to dim the ache. How much easier it was to imagine him as the victim, just like her. Swindled or threatened or brainwashed.

"So we just sit it out, do we?" Merle says. "Still not knowing who is entitled to stay and who has to leave?"

"According to Rav," David says, "there's a simple way to settle who legally owns the house and therefore has occupation rights: the Land Registry. There are no physical deeds anymore, but if the house has been registered to us, then we are the owners. If it hasn't been trans-

ferred for whatever reason, then the Lawsons' names will still be registered and they remain the owners. Emma will be able to tell us."

The Vaughans' solicitor, Emma Gilchrist, is finally out of her external meeting and a colleague is alerting her right now to the crisis in
Alder Rise.

"Don't worry," David reassures Lucy. "There's no way Emma would
have paid out two million pounds without the sale being registered."

"Really?" Merle says. "It wouldn't be the only disastrous error in
this situation, would it? Look, I'm sick of waiting for solicitors. Can't
we check the Land Registry website?"

"It takes a few days to appear online, apparently," David says. "We
do need Emma or this Graham Jenson character to confirm the exact
position. And this might be Emma now. . . ."

As his phone rings, he draws it from his pocket like a firearm. To
a person, the others stiffen in their seats, electrified. "Emma, at last!"
David cries. "We've got a very worrying situation here and we need
you to resolve it as quickly as possible. . . ." Catching Fi's eye, he looks
unexpectedly embarrassed and opens the kitchen door to take the rest
of the phone call in the garden. Icy air flows into the room like a threat
as he treads off down the path toward the playhouse.

This is it, Fi thinks. *My future, Leo's and Harry's too: it all comes
down to this.*

GENEVA, 5:15 P.M.

He is aching when he reaches Gare Cornavin, his hips and knees, even
his shoulders, as inflamed as his feet. His mind, however, is numb: the
city's streets have gifted him the balm of anonymity and, as he draws
to a halt to survey the bustle of the station concourse, it is almost as if
he has forgotten why he is here.

A group of young female travelers passes him, faces turned to one particular figure at their center, and as he watches he is speared with the knowledge that Fi will cope just fine. She will have *her* women around her.

The knowledge is clean, painless, absolute.

He always used to find the way the women of Trinity Avenue talked to one another exhausting. Even when you couldn't hear what they were saying, you could tell from their body language, their facial expressions, that it was all so intense. They acted like they were discussing genocide or the economic apocalypse and it turned out it was just about little Emily having been moved down a maths set or Felix not making the football A team. The plot of a TV drama or some outrage on *The Victim*.

Then, when really terrible things happened, like a sudden death in the family or a destroyed career, and you expected mass hysteria, they were a SWAT team, immaculately organized, focused on resolution.

"They're the worms that turned," Rog said once at the bar in the Two Brewers. "Remember the old comedy sketch called that? 'The Two Ronnies' with Diana Dors, about women taking over the world? It was supposed to be a dystopia."

"Sounds a bit un-PC," Bram said.

"Oh, completely. Wouldn't be allowed now," Rog agreed with pretended regret.

Funny that he should think of that now, under the DEPARTURES board at a train station in Geneva, but he's glad he has, because it makes him think things might not be so atrocious in London, even today, the day of discovery. Because it is Fi in charge now and not him. When the dust settles, the boys will be better off without him.

For the first time since he left Trinity Avenue he feels something closer to peace than to turmoil.

And there's a train to Lyon leaving at five twenty-nine p.m.

38

"FI'S STORY" > 02:22:12

This may come as a surprise to you, but there've been times when I've felt sorry for him. I really have.

Don't get me wrong. I'm not excusing what he's done. Obviously, I despise it: he's stolen from me; he's stolen his own children's future. It's just that a part of me understands how the situation might have become as extreme as it did. You know, an escalation of events, a momentum that couldn't be halted. A sense of cosmic irresistibility. A problem shared is a problem halved—we all know that—but isn't it also the case that a problem kept to yourself is a problem multiplied many times over?

And that's what he did, I'm convinced—in my calmer moments, anyway. He kept it to himself. Had he confided in someone, *anyone*, he'd have been dissuaded from his actions. Instead, he's wanted for fraud and maybe even worse, maybe even—

No, I won't say it. I won't say it until—*unless*—it's been proven in a court of law.

No, honestly, I can't make any statement about it. I'd get in trouble with the police myself.

What I *will* say is that Bram was not the blithe spirit people thought he was. He had his depressive moods, more so than most of us, which stemmed from his father dying so young. Not to criticize his mother—she's an amazing woman—but parenting a bereaved child isn't easy when you're grieving yourself.

I suppose the point I'm trying to make is that it's hard sometimes to tell the difference between weakness and strength. Between hero and villain.

Don't you think?

Timing was not on Bram's side—I admit that. In fact, it couldn't have been crueler.

Though I'd intended heeding Toby's advice and reining in my outrage about the attack, by the time Bram returned the following evening for his regular Wednesday visit with Leo and Harry, there'd been a development he could not have foreseen. I waited for him to come down from putting them to bed, led him into the living room and closed the door—I didn't want the boys hearing a word of this. As we settled on the sofa, wood burner glowing across the room, I thought how couples up and down the street would be doing the same, precious few caught in a fray like ours.

"About what happened last night," he began. As Toby had predicted, he was bashful, full of remorse. "I'm really—"

"I know." I shrugged off his apologies. "Toby doesn't want to escalate it. You're very lucky—he could have gone to the police. But he understands why you lost it like that."

Bram gaped, apparently stunned by this revelation. "What did he say?"

"Just that he appreciates the value of what you chose to throw away." A good wife, an attractive woman. I paused, enjoying his confusion. "Besides, what he and I do or say is none of your business—we agreed that."

"Oh-kaay." He extended the vowels, buying himself a second or two as he tried to guess what *was* coming, if not a postmortem of the previous evening's crime.

I produced an opened envelope from my cardigan pocket. "This came in the post today, Bram."

He took it from me. "It's addressed to me."

"I know, but I thought it might be to do with the insurance claim, with any luck a reversal of their decision, so I opened it on your behalf." In fact, the document was a DVLA form inviting Bram to reapply for his driving license following a disqualification in February. "A driving ban, Bram? *Months* ago, when we were still together. You went to court, you stood in front of a magistrate and you didn't say a word about it!"

"It's a criminal act to open someone else's post," he said sourly.

"It's a criminal act to drive while disqualified!"

"What?" He frowned at the document. "That's not what this says." The faintest of shrugs, all he could muster of the famous Bram bluff and swagger.

"No, but it's what *I'm* saying. Don't deny it. You've driven regularly since then—I've seen you with my own eyes. For Christ's sake, Bram, a ban is bad enough, especially in your line of work—you're lucky you haven't lost your job—but if you'd been involved in an accident these last few months, you'd have got in serious trouble. What were you thinking? How do you get yourself into these situations? Why can't you just follow the rules like the rest of us?"

I'd grown strident, disliked the sound of myself in this righteous mood. Never had I felt more like a parent than at that moment: *his* parent. "Well?" I wanted to hear it from his own mouth; I wanted to watch him confess.

Having chased each other's gaze around the room, we now connected properly and he narrowed his eyes at me as if he no longer trusted me (*he* no longer trusted *me*!). "Fine, so I made a few quick trips when I shouldn't have, but not as many as you think. And then the car was stolen and—"

"And you were spared further temptation thanks to someone behaving even more criminally than you," I finished for him. "So, on these 'few quick trips,' did you have the boys in the car?"

"Maybe once or twice, just a short journey to swimming or something, but they were never at risk—I swear."

I wanted to slap the idiot. "You involved them in an illegal act, Bram. Of course they were at risk! I honestly don't know where we go from here. It was a big thing for me to get past what happened when we split up, and when I did it was in good faith that you wouldn't put me through more distress. But not only have you just assaulted a friend of mine, but you've also been lying to me this whole time!"

A tremor started around his mouth. The noise in his throat was not quite human as he reached, yet again, for his excuses. "I know, you're right, but I didn't want to jeopardize my chance to stay with the kids. Please, Fi, I'm sorry. I really am. I know I've screwed up and you're probably thinking the bird's nest isn't working out—"

"How can I think anything else when one of us is a liar?"

"But it's good for Leo and Harry, isn't it? You've got to admit that. They're far happier than they would have been if we'd split up."

We both froze, each as startled as the other.

"We *have* split up," I said at last.

He shook his head. "I know. A Freudian slip."

"Is this why the insurance company didn't pay out?" I demanded. "Because you didn't tell them about the ban?"

"I did tell them. Of course I did."

"So, as usual, it's just *me* you've cheated."

To my horror, his face began to collapse in that awful spasming way it had once before, and this time he began sobbing, repeating over and over how sorry he was.

"Please, Fi, give me one more chance. At least until the end of the trial period we agreed back in the summer. *Please.*"

I waited for his tears to subside, forbidding myself to see Leo in him, but it was too late. He was the boys' father; they were in his face, his voice, his frailties. I couldn't banish him without banishing them.

"One last chance, Bram. I just . . . I can't have you making a fool of me." Again. Again and again.

"I promise," he said.

Which we now know was not worth the soundwaves the words traveled on.

BRAM, Word document

I honestly think if Fi had pushed a bit harder I would have broken. If she had demanded to know why I'd reacted to her new man the way I had, I might have split open and let the secrets ooze from me, foul and unpalatable as they were.

But where once she'd been fixated on the adultery and missed the driving, now she was fixated on the driving and missed the fraud. A letter had come from the DVLA laying bare the details of my ban and there was the predictable confrontation. I can picture her face now, its saintly horror as she told me off: *"If you'd been involved in an accident these last few months, you'd have got in serious trouble. . . ."*

I think I know that!

"Why?" I asked Mike, when I'd calmed sufficiently to phone him. "Why are you seeing her? Is it just to show me you can?"

"Bram," he said, making a sigh of my name. "You seem to think I have limitless time in which to amuse myself. There's a deadline here, remember? The police might be a bit slow, but they're not complete fuckwits. They'll get around to you eventually."

"They already have," I admitted. "A guy came to question me on Tuesday."

"Really? He asked you about the crash?"

"No, not directly. Just who saw the car last, the same ground they covered with Fi weeks ago, so I'm thinking they must have something new to need to look me up."

"Did he ask where you were on September sixteenth?"

"Yes. I had to use the alibi. I said I was in the pub at Clapham Junction, like we agreed."

"That'll work out fine. Don't worry about it. Even if they check the cameras, it's mental there on a Friday, easy to get lost in the crowd. You need to hold your nerve, Bram. As for your missus, rest assured I have no intention of getting down on one knee. But someone has to get her out of the way when the time comes, don't they? It's not going to be *you* taking her on a romantic getaway."

They were definitely sleeping together, then. (As if it were ever in doubt. Sex was important to Fi.)

"I know it's a blow to your male ego, but it's nothing personal, so don't go plunging into a gloom about it, all right? You need to stop drawing attention to yourself with these petulant outbursts."

Petulant? As if I were an infant frustrated by the word "no."

"Just keep away from my kids," I said. "Promise me that."

"Pinkie promise," he mocked. "Can we get down to business now, please? There must have been some offers after those second viewings. I thought they'd be biting your arm off at this price."

I exhaled, a sound humiliatingly close to a whimper.

"Don't even think about holding out on me, Bram. One word from me, and Mrs. Lawson will call the agent herself."

"She's not Mrs. Lawson."

"Just give me the fucking update, will you?"

I swear, it was like he pulled a string from my back and when he let go the words came out. "There've been two offers. The highest is from a couple who are still waiting to sell their own house. The lower one is from a couple who've already sold their place, so there's no chain—they're ready to go."

I'd met them at the open house, Rav said, though I couldn't place their faces among the genteel collection of identikit couples. David and Lucy Vaughan, upgrading from an East Dulwich town house and recipients of a windfall following a wealthy grandparent's death. Younger than Fi and me and ready to start a family.

"How much?" Mike demanded.

"Two million. That's the best they can do—they can't get any more from their lender. Rav recommends we accept the higher one, give them a reasonable period to agree a sale on their place."

"There's no time for that," Mike said. "Two mill will have to do."

Like it was pin money, like beggars couldn't be choosers.

"So you want me to accept?" I said.

"I want you to accept."

I couldn't have designed weather more minutely matched to my psychological state as I walked through Alder Rise to the doctor's practice on the north side of the Parade. The skies drooped so smotheringly low they almost touched the rooftops, while, underfoot, the leaves disintegrated to dust.

I'd booked a session with the head of mental health services, Dr. Pearson.

"I can't go on," I told him, truthfully.

To his credit, he did his best to uncover the issues, but I stuck to broad strokes: I can't cope; I constantly feel like I'm about to have a panic attack; everything's falling apart; I want to cry all the time.

"I'm going to write you a prescription for an antidepressant," he said. "We'll start with a month and, if you're happy with it, we'll extend the prescription in the new year. But medication is only a part of treatment, and I strongly recommend that you talk to a therapist as well."

I made some indecipherable response, noncommittal, already adding him to my list of people I would never see again.

"I can refer you through the NHS or, if you'd like to get started sooner, you can use a private therapist."

"I'll use a private one," I said to get him off my back, and he gave me a link to a website that listed the local options. I imagined being probed about poor lifestyle choices and stress management by some earnest biddy the wrong side of fifty. "Listen, you stupid cow," I'd say, "I've caused a child's death. I've killed someone and now I'm being blackmailed into taking part in criminal fraud and if I don't cooperate I'll be jailed for ten years. The blackmailer is fucking my wife and threatening my children and I fantasize all the time about killing him, but if I do, I'll have to kill his accomplice as well, who, by the way, I've slept with, and even then the police might still get to me, because there could be other witnesses out there, not to mention the surviving party herself, who for all I know might have PTSD that's preventing her from remembering the incident properly, but that might lift at any time. . . ."

No, better to keep my troubles to myself.

39

BRAM, Word document

Since the collision, I had seen nothing of the story on the television news, either national or local; whoever the arbiters of death were, they had not judged it worthy of so high-profile a medium. I continued to watch, however, night after night (when I wasn't in the pub), for the single despicable reason that bad news made me feel better. A war atrocity, a serial killer's spree, a gangland knifing: each succeeded in convincing me that *my* crime wasn't so bad.

Sick, I know.

Then, one night in late November, when I was consoling myself with a bottle of wine and the tragic imagery of an Indian train wreck, thinking what did it matter that I made a terrible mistake two and a half months ago when there were seven billion other people who were just as fucked as I was, the local news headlines came on and turned me cold with horror:

> Tonight we speak to the mayor about safety concerns for
> construction workers on a new building on the South

Bank that will dwarf its neighbors. . . . Also this evening: following the government's announcement of sterner sentences for dangerous driving offenses, we ask why it is that two months after the road rage incident in South London that killed ten-year-old Ellie Rutherford there have still been no arrests. Ellie's father talks to Meera Powell in an exclusive interview. . . .

I waited in breathless agony for the segment about the skyscraper—excruciatingly in-depth—to end. Then, after ten seconds of a studio talking head, a long shot of Silver Road filled the screen and a voice-over began recapping the known facts about the collision over archive footage of Thornton Heath traffic and the entrance to Croydon Hospital. Next came a sequence of images from the funeral—children in yellow clothing, flowers arranged in the shape of a butterfly—followed by video of the Rutherford family gathered in a well-appointed living room, a large fern in the window and shelves crammed with books. Ellie's teenage brother was helping his mother up from her seat and supporting her as she moved painfully to the mantelpiece to look at a framed school photograph of Ellie. Then the camera picked out a fold-up wheelchair in the corner and a small pile of wrapped presents on a side table. "It's Ellie's birthday this week. She'd be turning eleven," the voice-over explained.

Finally, there was an appeal by Tim Rutherford, admirably, miraculously composed: "We're not saying the police aren't working hard on this, because we know they are. We're just asking that everyone watching this go over that evening one last time. Look back at your diary and see where you were after work that day. It was a Friday, mid-September, so still light. You might have been coming home from the office or heading out for a drink. You may not have witnessed the collision itself, but you may have seen a black hatchback Audi or VW leaving the area at speed. You might have noticed if it was a man or a woman at the wheel, what sort of age they were, how they were dressed. A little detail like that might be the breakthrough the police need."

And that was it. Though shocking enough to cause me to shake, the interview nonetheless confirmed my instinct that the police didn't know enough—if much at all—to build a case against me, and I could only assume that any case they *were* putting together was against either the suspected thief of our car or someone associated with a different vehicle altogether.

No one was going to remember anything new about a routine evening two and a half months ago, were they? Was it really possible I was going to get to the finish line undetected? Or was the human mind the erratic weapon the Rutherfords prayed it was? ("Wait. There *was* a car—I thought it was going to hit my wing mirror. *Definitely* an Audi. The guy had curly hair. . . .")

Turning off the television, I found that opening a second bottle of wine helped me err on the side of optimism. (The fact that mixing alcohol with my new medication was strictly forbidden gave me no pause whatsoever.)

Waking the next morning, however, I couldn't get the image of little Ellie from my mind, that photo of her in her bottle green school jumper. She was like the girls in Leo's class, not the golden one—the popular one—but smart, good-natured, probably a little shy until she was with her friends, and then she was bolder, more confident.

Just a sweet kid like yours or mine.

"FI'S STORY" > 02:30:15

No, I'm ashamed to say I didn't give the Silver Road accident a second thought. In my defense, the police officer who'd come to question me about the car had never contacted me again, and I'd probably read of countless other accidents since, countless other misfortunes. They weren't exactly in short supply last year, were they?

Not once did Bram mention the Rutherfords to me, no. It was only after everything came to a head in the new year that I heard their name at all.

40

BRAM, Word document

It was mind-boggling how far the conveyancing process could progress with neither Wendy nor me having face-to-face contact with a lawyer. Graham Jenson of Dixon Boyle & Co in Crystal Palace was selected by Mike, of course, presumably for his lack of reputation for excellence (indeed, on the legal-ratings website I looked at, Jenson did not score spectacularly in client satisfaction). Like Rav, he was not part of our conspiracy, and so once again I was simply to proceed as if the sale were happening normally. I set up a new e-mail address in the name of A & F Lawson, shared the password with my overlords, and gave my pay-as-you-go number to Jenson and his trainee.

By early December, I'd collated the required paperwork and proofs of ID, filled in all the questionnaires, and supplied a mortgage redemption figure, which would be paid automatically on completion. Documents were shuttled in and out of the Trinity Avenue filing cabinet as I came and went according to the bird's nest schedule. (In the unlikely event that Fi would want to look up something I'd removed, I knew she would simply assume it had been misfiled.) To avoid having packages arrive at Trinity Avenue in the post—I already knew that Fi had no qualms about opening mail addressed to me; well, *these* were addressed to her too—we agreed that Wendy should pick them up from the solicitor's receptionist in person, using her practiced Fiona Lawson signature whenever called for. She would then hand deliver them to me at the flat and wait for me to add the requisite information or coauthorization before returning them to the solicitor at the next opportunity. The few documents that required witnesses to our signatures were rerouted to Mike to add whichever fabricated names and professions he saw fit. In the meantime, Wendy supplied to Jenson details of the holding account that would feed the closing payment to whatever offshore alternative Mike had opened via his fabled dark-web contacts.

All of which was both insanely risky and insanely easy—considerably easier than it would have been had not one of the conspirators been a fifty-percent owner of the property. That was the genius of the scheme—I have to hand it to Mike.

Though the buyers' queries were minimal, their mortgage company required an on-site valuation, a nonnegotiable element that could be scheduled only for a weekday. Though not without its stresses, this was child's play compared to the open house: I arranged to work from home and requested that the surveyor come at noon, so he'd be gone well before Fi or her mother could return with the boys after school. The street was quiet, but I had an excuse prepared about roof repairs should anyone approach me with questions.

By mid-December, draft contracts had been drawn up and sent to the buyers' solicitor.

Good work, amigo, Mike texted me, and there was a disorienting moment when I completely forgot myself and experienced pleasure in his rare praise. Then the horror returned, more oppressive, more sanity eroding than ever.

The drugs weren't working yet, evidently.

"FI'S STORY" > 02:30:45

I know it's going to sound like I was making concession after concession, but you have to remember I was engaged in realpolitik here. I was not in a position to take a strictly ethical stance. What I took was a strictly maternal one, and on that score I have no regrets.

Because Bram was right about Leo and Harry being happy. They were *really* happy. I even saw them being nice to each other, like proper brothers in a book—I mean, not quite the Weasley twins from *Harry Potter*, but nice by *their* standards.

There was a cold snap in early December and Trinity Avenue was a picture of iced shrubbery and shimmering mists. Christmas was in the air, always my favorite time of year. Once home from school, the boys preferred to stay there, abandoning the garden for the living room, with its wood burner and burrows of fur throws. Seeing them snuggled up together, pink cheeked and sleepy eyed, I was convinced anew of the beauty of our bird's nest. That half-witnessed skirmish with Toby was likely nothing compared to the conflict Bram and I would be exposing them to if we'd remained together.

At parents' evening, for which Bram and I both cleared our diaries, neither Leo's nor Harry's teachers reported any evidence of the kind of anxiety or disruptive behavior often noticed when a child's parents have recently separated.

"Whatever you're doing at home, carry on doing it," Harry's teacher Mrs. Carver said. "He's a real bright spark."

Buoyed, Bram and I arranged to go to the end-of-term Christmas carol concert together.

BRAM, Word document

Even as I plotted to steal their future from them, I prioritized the boys. For the first time in their lives, I attended every last school event of the festive season, even Harry's drop-in Christmas decorations session, from which every parent departed for his day's meetings with glitter on his earlobes. Work was no longer relevant—I'd be gone soon—and wherever possible I delegated or canceled or passed the buck. Three times in December I called in sick or left early unwell (not entirely dishonest, since nausea was never far away).

"I think there's something wrong with me," I told Neil (again, not entirely dishonest). "It's maybe some sort of virus."

"So long as that's really what it is and you're not just taking the piss," he said, which was his equivalent of a first warning. The situation was not helped by my decision to skip work Christmas drinks in favor of the boys' carol concert in the last week of term.

"Quitter," Neil said, which we both knew was how Keith Richards baited Ronnie Wood when he checked himself into rehab.

If only addiction were my greatest problem, I thought, woefully. The effects of rock 'n' roll excess.

The carol concert almost undid me. "It Came upon a Midnight Clear" was Fi's favorite and, by chance, the children sang it as their finale, their sweet, hopeful little voices almost too much to bear. It was the closest I came to breaking down in public.

"Absolutely gorgeous," Fi said as the classes filed down the aisle afterward. "Were you filming that, Bram?"

"Just the last song," I said. "It was allowed, wasn't it? All the other dads were doing it."

"Yes, I think so. Anyway, I'm not a security guard."

There was a message there, I thought, or at least chose to think. She was saying she'd finished threatening war and now she wanted a return to the peace process.

We waited for the pew to clear before we shuffled out. To my right, there was a fresco showing the trial of some martyr or other, and in all my years as the son of a God-fearing mother, I had never felt such a sense of connection in a church as I did then.

"In the spirit of goodwill to all men," I said to Fi, "can I ask you a favor?" Only a man who no longer has anything to lose makes a wish that he has never been less likely to be granted. "It's the last one I'll ever ask you," I added.

She rolled her eyes. "There's no need to overdo it, Bram—you're not terminally ill. What is it?"

"Could I have the boys for Christmas? It would . . . it would mean a lot to me."

Because it might be the last time. It *will* be the last time. This time next year, I'll be on trial like our friend the saint, or in prison or living in a hole in the ground like a terrorist. I hadn't decided on my current course of action then—that presented itself later in a near-holy moment of revelation—but presumed I would want to carry on living, however pitifully.

Fi didn't reply at first. I could see her natural response surge through her, about to explode into opposition, my crimes past and present on the tip of her tongue, but then she swallowed it, remembered her renewed commitment to the cause. Maybe it was also the sight of all those other parents with their symmetrical still-married smiles and cashmere-scarf-wrapped togetherness, but suddenly she was saying something wholly unexpected.

"Look, why don't we *both* have them? At the house, like every other Christmas they've known?"

"What?" I felt myself flush. "Are you serious?"

"Yes. They'd love us all to be together. It's on a weekend, so why don't we both just stay in the house for Christmas Eve and Christmas Day? On Boxing Day, I was hoping to take them to my parents', so perhaps you could visit your mum with them during the day on Christmas Eve. Does that sound fair?"

Euphoria gushed through me. "Yes, more than fair. Thank you." The only thing better than spending my last Christmas with my sons was to spend it with my wife and my sons.

"Let's walk to Kirsty and Matt's together," she said. "You know they're doing drinks now?"

Another almighty concession; it was understood that as the injured party in our split—as the *woman*—she had first refusal on neighborhood social invitations.

"Harry forgot the words to 'We Three Kings,'" Leo said when the two of them were released to us by their teachers. "It was *so* obvious."

"Not to us," Fi said. "We could really hear your voices, couldn't we, Dad?"

"Absolutely," I said, helping Harry with his gloves. The end of his left thumb stuck through a tear and I kept that hand in mine, covering the hole.

"I *didn't* forget the words," he grumbled, as we headed into the street, and I waited with disproportionate dread for him to snatch away his hand. But he didn't; he kept it in mine the whole way.

Passing along the Parade, we walked four abreast where the pavement was wide enough, as we often had when the boys were young.

Them in the middle, one of us on either side.

"FI'S STORY" > 02:32:16

"We've decided to spend Christmas together, for the boys' sakes," I told Polly.

"You've got to be kidding me," she said. "Whose crazy idea was that? Yours or his?"

"Mine. He looked so awful, Pol." He'd looked, in fact, like a death row inmate being given news of a temporary reprieve. (And his horror when he'd thought he'd filmed the concert without permission: the old Bram would have exulted in such small rebellions.) I'd been embarrassed by both the intensity of his gratitude and the melancholy that seemed to underlie it, as if he thought he'd never live to see another festive season. "And you know what Christmas would be like at his mum's."

"What, a sincerely religious celebration? How bizarre." Polly gave me a warning look. "Just so long as your Christmas present to him is a letter from your divorce lawyer."

Alison was less harsh. "I think that's a really nice thing to do," she said. "You're such a kind person, Fi. I know how tempting it must be to punish him by leaving him out."

"I'm not sure I need to punish him," I said. "He seems to be doing that himself."

#VictimFi

@tillybuxton #VictimFi is her own worst enemy, isn't she? Bit unfair to blame the victim, I suppose.
@femiblog2016 @tillybuxton V unfair, but also v common. It's called the "just world hypothesis": we get what we deserve.
@IanHopeuk @femiblog2016 @tillybuxton I don't believe that for a second #lifeisshit

BRAM, Word document

As I say, I devoted myself fully to the family those last weeks. No Christmas dos, no work drinks. Tuesday nights at the Two Brewers had fallen by the wayside of late and I saw the Trinity Avenue guys for a drink only once in December, that night after the carol concert at Kirsty and Matt's. I had to be careful about what I said now. I had to isolate myself from the pack.

By contrast, I was connecting to the place like never before, appreciating the details of Alder Rise as if I'd just arrived from the slums—standing in the park and closing my eyes and feeling freedom on my face, blank and pure and kind of *sheltering*. Perhaps it was just the relief of escaping the house I was stealing and the flat that was the HQ for plotting that theft. The siren call of devices on which I might browse articles about the brutality of prison life.

I remember the weather spiked constantly between chafing cold and golden mild, a sense of punishment and reprieve. There were times when I found a weird comfort in this—if you can't take the good for granted, then you can't take the bad either. *If you can meet with Triumph and Disaster / And treat those two imposters just the same . . . you'll be a Man, my son!*

We learned that at school.

They didn't tell us that the worst disasters would be those of our own making.

41

BRAM, Word document

"Why are you doing this, Wendy?"

"What?" Caught off guard, she gave a half-embarrassed laugh, gripped the tissue in her hand a little tighter.

"I'm serious. Why are you hitching your wagon to his star like this?"

Normally, on her visits to the flat, I kept social interaction to a minimum, grunting my responses to her attempts at flirtation and evading her eye for fear of the violent hatred she might provoke in me. As a go-between, she liked to present herself as girlish, almost simple, but it would be I who was the simpleton if I allowed myself to forget previous evidence of her guile: that emotionless steel when she phoned the hospital in front of me to test my nerve; the malicious way she had toyed with me after our night together.

But on her last call before Christmas, I found I was in the mood to engage. Maybe it was because she had a cold, sniffing pathetically every ten seconds and kneading sore eyes with her knuckles, or maybe the pills were finally blunting my rage, but I found myself feeling half-sorry for the woman.

She was pouting at me now, her expression querulous. "What does *that* mean?"

"You know, riding on his coattails. Trusting he's right when he says it will work. What the hell does *he* know? He's an amateur, like us."

A shrug. I sensed I'd hit a nerve, though, because she wasn't so quick with that fake giggle of hers.

"This whole idea *was* his, wasn't it?" I pressed. "Have you done scams together before? Probably just petty stuff, eh? Nothing like this. This is hard-core. More of a long game."

The very blankness of her gaze confirmed my guesses to be correct. Making her wait for the building regulations form the Vaughans' so-licitor had requested (and which I'd found exactly where I'd expected to, in the Trinity Avenue file marked HOME IMPROVEMENTS), I went on. "How come you have such faith in him? Are you two married? Going out? You know he's screwing my wife, don't you?"

I thought I read a negative message in her eyes then. She was in his thrall, somehow. Did he have something on her too?

"Don't you care that you're destroying my life and my children's lives?"

She shook her head. "No, *you're* doing that, not me."

"Right. So you're a monster like him. You take no responsibility for your actions. How admirable."

She gazed at me, clearly struggling between the dim-witted act she'd been cultivating and the more complex intelligence she surely realized I knew she possessed. "It's so boring the way you think, Bram."

Boring? Sorry, love. I'll try to be more sparkling in my efforts to claw myself from the stinking bowels of hell. "I'm just trying to understand why you would get mixed up in blackmail and fraud. They're really serious offenses, you know. Fine, so you don't give a shit about me and my family, but you must see the risk you're taking personally. This isn't nicking a hundred quid from someone's wallet. You said you had a decent job—don't you earn enough to get by? You'll get a promotion, a pay rise. You seem pretty smart to me—other than going along with *this*, of course."

She suffered this pitch in silence, other than to cough at me, a natural repellent. Her nostrils were raw from rubbing. No doubt she wondered why I hadn't researched her and Mike as they had me. Hired a PI to follow them—or even the services of the same underworld scum they'd used themselves. The truth was, I'd considered it a hundred times, but on each occasion allowed the delusion to persist that my ordeal would end before I needed to act myself. The truth was, I was gutless.

Until now, evidently.

"Are you scared of him, Wendy? Is that it? He's intimidating, I know—a big guy. Believe me, I've felt how solid he is—no doubt he told you about our little wrestling match at the house. But there are ways of protecting yourself, you know. If we both tell him we're backing out, we can stand up to a thug like him, don't you think?"

But I understood I'd made a mistake before I'd finished the sentence. She went rigid with objection, her upper teeth snapping shut like a portcullis. "He is *not* a thug," she said through her teeth. "That's my brother you're slagging off."

"Your brother?" I exclaimed. It was the one possibility I'd failed to consider. "You look nothing alike."

"We're not twins, for fuck's sake." She gestured to the document in my hand with new belligerence. "Can you just give me that? I need to get back."

To the solicitor or to Mike? Her brother. Jesus. Would she tell him what I'd said? And if she did, would he care? What could he do now that he hadn't already done?

It wasn't hard to imagine. After she left, I texted Fi with trembling fingers:

> Just reading about an attempted abduction in Crystal Palace, a guy in his thirties in a white car cruising school gates.

Don't worry, Fi texted back. *The boys know how to keep safe. I'll mention it to the school tomorrow, though. Thanks for alerting me.*

You're welcome, I typed.

"FI'S STORY" > 02:33:36

On the Wednesday evening before Christmas, Bram fetched the stepladders and strung fairy lights in the magnolia, while I hung a hundred silver baubles from its lower branches. We do it—I mean, *did* it—every year, and though I say so myself, it always looks beautiful (people have stopped to film it, seriously). Ideally, there would have been the decorative frosting of snow we'd had earlier in the month, but the second half of December had turned oddly mild, a false spring that had even encouraged daffodils to sprout.

The playhouse lights we'd kept up all year. Bram had built the house the previous Christmas Eve while I took the boys in to the West End to see *The Snowman* at the theater. After they'd gone to bed, we rigged up icicle lights and put little seats draped with sheepskins on the deck so it looked like a miniature mountain lodge. It was still dark when they got up on Christmas morning and we took them to the window for the big reveal.

"That is just *nauseatingly* cute," Merle said when she and Adrian came for drinks on Boxing Day and we presented our new attraction. "I almost wish you hadn't shown me."

"You're funny," I said, giving her arm a little squeeze.

BRAM, Word Document

"I almost forgot," Fi said during my last Wednesday visit to Trinity Avenue before Christmas Day, after we'd pimped up the magnolia tree in the traditional way (there may have been no formal prize, but believe me, there was a competition on the street for the best decorations—and no one understood this better than the woman who worked in homewares). "This came for you today. By hand."

She passed me a white envelope with my name scrawled in slapdash capitals. The flap had not been sealed, only tucked inside. It couldn't be anything to do with the house sale, I thought. Mike wouldn't take a risk like that, surely?

"I didn't look," Fi added, seeing my face.

"Thank you."

I opened it as I walked back to the flat. It was from him of course, a reprisal for my overtures to Wendy. There were two items, the first a download from a news site, the *Telegraph* site no less. (I imagined him being pleased with himself about that. "I'm not some oik. I read quality news, don't you know?")

DANGEROUS DRIVING RUNS IN FAMILY, STUDY FINDS

Young drivers who have witnessed their parents speed or drive drunk are three times more likely to commit the same offense themselves, according to a study published today. . . .

The second was a single-page printout from a government website, a dense table of names, my father's among them. My vision actually blurred: the shock at this display of knowledge was even more breath stealing than at any of the previous ones. How could he possibly know—and why would he send this? What was going on here? Surely what my father did decades ago could have no bearing on any prosecution of *my* crimes—could it? Was it admissible at trial as background information?

Not for the first time, it crossed my mind that he might be with the police and only posing as a fraudster. But wouldn't his actions to date constitute entrapment? Not a defensible practice—everyone knew that. No, what other purpose could there be for goading and intimidating me in this way if not for financial gain?

What this was, was a turning of the screw, a declaration that I could go on resisting, I could attempt to groom Wendy till the cows came home, but he had no intention of letting me go.

I threw the *Telegraph* printout in the bin by the park gates, but kept the second sheet, folding it into my wallet. I couldn't just toss it in the bin and see it on the pavement the next day, scavenged by a fox or maybe the wind.

"FI'S STORY" > 02:35:10

Christmas was a big compromise, yes. Did my sympathy for him have anything to do with his father? All those Christmases Bram spent without him? The delight he'd always taken in ours?

I don't know. Maybe. It was always there in my feelings for him, a complexity, a nuance, that had to be considered.

I wasn't going to reveal this, but now we've come this far I think it's relevant to mention that Bram's father served a prison sentence for drunk driving. He hit a pedestrian, an elderly man—no, he wasn't badly injured, nothing like that, but this was the 1970s and society was just starting to understand how frequent a factor alcohol was in road fatalities. As part of a crackdown, Bram's father was made an example of, given a custodial sentence.

Talking about prison, or watching a news item about overcrowding and violence in our jails, was probably the only thing that truly unnerved Bram, or so it seemed to me. I remember we took the boys to the Clink Prison Museum once—you know, the medieval jail by the river? You can see the old cells and instruments of torture, that sort of thing—the boys loved it. Anyway, Bram wouldn't go in. Seriously, he had to wait outside. They call it carcerophobia, someone told me.

His father died not long after that and so it's possible his prison stories were the last Bram remembers him telling. Such a sad thought.

The reason I'm sharing this is to show that there's a context to all this: Bram learned his lawbreaking from the backseat. (Actually, in those days, small kids were allowed in the front and weren't even made to wear a seat belt. Bram was playing with his Action Man when his father was pulled over by the police.)

I remember him saying to me soon after we met and he'd told me about his father's prison stretch, "Are you sure you want to take on someone from criminal stock?"

"Oh, I imagine we're all from criminal stock if you go back far enough," I said.

"Good answer," he said, as pleased with me as I was with myself. Back then, I wanted him as much for his edge as in spite of it.

But we grow out of those sorts of tastes, don't we?

At least some of us do.

#VictimFi

@deadheadmel So is #VictimFi saying Bram WAS in that car crash and he was wasted at the time?
@lexie1981 @deadheadmel Sounds like it. Prison's not that bad, is it? Don't they watch TV all day and smoke crack?
@deadheadmel @lexie1981 Sounds a whole lot better than *my* day LOL.

42

And then finally, *finally*, the pharmaceuticals took effect—oh my God, the beautiful mood-influencing neurotransmitter that is our friend serotonin—and not a moment too soon either. It felt like a Christmas miracle. Gone was the perpetual agonizing, the cartoon pumping of my heart, forceful enough to move the shirt on my chest, whenever the buzzer or the doorbell went. The twisting pain of panic when I weighed up my options (give myself up for one crime or persist with a second that I hoped—but had no guarantee—would camouflage the first?).

No, now I was quiet, optimistic, back to my short-termist, compartmentalizing best.

Thank you, Father Christmas.

Thank you for the hours spent making a Star Wars Clone Turbo Tank out of Lego; playing "retro" Pokémon games on the Nintendo and having a heart light enough to joke that I was more vintage than they were; eating sweets from a glass jar of old-fashioned pick 'n' mix the size of Harry's torso. Thank you for Fi smiling constantly—even at me, because I was pleasing her in my own right, not just as her sons' father.

"It's like Richard Curtis is directing us," I said as all four of us assembled in the kitchen to peel sprouts, baste the turkey and stir gravy, though we all knew it was Fi who was directing us, that this slice of old times was her Christmas gift to me.

"Yes," she agreed. "Either that or we're the England-Germany football match during the First World War. You know, the Christmas Day truce."

I laughed (I hadn't laughed in a long time). "A war analogy, hmm. Is it that bad between us?"

I interpreted her silence as a "no."

I waited for the boys to pass out for the night before presenting her with my gift.

"We said we wouldn't do presents," she chided me, but she didn't utter the words "car insurance" or "lies"—hadn't all day—and that was an expression of grace in itself.

"It didn't cost much," I said.

"Well, in that case . . ." She slid a fingernail under the flap of the envelope and removed the card. "An adoption certificate for a tree in the royal parks? What a lovely idea!"

"Well, I know how much you love the magnolia."

And will miss it when I've—

Stop. Seal the thought in its tomb and turn back to the living world. Stare directly at bright light, if necessary—whatever it takes to erase the image of Fi admiring her beloved tree only from the other side of the gate, the new owners watching from the window—

I said stop.

"Thank you, Bram." She was about to kiss me on the cheek, but then she remembered it was different with me. No longer a husband, but not a friend either.

I wanted to ask what *he'd* given her. Underwear, I guessed. Something that looked expensive but was actually cheap. Something fake or stolen. Something he'd got his sister to choose for him. If only someone could administer electric shock treatment to the pair of them, void their wicked scheme, their memories of all contact with me: what a gift that would be.

"Look how sad you are," Fi said tenderly, and then, in sudden wonder: "Wait, is this how it works?"

I blinked, returned my attention to her. Her skin was flushed, her posture slack from the labors of the day—and the alcohol. She'd drunk a lot and, believe me, it takes one to know one. "How what works?"

"You. I bet you're not the predator at all."

"I don't know what you're talking about," I said.

"Women, Bram. I'm genuinely interested. Now you're free to do exactly what you like—*who* you like—do you actually have to pursue them? Or do you just look all sad and appealing like *you're* the prey?"

I didn't answer, but the question remained between us as her face came closer.

"What are you doing?" I said, but not in protest. *Let her prove her point,* I thought. Our mouths met. They knew each other's shape and flavor, the way the muscles and nerves responded. I've always thought rediscovery is sweeter than the original discovery: you notice more without the distraction of novelty. Why else would people go back to the same place on holiday or remarry the same wife or move back to their childhood street when they can choose any other in the land?

"You're very drunk," I pointed out, gently.

"Thanks for the heads-up," she said.

No, it's not just the sense of coming home. It's the understanding that what or where or who you love is only ever borrowed. There is no permanent ownership, not for any of us.

"FI'S STORY" > 02:36:52

Christmas *en famille*. Our last—at least I assume now that it was.

To cut a long story short, I drank far, far too much and we slept together. I really let myself down—I know that.

#VictimFi

@ KatyEVBrown Well, I saw *that* coming a mile off #Throw-backSex

BRAM, Word document

It transpired that the Christmas miracle had deprived me of neither bodily function nor hormone-drenched postcoital optimism. This business with Mike and Wendy—I could make that go away, surely? Tomorrow, yes, I'd sort it and look back on this period as a blip, a quirk in the space-time continuum, a horror experienced by a parallel Bram, a hapless, unlucky version of this one.

"What are you thinking?" Fi said. Not a line I welcomed as a rule, but that night, with her, in the bed that used to be ours and was now hers, it was exactly what I wanted her to ask me.

"You really want to know?"

"God, maybe I don't, but go on—tell me anyway." She was completely relaxed, her guard down, her heart . . . open?

"I'm thinking, is there really no chance?"

"No chance for what?"

"For us," I said, smiling. And I thought, in a simple, almost dreamy way, if she says yes, I'll confess everything here and now, because it will mean she loves me no matter what, and when you love someone *that* much, you do everything in your power to save them.

But if she says, "No, I won't," then nothing will have been lost that wasn't already.

"*Us?*" The abruptness of her distaste shocked me. She all but physically recoiled, pulling herself upright, her shoulders tense with indignation. "You're in a dreamworld, aren't you?"

I sat up too, feeling the drench of humiliation, the loss of hope. "I'm not in a dreamworld. If you must know, I've been in complete hell."

"If I *must* know? What do you expect me to say, Bram? Poor you that you don't like being on your own, that you fucked up your marriage by fucking other women? If it's hell it's because *you've* created it, no one else."

And she reached for the nearest item of clothing and covered herself, not only withdrawing the goods but doing so with an air of great regret that she'd offered them in the first place.

"FI'S STORY" > 02:37:08

By the morning, I'd decided it was inevitable. A necessary memento.

"Listen, I don't want Toby finding out about this," I told him. Woman asks husband not to tell new boyfriend she's slept with him: I wasn't sure if it was low-rent or aristocratic, but I was fairly certain it was not an exchange taking place anywhere else on Trinity Avenue that Boxing Day morning.

"You're still seeing him?" he asked. "I thought it wasn't serious."

"It's *not* serious. But it's also none of your business."

I was relieved when he made his departure at the prearranged hour, in good time for me to organize the boys for our visit to my parents.

As the taxi drove through the eerily empty streets of South London, the thought of that First World War football match lingered in my mind. The way those poor men cleared the bodies from no-man's-land so they could play, and then the next day the horror resumed as if there'd never been any pause.

#VictimFi

@themattporter Not sure #VictimFi is quite in the trenches of the Western Front, but she's got herself a bit of closure there. @ LorraineGB71 @themattporter Lawson vs Lawson's not over yet, remember?

BRAM, Word document

On Boxing Day morning, she kissed me good-bye and I could smell the detachment on her skin. It was like laying flowers at a grave when the grief is no longer fresh.

A tribute in my memory.

43

The kitchen door flies open and David draws himself to his full height before making his announcement: "The title is in our name. Ownership has been transferred. It's definitely ours."

To be fair, he speaks with less exultation than he might. There is no victory salute.

As Lucy cries out her thanks, Merle's face expresses all the devastation that Fi's own must—or should, if she were not too winded to react. The other three adjust their expressions and gaze at her with varying degrees of the same emotion: pity.

"I don't believe it," Fi whispers, finally, almost experimentally, as if the news might have robbed her of her voice as well as her property. She has the faint thought that even a judgment against you is preferable to the purgatory of not knowing, though she'll think differently tomorrow, she knows, when the shock has lifted, when the true magnitude registers.

David resumes his update: "Emma is going to phone Dixon Boyle now and get to the bottom of where the money is, but it's an incontro-vertible fact that the required amount left her client account this morning and was confirmed as clearing theirs before noon. If someone got a digit wrong in sending it on to the Lawsons, that will of course be followed up and rectified—realistically, on Monday." He meets Fi's eye, not without compassion. "In fact, this could be your chance to jump in and get them to hold the funds while you sort out your situa-tion. Or if it's too late for that, Emma suggests you continue talking to the police and find a lawyer to help you with any fraud claim against your husband—or whoever the guilty party is—and try to recoup what's owed to you that way. We're all really sorry you're having to go through this ordeal."

When Fi fails to find any words, he looks to Merle for a response.

"It's not the money," Merle says in a new tone, no longer adversarial but as one equal to another, resident to resident. "It's the house. I'm sure you understand that. This is Fi's home, her children's home, and it has been for a long time."

"I'm sorry—I really am—but it isn't anymore," says David.

There's a silence.

"We need to leave," Fi tells Merle, numbly.

"You said there's a flat?" Lucy says. "Could you stay there tonight?"

"We'll go to mine," Merle says. "We need to be on the spot in case anything else happens."

"Perhaps we should meet again on Monday morning, like you sug-gested, try to make some more sense of it all. Whatever we can do to help unravel this, we will, won't we, David?"

"Of course," he agrees.

It's already unraveled, Fi thinks, picking up her handbag. She re-members her overnight bag, on the floor in front of the oven, the only tangible evidence that her life before existed.

As she and Merle leave, it seems to her that the mood of the house has changed, as if it's accepting the fact of its new owners. The Vaughans will soon start unpacking, treating it as their own, this mesh of complications slowing their transition, but not stopping it. She doesn't allow herself thoughts of Leo and Harry, how they might never again come tumbling down the stairs, arguing, yelling, demanding to stay up late; how they've been deprived of the right to say goodbye to their bedrooms, to their first home. She does not allow those thoughts, but she is aware of a lurking instinct that they *will* arrive. Adrenaline will burst through the dam and drive her back to this door, fists beating.

It occurs to her that the Vaughans have not asked her for her keys; she wonders if they will change the locks for fear of her letting herself in, in the days to come (she could camp out in the playhouse, perhaps, closing the circle that began that evening last July).

She can't bring herself to shut the door behind her, using the edge of the lock to pull it gently toward her as she's done thousands of times over the years, and it is left to Merle to do this for her.

"Don't give up," Merle says, her eyes fierce. "It's not over yet."

BETWEEN GENEVA AND LYON, 6 P.M.

The train is tearing through the darkness, passing from one land to another, neither one his own. It's too dark to see the sights of the route, even if he cares to, though he is aware of the alteration in sound and pressure that marks the stretch of tunnel through the Alps. He makes no eye contact with the other travelers, the families and the skiers and the silent majority whose reasons for traveling he can only guess at.

His phone, SIM-less and, strictly speaking, the property of his (former) employer, delivers a slide show of photos and videos of the boys. He starts to watch the film he took of the carol concert, but the sound of their eager voices, the sight of their guiltless faces, is too painful and he has to close it.

Music, then—no pictures. He hits SHUFFLE and the first song it brings up is an old one, "Comin' Home Baby" by Mel Tormé. He owns so few sentimental songs among the concept rock and the folk and the eighties and nineties favorites from his younger days, it seems cruel that this should be the one to play. It might have been selected by Mike himself to torment him.

I hate you, he thinks. *I hate you with a depth that makes me see I have never hated before in my whole life. Only you.*

Even now, if he could think of a way to do it without making things worse for Fi than they already are, he would get off this train, fly home and kill him.

44

BRAM, Word document

New year, new arrangements to make regarding the execution of a criminal fraud.

Wendy and I met our solicitor for the first and only time, to sign the contracts prior to their exchange, on Friday, the sixth of January. We sat side by side at his desk in the small, down-at-heel practice above a cheese shop in Crystal Palace. Graham Jenson, with his faded eyes and posture of near collapse, had an air of having met middle age with a more crushing experience of defeat than he'd hoped, which reflected my own mood to an uncomfortable degree. In different circumstances, we might have traded war stories over a pint and vied for the attentions of his perky trainee, Rachel.

Instead, I laid two passports on the desk in front of him: mine and Fi's.

"Lucky they don't ask for driver's licenses for ID," Wendy said to me, in an affable aside. Her fingers reached to pick up my passport and, as she flicked to the photograph, she touched my arm as if remembering with fondness this younger version of her husband. In her interpretation of our twisted role-playing, we were not estranged but very much together.

As for "her" photo, I did not need to hold it up to her face to know that she'd done enough. Though considerably less attractive and at least a stone heavier than Fi, she was of a similar-enough facial type to pass herself off. They both had dark eyes and blond hair—Wendy had had hers tinted to ape Fi's less strident shade and a fringe cut to conceal her thinner, higher eyebrows. Fi had a sweetly pointed chin, but it wasn't a dominating feature and not something a casual observer—a qualified conveyancer, for instance, with the authority to handle millions of pounds—would pick up on. (They should make blood tests compulsory, I thought, or fingerprinting.) In the event, only the most cursory comparison was made between passport Fi and fake Fi, the filing of photocopies evidently considered due diligence enough.

I pocketed the passports. Both would be returned to the file at Trinity Avenue at the first opportunity.

"Right, I think we're pretty much there," Jenson told us. The paperwork was in order, all queries dealt with, the vendors' multiple searches now complete. Wendy double-checked the details of the bank account into which funds were to be paid on completion, once the mortgage had been redeemed and agent's and solicitor's fees automatically deducted. (As I understood the scam from research of my own, the funds would spend a matter of minutes in a UK-registered account before being spirited to an untraceable offshore alternative.) We confirmed that Challoner's would be taking care of transferring the utilities, having been issued with strict instructions that all final statements should be paperless and, like the rest of their correspondence, sent to the secret "joint" e-mail account.

"Let's sign these contracts," Jenson said, and I know it was only my imagination, but he made it sound like a set of death warrants.

"Exciting," Wendy said to me, with a little tremble of glee.

"Hmm." As I made eye contact with her, I imagined Fi's disgust in place of Wendy's phony devotion, the wholesale retraction of any remaining benefit of the doubt, any last positive regard for me.

I'm signing away our house! Right here and now, that's what I'm doing.

There was a sudden jolt of grotesque lucidity: How had I *ever* been so shortsighted? If I'd handed myself in after the Silver Road incident, I'd have been jailed, but the crime—and its punishment—would at least have ended there. Instead, it had grown and mutated. This was how human disaster worked: you began by trying to conceal a mistake and you finished up here, the perpetrator of a hundred further mistakes. To avoid a few years in a cell, you sacrificed your whole life—for as long as you chose to go on living the miserable piece of shit.

Go now, I urged myself. *Go before you sign anything, before the exchange of contracts.* I wouldn't get the counterfeit passport conditional to the sale completing, but there was nothing to stop me using my own or vanishing somewhere in the UK—it wasn't like I was on police bail.

Do it now. Go!

Mike would go after Leo and Harry, though, wouldn't he? Could I alert the police? Get some protection for them?

No, the police would be more interested in *me*.

"Your turn to sign, babe." Wendy showed me the space next to her signature, an impressive facsimile of Fi's that she had honed over the last few weeks. "You're shaking," she added, tenderly. "You must still have a bit of that flu. He was wiped out over Christmas and New Year," she told Jenson.

"I'm fine," I said. Crazy, when you considered the scale of her theft from me, but I objected just as strongly to her fabricating the intimacies of our life as a couple.

I signed.

Our legal representative's tiredness and cheapness was evident in his lackluster congratulations. "A bit early for a celebratory drink," he added, with discernible dismay.

"Thank you," Wendy told him, mimicking his low-key tone. "We'll wait to hear from you that we've exchanged." She was very good. Relaxed, polite, but somehow bland. Unmemorable. Not the woman who had caught my eye across the bar at the Two Brewers.

"Cheer up," she said as we reached the street. "Here, let me give you a quick kiss, in case what's his name is watching from the window. Not that he will be. He was phoning it in, I thought—didn't you?"

"That's why Mike chose him," I muttered. "Don't act like you don't know that."

"There's no need to be so grumpy," Wendy said.

No need to be grumpy? Was this woman serious? As she craned to kiss me on the mouth, I pressed my lips shut. The traffic braked at the changing lights, the drizzle turning the usual roar into a kind of asphyxiated howl.

"Spoilsport," she said. "If I'm your wife now, I should demand my conjugal rights, shouldn't I? We're not too far from your place."

"We just stole a house together," I said grimly. "We didn't get married." I thought, fleetingly, of Christmas night.

Shove the thieving bitch under a bus, I thought. The way the traffic was accelerating from the lights, bearing down on us right up against the curb, drivers unseeing behind steamed-up windscreens, passengers staring at their phones, it would be easy.

OK, so I'd be wanted for two deaths instead of one, but what was the difference?

I had one last meeting with Mike, a surreal affair that began cordially enough for me to experience the illusion of mixed feelings, as if we were partners winding down a business about which we'd once been equally passionate.

"What about Fi?" I said. "You said you were going to take her away, but she hasn't said anything about it to me yet."

"All in hand," he said. "I'll take her from Wednesday afternoon to Friday evening. As soon as the money lands, early Friday afternoon at the latest, Wendy will deliver your bits and pieces to the flat. Then you can skedaddle."

For once his cavalier language was soothing. "Bits and pieces," not illegal passport and blackmail materials he'd dangled over me like a noose for three months; "skedaddle," not flee for my life. Presumably, he and Wendy would be skedaddling off to Dubai on Friday night to cash in their winnings, buckling themselves into their seats at Heathrow as Fi arrived to find strangers living in her home.

"Where are you taking her?"

"Let me check the kitty," he said, "see what we can afford."

The kitty I had supplied.

I'd already begun a fund of my own and had cashed in my last remaining investment. Between now and my last day, I would withdraw every last penny from my individual account, minus the portion to be debited to the joint account at the end of the month. The joint account I wouldn't touch—clearly no noble act, given what I *would* be taking, but still, a gesture, however minuscule.

"So, on the Thursday," Mike said, "you're all booked for taking the day off work and getting the place cleared?"

"Yes, but we should expect Fi to get messages from neighbors that something's going on. I'm not going to be able to empty a huge house without being noticed."

"Good point. Tell any nosy neighbors you're redecorating as a surprise for her and if they speak to her they should keep schtum. Will that work?"

Yes, that would work. Those on the street who knew about the separation would know we were cordial. They would also know I was the guilty party—it wasn't so extraordinary a leap for me to try a grand, symbolic gesture to win her back. "What if Fi can't take days off at such short notice? And so soon after Christmas?"

"Then I'll persuade her to pull a sickie. Shouldn't be a problem."

I stiffened. He was offensively confident of his powers of persuasion, offensively confident that he could take my house from me and, at the very moment that he took it, distract my wife by checking her into a hotel and fucking her.

"Oh, Bram," he said, sensing my dip in mood and taking pleasure in lowering it further. "Who would have thought you'd end up as much of a loser as your father?"

Any illusions of camaraderie vanished at a stroke and I grabbed him by the collar, my knuckles pressing into his throat. Had I been the stronger I would have taken his head in my hands and smashed it into the wall. But I was not and he held me at arm's length like a weakling until I shook myself off and staggered back. "Why did you deliver that list to the house?" I hissed.

"What? It was addressed to you, wasn't it?"

"Did you think Fi doesn't know? Of course she knows—she knows everything about me."

"Not everything, Bram. Not the assault conviction, eh? And not *us*. At least I hope not." He chuckled, genuinely amused. He was venal, completely and utterly immoral. Almost as horrific as what he was doing was the knowledge that none of it, not a single penny from the house, not a single moment with Fi, was personal.

I could have been anyone.

"FI'S STORY" > 02:38:27

New year, new level with Toby. He was taking me to a smart hotel in Winchester for a few days. I won't use the term "romantic getaway," not now. I realize the horse has bolted in terms of any credibility I may have as a judge of character. Can I just say that it was by no means a foregone conclusion that I should go? I did waver: our regular Saturday nights were one thing, but two nights away from home was another. I even chose Polly as my adviser, subconsciously expecting her to discourage me.

"Go," she said. "What's the big deal?"

"You've changed your tune," I said.

"It's a holiday! If I were you, I would use it."

"Use it?"

"Yes. To dig for the truth. Look in his wallet, check his phone."

"What for, Polly?"

"For photos of his wife, Fi."

I groaned. "Maybe I could wear a wire as well?"

"It's a no-lose situation. If you find out he's not married, great. If you find out he is—and I mean living with her at the same time, not bird's nesting or some other trendy setup—well, it's better to know."

"Perhaps you should go in my place." I laughed.

She reminded me of that later. "Bram could never have done what he did with you there in the house all the time," she said. "He used the custody arrangements against you."

"Hindsight is twenty-twenty," I said.

Was I falling in love with Toby? I don't think so, no. Oh, I don't know. Maybe a little, during that trip away. But what does it matter? Other than talking to you, I've done my best not to think about him.

As for work, the timing was perfect in that a presentation I'd been working on with Clara was about to go to our design agency, with feedback due the following week, creating a natural break for me.

"I'll need to sort out cover for the boys," I told Toby. "Otherwise I won't be able to do it."

"Your ex'll step in, won't he? I take it he's moved on from his initial disapproval of us."

"You could say that."

If Bram couldn't, I knew one of the grandmothers or neighbors would help, but he agreed without question, happy to prioritize family over work and handle every detail of their care. Even so, I lined Alison up for contingency.

"You didn't tell me how it went at Christmas," she said when I popped in for a coffee. "With Bram."

"It was good. To be honest, I'm still trying to forget how good."

"I see. But nothing's changed?"

I paused, admiring the polished stone of her breakfast bar, the vintage roses arranged in the flared vase I'd chosen from our recycled ceramics line a few years ago.

She gave a rueful sigh, forked fingers through her blond hair, like mine highlighted to deny the gray. "I'm not saying I held out hope, but, you know, when you arrived at Kirsty's together after the carol concert . . ."

"I know. It felt like old times." I looked up. "But no, nothing's changed. It's too late."

We lapsed into silence then, almost in tribute.

You know, speaking of falling in love, it's almost as difficult to say when you've fallen *out* of it, isn't it? I feel very strongly that just because you do, it doesn't give you the right to deny the love existed.

I may be many things, but I'm not a revisionist.

#VictimFi

@DYeagernews So heartfelt, so true. Starting to wish they might get back together . . . #Bram&Fi
@crime_addict@DYeagernews Are you kidding me? You're as bad as she is!

BRAM, Word document

The solicitor e-mailed to say that contracts had been exchanged. The vendors' ten percent deposit—two hundred thousand pounds, a sum that the medication helped me visualize in Pokédollars—had been received and the final statement sent out to their solicitor. Completion was confirmed for Friday, the thirteenth of January (it was far, far too late to note the unluckiness of the date), the balance—minus mortgage settlement, estate agency fees, legal fees and other reimbursements—expected to land by one p.m. It would be close to one point six million pounds.

Rav met the Vaughans at the house on Saturday, the seventh, for a last check of fixtures and fittings, but I elected not to be there, taking the boys straight from their swimming lesson to PizzaExpress for lunch.

"It's not real" was my new mantra.

The next day, my final Sunday morning at the house, Sophie Reece came to the front gate as I was letting the boys back into the house after a bike ride in the park.

"Everything all right?" I said, approaching.

"Yes, fine. Except I almost called the police yesterday!"

Why the fuck would you do that? "Why?"

"There were some people standing right in your front window and I knew you were out at swimming. They looked innocent enough, but burglars are very sophisticated now, aren't they? Carrying tools as if they're on a plumbing job, pretending to measure up for curtains, that kind of thing."

I smiled at her. "That must have been my friend Rav. He runs a decorating business. He's doing some work for me next week, so you might see some of his team then as well. He was here with some other clients, talking them through his plans."

"Ah, that makes sense. Just as well I left it, then. They say you can't be too careful, but actually you can, can't you? He's very well-dressed for a decorator," she added.

"Yes, isn't he?" Decades of sales work had taught me that there was no more efficient way of shutting down an unwanted line of inquiry than to agree. "He's more of a creative director—he doesn't get his own hands dirty. By the way, I wanted it to be a surprise for Fi, so if you don't mind . . . ?"

She did that wide-eyed thing women do when a secret is spilled, breathed the little "Ooh!" "Of course. I haven't bumped into her for ages. You know how it is."

"Everyone's so busy," I agreed.

All that remained was to book the storage space and removals service and pack up our lifelong possessions without the other members of my family, or my colleagues, knowing anything about it.

Though I did my best to be discreet, Neil overheard me taking a call and hovered by my desk, waiting for me to finish. "What's this? You're not moving house, are you?"

"No, no, just helping my mum out. She's putting some stuff in storage."

Might the police interview him, I wondered, and discover there'd been no such arrangement? It didn't matter. He could tell them what he'd heard verbatim; I'd be long gone.

"Might as well bin it," he said. "I know that sounds harsh, but apparently the vast majority of people who put stuff into storage never bother getting it out again. Surprised she doesn't donate it to charity, a good Christian woman like her."

"It's just knickknacks," I said vaguely. "No one would want it."

"Is that why you're taking Thursday and Friday as holiday?"

"Partly."

He narrowed his gaze. "Nothing wrong, is there? I mean healthwise."

"No, she's fine. Other than the delusions of eternal life, of course."

"Not her, you mug, *you*. And I don't mean this mystery virus."

What he did mean was the booze, I supposed. The loose jowls and bloodshot eyes, the afternoon beer breath. "No, I'm much better now," I said.

He was keeping an eye on me—that much was clear—and not only as a revenue-protecting sales director, but as a mate. The fact that I was going to let him down on both counts was somehow worse for knowing that he would bear no malice. He might even find a way to grant me pardon.

45

It's one of the well-known ironies of parenting, isn't it, that to arrange time away alone with someone who isn't your spouse is a thousand times simpler than with the one who is. In the old days, a trip with Bram spanning three school days would have called for Churchillian cunning and an army of helpers, but now he was my ex all I had to do was issue a five-minute briefing and I was free as a bird.

On the Wednesday morning, after school drop-off, I popped into the flat to retrieve a pair of boots I'd left there at the weekend and needed for Winchester, assuming, correctly, that Bram would already have departed for work. Given the strict rules regarding access to Trinity Avenue on an "off" day, there were laughably few, if any, for Baby Deco. Why would we want to go there unless ejected from the house? That had been the original thinking, and yet that tiny studio flat had, in its own way, become a home.

Letting myself in, I was struck immediately by the smell of cigarettes. Bram was still smoking, clearly, and must be going to some lengths to air the place each time he left, since I never noticed the smell on my Friday arrivals. The bathroom door was open, water pooled on the tiled floor from his shower, and worn clothes scattered on the floor by the unmade bed. On the nearby table lay a green and white paper bag from the pharmacy on the Parade.

I shouldn't have looked inside—you don't have to tell me that; it was both an invasion of privacy and an act of hypocrisy—but I did. In it were half a dozen identical boxes of prescription medication, and I slipped one out to take a closer look. I didn't recognize the name of the medication—sertraline—that Bram was being directed to take in a daily fifty-milligram dose, and of course by the time I'd reached for my phone I'd convinced myself that he was gravely unwell. The lies he'd been telling, his excessive anguish when confronted: Had he been protecting me all along from something far, far worse than fecklessness?

And that remark I'd made at the concert about him acting like he was terminally ill! How could I have been so callous?

I Googled "sertraline," thinking that if I was right I would cancel this break with Toby and wait for Bram to arrive, as planned, to pick up the boys; we'd talk through how we were going to manage the situation, get through this together.

The search results were up: it was an SSRI, an antidepressant used to treat anxiety and panic.

I sat on the bed for a moment, immobile. Anxiety and panic caused by what? My having left him? I have to say the thought provoked feelings of sadness rather than guilt; after all, he'd brought his losses on himself, as I'd rather cruelly emphasized on Christmas night, and he'd been lucky to be forgiven that fracas with Toby. But he was still a human being and we all made mistakes; we all hurt.

I decided there was no need to cancel the break, but I'd talk to him on Saturday, as scheduled. I'd subtly discover if there was anything I could do to help lessen his load.

By now, I was running late. I gathered up my things and headed for the door, abandoning the pharmacist's bag on the table where I'd found it.

BRAM, Word document

On the last Wednesday, the day before I cleared the house and—unbeknownst to my colleagues—my final day in the office, I had a call on my mobile from an unknown number.

"May I speak to Mr. Abraham Lawson, please?"

It was midmorning and I was at my desk. I wasn't hungover, at least not notably, and my brain was sparking normally. *Abraham,* I thought. No one used my full name, so this meant someone in an official capacity. The police—it had to be. Female, so not the detective who'd come to see me at the flat—

"Hello?"

Speak, Bram!

"I'm afraid he's not in this week," I said in my own voice, casual, courteous. "Who's calling?"

"This is Detective Sergeant Joanne McGowan of the Serious Collisions Investigation Unit at Catford. So this isn't his mobile I'm calling?"

"It's his work mobile," I said. "Company policy is to hand in your phone when you go on holiday." A lie—what company in 2017 would require that? "I can leave a message with his team, though, and have someone call you if they have another contact number for him."

Don't give her the landline at the house: Fi might still be there!

"We have his landline number, but there's no reply at the moment."

"I guess they're not at home," I said with a polite sympathy that belied the succession of terror and relief her last remarks had caused. "Maybe his wife's mobile?"

Quick thinking, Bram. If she believes Fi's away with you, she might delay any plans to phone her separately.

"Thank you. We have her number already. How long is Mr. Lawson away for?"

"I think someone said he's back on Monday."

"Is he in the UK, do you know?"

"Er, Scotland, maybe?" Best not to give a destination that might send them checking the airlines' passenger manifests.

"Thank you." She hung up.

I remained calm. They knew nothing, I reasoned. At most, they'd discovered the car and had a few additional questions for me—few enough to ask over the phone. Even in the worst-case scenario, they'd give me till Monday. They'd wait till I was back from the Outer Hebrides before clapping handcuffs on my weather-beaten wrists.

"Why are you putting everything into these boxes?" Harry asked on Thursday morning when he and Leo came downstairs for breakfast. I'd got them up early so I could prepare them for the arrangements ahead.

"I'm about to tell you, but only if you can keep it a secret."

They gave their word.

"I'm arranging a surprise for Mummy."

If I'd anticipated that this would be one of the most unbearable moments, when I tricked my two sacrificial lambs into expressing delight at the prospect of slaughter, I needn't have worried.

"She doesn't like surprises," Leo said, pouring his Shreddies into a bowl. "I wouldn't do it, Dad."

"She hates them," Harry agreed. "Unless it's when we've made her a cake with caramel icing."

"She'll like this one. I'm going to have the house redecorated."

"When?"

"Today and tomorrow. So you're going to stay at Grandma Tina's for two nights and—this is the best bit—you get to have tomorrow off school!"

Now they were pleased, or at least Leo was.

"Did Mrs. Carver say it's allowed?" Harry asked. For one so raucous, he was oddly keen on permissions.

"Yes. I spoke to Mrs. Bottomley and everyone is fine about it. So when I pick you up from school today, we'll go straight to Grandma's on the bus. We'll call Mummy on the way, but remember, don't say anything about the surprise. Or about having Friday off school. I don't want her to worry."

I had booked my mother a week or so ago to (unwittingly) abet me these next days. Wholly approving of my decorating scheme, she'd offered to take care of the school run on Friday so the boys wouldn't have to miss their lessons, but I'd fobbed her off. I couldn't risk her dropping by the house and finding strangers moving in. Not with the boys. That was not how they should find out.

After breakfast, I suggested Leo and Harry pick their three favorite things to take to Grandma's. "I'll bring them after school with your pajamas and a change of clothes for your day off tomorrow."

Though it was an irregular request, they rose to the challenge, not noticing their father watching dismally from the door.

"I need more than three," Leo complained.

"I've only got two," Harry said.

So I said Leo could have Harry's extra one. Harry protested that he'd use his selections after all. Leo called him a selfish pig and I brought a halt to the argument by proposing we leave for school immediately and call in to the bakery on the Parade for chocolate croissants.

Just ignore how bleak and depraved and heartbroken you feel, I urged myself.

It's not real.

A passionate devotee of decluttering, Fi had purged the house regularly over the years, but it was still a gargantuan job to pack and remove our possessions. Even with two professionals to help me, it took all day to relocate the furniture to the short-term storage unit in Beckenham and to box up and deliver to the flat all our clothes and personal items.

It was raining, of course, as if the gods were sobbing in protest at my wickedness—either that or they were helping keep the neighbors at bay. Very few came out into the downpour to ask what was happening, and those who did swallowed my cover story with half an eye on their own dry hallways.

Only an early-afternoon encounter with Alison taxed my nerves to any dangerous extent.

"Not at work?" I asked her, concealing my horror at her approach. Rocky was by her side—she'd just been walking him, judging by her rain-slicked mac and wellies—and rather than tug her toward her door he settled obediently between us as if for the long haul.

"I only work Monday to Wednesday, remember?" she said. "Or at least I only get *paid* for those days."

Of course. She sometimes picked up the boys for us on Thursdays, Fi returning the favor on Fridays.

"What on earth's going on here, then? You skipping town or something?"

I gulped. "I'm doing some decorating."

"Decorating? Does Fi know about this?"

I petted Rocky's damp ears, praying I didn't look half as stricken as I felt. "No, that's the point. I'm surprising her."

"Looks like a serious job," Alison said, peering past her dripping hood to my removals van. "Why do you need to move stuff out?"

"Because I'm doing the whole thing at once—we can't move it from room to room."

"Can't you just pile it in the middle of the rooms and cover it with sheets? That's what we always do. Where's it going?"

"Just to a storage unit on the other side of Beckenham."

"Wow. This is quite an operation. When's Fi back from Winchester?"

"Late tomorrow night, but not back at the house until Saturday morning. It's a very tight schedule."

She narrowed her eyes, twisted her mouth to one side. "It's not tight, Bram—it's impossible. Something on this scale takes *weeks*. How have you chosen the colors without her input? You've gone for rich blues and greens, I hope. None of those greigy mushrooms."

Was it normal to keep answering questions like this or would it be more natural to call her out on the interrogation? "Alison, you'd have been great in the gestapo—has anyone ever told you that?"

She laughed. "Sorry. I'd like to think Fi would be on Rog's case if he pulled a stunt like this."

If she had any idea what a stunt it was!

"She's been wanting to redecorate for ages," I said, "as I'm sure you know, and an old colleague of mine is starting a new business, giving me a great rate. He's inside now with his team, cracking on."

At this show of enthusiasm, a trace of indulgence crossed her face and she put a damp-gloved hand on my arm. She thought I was trying to win Fi back, had heard about Christmas, perhaps. "Bram, I hope this isn't out of line, but you do know she's away with someone else right now."

"I do. M—" I caught myself. "Toby. Have you met him?"

"Not yet. I think she's waiting . . ." Tact prevented her from continuing, but she needn't have worried. *Waiting till she's sure it's serious,* I thought.

That would be never, then, because after tomorrow Casanova would be gone and the pain of a breakup would be lost in the horror of dealing with the loss of her home, the mystery of her children's father's disappearance.

"I'll let you get out of the rain. You want me to pick up Leo and Harry for you later?" Alison offered.

"Thanks, but I'm good. I'm taking them to my mum's, actually—it's a bit chaotic here." I didn't mention that I was keeping them off school the next day. The mothers of Trinity Avenue viewed a missed day of primary school as damaging to their offspring's Oxbridge prospects.

"Well, good luck. I hope it works," Alison said.

I had the (perhaps mistaken) sense that by "it" she meant something more than my decorating project, and I indulged in a momentary fantasy of how things might have developed in a parallel narrative. There were people like her and my mother, and maybe Fi's parents too, who would have supported a reunion—or at least not actively opposed it. If I'd kept my head down and waited it out, if I'd shown Fi I could change . . .

Soaked to the bone by then, I went back inside and arranged for the last contents of her bedroom to be boxed and removed.

"FI'S STORY" > 02:44:36

It was a nicely traditional dirty weekend in Winchester, albeit midweek: sex and room service, punctuated by visits to the cathedral and strolls through the old streets with half a mind on Jane Austen and half on each other.

I was tempted to tell Toby about the prescription pills, but I reminded myself that Bram was entitled to his privacy and, in any case, this of all times was not the right one to share with Toby my concerns about the mental health of the man who'd attacked him.

When I spoke to the boys on the Thursday after school, I thought nothing of it when Harry said he had a secret.

"A good secret or a bad secret?"

"A good secret. A surprise."

"A surprise for Leo?"

"No, not Leo, you!"

"I'm intrigued."

"Daddy's—"

"Don't tell me!" I said, laughing, but in any case Bram had cut him off at the other end.

Of course he had. In my naivety, I assumed it was some sort of "welcome home" cake—Bram was surprisingly willing to supervise baking—probably with blue icing and Maltesers or, failing that, a portrait one of them had done of me at school, all sausage fingers and ears down by my shoulders.

I imagined the swearing of secrecy as a lesson in trust, not an abuse of it.

BRAM, Word document

Even for those who aren't preparing to abandon their family to the wolves, there is a particular bittersweetness to the act of picking up your children from school.

I discussed it with Fi once and she said that not only did she know the feeling but she felt it even more keenly than I did (she always said this: it wasn't that mothers had the monopoly on parental devotion—

they just *felt it more keenly*). She said it's because small children are so unconditionally happy to see you at the school gate and yet you know even as they're bowling into your arms and nuzzling for treats that one day—maybe not this year or the next but definitely sooner than you'd like—they will be embarrassed to see you there, or angry, or even fearful, because why would you come when you've been expressly forbidden unless there's bad news of one form or another?

She said at least it wasn't an abrupt or vicious blow, but an incremental detachment: every day they need you less until the moment when they don't need you at all.

If only Mike had come along later rather than sooner. If only he'd come when my sons no longer needed me, when saying good-bye was not the worst crime of all.

On our way to my mother's on the bus, I took a photo of them together and then a second with me between them. Though I'd be destroying the SIM, I planned to keep my phone for music and the small depository of images of the boys. As I took the picture, cajoling Harry into the smile that Leo delivered obediently, I was aware of a young woman watching us from across the aisle, thinking, no doubt, "I hope *I* get a husband like that, a great father."

Be careful what you wish for, sweetheart.

I couldn't stay at Mum's long, because I was meeting cleaners at the house at six p.m. Believing they would see me soon enough, the boys tried to dash off, groaning when I reeled them back for a last hug.

"Come here. Before you go in, I want to tell you something."

They waited, only half listening.

"I love you and I will forever. Never forget that, OK?"

Then I kissed them in turn.

They were puzzled, distracted, though the word "forget" sparked an association in Harry, at least: "Dad, I forgot to bring my spelling book! I have to learn two from my list every night *without fail.*"

I kissed him again. "I'll find it for you and you can catch up at the weekend, OK? And if you can't, just say you're sorry and tell Mrs. Carver it's my fault."

I could tell he wouldn't. He wouldn't want to get me in trouble.

"Can we go?" Leo said, hearing his grandmother open the biscuit tin in the kitchen. And then she was there in the hallway with us, the open tin angled toward them, and they turned from me and I mouthed my last good-bye and closed the door and that was it.

The last time I saw my sons.

As I traveled back to Alder Rise, my brain wouldn't allow itself to process what this actually was. To do so would be to render myself incapable of fulfilling the rest of the duties before me.

I had planned to sleep at the flat, but I stayed in the empty house, a sleeping bag spread out on the carpet in Leo's room. I felt an irrational compulsion to guard it from intruders, though of course none were coming—at least not until the next day, when the legally sanctioned ones would be there. (They would meet their own share of agony these next days and weeks, I suspected. I understood about ripple effects, even if I had no emotion to spare for the outer rings of my own.)

There was no satisfaction to be had from touring the denuded rooms, no avoidance of the reality of my asset stripping. If anything, staying overnight was a punishment; maybe I hoped I'd die of a broken heart in that sleeping bag on the floor.

Enough wallowing.

At ten, I phoned my mother to check that the boys were in bed.

"You've just missed them," she said. "I let them stay up late because they don't have to get up for school in the morning, but they're asleep now."

"Thank you. Thank you for everything, Mum. I'm sorry if I haven't said that as much as I should."

"Don't be silly," she said.

I hung up thinking there was a comfort in those final words of hers.

How do you say good-bye to your own mother?

The answer is, you don't. Because it's kinder that way.

46

The last time I saw Bram, with my own eyes? It would have been on the last Sunday, Sunday the eighth, the noon handover at Trinity Avenue. Was there anything different about him, anything about his manner that augured betrayal—betrayal on a whole new level?

There wasn't. I'm sorry. He briefed me on the boys, asked how I was. I noted, and appreciated, the absence of any mention of Toby. Even now, when I try to make something significant of a small detail, I fail. It was raining and he had no umbrella? That could be a metaphor, I suppose.

He was just Bram, or at least the creature Bram had become. When he left, I had the same feeling I'd had every Sunday and would no doubt have continued to have had the sky not fallen in: disbelief that he could have done this to us, sadness that he wasn't mine anymore.

A weekly interlude of irrational sentiment, I admit. But I wouldn't be human if that didn't make me a bit sad.

BRAM, Word document

Fi, I'd said good-bye to in my own way—that is, without her knowing. (Very defining, you're probably thinking.) It was Tuesday the tenth and I knew from the diary app that she was doing what she usually did on a Tuesday, which was arriving at Alder Rise Station on the eighteen thirty from Victoria and going straight home, where her mother would have fed the boys and umpired their latest battle. She emerged from the tunnel on the edge of the commuter swarm, scratching the skin by her right eyebrow, adjusting the shoulder strap of her laptop bag. She didn't notice me there, didn't sense me following her down the Parade (she didn't even *glance* at the Two Brewers). On the corner of Trinity Avenue, she paused and turned her head. It wasn't an image that was "special": there was no breeze to flare her clothing, no seren-dipitously placed light to catch her in memorable silhouette. Nothing about her expression or posture betrayed the emotions she'd confessed to feeling on approaching the house after work: general excitement to see the boys, specific dread that they might be fighting, that her day's labors were about to begin just as she needed to rest.

She was exactly as she might have been any day at about that time. A woman with half her life behind her and the other half ahead.

Which, I know, was an unfair place for me to leave her.

Before dawn, I returned to the flat for the last time. I placed the keys on the kitchen worktop, along with details of the storage facility and Harry's spelling book, unearthed at the eleventh hour from one of the boxes.

No note, no letter.

All set, I texted Mike.

As usual, he responded instantaneously:

As soon as I get confirmation the funds have landed,
Wendy will deliver new pp etc to the flat. Cheers.

Cheers? Twat. I deleted the message, pocketed the pay-as-you-go phone, then picked up my prepacked bag and left. I took a minicab from the station to Battersea, where I had the driver wait while I posted through Challoner's letter box a package containing two sets of Trinity Avenue house keys (mine and the spares Kirsty kept for us, but not Fi's or her mother's—I hadn't been able to engineer that). I told the driver to take me on to Victoria Station and messaged my mother en route to ask her to kiss the boys good morning for me and wish them a lovely day. I'd already briefed her that she should phone Fi directly to liaise about their return on Saturday morning.

In the street outside Victoria, I removed the SIM from my official mobile phone and slipped it into a drain, then repocketed the phone. Careful to leave the pay-as-you-go turned on in order to receive the many further messages Mike would be sure to send me throughout the day, I turned off the ringer and dropped it into the nearest bin.

Inside the station, I found a cashpoint and emptied my bank account of its last funds before buying a ticket with cash and boarding the next Gatwick Express train. It was seven thirty a.m., the incoming throngs already thickening. I guessed Fi wouldn't be awake yet, even if the charlatan in bed with her was already checking his phone, eager for confirmation of his remarkable change in fortunes.

"FI'S STORY" > 02:46:45

"You keep looking at your phone," I said to Toby, over the hotel breakfast table. "Expecting a call?"

"Just an e-mail confirming something for tonight."

He had an important function that evening, an advance gathering of the commission before an announcement the following week of the initial findings of their report. Transport executives from Singapore, Stockholm and Milan would be present, as well as government officials. Though he would need to leave Winchester after lunch, he'd arranged for me to keep the room and return to London as late as I pleased.

God, what a patsy I was. I remember very clearly sitting there at the breakfast table when he'd gone to the bathroom, staring at the phone lying facedown next to his cappuccino and consciously disregarding memories of Polly's urging me to "dig for the truth."

That's the problem with actively disassociating yourself from life's cynics: you deprive yourself of their good advice.

BRAM, Word document

At Gatwick, I bought a return ticket to Geneva with cash. (My thinking: a return is less suspicious than a single. On the other hand, is cash more suspicious than a credit card? Then: neither is suspicious. Millions of people fly out of here every week, and airport staff have seen every last quirk of traveler behavior. *Get a grip, Bram.*)

I used the self-check-in, got through passport control without any trouble and bought a mix of Swiss currency and euros with the cash I'd amassed.

With no time left for self-doubt, I proceeded to the gate.

"FI'S STORY" > 02:47:37

As it turned out, it was I who got the pesky work call, when we were back in our room after breakfast gathering a few things for a guided tour of Winchester College.

"Where's the Spirals brief for the agency?" Clara asked, her degree of panic suggesting it might have been building for some time.

I frowned. "Didn't you send it to them yesterday?"

"No, they've asked for a briefing in person and we scheduled it for this afternoon. But it's not on the server. I've had IT down to look and they can't find it anywhere."

Calling me was her last resort, plainly. I saw exactly what was going on here. In my absence, she'd sensed an opportunity to present the work as her own. (Yes, irritating, but if you're good at your job, you have no need to feel threatened.)

"Don't worry—it's on my hard drive at home. I'll see if I can get it sent over to you."

"We really need it this morning, Fi. Early afternoon at the latest. The meeting's at three."

"Three?" A crazy slot to have agreed on for a briefing, last thing on a Friday. I did not point out that she was a little slow in noticing the file's absence—not to mention in rehearsing her presentation. I hadn't worked on it since Tuesday evening.

"Let me call you back. Meanwhile, have another hunt. I might have used a different file name."

"What is it?" Toby asked, glancing up from his own phone.

"Just a presentation I must have forgotten to put on the work server before I left. It's on my laptop at home. Clara's only just noticed."

"Can't she wait till Monday?"

"No, she's presenting it today. Not to worry—my neighbor Kirsty's got keys to the house, so I'll ask her to find it. I'm just trying to think where I left it. Maybe in my bedroom . . ."

"Why not ask Bram?" Toby suggested. "Didn't you say he was working from home today so he can pick the boys up from school?"

"That's true." I dismissed uneasy thoughts of the last time he'd been granted access to my bedroom, and I dialed his number. "How weird. It's saying his phone's out of service."

"Really? That's not very helpful, is it?"

"Let me try Kirsty. Otherwise I might have to head back a bit early."

Toby watched with dismay as I scrolled for Kirsty's number. It was flattering that he wanted me to stay, to eke out our time together. You know, there were many things I was enjoying about the sapling relationship, but the one that sprang to mind that morning was control. Balance. *I* was the one cutting short the break. *I* was the one deciding what came first—in this case my duty to my colleagues. And, yes, it *did* cross my mind that I was also the one who had strayed, but it wasn't as if we had sworn exclusivity, was it? The point is, it was all in glorious contrast to the uncertainty I'd felt during those last couple of years with Bram. It made me optimistic for our future, hopeful that we *would* be exclusive.

"Kirsty? Hi, darling. Are you at home, by any chance? Could you do me a favor and use the spare key to pop into my place? What I need is—oh, really? OK. No problem. I'll see you later." I turned to Toby, frowning. "She says Bram asked her for the keys earlier in the week. He'd lost his, apparently. He didn't tell *me* that—surprise, surprise."

"Fool," Toby said, with feeling.

"I know. This is the kind of thing that drives me nuts. I know it was him who lost those car keys." Remembering the antidepressants, I curtailed further criticism; perhaps the medication had impaired Bram's memory. (Well, if he was at home that afternoon when I returned, it would be the perfect opportunity to broach the subject.) "I'm sorry, but it looks like I'll have to shoot off early and save the day."

"Are you sure your laptop's not at the flat?" Toby said.

"What difference does it make?" I'd noticed that since the assault he often asked about the bird's nest logistics, presumably wary of bumping into the Neanderthal ex again. "There's no need for you to come with me. If you don't fancy the college tour, we've got that table booked for lunch—you could still go. Then head back in time for your drinks thing."

He surprised me then by crossing the room to kiss me. "At least stay a bit longer," he murmured, his fingers in my hair.

"It's already ten o'clock. I really can't."

"Come on. What's twenty minutes?"

When I finally made my exit, the taxi waiting to take me to the station, he kissed me again with such feeling the cabbie averted his eyes.

"How long does the train take?" he asked, finally releasing me.

"I'll change at Clapham Junction for Alder Rise, so I should be able to get the file to Clara by one-ish, which will be in good time for the briefing. I suppose I should be grateful she's only spotted it now and not earlier. It's been a great few days, Toby. Really. Let's do it again."

"Definitely," he agreed. "Text me that you're home safely."

Really, it was sweet how dejected he looked.

The gods were on my side and my train connections were smooth, getting me into Alder Rise Station before twelve thirty p.m. I texted Bram to say I was coming, but the message was undelivered, thanks

330 · LOUISE CANDLISH

to the out-of-service line. Not ideal if the school needed to get hold of him, but it didn't matter—I was back in Alder Rise, back in charge.

I turned into Trinity Avenue with a smile on my face. The sunlight was unusually rich and golden for January. Lovely, truly lovely. Focusing on the van about halfway down, I thought, *I must be mistaken, but it looks exactly as if someone is moving into my house.*

#VictimFi

@Leah_Walker Here we go . . .

47

Friday, January 13, 2017

LONDON, 7 P.M.

They are no longer in her house (correction: the Vaughans' house), but in Merle's. They've finally spoken to Graham Jenson and informed him of the situation, though Fi became too distressed to reason effectively and when Merle put the call on speakerphone, her accusations about identity theft and fraud sounded wild even to Fi.

"I've been through this with the buyers' solicitor and with Mrs. Lawson herself," Jenson said, "and I've explained there has been no error on our part. Beyond that, I cannot discuss this. I have to respect client confidentiality." He has, however, agreed to a meeting on Monday morning.

They've spent the last hour ringing the hospitals of South London and beyond and drawn blank after blank, which is, they repeat to each other, good news, good news.

And now they've come into the living room at the front with large drinks. It's a bit of a mess, as Merle's place usually is. There are pine needles by the skirting board, the loose ends of Christmas that never got vacuumed away, and Fi stoops to collect one, pressing its point into the flesh of her index finger. It feels crucial that she see a bubble of her own blood, just one drop, to prove that she is still alive and this is really happening, but the needle bends before it can puncture the skin.

She has not been in this room since the meeting with the community officer back in September, when those forensic pens were handed out (she should have used hers to mark the house itself). They thought they were being so clever, the ladies of Trinity Avenue, to inform themselves about cybercrime, to pledge to protect one another from invaders and scammers. It hadn't occurred to them that the enemy might be within. "You don't seem very interested in this," she'd complained to Bram when he'd dismissed poor Carys's suffering. "Irony" wasn't a strong enough word.

"Should I get Alison to come over? Rog can stay with the kids," Merle suggests, but Fi thinks not. She doesn't have the energy to explain her catastrophe an additional time, or to hear poor Alison's apologies—for she has confessed to Merle she saw Bram moving their things out yesterday, that he spun her the same redecorating line he did Tina. He's taken them all in, every last one of them.

It is hard enough talking to Tina again, which she does next. "So, you agreed with Bram you'd keep Leo and Harry tonight as well?" This is helpful. She's in no condition to see the boys, must sustain herself on the hope that their sleep tonight is innocent. "Things are a bit behind schedule here."

"But you're pleased?" Tina says eagerly. "Is Bram there with you?"

"I'm not sure where he is right now," Fi says truthfully.

"When are we coming home?" Leo asks, when she has a word with him.

"Probably tomorrow."

"Will we be back in time for swimming?"

"No, I think it's been canceled. You and Harry just have a nice, lazy morning."

Already she is thinking, *One lie at a time.*

"I feel really terrible," she tells Merle. "The vodka isn't working."

"You're exhausted," Merle says, and she too looks bone-tired. "It's been like a hundred days rolled into one. Sleep will help."

Fi chuckles mirthlessly. "There's no way I'm going to be able to sleep tonight."

"I can help you there." Merle has a few sleeping pills, she remembers, and fetches them from upstairs. "They're from last year when I had a bout of insomnia, but they're still in date. You might need them over the next few weeks. Take them, just in case."

"Thank you."

They become aware of squealing brakes in the street, of a car parking with much noisy revving and a door crunching shut.

"What's that shouting?" Merle goes to the window. "I think it might be someone at your place, Fi. It'd bloody better be him."

It won't be, Fi thinks, but she shows willing and follows Merle to the front door. She's glad she does: swallowing the night air, feeling the sharp chill penetrate her lungs, she gets the bodily pain she's been craving. It's dark in the street, a night frost forming on the car windscreens, and as they peer out to the left, across the Hamiltons' front garden toward hers (correction: the Vaughans'), a male voice carries through the stillness, brittle and hostile:

"Where the fuck is Bram? I'm not leaving without an answer!"

David Vaughan steps into view on the front path. "Now who are you, exactly?"

"Never mind that—I need to speak to him right now!"

"Join the queue," David says with a bitter laugh.

It takes a moment for Fi to recognize the second figure, the other voice. "It's Toby," she tells Merle, confused. "The guy I've been seeing.

We've been away together. I said I'd text when I got back—he must have been worried and come to see if I'm all right."

Unless she *did* text him, sent him an SOS during those befuddled hours in the house? It's possible: whole chunks are inaccessible to her. These have been both the heaviest hours of her life and the most slippery.

"I'll go and get him," Merle says. "You wait here in the warmth."

She hurries out into the cold, coatless, leaving Fi on the doorstep. "Hello, can I help? Bram isn't here, but Fi is, if you want to come in."

As Toby turns on his heel, David withdraws, his gratitude palpable even from this distance. He's done with today—that is clear.

When Toby comes striding into Merle's hallway, Fi falls against him like a collision. She doesn't care if it's wrong to show her need for his comfort, for some uncomplicated masculine strength.

"Toby, it's so awful, the worst possible thing! I've lost my house."

"We don't know that for sure, darling," Merle says, fingers patting Fi's upper arm.

"We *do* know. The Land Registry has transferred the title deeds. I've lost it."

"Where is he?" Toby growls and disentangles himself from her. He scopes the hallway, the succession of doors that lead from it, as if expecting to find Bram cowering in the shadows.

"He's vanished," Fi says. "The boys are fine, though—thank God. That's the main thing, isn't it?"

"Of course it is," Merle says soothingly. "No one's died. It's a mess—someone somewhere has made an epic cock-up—but we'll get it fixed. Would you like a drink, Toby? Vodka?"

"Thanks."

Merle delivers the drink, tops up Fi, and the two of them tell him what they know about the house sale: Bram's open house, the woman purporting to be Mrs. Lawson who has complained that the Vaughans' payment has not yet reached her, the erroneous transfer that Graham Jenson denies but that may end up giving Fi time to register her claim on the money, the scramble to mitigate the crisis that will resume after the weekend.

"So the money's not in any of your accounts?" Toby asks Fi.

"No, I checked straightaway. Not a penny. The solicitor won't disclose the details for the account he did use, but it's possible it was Bram's individual account. I don't have access to that."

"At least the mortgage and all the seller's fees were paid separately," Merle reminds her. "There've been no errors there, which is something."

Fi shudders. Insane though the suggestion is, this *could* be worse. She could have lost the house and been left with a huge debt.

"This is stating the obvious," Merle says, "but you don't think Bram could be at the flat? You know what they say about hiding in plain sight, and it's not like the police are bursting down doors at this stage. It was hard enough getting them to come here and take the preliminary report," she tells Toby.

"He's definitely not at the flat," Toby says. "I went there before I came here."

"You did?" Fi says, surprised.

"He might have been there but not answering," Merle suggests. There is something about her grave, gentle authority that is making Toby seem a little crude. Fi can tell that Merle is taken aback by his anger. She didn't know Fi had such a firebrand for a new partner.

"I got a neighbor to let me into the building," he says, "and I went up to try the door. There was no answer and the lights were out. He's definitely not there."

"I'll go over in a while," Fi says. "I might have to sleep there tonight."

Merle intervenes. "Fi, I really think you should stay here. You've had enough to contend with for one day. Alison's keeping Robbie and Daisy for a sleepover, so they won't be back till tomorrow. We'll be on our own. We can ring around the hospitals again in the morning, make a proper list for Monday, discuss how you're going to handle this with the boys. Then you can go to Tina's when you're calm and rested."

"Who's Tina?" Toby asks.

"Bram's mother."

"You think he might be there, Fi? Let's go!"

"No, he definitely isn't," Fi tells him. "She's convinced he's *here*." Talk of the boys focuses her. "I'll wait till the morning to see them— you're right, Merle. And I'll need to go on my own, Toby. No offense, but the boys don't know you and now isn't the time for them to meet new people. They'll need their family."

"Fi, when you do see them, I wouldn't say anything about Bram being missing," Merle says. "While we still don't know all the facts, you don't want to upset them."

"You know something we don't, Merle?" Toby says, his mistrust of her unconcealed.

"Of course not," Merle says evenly. "But he's their father. They'll be distressed to think something might have happened to him."

"I won't say anything to them," Fi promises. "Or Tina. But I think I *will* sleep at the flat tonight. Find some fresh clothes, see if Bram left any of our stuff there."

"Right." Toby is on his feet in a bid to take charge. Already he has the keys to his Toyota in his hand. "I'll drop you there."

Merle eyes his empty vodka glass.

"I've only had this one," he tells her. "I'll be fine to drive."

Merle tails them to the door. "Phone me if you need anything," she says to Fi. She squeezes her and then says a second time, with feeling, "Anything."

LYON, 8 P.M.

He goes straight from the station in Lyon to the first bar he sees and orders a beer. He's not the only traveler in the place and the mood is impersonal, but that's fine—he's not looking to make friends. The beer comes quickly, the bill with it. Retrieving his first euros from his wallet, he notices the folded sheet Mike posted through the door at Trinity Avenue and feels oddly comforted to have it in his possession.

He's aware that something has changed during the train journey, the passing from one realm into another. A shoot is pushing through him, but it is not looking for the light; it is looking for the darkest part of him. This bad shoot makes him feel calmer, which is ironic.

He needs an alternative adjective to "ironic," he thinks, a stronger, deeper one. What would Fi choose? "Twisted," maybe. No, not "twisted." "Destined." "*Doomed*."

He snaps shut the wallet, downs the beer and leaves.

48

There's no need to pity me, honestly. I don't want that. I'm not the worst punished by this—or the most bereft. Yes, I have lost my home and my children have lost contact with their father. We are suffering, but the bottom line is that another family is mourning a child: little Ellie Rutherford, who died in that car accident in Thornton Heath, an accident that Bram may or may not have been involved in.

The police certainly think he was. A week or so before he went missing, they found our car in a backstreet in Streatham. There were no signs of theft or misuse, no forensic matches with any of their joy-rider suspects, and so they returned their attention to the owners of the vehicle, specifically the one whose driving ban meant he had good reason to leave the scene of an accident, whether he was directly involved or not.

They'd interviewed him before—not that he'd thought to tell *me* that—and had a sense that he was withholding something, perhaps to do with the missing key, but the security footage at Alder Rise Station from the morning of September sixteenth clearly identified him among the waiting commuters on the platform and they put his name to one side. Other leads were more plausible. But now they talked to his employer's HR department about his attendance at the sales conference and were told he'd only disclosed his driving disqualification *after* that date. The very next working day, in fact: quite some coincidence. They decided to reinterview him as soon as he returned from "holiday," which he obviously never did. Then, about a week after he disappeared, they were sent an anonymous tip, a photo of our car on Silver Road, taken the same day as the collision, a dark-haired male visible at the wheel. Facial recognition technology confirmed a match for Bram.

What they suspect happened is that he ran the victims' car off the road in some sort of road rage incident, then secretly put our house on the market to fund his escape. The fact that he had been driving while disqualified only confirmed his bad character.

It shames me that while a family was grieving, I was more concerned that our insurance claim had been rejected, about the impact this would have on our finances. The parents of that little girl would swap a thousand new cars, a thousand million-pound houses, to get her back! As would I in their situation. In the end, establishing the facts about how Ellie died is the only thing worth pursuing, the only thing worth crying over.

Easier said than done, of course, when your own life is in tatters.

How much do the boys know? At this point, very little. I've told them Bram has gone to work overseas and that if anyone says differently, they should walk away and think about something else. They're still at Alder Rise Primary, but we're living at my parents' place in Kingston and the long commute isn't really sustainable. By the time this is aired, they will have moved schools. Everyone in Alder Rise will be talking about Bram then—and perhaps people in their new neighborhood too. Basically, a loss of privacy is the price I've paid for getting this story out there, for helping other innocent homeowners avoid falling victim to fraud on this scale.

I gave notice on the Baby Deco flat as soon as the contract allowed, and the landlord was very understanding about it. No, I've been asked by the police not to comment on what happened there the day after the house sale. Nothing will persuade me to say any more—Lord knows I've probably already revealed details the police would have preferred to keep confidential at this stage. I don't want to be charged with perverting the course of justice. But I also feel strongly that we have to trust them to investigate.

Your guess is as good as mine as to whether this will ever go to trial, if they ever find this other me—this second Fiona Lawson. Neither the estate agent nor the solicitor had a phone number for her, only for Bram, and the address and date of birth she gave were mine. We know she used my passport as her ID and that she and Bram attended a meeting together, posing as us. Both her appearance and signature were credible enough, evidently. No, it's hard to imagine she will come forward anytime soon and get herself slapped with some sort of conspiracy-to-commit-fraud charge. I mean, would you?

As for where the money is, that remains a tangle. Graham Jenson and his colleagues at Dixon Boyle still deny any misconduct, and they have e-mails and phone logs to prove that the details for the receiving account were supplied by Bram himself. The sale proceeds duly landed in a legitimate UK high street account in our joint names: so far, so simple (if you overlook the fact that I knew nothing about the opening of said account). But, within hours, the same sum was transferred offshore. Not so simple. There's talk of anonymous accounts in the Middle East and God knows where else—banking nations with no reciprocity agreement with the UK.

You know what upsets me the most about that? He didn't need to hide it offshore for tax evasion reasons—there's no tax owed to the government on this sale. It was purely to hide it from me.

Anyway, the police say they are hopeful of recovering *something* for me, but my solicitor is more guarded. She says the Serious Fraud Office have bigger fish to fry. Far bigger.

David and Lucy Vaughan are still in the house. It's legally theirs, after all. Everyone uses that term. They're the "legal" owners, as if we all agree that I remain the moral one, the spiritual one. They won't mind my telling you they've said that as soon as I am in a position to do so, I can buy it back for market rate, even if we all know I'll never be in a position to do that. With all of this going on, I've been lucky to keep hold of my job.

Toby? No, I'm not seeing him anymore, let alone planning to set up house together. I'm glad your listeners can't see me blushing, because it will come as no surprise to hear that I haven't laid eyes on him since the day of the theft. I guess I was less attractive to him once it became clear I'd lost my big house on Trinity Avenue.

What can I say? Gentlemen prefer homeowners!

Obviously, I'm making light of this. A coping mechanism, no doubt. I've already told you I was starting to trust him, to believe I could love him. All I know for sure is that we parted that Friday with him promising to phone me at the weekend, but there was never any call. His phone, like Bram's, has been out of service ever since. At least his vanishing is explicable in a way Bram's never will be—imagine if I'd had to make a missing-persons report on him as well! They'd think I was some sort of black widow.

"He's probably spending a bit of quality time with his wife," Polly said when I told her. "Have you tried putting his picture into Google to see what comes up?"

I had to admit I had no photo to try.

"He wouldn't let you take one, would he? Oh, Fi, how could you have missed all these obvious signs? You know what I think? I think the wife was pregnant and you were his maternity cover fling. And I bet he didn't work for any Department of Transport think tank. I bet he was a car salesman. No, a *traffic warden*."

At least she didn't say "I told you so," not in those exact words—though if she had, it would have been as good a line as any to end my story.

Because this *is* the end. There is nothing more.

#VictimFi

@deadheadmel No way, that's it?
@IngridF2015 @deadheadmel Like she says, it's still a live investigation.
@richieschambers @deadheadmel @IngridF2015 I think we're looking at a part deux, people.
@deadheadmel @IngridF2015 Where is he, then? Come on, join the chat @BramLawson!!
@pseudobram @deadheadmel @IngridF2015 I'm right here, ladies! Just cracking open my third bottle of red.
@deadheadmel @pseudobram @IngridF2015 Ha, a parody account already. Love it.

BRAM, Word document

I'll be signing off today with digits, not letters—with the confirmation that I've returned the money. You'll find it in the same account the solicitors paid it into in the first place, just a regular joint savings account, opened online with the requisite forms of ID easily "borrowed" from Fi's files at Trinity Avenue. It's accessible to either account holder individually, which I hope will help.

You don't need to know where it's been these last weeks, only that I transferred it somewhere untraceable by *him*. Him and his contacts.

But with this confession, this *warning*, I trust you to keep it safe now for Fi and the boys.

You will have deduced by now that I defrauded the fraudsters. The crucial act of double-crossing took place while I was in the air between London and Geneva, but I didn't know for sure that I'd succeeded until several days later, when I located an Internet café here in Lyon and satisfied myself that there were no cameras or unusually suspicious staff and I could probably risk fifteen minutes online.

That was probably my final moment of earthbound joy, connecting to the Internet for the last (sorry, penultimate) time and seeing that the money was there—it definitely was—sitting in an anonymous offshore account outside the search capabilities of the UK government. Beyond their tentacles, as Mike put it. Beyond *his*.

A little under one point six million pounds. It doesn't sound like much, does it, after all this?

It was relatively recently that I decided that two could play at Mike's game. It was just after Christmas, when I understood Fi was never going to save me, save *us*, never going to fix the abominable mess I had created for our family, never going to take the torment out of my hands, out of my head. That had been a pipe dream.

She really was done with me.

Using an agent whose details you'll find on no legitimate search engine, I bought myself a counterfeit passport, and then I furnished Graham Jenson with the innocent details of that new bank account. You see, the strength of Mike's plan—the legitimacy my involvement gave it—was also its weakness. I didn't need the aid of phishing to "correct" the details—I could simply e-mail Jenson myself. Obviously, I couldn't use the e-mail account Mike and Wendy had access to, so I sent the new instruction from my work e-mail.

Dixon Boyle & Co weren't nearly as slapdash as I'd hoped, how-ever, and Jenson's trainee, Rachel, rang to query the last-minute change of receiving account. Naturally, I reassured her that the instruction was genuine and I hadn't had my e-mail hacked by crooks.

"We have to be very careful," she said. "We just had a warning from the Law Society about criminals intercepting e-mails between solicitors and their clients. There was even a case recently where they set up a fake branch of the conveyancing firm."

"Unbelievable," I said. "Thank you for being so thorough."

I take pleasure—measly, hollow, but pleasure nonetheless—in Mike's defeat. In the thought of him canceling his flight to Dubai—canceling *everything*—checking his balance day after day, waiting for the one point six million pounds that will never come. Firing off threats, discussing with his sidekick what torture they will visit on me when at last they track me down.

But that won't happen. I'm off the grid now. Let his texts pile up, never to be delivered; let the e-mails gather, never to be read.

Let the boys cry only briefly.

Because in a few hours I'll be off the grid old-school. If you know what I'm saying.

You know, maybe I was wrong to call it a divine revelation. The deci-sion to take your own life doesn't come upon you as an epiphany. I do know a bit about suicide, including the fact that it's the biggest killer of young men in the UK. Undiagnosed depression, the alcohol and drugs factor . . . I won't lecture you. It's not like I haven't just spent a hundred pages explaining the context of *my* decision.

I really believe it has been there in me, dormant, for my whole marriage, my whole life—or at least since my father died. It wasn't only the drinking that camouflaged it (or expressed it), but also the sex, the risk-taking, the fights, the recklessness. Wasn't it all just self-destruction by a thousand cuts?

A slow slicing.

You know, on the speed awareness course I took a couple of years ago, there was an exercise in which the instructor went around the room and asked us to say in one word why we'd been speeding.

"Ignorance."

"Lateness."

"Impatience."

"Overtaking."

"Habit."

On it went, all the predictable culprits, until one guy said, "I was chasing my brother," and we all cracked up.

Then it was my turn. I could make something up ("noble causes" seemed to go down well, even if it *was* two words: taking a heavily pregnant wife to hospital, for instance, or a child with something stuck in his throat). Or I could tell the truth.

"Bram?" the instructor said, making a point of reading from my name tag, a little touch of ceremony. "Why do you think *you* were speeding?"

I could tell the truth in one word, and it's the same one I'll use now to account for this, the end of me:

"Pain."

49

It has been a very long day, but both the producer and the interviewer of *The Victim* have been exemplary in their professionalism and Fi leaves the Farringdon studio with a sense of accomplishment, of good having been done. There's a freeing feeling too, though she of all people knows freedom is an illusion.

In a café on Greville Street near Farringdon Station, Merle is waiting. It's one of those self-consciously hipster places with bulbs hanging bare from cables, and chairs salvaged from skips. Each of their coffees has a love heart sketched in the foam and comes with a chocolate-covered edamame bean on the side.

"Is it Valentine's Day or something?" Fi says, obliterating her love heart with the back of her spoon.

"We've passed that," Merle says. Like Fi, she wears black. They always do when they meet, as if the two of them mourn not an individual but an ethos or a state of being. Privilege, perhaps, or control.

"What did Adrian give me? Oh yeah, I forgot." She glances down at her own body, the growing baby bump, and Fi thinks suddenly of poor Lucy Vaughan and the way she eyed Merle's red smock that day at the house, wondering whether she should offer her congratulations.

Merle checks there's no one in earshot. "So, how did it go?"

Fi nods. "Really well. Tiring, though. I feel like I could sleep for a week."

Merle reaches to take her hand. They've done this a lot, lately, grasped hands in sisterly support. "Well done, darling. Concentrating for that length of time *is* exhausting. Any idea when they'll be releasing it?"

"The first week of March, the producer said. They have a really quick turnaround."

"They didn't ask anything too awkward?"

"They *did*, but I stuck to the house sale, obviously. I said I've been advised by the police not to discuss anything else."

"Which is perfectly true. Excellent. Look what I've just found." Merle has open on her phone a page from a missing-persons website. Thumb and forefinger enlarge a face as familiar to Fi as her own:

ABRAHAM LAWSON
(KNOWN AS BRAM)

Reported missing after the weekend of 14–15 January 2017, when a crime took place at Mr. Lawson's residence in Alder Rise, South London. Has not been seen since Thursday, 12 January, when he spoke with neighbors and with the staff of a storage facility in Beckenham.

If you know of this man's whereabouts, please call the Metropolitan Police on the number shown below.

"Interesting that they don't say what the crime is," Merle says.

"Maybe that's standard policy." Fi sighs. "But after this interview goes out, everyone will know what he did."

"You realize that *he* might hear it? You can download *The Victim* from anywhere."

"That's what the producer said. It's happened a few times that the accused has come forward to deny the allegations. Very helpful to the police, apparently."

"Well, if he *did* get in touch, it would only be his word against yours."

"It always has been, hasn't it?" Fi says. "All those years together, his word against mine."

"That's what marriage is," Merle says with a trace of her old smile, playful, wicked.

"I spoke to the police this morning," Fi tells her. "Before I did the interview. They told me something interesting."

"Oh yes?"

"They've found a phone they think was Bram's. It has the numbers of the Challoner's estate agent and the solicitor, plus searches relating to Silver Road. Obviously, they'll check out all the other numbers, but the main thing is, this phone had the forensic code from *our* address. It was marked with our security pen."

"The pens we gave out at the meeting? With the fluid that shows under UV lamps?" Merle stares at her, a smile creeping across her mouth. "That's an incredible piece of evidence. It obviously *was* Bram's phone, then."

"Must have been. Harry went around the house marking everything that wasn't nailed down. Bram must have had it in his pocket or left it out on the side or something."

"Where did they find it? In the flat?"

"No, it came in with some petty criminal. He had a haul of stolen phones, claims he found Bram's in a bin in Victoria."

"Wow." Merle exhales. "That's it, then. He'll be arrested the moment he's found. Where the hell is he? Do you think he's still in London?"

"I wonder that all the time," Fi says. "One thing's for sure: he'll never go back to Alder Rise."

"But *you* will, won't you? As soon as they find the money."

"*If* they do. And apparently, any accounts involved will be frozen while they investigate, maybe for years. Then there are all the costs."

"But after all that, you might be able to come back to Trinity Avenue?"

Again their hands touch. "I don't see how," Fi says. "Property prices will have gone up even more by then." There's a bittersweet moment when she's plunged into the past, to simpler times, when she and Merle and Alison and the other women of Trinity Avenue talked about house prices, how their properties had saved them, ensnared them, obsessed them. "It'll be a long time before I buy again, Merle, but that's fine. It's not my main concern. The boys are. They're my *only* concern."

"Of course they are. Fi, did you . . ." Merle falters. It is a rare moment of self-doubt. "I have to ask: Did you say anything about me during the interview? Do I need to prepare myself for when this goes out? All the women at work listen to it."

"Of course not," Fi says. "The occasional bit of conversation from Kent, that kind of thing, but nothing else."

They pay for the coffees and walk together to the station. At the barriers for the overland train, which Merle will take to Alder Rise, they hug good-bye. It's still odd knowing she will take a different route, the tube to Waterloo and then the train to Kingston.

"We'll come and visit you soon," she promises. "I've told Leo and Harry about the baby, and they're very excited."

"That's sweet," Merle says. "Give them a kiss from me. It sounds as if you did brilliantly today, Fi. I'm really proud of you."

Fi watches her friend make her way toward the stairs to the platform, her movements, like her mind, lithe and elegant. She's pleased that Merle is proud of her; she's proud of herself, if it's not too immodest to say. Yes, it was painful having to relive the events of the past six months, but it was also, as Merle warned, a necessary preemptive strike.

They say all confessions are self-serving, don't they? Well, hers was no exception. And, hand on heart, she can recall only a couple of lines in the whole interview that were outright lies.

She wonders sometimes why it was Merle she phoned that night and not Alison. It couldn't have been simply because she'd seen her during the day, accepted her help in battling the Vaughans, in contacting solicitors and police and hospitals. Or that she'd said when Fi had left, "Phone me if there's anything I can do. Anything."

I owe you.

Had she actually said that, in a whisper, or had Fi's ears conjured it on the breeze?

Because Merle owed her, all right. And now she has repaid her debt with interest. In the aftermath of it all, when Fi's mind had been clogged and useless, Merle's worked with clarity and verve.

It was Merle's idea for her to get in touch with the makers of *The Victim*. The police had been progressing so tortuously in their attempts to prove that the fraud was linked to the collision and other crimes, their questions for Fi probing so little, that it was messing with her mind. It was making her think they were withholding what they knew, lulling her into a false sense of security before staging their ambush.

"There needs to be a statement out there," Merle said. "What you knew and when. We need to establish you as the injured party before anyone thinks to suggest otherwise."

Fi had found the idea terrifying. "Why would I draw attention to myself like that? Those stories on *The Victim* get followed up in the *Mail*, all over the Internet."

"Exactly. Why draw attention to yourself if you're in any way at fault? This is public service, virtually an act of charity."

She is a born strategist, Merle.

There's a game Fi plays when she can't sleep: she tries to remember her last moment of innocence, of ignorance—because they were, in the end, the same. The day is not in doubt: Friday, the thirteenth of January, of course, when she discovered Lucy Vaughan in her house— her furniture, her belongings, her *rights*, replaced by a stranger's. But when, precisely, that day? Not when she heard about Challoner's open house, nor when it emerged that Bram had a female accomplice, nor even when David announced the transfer of title deeds from the Lawsons to the Vaughans. No, it was in the evening, after she'd decamped to Merle's house and Toby had arrived, and he was holding her, comforting her, listening to their story, the three of them cursing Bram and discussing where he might be hiding. Over the course of the afternoon, her last sense of possession of him had disintegrated, but Toby was there. Toby was her rock.

She'd forgotten that rock forms over many years, not in a matter of months.

Leaving Merle's house that evening: that was probably the moment. Walking down the path, not allowing herself to turn toward her own beloved property, to see the lights blazing through old glass for the new owners.

Yes, she was still ignorant, still innocent, when she followed Toby to his car. She was like Leo's old favorite Jemima Puddleduck, when she followed the fox to his kitchen, witlessly carrying the herbs to be used for her own stuffing.

50

Friday, January 13, 2017

LONDON, 8:30 P.M.

She's in Toby's Toyota in the passenger seat and they've reached the junction with the Parade, but for some reason he's turning left—not right—which isn't the way around the park toward Baby Deco.

"So, where do you think he is?" Toby says, his tone so tense she glances up, startled. His jaw is set very tight, his shoulders clenched. Like Merle, he's feeling the fury she can't yet feel. She wants to capture his left hand in her right one, lace her fingers through his, but both his hands are busy at the wheel.

"He could be anywhere," she says. "He'll know the police will want to speak to him. At least they will once they have the evidence he's acted criminally." She remembers the circumspection of the two officers, how they stopped well short of agreeing there'd been any wrongdoing. And the solicitor, Graham Jenson, was adamant that he had followed his clients' instructions to the letter. There is going to be nothing swift about this process, no justice guaranteed.

"There'll be evidence, all right," Toby says with a conviction bordering on viciousness. "Don't worry about that."

Her mind lags, her powers of reason are delayed and she's still stuck on "why?" If Bram needed money in a hurry, why didn't he make his case to her? Why didn't he give her the chance to buy him out of his share of the house? And even once he'd convinced himself to act alone, wouldn't the easier deception have been an application to remortgage and release equity, not sell the place outright?

The oncoming headlights are unnaturally clean in the dark, as if the air is purer than usual, and she stares into the dazzle. There is no music or radio on in the car and she can hear Toby breathing beside her.

She remembers a work event, a discussion about dignitaries from overseas. "Shouldn't you be at your drinks thing? With the people from Singapore?"

He does not answer, but only repeats his earlier question: "Where else could he be?"

"I've told you, I have no idea. Where are you going? Aren't you taking me to the flat?"

"In a while. *Think*, Fi."

Only then does she understand that he is circling the roads of Alder Rise and its environs, physically patrolling for Bram. "He won't be anywhere near here—that's for sure. Toby, I know you're trying to help and I'm really grateful, but I just want to get to the flat and rest for a couple of hours. My head is killing me."

"*Your* head." He sniggers unpleasantly. "Well, in *that* case . . ."

She frowns. Something is not right. It wasn't right in Merle's house either, she realizes. It's as if he's raging not on her behalf, but on his own.

She rewinds. "How did you know something was wrong? OK, I didn't text you that I'd got back, but that's no big deal. Definitely not enough for you to ditch a work event and come and find me." To go to the house and look for *Bram*, not her. *"Where the fuck is Bram?"*

"What's going on, Toby?"

He sighs, too impatient to explain, his eye scanning the passing pedestrians with professional attention.

It doesn't take long, even for a pulverized brain, to locate the only imaginable link. "Is this to do with your job? You know Bram from some work situation?"

He says nothing, lips sucked shut. She extracts from memory an image of the only occasion the two men met, when Bram was so threatening, unforgivably so, and Toby so controlled. Had he been a little *too* controlled? Like someone with *training*?

"You don't work for that think tank, do you? You work for the police. You've been investigating him. All this time, you've been investigating him. Is that why you've been seeing me? To get close to him?" She flushes, unsure if the heat is from shock or shame. "Is it to do with this house situation? Do you work for the Fraud Office?" As her brain misfires, her voice rises. "Couldn't you have stopped this? Before the contracts were exchanged? *Why didn't you stop this?"*

"Stop asking questions," Toby snaps. "For fuck's sake, shut up for half a minute, can't you? You're doing my head in with your whining."

She gasps, shrinks against the seat as if thrown by force, but her alarmed response does nothing to dim his anger.

"Seriously, you're spewing out questions and not waiting for the answers. Calm down, Fi."

She whimpers, "I can't believe you're speaking to me like this. You're the one who—"

"Just *listen*. If you want to know, I'll tell you, but you've got to shut up and let me speak." He pauses, eyes fixed ahead, though they are sitting now, going nowhere, in a queue of cars at a set of red lights. "I'm not a fraud investigator; I'm not a detective; I don't work for the government or any other organization. There are no dignitaries waiting for me in town with a glass of fucking champagne!"

"But you said your work was about traffic congestion. You said—"

"Jesus Christ, I haven't got time for this." He turns, sneering at her. "Read my lips: *I made it up*. Every word I said came from an article in the *Standard*. I couldn't believe it when you believed me. I mean, how gullible are you? No wonder you've just been shafted the way you have. And that whole bird's nest thing—what kind of a dumb fuck would do that with a guy like *him*? It wasn't even his idea—it was yours!"

A shake is starting up in her arms, tears rising in her eyes. He's a different man: he's sharp and menacing, full of loathing.

He's not on the side she thought he was on.

And now he's through the lights and turning from the main road into a side street; he's pulling over far from any streetlamp. She doesn't know the road, has lost track of how far they've come, and there is no other traffic, no one passing on foot. The lit windows of the houses are set back from the road. Oh God. She scans the switches in front of her, searching for the door lock release.

"Now," Toby says, unbuckling his seat belt and drawing closer, "bleed though my heart does for you, I need to know where your husband is. I'm not interested in anything else—do you understand?"

She's sure she's located the switch, down there by the gear stick. If she reaches with her right hand before opening the door with her left . . .

But then she has the thought that immobilizes her once and for all, the worst thought of any: "Were you . . . Were you in on this house scam?"

Toby throws up his right hand, face enraged afresh, and she recoils. "I'm the one who's been scammed! Where's the money?" The hand lands on her left shoulder, pins her painfully to the seat. "He's told you, hasn't he? He's tried to hide it for you and your fucking rug rats. Are you joining him somewhere? Where? *Where?*"

She stares at him, terrified. "I know nothing whatsoever! The solicitor said the sale went through exactly as it was supposed to. He said—"

"That's bollocks!" His voice explodes in the sealed car. "We spoke to them, and they had an order from him to change the account at the last minute. So where the fuck is it? What other accounts do you two have?"

She thought she'd used every last drop of adrenaline, but a valve opens and thrusts her forward to take him on. "There *are* no other accounts, Toby. How on earth would I know where the money is, when I don't know a single other thing about this mess? And if you *are* involved, you can't seriously have expected to have a huge sum like that land in your account and just be able to start spending it. The Inland Revenue would want to know where it came from, probably the police too. It would never have worked—the money would have been seized. It still will be—half of it is mine, not his!"

Toby jeers at this. "If he'd used the account he was supposed to, it would never have been traced. We find him, we get the money."

"We? You mean—?"

"Not you," he cuts in.

The fake Mrs. Lawson. The imposter.

"Who's the woman?" she demands.

"You don't need to know."

"I don't need to know? It's my house, Toby!"

"Not anymore, love."

"Who is she? What's her name?"

"Fiona Lawson," he says, smirking. "A slightly younger, sexier model, admittedly. Don't take my word for it. Ask Bram—he's the one who fucked her."

At last he releases her shoulder from his grip and she can breathe freely. The pounding of her heart is louder than their voices.

"How did this start? How do you know Bram? Tell me, Toby— you owe me that!" She begins to cry and he eyes her with disdain. She can tell her display of emotion repulses him. *"You owe me that"*: so weak and plaintive and female.

"He ran another car off the road and it crashed. He wasn't supposed to be driving—he'd been banned. There was a kid in the car who died."

"What?" The air is sucked from her chest. "You mean that accident in Thornton Heath?" The one she'd read about, the one the detective was investigating—he'd come to the house. If she'd thought to ask *him* some questions, would she be here now? "You mean you were there? You witnessed it? You found out about the ban and you blackmailed him?"

"Correct." Toby shrugs. "Turned out I struck gold. He hated the idea of prison more than he loved his wife and kids. What can I say? We all have our Achilles' heel."

Fi shakes her head. "That's not true. No way. Maybe he started out scared of going to jail, but he wouldn't take it this far."

"He would if he thought he was going to get ten years, maybe fifteen. He's a pretty nasty piece of work on paper, had a conviction for assault—did you know that?"

"Rubbish," she cries.

"He beat up some guy outside a pub, put him in hospital. Just a few years ago."

"I don't believe you."

"No, I don't suppose you do. The thing is, the police won't give a shit what *you* believe. It's a past record of violence, isn't it? Once the kid died, he was looking at a maximum term."

Fi feels her breath thinning. "Even so, he wouldn't choose this. He wouldn't abandon his boys. You must have . . . you must have *broken* him."

He regards her with genuine curiosity. "He broke himself. He's a loser. It's in his blood—you know that."

She gazes at him, appalled. Until this moment, she has been aware of only one other person in her life knowing the truth about Bram's father, and that is his widow, Tina. Never has it been discussed between the two women, and only once, in the beginning, between Bram and her. "How can you be so heartless?" she whispers. "He was a child when his father died. It destroyed him."

"Boo-hoo. Some of us have had it a lot worse than him. You should have seen what *my* old man was like."

Fi inhales. There is no path through this conversation, no route to reason or mercy. "Whatever happened in that accident, he wouldn't have hurt anyone intentionally. He doesn't deserve this."

"Oh, Fi, are you really qualified to say what that cunt deserves?"

She gasps. "Don't call him that."

He laughs and there is spite in it, a sadistic edge. "Do you know how much you used to talk about him? You wouldn't hear a word against him. Only *you* were allowed to criticize him, and in such a self-righteous way. It was pathetic how you couldn't get over him. Always comparing us."

"I never compared you!"

"Don't worry, love—you didn't hurt my feelings."

She has stopped shaking, stopped crying, and is very still now, possessed by an energy she doesn't recognize, a response to this degradation deeper than fight-or-flight, something from the soul, not the brain. "In Winchester, I thought we were . . ."

"What? *Falling in love?*" he sneers.

"Did you not care at all? About me?"

"Honestly?"

"Yes."

Toby's mouth moves cruelly before he answers. "It didn't cross my mind. You were just another way to keep him in line. Show him I had all his exits covered. Mind you, I thought he was going to blab that night he found me in the house."

But he didn't blab, she thinks. He left her in this monster's clutches, when she might have been the one person who could have rescued *him* from them.

"What about your ex-wife? And Charlie and Jess? Do they even exist?"

"Who are Charlie and Jess?" he says. He reaches for the key in the ignition, turns it on. "Now, unless you've got any useful contribution to make, you might as well get out here. I need to get on."

"You were supposed to take me to—"

"I'm not a fucking Uber. Get out of the car. You're obviously no use to anyone."

She stumbles out, her bags with her, feels the door pull away from her hands as he tugs it closed. There is the faint clunk of doors locking and then the Toyota jerks away from the curb, its acceleration breathtaking. There are cars parked on both sides, barely space for one to fit down the middle; if he met someone coming the other way he'd kill them both.

LYON, 9:30 P.M.

He's settled in his room in another insipid chain hotel, his second within twelve hours. Tomorrow he will find something semipermanent. On the desk, there is the standard-issue directory of local attractions and accommodations, as well as a map of the city, and he studies both. He decides to try an aparthotel on Rue du Dauphiné that boasts discounted weekly rates for smoking units with a kitchenette, cleaning service, and free Wi-Fi.

He won't need the Wi-Fi.

He tears the page from the directory and stores it in his wallet for the morning. Masochism, or maybe even sentimentality, prompts him to extract Mike's printout from the same place. He pauses before unfolding it, pauses a second time before reading the title:

DEATHS IN PRISON CUSTODY 1978, ENGLAND AND WALES

There are approximately sixty names on the list. A bleak tally of souls. His eye finds the one he recognizes about a dozen lines down and absorbs the given facts:

SURNAME: Lawson

NAME: RL

SEX: Male

AGE: 34

DATE OF DEATH: 24/07/1978

ESTABLISHMENT: Brixton

CLASSIFICATION: Self-inflicted by hanging

The prison authorities had forwarded a letter to his mother that he'd never been permitted to read, but which had been summarized for his young ears. "He thought it was better for us this way. He was convinced it would be easier for you if he wasn't here to bring more shame on you."

Privately, sharing nothing with his mother or, later, Fi, he'd done what research he could. There'd been a rise in suicides in British prisons in the 1970s, an increase in excess of the rate of rise in prison population and put down to overcrowding and mental health problems like depression and anxiety—factors that had got far worse since. It wasn't easy to discover details of his father's case, but he'd found someone who'd been at Brixton at the same time and had known his father's cellmate. Lawson had been agitated from arrival and unable to adjust, he remembered. There'd been an inmate with a neighborhood connection to the elderly man he'd injured and this had resulted in bullying. ("He got a kicking most days.") He'd begged to be moved, but this was never facilitated. He'd hanged himself with a bedsheet in the night, had had no pulse when he was found and cut down.

Bram feels a sharp smack of pain through his center, followed by the one feeling he's been craving all day—longer than that, for weeks, months, years: the knowledge that the final destination he has chosen for himself is utterly right.

Not just for him; for all of them.

51

The temperature has plummeted and it's deathly cold now. Rage insulates her only so far, and she digs into her coat pockets for the gloves and hat she used in Winchester. Before putting them on, she bundles them to her face and inhales the scents of yesterday, of cathedral and woodland and ancient cobbled alleys. Of a lifestyle—a life—that's gone.

It takes a moment to figure out where she is. There's a bus stop on the main road and she sees that she is several stops south of Alder Rise, with no service due in the next fifteen minutes. Her mind churns. Faster to walk? Or wait for a taxi? Can she afford one, now everything is lost? Where is the money? What has Bram done? What will Toby do? Will he turn back and come after her, dish out some of the violence that was all too implicit in the car?

She walks. When she reaches Baby Deco, the building is alight with Friday-night humanity, people whose lives have been improved by the arrival of the weekend, a laughable notion if it didn't make her want to sob. She takes the stairs to the second floor. She's moving strangely, sluggishly, and the light times out before she reaches the door. Any other time, she'd be unnerved by the dark, the hollow silence of a stairwell, but tonight she embraces it for what it is, a respite from scrutiny, exposure.

When she opens the door to the flat, she actually stumbles back out again. The whole unit, barring the kitchen area immediately inside the door, is crammed with heavy-duty removals boxes, a ceiling-high rock face of brown, stamped with the blue of a brand logo. The glazed doors to the balcony can be seen only through a single fractured line, though a wider gorge has been created to allow access to the bathroom. The bed must be hidden under the boxes, while, thoughtfully, the two gray armchairs have been relocated to the kitchen area.

Her fingers probe the items on the kitchen worktop as if her eyes are no longer to be trusted: Bram's keys to the flat; a yellow A4 sheet, which proves to be the paid invoice for a self-storage company in Beckenham that she guesses contains her furniture; also, inexplicably, Harry's little blue spelling book. What was going through Bram's mind, she wonders, to cheat his family on such a scale and yet think to pull aside a school exercise book? When did he last speak to the boys? Did he prepare them for this trauma? Can he *really* have said good-bye to them and intended it to be the final time?

There is no note, nor any details of bank accounts, but she had not expected that. This is not a puzzle set by Bram for her edification; this is the last act of a desperate man.

With no true instinct as to what to do next, she dislodges the nearest of the boxes and looks inside. Ornaments, photographs, books: all from the Trinity Avenue living room. The next three contain more books from the same room. The fifth holds items from the study, including files and documents from the cabinet, a lucky find so early—if anything can be described as lucky on this most diabolical of days—

because she'll need financial documents for her meeting with the solicitor on Monday. When she pulls herself together, with her parents' help, she'll need them to prove her ownership of the house. She starts to sift, removing anything useful, including the blue plastic folder that contains the family's passports. She is stunned to find Bram's, untouched, intact—so stunned that she sits for a moment to think.

He must still be in the UK, then. Though bludgeoned by fatigue, her brain seems to know that a passport is required of UK citizens even for France or Ireland. Of course, he may have acquired a false one. If he can steal a house (half a house, technically), then he can buy illegal ID. The criminal underworld is his oyster, evidently, and Toby his erstwhile traveling companion.

She experiences a rush of fury at the thought of Toby, which at least energizes her next spell of unpacking. Kitchen utensils, clothing, shoes, toys . . . on it goes. After an hour or so, she breaks to find something to eat and drink. There is nothing in the fridge, not even milk or water, just a bottle of red wine in the rack on the counter, and so she tries the top shelf of the cupboard where they keep pasta and other groceries. Instant noodles will do, or soup.

Immediately, her fingers find something flat and plastic. Behind the stocks of tinned tomatoes and crackers and tea bags, there is a phone, a battered-looking Sony belonging to Bram, since it is definitely not hers, and with a charger lead attached. It's dead, so she plugs it into the nearest socket, eats the crackers and drinks a glass of water while waiting for it to come to life.

When at last it responds, she finds herself looking at a home screen with neither pass code to crack nor contents to protect. No photos, no e-mails, no history of Internet searches. There are, however, two text messages from an unnamed number. The first, dating from October and opened, reads, *Uh-oh, looks like someone's getting her memory back . . .* and links to an article about the Thornton Heath accident:

ROAD RAGE CAUSED SILVER ROAD CRASH,
SAYS VICTIM

She knows who must have sent it even before she remembers those grotesque words in the car—*"He ran another car off the road and it crashed . . . The kid died"*—and even before she opens the second message, sent earlier today and until now unread:

> Wtf going on with your phones? No answer from usual number. Fi on way back to London. Call ASAP.

Her anger returns in a torrent.
"You're obviously no use to anyone. . . ."
"A younger, sexier model . . ."
"What kind of a dumb fuck . . . ?"
Almost immediately a new alert sounds and she sees that by opening the last message she has announced her presence—or Bram's—to *him*.

> I know you're there. Big problem, solicitor paid wrong account. Know anything about that?

She waits, breathless, for the next to land:

> No money, no passport. You know the deal. You have till Monday morning to sort this out or the evidence goes to the police.

"No money, no passport." And yet Bram's passport is here, in the flat. She can see the folder from where she's standing. She was right, then—there must have been a replacement one, procured by Toby and withheld until he'd received his payoff. How cunning he has been—

thought he had been. And yet he finds himself with nothing, because somehow Bram has triumphed, triumphed over all of them. And either he's forgotten this second phone exists or he's deliberately left it. Should she dispose of it? What is he expecting her to do?

Then she has a thought she hasn't had before: this couldn't have been . . . this couldn't be Bram's revenge for her having chosen Toby over him?

But no: Bram must have understood Toby's interest in her was merely a pretense. She is ashamed to remember her own vanity that night Bram found Toby at Trinity Avenue: all her feminist faith, all her pride in her independence, and it comes down to the cavewoman excitement of two hunter-gatherers fighting over her.

Which it turns out they were not.

How pathetic she is. Homeless and defeated and debased.

As her eye rests on the bottle of wine, the phone starts to ring.

LYON, 10:30 P.M.

He thought he would never sleep again, but in fact he passes out early and sleeps deeply that first night in Lyon, yanked to the surface only twice. The first time, the pea under his mattresses is a phone. The third phone, to be precise—the Sony Mike delivered to him at the office to replace the Samsung he'd smashed. He knows he never used it, but where did he leave it? In the office? In the flat?

Is there any way it could lead Mike to him here? No. His searches on Geneva and Lyon were made in the Internet café in Croydon and his calls to Mike were from the pay-as-you-go, now sitting in the bottom of a bin in Victoria.

His eyes close.

His eyes open once more. There was that one text, wasn't there? A

368 · LOUISE CANDLISH

link to a news piece about the Silver Road investigation. Is there any way that could lead the police to Mike?

Possibly. But maybe that would be no bad thing.

LONDON, 10:30 P.M.

She declines five calls from him before sending a text of her own:

> *Calm down. I'm at the flat.*
> You fucking twat. Where's the money?
> *I have it, don't worry. Mix-up with account numbers. Come to flat and I'll do the transfer while you're here.*
> Not sure flat is safe. Fi has been to house, had the police out.
> *It's clear. Police won't come this late.*
> You think?
> *Come if you want the money. Your choice.*

He must have driven like a bat out of hell, because he arrives in minutes. When she presses the intercom button, he barks into it without waiting for a greeting: "Mike. Let me in."

"*Mike?*" So Toby has been a fake right down to the name he fed her.

"*I mean, how gullible are you?*"

"*Read my lips: I made it up.*"

She buzzes him in.

Remarkably, given all that has passed today, she experiences a sensation close to relish when she sees the astonishment on his face as he approaches the open door and catches sight of her waiting inside.

"What the hell are *you* doing here?"

"I told you I was coming here. This is the only home I have, remember?" Her tone is as abrasive as she can muster, but nothing she has to say can wound him. He sees her only as an obstacle to be kicked aside. "I'm looking for Bram," she adds. "Same as you, I assume, since you clearly haven't returned to propose marriage to me."

Have you, Mike?

He curls his lip with contempt. "Where is he?"

"He just texted me, said he'd be here in ten minutes."

It strikes her that she hasn't muted Bram's phone, concealed under her bag on the worktop, right next to the knife she's taken from the drawer, just in case. Just in case this bastard tries to hurt her.

But she can't reach for the phone with him standing here.

"He told me he was already here," Toby says. Mike says.

"He must have texted us en route. He'll be using public transport, remember."

"For fuck's sake!" His fuse already blown, he looks about him for something to hurt. "Well, you're going to have to wait till I've finished with him. Catch up on your way to hospital, eh?"

How could she ever have found this man attractive? He is a brute, a vile, ugly monster. "I've got all the time in the world. Take a seat." She gestures to the armchairs, side by side in their sad, makeshift lounge. "Drink?" she offers, gripping the bottle of red wine she's already begun.

"Got any vodka?"

"I've only got this."

"Fine."

Hers is already poured and she fills a new glass, passes it to him. She can't connect this act of hospitality to the dozens like it when he visited her here during their relationship. The conversation and the flirtation and the sex: that was with a different man. A man who'd pitted himself as the uncomplicated and restrained challenger to a famously uncontrolled ex. Was it the reined-in aggression that she'd sensed and responded to? How does he behave with women when he has no ulterior motive, no agenda that relies on his gaining trust? Unpleasantly, she suspects. Forcefully.

He swallows the wine in impatient gulps, complains it tastes like shit, but continues drinking. She pours him a second glass and a third, while continuing to sip her own.

"It's been way longer than ten minutes," he grumbles, then suddenly sparks. "What did you mean, 'en route'? Where was he coming from?"

Fi shrugs. She is not scared of him now. "I don't know—he didn't say in his message—but he's obviously hit a delay."

"Show me the message he sent you." He rises, stumbling slightly, and she leaps to her feet, blocks his passage past her to her bag.

"Don't you come near me."

He regards her with disdain, before reaching for his coat and trawling through the pockets for his own phone. As he stabs at the keypad, she is just deft enough to locate and turn off Bram's phone before he eyes her once more. A fraction slower and it would have given her away.

"He's turned it off," he mutters. "Don't know what the hell he thinks he's playing at."

"He'll be here."

"You're suddenly very trusting," he mocks. "Have you forgotten he's just shafted you for every penny you've got?"

She holds his eye, her expression so hostile, so sour, her face doesn't feel like her own. "Look, if you don't mind, I'd rather not talk anymore until he comes."

He scowls, reclaims his glass, helps himself to the last of the wine. "You'd be doing me a favor. You bore my tits off, if you must know. Fat old Mrs. Holier-than-thou—I don't know how Bram stood it all those years. No wonder he played away. I would have done the same. With that foxy neighbor of yours, for starters—what was her name?" He takes one of the chairs, angles it toward its mate as if inviting her to sit and subject herself to more abuse.

I hate you, she thinks. *I can't be near you for another second.*

"I'm going to the loo," she says. "I'll wait there."

She locks the bathroom door behind her and slides to the floor, sits with her chin on her knees. She is shaking so badly her teeth chatter, and she clenches her jaw to stop the sound of it.

At last, she reaches to pull the light cord, puts her fingers in her ears and closes her eyes.

LYON, AFTER MIDNIGHT

The second time he wakes up, it is Mike he sees, just as it is Mike who will wake him most often during the next few weeks. If he has learned anything from his own demise it is that he must not underestimate this man. He has, after all, seen him at his best, in command, flying. How will he behave when he learns he's been deceived? Will he try to harm Fi? *"She will suffer."* Will he kidnap Leo or Harry and issue a message on YouTube like some hooded radical—"Pay me my money and I'll let him go"—a knife held to the precious boy's throat?

No, he has to have faith in the police. The moment the property scam came to light Fi would have been in touch with them, and now she'll have access to their protection. Mike wouldn't take the risk.

In any case, he is a chancer, a bounder. He'll kick a wall or two and then he'll move on to the next opportunity, hardly limping.

52

Saturday, January 14, 2017
LONDON, 3 A.M.

Though her ears ache, her fingers no longer seal them shut and she can hear awful grinding sounds on the other side of the wall. It's a monster clearing its throat and preparing to devour her! No, that's just one of the kids' stories, the one Harry likes with the greedy sheep that swallows the world. *"I'm still hungry!"*

She struggles at first to understand the stiffness in her body, its proneness on a cold, hard surface. Has she been dozing? Her hand moves across tile, probing, and reaches a wall of smooth plastic: a shower screen. She is on the bathroom floor, in the flat.

No, not a story.

She heaves herself into sitting position, back against the screen. Light-headed, she counts to ten, twenty, fifty, before attempting to stand. Her legs are dead, buckling under her weight, and she grips the door handle for support. At last, she finds the light cord and pulls— the dazzle makes her flinch—before unlocking the door and opening it as noiselessly as she can.

It is silent in the main room. As she creeps between the cliffs of boxes, particles of light overtake her, flowing from the bathroom toward the kitchen area. On the worktop, she can make out her handbag, a bottle with the residue of red wine, a sheet of yellow paper, a little blue exercise book.

At the mouth of the passageway, she sees him. He is still seated, his legs outstretched, but his head is tipped right back, his face pitched skyward. She takes a step toward him. His eyes are closed. The skull bones are sharp beneath the skin and there's blunt stubble on his face and throat. There is a crust of vomit on his chin and part of his neck, dirty pink drops of it congealing on the chair. The noises she heard were of him choking, presumably in his sleep, unable to gain consciousness, for there is no evidence that he had woken and done anything to try to save himself.

Nor did *she* do anything.

He is dead, surely, but she can't bring herself to touch him.

Her heart begins to punch against her chest, her hands to spasm and twitch. She has an image of herself from last night that cannot be hallucination. Of taking Merle's sleeping pills from her bag and crumbling them into the wine bottle. She appears almost absentminded in the image, like when she looks after Rocky and gives him his anti-inflammatory for his arthritis. Just half a tablet, broken into two.

But she wasn't absentminded, was she? She was attentive to the point of frenzied. There were six sleeping pills in the pack and not only did she use them all, but she also decided they might not be enough. She went back to her bag and took out the box of antidepressants she'd taken from Bram's package on Wednesday morning. Not that she'd intended to keep them, but after Googling and reading and worrying she'd been running late, she'd still had to go home and shower and dress and get to the station in time for her train to Waterloo to meet Toby, and she'd swept the pills into her bag without thinking.

So she'd added several of those to the wine too.

I killed him and it was premeditated. I prepared the poison.

But no, that can't be right! How was she to know he would drink most of the bottle? How was she to know he'd drink *any* of it? She'd been delirious with shock, her actions reflexive, involuntary, hardly more than a child's playacting.

Except she'd poured herself a glass of wine before she added the pills, hadn't she? Because she needed a drink, or in malicious deception? If *she* was already drinking, then he'd be more likely to accept a glass, less likely to suspect foul play.

Except she'd worn rubber gloves to handle the pills, hadn't she?

I am a murderer. She claps her hand to her mouth to catch the vomit. Swallows.

Her phone is in her bag. She brings up the numbers keypad and her finger hovers over the 9 before she gasps and stops. The police can request phone records, see where calls were made. There was that one episode of *The Victim* where the whole thing hinged on mobile-phone masts. She's read about it in the paper as well, how the police can trace emergency calls to within thirty meters; they use computerized mapping, national grid coordinates.

She blinks. Her brain is working better, then, if she can remember *that*. And now it wants her to turn, take a closer look at the hideous thing still sitting there.

Don't.

Think.

Move.

Leave.

She takes her handbag and leaves the flat, tears down the corridor and the stairwell, through the lobby, out into a freezing mist. Hurrying through the smothered streets, she calms. The world is quiet, the fog benign, not eerie, as if the streets are respecting her need for anonymity. She avoids the main road around the north of the park and instead loops south around Alder Rise Road and up toward Wyndham Gardens, into Trinity Avenue that way.

At number 87, she rings the bell, just once, balling her hands to stop her from doing it over and over.

At last the voice comes—"Who is it?"—and she dips to her haunches to call through the letter box. "Merle, it's me. Are you still on your own? Can I come in?"

"Fi!" The door opens and heat rushes toward her. Merle is there, sleepy and rumpled in sky blue pajamas, feet bare. "I thought you were at the flat. Are you OK?"

Say it now or you'll never say it.

"I think I've killed him," she says.

Merle's face twitches with fear. Her hand goes to her abdomen. "What? Bram?"

"Toby. But he's really called Mike."

There is a sickening moment when she thinks it's going to go the other way, when she feels sure Merle will decide against her. And she will accept it; she will not run.

"Quick, come in." Merle pulls her over the threshold, closes the door. They face each other in the hallway. The stricken innocence of her friend's face is something Fi herself will never again convey, not without acting. "You mean that guy from last night? You said he was your boyfriend. . . . I don't understand."

"He stole the house, Merle. With Bram. He made Bram do it."

"What are you talking about?"

"He told me in the car. He blackmailed him." Now she's saying it, she's understanding the hideousness again, feeling the wrongness swell inside her, ready to split her open. "He threw me out of the car. He said I was dumb and useless. He only took me to Winchester because— Oh God! I've left my bag in the flat!"

Merle touches the strap of Fi's handbag in the crook of her elbow. "No, you've got it—look."

"I mean my overnight bag. I need to go back. I need to get it!"

"Breathe," Merle says gently. "Come and sit here."

They sit on the stair side by side. Merle is a radiator, her face flushed, breath hot. "Go back a bit. What happened after you got out of the car?"

"I went to the flat and I sent him a text."

"From your phone?"

"No, from Bram's. There was one at the flat, an old one—he must have forgotten it. That's all he was interested in, getting to Bram. Bram must have the money."

"Where is he now? Toby? Mike?"

"Still there. At the flat."

"What did you do, Fi?"

She sucks in warm air. "I gave him the sleeping pills."

"The ones I gave you last night? *All* of them?"

"Yes. And other pills as well. Bram's medication. He must have OD'd. He didn't wake up when he was sick, and he choked."

Merle's throat convulses. "You saw this?"

"No, I was in the bathroom. I was scared—I locked myself in. I sat in the dark just shaking, and then things went quiet and I must have passed out. It was hours before I came out and found him."

"And he's definitely not breathing now?"

"I don't think so."

Merle remains very still. "Did you mean to kill him, Fi?"

"No. I don't know. I think I did, but then this morning I don't recognize that person as me."

"You must have flipped. You were in shock yesterday—I can vouch for that. You acted in a fugue state—that's what they call it, don't they? It's diminished responsibility."

Fi begins to cry. "Merle, I can't. I can't go to the police."

Merle is silent then, consciously choosing her path at the crossroads before rising from the stair. She hurries upstairs, reemerges in jeans and a jumper and then adds boots and a long black coat, a knitted gray hat low to the brow. She pulls Fi's hat low too, almost to her eyes, and uses her fingers to brush aside the tears.

"We have to go there, Fi," she says. "I need to see him for myself."

53

Out on Trinity Avenue, it's still dark, still misty; the same haze that conceals the windows they pass must also be concealing them. Merle has said not to talk, that Fi shouldn't think about anything now, just empty her mind and concentrate on moving and breathing.

Only as they approach Baby Deco does Merle speak again: "Are there CCTV cameras here?"

"I don't think so."

"Good. I've been checking along the way and I don't think there's been anything—it's all residential. Plus the fog. Don't use the lights, though, just in case."

Climbing the stairs, Fi can't feel her legs, as if she's gliding. There is no sound as her feet move along the carpeted hallway, no sense of breath entering and leaving her body. As they step into the flat, there is a smell of vomit and wine and he is right there in front of them, still sitting with his neck stretched backward as if broken. Her overriding feeling is of shame, shame that he was her boyfriend, shame that he duped and humiliated her. He makes the place squalid.

"Oh God," Merle says. "I thought you might have been, I don't know..."

Deluded or confused, she means. Still in that fugue state. Not herself, but some ghostly, other Fi. But no, this is death, and *she* has caused it. She must now face the consequences, consequences that make the loss of her home negligible.

The boys. What will happen to them? One parent missing, the other in prison.

"What am I going to do, Merle?" Her voice is a thin, pathetic wail.

Merle looks at her and it seems to Fi that nothing in her eyes has changed from yesterday: *Fi* is still the victim, the human sacrifice. "I don't know yet. Let me think. Tell me why he's Mike and not Toby." As Fi explains, Merle picks up the coat draped on an open box near the kitchen, interrupting her to ask, "Is this his?"

"Yes."

Merle's fingers disappear into its folds and emerge with a brown leather wallet. "Michael Fuller. OK. That's good, I think."

"Why's it good?" Fi asks.

"Because you called him Toby. You've probably never mentioned Mike or Michael to anyone, have you?"

"No. I didn't know it was his name until last night."

Merle continues to poke through the wallet. "And I remember Alison saying you haven't met his family yet. Is that true?"

"Yes. Or friends."

Merle glances up at her. "Not a single one? No colleague or neighbor? Kids?"

"No one. We didn't share lives like that." Because "we" didn't exist. She has no idea who Toby—Michael Fuller—is. Who he *was*. Because he's not a man now—he's *remains*. As Fi suppresses the need to retch, Merle looks oddly heartened.

"I'd say that's very fortunate," she says, and places the wallet on the worktop before searching the coat pockets for other items. Car keys. Nicorette chewing gum. Two phones. Both are charged; both present security screens requiring pass codes the women have no way of guessing. "Which one does he use when he calls you?" she murmurs, to herself as much as to Fi.

"I don't know, but if I call it from mine, it will ring and we'll find out," Fi suggests.

"No!" Merle grips her arm. "Don't make any calls from your phone while you're here, OK?"

Fi nods. Merle's mood is commanding, constructive, and Fi has a childlike desire to please her. "What if I call the number I have from *Bram's* phone? The one I used to text him? Then we could assume it's the other one that he uses for me."

It is as if he has no name now; she can't bring herself to use it, as if to do so would be to rekindle his life force.

Merle pauses, before thinking aloud: "For all we know, he might have your number on both these phones. We'll get rid of them both and hope they're not traceable. This man is a criminal, right? He uses false names. Someone like him isn't going to have a nice family plan, is he? Will it look weird, though? He came here because Bram texted him, so where's the phone he got the text on? Still, there might be a hundred reasons why he's ditched his phone on the way." She finds a plastic bag in one of the drawers, drops the two phones into it, then pulls Fi into the passageway between boxes, as if removing the two of them from the dead man's sight line. She speaks in low, clipped utterances: "Listen to me, Fi. Does anyone else know you came here last night?"

"No. Only him."

"Did you call anyone when you were here? Bram's mother, maybe? To speak to the boys?"

"No, only from your place earlier. Well, I texted *him*, like I said, but only from Bram's phone."

"Did you use the Internet?"

"No."

"Where's your laptop? You haven't used that here, have you?"

"No. I don't know where Bram put it. In one of these boxes, I'm guessing. I haven't used it since before I went to Winchester. Tuesday evening."

"Good." Merle backs out of the passageway and scans the items on the counter before wiping the wine bottle and glasses with a tea towel. She does the same with the discarded packaging from Bram's pills. Without explanation, Fi hands her the knife, which Merle cleans and returns to the cutlery drawer.

"Anything else? Where's this other phone you texted from?"

This too is wiped. Fi wonders if it will join Toby's in the bag, but instead Merle places it on the yellow paper.

"Why are you leaving it? That's the one I've used!"

"Exactly. Listen, Fi. There's a way out of this. The police find him. Maybe even you do, or we do together—that's better! Later today, OK? We'll find his body and we'll call the police and we'll say we recognize him from yesterday, that he caused a scene at Trinity Avenue when he came looking for Bram. We spoke to him inside for a few minutes but he got aggressive and we asked him to leave. Before that, we'd never laid eyes on him in our lives. Do you see where I'm going?"

There is a slow, spreading sensation through her stomach and chest: it takes a few moments to recognize it as hope. "You mean Bram came back and sent the text? Bram gave him the pills?"

"Yes, or left him here in such misery that he took an overdose himself. I don't know—I wasn't here. And neither were you. They're Bram's pills, not yours."

Fi stares, her mind sifting images of the early hours. "The sleeping pills, though, Merle. Oh God, were they from a prescription made out to you?"

"Yes, but so what if they were?" Merle's focus is intense. "There's no box with my name on it. If anyone gets that far, I'll say I gave them to Bram. A few weeks ago—I don't remember exactly when, but when he was complaining about insomnia. He didn't tell me he had any other prescription medication, or I would never have given them to him."

Fi stares at her, struggling to keep up. "Thank you."

"The point is, you didn't touch the wine or the pills. And anything else in this place with your prints on it is purely because you live here half the time. This stuff is yours."

"I wore gloves to break up the medication and push it through the neck of the bottle," Fi tells her.

"Good."

"But I searched through some of the boxes without wearing the gloves, and they've only been here since Thursday. But that's OK, isn't it? I needed to find financial records to show the police and the lawyers about the house."

"Exactly. It's natural to look for essential things Bram packed without your consent. You might need stuff for the boys as well. But you do that when you come back later today, all right? *That's* when you touch things. Last night, you stayed with me. Then this morning I took you to Bram's mum's to pick up the boys, which I'll do at, what, eight o'clock? Nine? Let's go back to Trinity Avenue until it's time to leave."

"I can't bring the boys back here," Fi objects in horror.

"Of course not," Merle agrees. "We'll go straight on to your parents, shall we? You'll want to tell them about the house, get their advice, right? Focus on that. You haven't been here since . . . when?"

"Wednesday. I picked up some shoes."

"Good. Adrian's back today, so he'll look after Robbie and Daisy when I come back to meet you here. Lucky I was too tired last night to speak to him. Shall we go, then? Fi?"

Go? Fi is rooted to the spot, staring at *him*. Is he really cooling and stiffening, existing for the first whole day as a thing, an entity that is finished with life forever? How can it have been so easy to do this? How could he have drunk the wine with all those pills dissolved in it? Didn't it taste bitter? *Poisoned?*

Her heart stops. "I Googled the medication. On my phone, when I was here on Wednesday."

Merle frowns. "OK. Well, just because you saw it and wanted to know what it was, it doesn't mean you took it. Keep this simple, Fi, in your head. Keep it as simple as possible."

"Yes."

How unfaltering Merle is. She has all the answers, all the lines. She is Fi's savior, her all-seeing angel.

But there's something else. "Lucy saw Bram's pills. She saw them today, in the kitchen. They fell out of my bag."

"Did you tell her they were Bram's?"

"No, she thought they were mine—she kept saying it even though I told her they weren't."

"Good. Have you had any other prescriptions recently?"

"No."

"Has anyone in the family?"

"Only Leo. He has those allergy tablets. It's a repeat prescription—we use them as needed. But we haven't had a new batch for ages."

"That doesn't matter. Do they come in a packet like Bram's?"

"Maybe a different color. I can't remember."

384 • LOUISE CANDLISH

"Show me," Merle says.

"I can't—I don't know where they are." Fi hears the panic in her voice, the sense of salvation slipping from her grasp. "They were at the house, in the bathroom cabinet."

Together they survey the mass of identical boxes, not a single one labeled.

"This isn't everything," Fi says. "There's another lot in storage."

"Then we look." Even Merle's sigh is abbreviated, efficient. "And we do it quietly. We can't have anyone in the block hearing us bumping around."

It takes over an hour to find the boxes containing the items from the family bathroom, but Leo's tablets are among them. There is one half-used blister pack and one intact, still in its box. Fi puts this into her handbag. "I always carry a box with me in case Leo develops symptoms when we're out," she tells Merle.

"Excellent."

At last they leave, Fi with her overnight bag, the carrier containing Toby's phones in Merle's coat pocket. The fog has lifted but still the morning feels gentle, supportive of their cause, delivering them back to Trinity Avenue under its protection. The script continues to be written as they walk back, Merle speaking in low tones, not quite murmuring.

"Did any of your neighbors in the building ever see you together?"

"I don't think so. I've hardly ever bumped into anyone, even on my own. When he arrived, I buzzed him in and he usually let himself out, so anyone who saw him wouldn't necessarily have known it was me he was visiting, not Bram."

"And when he came to my place yesterday, he said he'd already been to the flat, didn't he? He'd got a neighbor to let him in and then he'd hammered on the door. I bet he was pretty unpleasant about it, probably made it clear he was angry with Bram."

They are almost at Merle's house, just passing Fi's—the Vaughans'—and her peripheral vision registers only stillness.

She stops dead, clutches Merle's arm. "The Vaughans, Merle! The Vaughans saw him."

"Keep moving," Merle says. "Yes, they did, but he was looking for Bram, not you. Remember, he was shouting for Bram, and David said something like, 'Join the queue.' Then I went out and invited him in. So the Vaughans have no reason to think he's connected to you. They might have seen you leave with him, but I doubt it—they were camped out in the kitchen. We can deny that, anyway."

There is not long to wait before it's time for Merle to gather her car keys and Fi to text Tina, and then they are retracing their steps toward Wyndham Gardens, where Merle's Range Rover is parked.

"So, tell me what's going to happen later."

Fi recites the plan: "You'll phone me at four and suggest we go to the flat and see if Bram's left any documents to do with the house, any clues that might help us with the police and solicitor on Monday. We'll discover the body together and say we think he might be the same man who came to Trinity Avenue last night looking for Bram. We looked in his wallet to find some ID."

"Perfect. They'll see the wine, check Bram's phone, start to make their own connections with the house theft."

The mist has turned to drizzle and the wipers swing back and forth across the windscreen. "And how do I explain that the man I've been dating has disappeared?" Fi asks.

Merle glances in the rearview. "Easy. He made himself scarce when he discovered you'd lost the house. Only interested in your money."

"I think he might have been married," Fi says. "He never took me to his place or even told me his full address. My sister was suspicious from the start."

"Exactly. You'd be happy to have the police track him down, but to be honest it's the least of your worries given the fact that your ex-husband has just killed someone and stolen your house."

The more they look into the details, the better it becomes. It is self-supporting; it has a central strength.

Then Fi remembers Alison. "Oh, Alison."

"What about her?"

"She saw him. She saw Toby the night we met."

In the bar at La Mouette, all those months ago.

Well, you certainly have a type.

"Alison won't say anything," Merle says. "She may not even be questioned. If she is, it was how long ago?"

"September."

When it all began. Her new dawn.

"So ages ago. She'd had a few drinks. The place was dark, a total mob scene. It's not a deal breaker, Fi. If it came to it, she wouldn't testify against her best friend. I know I wouldn't."

They hit a succession of red lights. The engine turns itself on and off. Stop, start; stop, start. Question, answer; question, answer.

Fi sinks into the seat, wishing herself invisible, an apparition detectable only to the woman next to her. "Merle, you'll really do all this?"

Red light. The engine stops.

"I really will," Merle says.

"Why?"

"Come on, Fi. You know why." She smiles at her sideways, wry, a little sad. "I didn't envisage *this* to be what got you talking to me again, but there you go."

Amber light. The engine starts.

Fi knows why.

54

It has not been easy, coexisting in a close community with a friend and neighbor who betrayed her in the most fundamental of all ways. The knee-jerk desire to punish subsided soon enough, but it left Fi with something bleaker and more enervating: a double bereavement. Bram *and* Merle. And the fact that life in Alder Rise is so tribal made it all the more painful, because now there were subdivisions of people who knew, people who didn't and people who she wasn't sure knew or not.

Kent was a particularly painful exercise. She'd thought repeatedly of pulling out, but in the end, she didn't want to let Leo and Harry down—or the other kids in the group. They were a tribe of their own. Surviving it (half enjoying it, if she was honest) made her appreciate the importance of appearances in neighborhood life, of personal sacrifice. The greatest happiness of the greatest number and all that.

In the days after the playhouse affair, a plea arrived. Handwritten and hand delivered, pushed through the letter box with stealth, so as not to make a sound.

"There's a card for you, Mummy," Harry told her. "Even though it's not your birthday."

"People send cards for other reasons," she said.

She read it just once before destroying it and so can remember only fragments now:

"Crazy and despicable . . ."

"I will never forgive myself. . . ."

"Is there any chance we can be civil, for the sake of the kids . . . ?"

"I need you to know that I would do anything to repay you. . . ."

The word "repay" stuck in her craw. As if Fi had lent her something, given of herself freely. Issued her with a permission slip to sleep with Bram. "The evening of your choice, my friend, the venue that works best for you. I'll make myself scarce."

In a funny way, she can imagine Bram rewriting the episode that way. He has a knack for repurposing his own misadventures.

But not Merle. Problem solver extraordinaire, strong and spirited Trinity Avenue wife and mother.

"You name it," she wrote, *"and I will do it."*

It is only after Merle has stopped the car on the way to Tina's flat to dispose of the phones that Fi asks why a second time. They are in the car park at Crystal Palace Park and Merle has just returned empty-handed from the boating lake, when it occurs to Fi that she might never see her accomplice again—at least not until they appear in the dock and the witness box respectively.

"I told you," Merle says. Not impatient, but focused on the day's demands. "You know why."

"No, I mean you and him. You'd known each other for so long. That *was* the only time, wasn't it?"

Now Merle follows. "Yes. Yes, of course."

"Who initiated it? Was it him?"

A pause. "No, it was me. That's the truth. He didn't invite me over. He wasn't expecting me. He had no choice but to ask me in."

Fi holds her eye. "He had a choice about fucking you, though."

Merle does not flinch. "I'm not sure he did, Fi. I was on a mission."

"Why? Why would you do that?" She can't argue that it was out of character, because Merle's character was not known to her until yesterday, this morning, not truly. "You *knew* how upset I was about what he'd done before. You comforted me. You advised me to give him another chance."

"I know," Merle says, her voice low. "There's no excuse. No justification. I still can't believe it myself."

To her credit, she does not try to diminish it. Sex, adultery, the institution of marriage: their importance *is* diminished now, to the point of irrelevance—how can it not be?—but Fi still has to know. She still has to understand.

"Was there always an attraction, then?"

A pause. Merle's fingers grip the edge of the leather seat. "I think there was, yes, but neither of us was ever going to act on it."

"So why did you act on it that night? If you'd managed not to for years before? What was this *mission*?"

Now Merle's fingers touch her mouth, as if monitoring her own words. The car is sealed and silent; there is the sense that its atmosphere will tolerate nothing but the truth. "That evening, I had a babysitter at my place—I was meeting Adrian at La Mouette. A belated wedding anniversary dinner. We hadn't been getting on that well—I probably told you that at the time. I'd had a few drinks at the bar when he texted and said he couldn't come. It was one of those quick texts, not even sorry, just 'can't make it—working late.' I was so angry with him, how casual he was, no thought to the arrangements I'd made with the babysitter, all the hoops you have to jump through just to get the kids sorted and get yourself out the door, let alone dressed up and in the mood for being an adult, a *wife*. It was like this one cancellation was an accumulation of all the cancellations, all the wrongs. I remember sitting there fuming, literally plotting to divorce him. There was a guy at the bar and I tried flirting with him and he just rejected me—he wasn't even tempted." She flushes at the memory. "It was so humiliating. It felt like the most humiliating moment of my life. Like a turning point."

Merle takes a breath, stares through the windscreen at the green beyond. "So I walked back down to the house and I felt so reckless. I wasn't in my right mind—that's the only way I can describe it. Something hormonal was going on, I suppose. I felt like my life was just sliding toward the end, you know, picking up speed, completely unstoppable, and I needed . . . I needed to make something happen to keep myself alive. Even if the only thing I could think of was completely self-destructive. Destructive to *you*. Both of you. Leo and Harry too. God. So I walked past my door and I went on to yours."

Fi absorbs this. If she understands correctly, it was a disposable moment of marital crisis, a rush of midlife hormones, that set this apocalypse in motion. Would it feel any different if it were something more recognizably momentous? A diagnosis of terminal illness, the loss of a parent, a career-ending degradation? It is impossible not to draw a parallel between Merle's crime and her own, not least because they have a cause in common: a reaction against humiliation.

"Fat old Mrs. Holier-than-thou—I don't know how Bram stood it all those years. No wonder he played away. . . ."

There had still been time to stop it when he said that to her. She could have poured the wine down the sink. Instead, she poured it into him. She killed a man.

I killed him!

They sit for a minute in silence.

"Merle?"

"Yes?"

Fi feels emotion welling like liquid, swallows before she speaks. "I want to make it clear that if the police come after me, if there's some forensic thing I can't possibly deny, I'll keep you out of it. You've had no part in this at all. You didn't come to the flat with me this morning. I turned up and asked you to drive me to Tina's. That's it. You had no idea what I'd done."

Merle shakes her head. "It won't come to that."

"But if it does, if I'm arrested, will you look out for Leo and Harry? I mean, my parents will take them in; they'll be the best guardians I could wish for, but will you keep the friendships going? Be there for them too? They'll need another family that feels like *theirs*. Not straightaway—I know you'll be busy with the new baby—but later. I could be gone for years."

Merle straightens her shaking shoulders, refastens the seat belt over her swollen body, starts the car. "Of course I will."

Fi had guessed after the Kent weekend, of course—that flippant excuse for not drinking—and had sought Merle out at the gym the following Sunday. They each had their regular class now: Pilates for Fi, yoga for Merle.

She'd need to switch to pregnancy yoga soon.

"Fi?" Merle was startled by her approach. "I didn't think . . ."

Didn't think Fi would address her outside of the group, outside of the agreed civilities of child delivery and collection.

"I have a question," Fi said.

Merle waited. Two women arriving for yoga class greeted her, beating a retreat when they saw her stricken expression.

"Is it Bram's?"

Fi saw that Merle was considering denying the pregnancy itself, but decided there was no sense in that. You could deny new life for only so long, and in any case, in her yoga kit she was starting to show.

"No," Merle said at last. "It's Adrian's. It's due in May."

"You swear that's the truth?"

"I swear."

"Then I won't ask you again," Fi said simply.

Not even if the baby comes in April, not May? she thought, walking away. Maybe. She would certainly keep an eye on events.

But all sorts of things could happen before then.

LYON, 2 P.M.

He has made his final move and is settled now in the aparthotel. His new accommodation is not unlike the studio in Baby Deco, as it happens: hard-wearing and neutral, designed with a sense that the bare minimum deserves as much respect as deluxe—hell, you might even make a virtue of it. Yes, exactly right for Custer's last stand and a decent writer's base, besides: well heated and soundproof; there's a Nespresso machine with a collection of pods and some of those individually wrapped tea bags the French go in for. A fridge for his beers. The reassuring trace of previous smokers' cigarettes.

The most important thing is that he has destroyed the information sheet with the Wi-Fi password and he is certain his willpower will not fail him. He would only be tempted to Google the collision investigation, the components of his old existence. To e-mail Fi and start explaining about the money, begging her to forgive him, even advising her how to go about reconstructing the family life he has destroyed.

Unforgivable—that was what Merle called him. Just another unforgivable man.

It interests him that even with his whole story ready to be told, the emphases and nuances entirely his, he does not expect to devote much of it to her (he's already decided he's going to give her a pseudonym). In the end, she hasn't mattered; she hasn't played a part. He's gathered that Fi chose to sweep it all under the carpet for the sake of the children's friendships (Leo and Robbie are thick as thieves, always have been), for the sake of neighborhood harmony, for the sake of continuing to live in the house. Not once did she mention Merle to him after they separated, and if she could exercise that sort of blank restraint with one guilty party, then she probably could with two. And she went off to Kent, didn't she? No one came back with stab wounds.

It will be a while before news reaches Merle about the loss of the house, but once it does, she certainly won't be gloating about it. Their liaison in the playhouse had never been about her coveting what Fi had, because she already had all those things herself—more, in fact, since *her* husband had been faithful, if sometimes a little disinclined to appreciate what he had, in Bram's opinion. No, for her, that night had been about doing something reckless to force a moment of crisis. To remind your blood that it still has a reason to circulate, even if the body it flows through is aging faster than you'd prefer. To restore your conviction that you still have something good to give.

That was the difference between Merle and him. She had faith that she made life better for those around her, whereas he had no faith that he did.

Or at least what little faith he'd once had, he'd lost.

55

The worst moment, she thinks, the most heartbreaking moment of the whole thing, is when she and Merle walk back through the door to the flat. Worse, even, than when Harry asks her if she is happy with Daddy's surprise and faith shines from him in rays. The belief that his father has succeeded, that his mother is pleased.

"Did he paint the right colors? Did it dry in time? Were you *really* surprised?"

She can do nothing but hug him, tell him everything is lovely, that the only thing that matters is her being with him and his brother because she's missed them, and the two of them *haven't* got a fraudster for one parent and a murderer for the other.

She extracted them with relative ease from Tina's, not staying long enough to be tempted to blurt the news about Bram's departure and suspected embezzlement. She feared the more complex strain of being with her own parents for the rest of the day, not least for the fact that, if Merle's plan was to work, they would be called upon to vouch for her state of mind in the aftermath of a crime.

But, as it turns out, the effects of severe trauma are the same whatever their origins. Losing your mind because you've killed someone does not differ vastly from losing your mind because your husband has stolen your home and absconded. If anything, the managing of her parents' bewilderment and anger about the house sale is a welcome focus, their fiercely protective stance regarding the boys a reminder of how the authorities will be expecting *her* to present herself. It is agreed that Leo and Harry should remain in Kingston for the time being, a fib about delays with the decorating used to explain the impossibility of a return home. They've never been to the flat, and it would be unsettling to take them there now.

(To put it mildly.)

As Merle has instructed, she showers, puts both the clothes she wore yesterday and those from her break with Toby through the wash, then changes into the jeans and jumper Merle has lent her. At four p.m., as agreed, Merle phones and Fi announces to her parents that she needs to go to the flat. "Merle thinks Bram's probably stored some of our stuff there and I think she might be right. I need to find all our mortgage and banking paperwork so I can start to talk to a lawyer."

The reappearance of Merle in Fi's life is met with raised eyebrows, but no special interrogation: extraordinary times call for extraordinary measures, is the message. Whatever—whoever—helps her untangle this unholy mess. Her mother agrees to drive Fi to the flat, a journey lengthened painfully by rain and Saturday traffic, and when they pull up at Baby Deco, Merle is already waiting outside.

"Shall I come in and help?" her mother asks, turning off the engine.

"No, no, you go back to the boys. Thank you, Mum. Thank you so much." Fi wants to say more; she wants to say, "Take care of Leo and Harry, because I might be arrested in a few hours."

"It will all work out fine," Merle says as they wait for the lift; no need now to skulk in unlit stairways. "Adrian is just back from skiing. He's with the kids at home. I've filled him in—on Bram and the house, I mean. He's completely appalled, as you can imagine. And Alison has given me a recommendation for a lawyer, by the way. She and Rog think we shouldn't deal directly with this Jenson character, because his loyalty will be to his client, not us."

"*Us.*" "*We.*" It's still evident in Merle's words, in her manner: the unconditional fidelity.

"Seeing them hasn't . . . hasn't changed your mind? About helping me?" Fi speaks in gulps. "I'd understand if it had." Who, even the most guilt-stricken, would want to get embroiled in this? "You've already helped me enough, Merle. You need to concentrate on yourself and the baby."

"Here's the lift," Merle says firmly.

Inside the flat, nothing has changed from the scene they abandoned that morning, except the smell, which has grown richer, more fetid. It must be the vomit . . . unless *he* is starting to decompose. Is that possible?

Fi eyes the body as if for the first time. It's not the way she's read a decaying corpse is supposed to make you feel, that profound sense of the departed, an empty vessel, the soul stolen.

Maybe because he didn't have a soul.

Merle strides forward, thinking aloud. "What would we do first if we were just finding him now? One of us needs to check his pulse. Best it's me. You're still very distressed after what happened yesterday with the house." She touches his neck and wrist with her fingertips. "I don't think anyone would expect us to try CPR or anything, would they? I think I'd be sick if I had to put my mouth on his."

Fi hangs back, avoiding looking at his face. "Is he cold?" she asks, shivering.

Merle takes her hand, passing on the touch of his skin. "Yes, but I think he's warmer than you are. Can't you feel the heating in this building? It's suffocating. I'll try to get through to the balcony doors, let some air in. Otherwise I'm going to throw up."

"Careful," Fi says. As Merle squeezes between the towers of boxes, she runs her icy fingers under the hot tap in the bathroom. She does not look at the murderer in the mirror.

When she returns, Merle has succeeded in opening the balcony doors and has her mobile phone in her hand. "Right. Shall I call, or will you?"

Fi says she will do it. Her hand trembles as she uses the phone; her voice is dull with shock. "Hello? Please, I need someone to come to my flat. . . . There's a man here. . . . My friend and I have just arrived and there's a body. We think it's someone my ex-husband knows. We think he's dead."

"Good," Merle says when she's finished. "That sounded exactly right."

Because she's not acting. That's the unintended beauty of this plan of theirs: none of it has to be manufactured. The feeling that she might sob or be sick or wail and wail until someone puts a needle in her arm and blacks the world out: it's all real.

LYON, 6:30 P.M.

It is evening now and he is smoking a cigarette, ready to begin. He is not a fluent writer and he expects it to take him weeks, perhaps even as long as a month. When it is done, he will collect his remaining antidepressants, plus any other medication to be had over the counter from the French pharmacies, and he will swallow them in fistfuls with the strongest vodka he can find. And he will die. He will go where he put little Ellie Rutherford.

He writes: *Let me remove any doubt straightaway and tell you that this is a suicide note. . . .* And at once, he understands why he is doing it, why he is delaying the inevitable. He wants to spend his last weeks with them, with Leo and Harry and Fi. Writing about them is not the same as being with them, in the flesh, in the house, but it's still time together, isn't it?

He can give them that, if nothing else.

LONDON, 6 P.M.

While they wait, they retrieve the paperwork Fi unearthed the previous night and dig through some of the boxes to assemble the rest she might need to start investigating Bram's embezzlement.

"Would we do this?" she asks Merle. "Would we not be too shocked by what we've discovered to want to go hunting through files?"

Merle considers. "Maybe, but the whole place is going to be sealed off, so now's your only chance to take your passports and financial stuff. Like we said, we might need to explain why your prints are inside some of the boxes."

Fi nods. "Do you think there'll be sirens?"

"Yes, I think an ambulance will come first. They won't just take our word for it that he's dead. We're amateurs. They'll want to see if he can be revived. Then they'll bring in the forensics people."

"You definitely got rid of the phones?"

"Yes. I threw them as far into the lake as I could. No one saw—I'm sure of it. If it turns out someone saw us in the car park, we pulled in because I felt sick, OK? It's happened a lot lately."

What with her being pregnant—being pregnant and yet still choosing to do what she is doing. There is atonement and then there is *this*.

With the distant scream of a siren, they sidestep once more through the gully between the boxes to wait on the balcony. The street below is slick with rain, reflecting in lurid flashes the colors of the passing car lights. The smell is unexpectedly fresh and renewing, as if the nearby park is on the cusp of spring, the worst over.

The first vehicle, an ambulance, runs the red light at the junction and approaches Baby Deco in the near lane, while the oncoming traffic gives way and waits.

"Last chance to change your mind," Merle says.

Fi knows no answer is required. It is an illusion that she can change her mind now; they both know there is only one narrative ahead. And it's a good one. The bottom line is that as long as no link is made between the Toby Fi has been dating and the Mike sprawled lifeless in her flat, she has a fair chance of getting away with it. Freedom—if not for Bram, then for her and their sons.

As the paramedics exit their vehicle, Fi and Merle return inside. Merle positions herself in front of the intercom before the buzzer goes, a conductor taking charge of her stage.

"Ready?" she says, her fingers poised to press.

"Ready," Fi says.

The buzzer goes.

56

The pills are already assembled in the kitchenette when he writes the last line. Enough to kill a horse, in his nonprofessional judgment. Less grisly to stumble upon than a hanging.

"He was convinced it would be easier for you if he wasn't here to bring more shame on you."

He has left no message, nor taken any precautions to spare the sensibilities of the poor cleaner, his most likely discoverer, whose next shift is in two days' time. Far too late to pump him empty and save him.

The last words are written. A story about his speed-awareness course: not how he would have predicted he would sign off when he started this account, but it's as illuminating a tale as any. It's in his voice; it gives the reader the measure of him.

Plus the bank details, of course. No doubt there will be delays, but he trusts the police and the lawyers to determine that the money is rightfully Fi's and to allow her due access to it.

He titles the file "For the attention of Detective Sergeant Joanne

McGowan, Metropolitan Police," copies it to a memory stick, and turns off the laptop. Of course, he could safely use the Wi-Fi now—no police officer on earth would get here quickly enough to stop him—but after six weeks offline he has no appetite for reconnection with the world. Besides, he feels like getting some air, taking a last stroll.

As he walks to the Internet café, he thinks how funny it would be if he found the place closed down, forcing him to search for another, bringing him back into contact with humanity, happenstance, a last chance at life.

It is open.

He is less than five minutes at the computer terminal. He noted and memorized the e-mail address before he left London, but for good measure he copies in a general address for the Serious Collisions Investigation Unit at Catford. As he waits for the document to upload, he reminds himself that he needs to make a decision about which music to play while he loses consciousness. It should be a requiem, by rights, or opera, perhaps, but he has none in his collection.

Maybe Pink Floyd.

No doubt it's disingenuous, but he really does think of this as his last gift to Fi. Not only in divulging the means by which she can retrieve the proceeds from the house, but also by exposing Mike: his criminal acts, his coercion of Bram and deceit of Fi. Especially his deceit of Fi. Because the police need to know that she became entangled with this evil man only because he targeted her—she has done nothing wrong herself, not a step, not a breath.

Once the police know that Mike is Toby and Toby is Mike, they only need ask Fi how and where to find him and then she and the boys will be safe.

At last, seeing that the file has successfully attached, he presses SEND.

Acknowledgments

Our House was written partially out of contract, which, as writers know, entails a cash-starved and yet exhilarating work period during which there is really only one person in your corner: your agent. So a huge heartfelt thank-you to Sheila Crowley: I will not forget your encouragement and support during a time when you had far, far more important things to think about.

My thanks also to Team Crowley at Curtis Brown (UK): Becky Ritchie, Abbie Greaves and Tessa Feggans. Also at CB: Luke Speed, Irene Magrelli, Alice Lutyens and Katie McGowan.

Thank you to Deborah Schneider of Gelfman Schneider for US expertise. It is a pleasure to work together and long may it continue. I consider myself privileged to have been present at the unveiling of the Opals.

A very special thank-you to Danielle Perez at Berkley for extraordinary skill and patience in the editing of this book. Danielle, we both know how significantly you've improved it and I couldn't be more grateful. Your ongoing faith in the book and championing of it in the US means the world to me.

Thank you to the rest of the crack team at Berkley, including Sarah Blumenstock and Jennifer Snyder, and Katie Anderson, who designed the beautiful cover (with a special mention to Alana Colucci for her earlier incarnation).

At Simon & Schuster UK—I'm so happy to be reunited with fiction legend Jo Dickinson and to be working for the first time with a team I've admired from afar for years: Gill Richardson, Laura Gough, Dawn Burnett, Hayley McMullen, Dom Brendon, Jess Barratt, Rich Vliestra, Joe Roche, Emma Capron, Maisie Lawrence, Tristan Hanks, Pip Watkins, and Suzanne King. Last but never least, Sara-Jade Virtue, to whom this book is dedicated. You have been a great friend and powerhouse supporter for more than ten years and I still can't believe we are *finally* working together.

Thank you to John Candlish for legal know-how as well as for great book recommendations to take my mind *off* property fraud. And to the rest of my family and friends, who listen to my moans and groans with straight faces, as if books were blood diamonds and I might one day not come out of the mines alive. I won't list you for fear of missing someone and doing more harm than good—except for Mats 'n' Jo, which is traditional.